Also available from Christi Barth
and Cari~~~~

Ask Her At~~~~

And coming soon f~~~~
and Carin~~~~

A Fine Romance
Friends to Lovers

CHRISTI BARTH

earned a master's degree in vocal performance
and embarked upon a career on the stage. A love
of romance then drew her to wedding planning.
Ultimately she succumbed to her lifelong love of
books and now writes contemporary romance.
Christi lives in Maryland with her husband.

Planning FOR Love

Christi Barth

CARINA PRESS™

CARINA PRESS™

ISBN-13: 978-0-373-77812-6

PLANNING FOR LOVE

www.CarinaPress.com

Printed in U.S.A.

Dear Reader,

I'm thrilled to share Book One of my Aisle Bound trilogy with you. My hope is that you'll adore the characters as much as I do. Ivy, my über-romantic wedding planner, wants nothing more than to find true love. And then there's Ben, an unapologetic flirt of a cameraman with a semisecret past. He's allergic to love. But at least he's upfront about it! They've got a handful of quirky, funny friends. Last but not least, there's the city of Chicago itself, such an integral part of this story. It couldn't take place anywhere else. So many beautiful wedding locations, world-class museums and a majestic lake as far as the eye can see. Oh, and I hear they're pretty famous for their sports teams, too.

One of the questions that authors dread in interviews is, "Where do you get your ideas?" As if there's a magical writers'-only store, or an idea tree you can shake. Happily, with this series, I have an answer! Nine out of ten people who learned I was a wedding planner would say, "You should write a book!" Then they'd launch into elaborate eye winks about bridezillas and mother-of-the-bride horror stories.

Except in my experience, at least 90 percent of weddings are wonderful. They are a celebration of friends and family and enduring love. Most people do pull it together and behave like grown-ups. So I didn't want to write a scathing tell-all. But a trilogy that focuses on the wedding industry, showcasing people who spend every day creating the perfect happily-ever-after? That felt like a good place to start. And maybe a few crazy real-life hijinks did slip into my manuscript. It is a comedy, after all! You'll have to guess which ones happened and which are just figments of my imagination....

If you like a sassy and sexy happily-ever-after, this is the book for you. Along with the rest of the trilogy, which will be released in 2013. Book Two, *A Fine Romance*, is the story of Sam the baker/aspiring chocolatier and Mira, the manager of Ivy's new romance store, who doesn't like chocolate. Spoiler alert: there is a *very* hot sex scene that just might involve melted chocolate.... Book Three, *Friends to Lovers*, follows Daphne the florist and Gib the British lothario as they journey from—well, friends to lovers! I just finished writing their aphrodisiac dinner. It actually works, to their shock and dismay, far better than either of them expected. But first, in the harsh spotlight of reality television, a romance-a-holic wedding planner tries to snare the anti-Cupid. Enjoy *Planning for Love*. And if you do, please let me know at www.christibarth.com—I'd love to hear from you!

Christi

ACKNOWLEDGMENT

Thanks to the MRW Critters for helping me become a better writer with every meeting. Thanks to Angela James and her entertaining Twitter feed for the heads-up about her yen for a book just like this one. Her pain-free polishing makes the work of writing fun. And, therefore, thanks to Eliza Knight for forcing me onto Twitter.

DEDICATION

To my husband—
so much more than I ever planned for,
and a die-hard romantic!

CHAPTER ONE

All weddings are similar, but every marriage is
different.

—John Berger

IVY RHODES LAY sprawled at the bottom of the stone
steps, feet tangled in the straps of a large black duffel
bag. Everything hurt and, to top it off, she thought she'd
heard her dress rip. At the very least, the pale pink satin
had to be smudged from her ungraceful slide down the
sweep of old stones dominating the foyer of the Great
Hall at Café Brauer. Worst of all, the round lens of a
video camera bobbled less than an inch from her nose.

"Are you kidding me? You're filming this?" Ivy's
voice rose to a high squeak on the last word. Her famous, unflappable composure threatened to crack. Because who wouldn't be flustered when their humiliating
clumsiness got recorded for posterity on a wedding
video? She dropped her cheek back to the cool stones
and waited for a wave of dizziness to subside. Hopefully, if any of the caterers needed to walk by her to
finish setting up the ballroom, they'd avoid stepping on
anything important, like her dress or her head.

"Ollie, you idiot! Get out of the way." The deep, bari-
tone voice issuing the command buzzed with almost as
much annoyance as Ivy felt.

A pair of highly polished dress shoes entered her limited field of vision, replacing the scuffed loafers belonging to the cameraman. Hoping this indicated the camera was gone, Ivy lifted her head once more. Not only had the camera disappeared, but an incredibly handsome man now crouched in front of her.

Although it was true almost every man looked good in a tux, this one in particular was downright yummy. Broad shoulders filled out his jacket. Impeccable tailoring emphasized the vee shape of his torso. His chin had a movie-star cleft deep enough to anchor a small boat. A streaky thicket of blond hair set off piercing blue eyes. Combined with his unusual-for-April-in-Chicago tan, it gave him a bit of a surfer look.

"Are you okay? Here, let me help you up," he said, without waiting for an answer. Strong arms lifted her off the floor, cradling her against a very firm chest. Her long dress, albeit possibly streaked and torn, cascaded down to his knees. It was like a scene out of a movie: the formalwear, the romantic pose, the Prince Charming look-alike carrying her. Or, to be perfectly honest, one of several favorite fantasies she mentally thumbed through instead of counting sheep. Ivy's heart did a quick flip flop. These things never, ever happened to her. This moment was well worth a few scrapes and bruises.

"Not that I'm complaining, but where are we going?" she asked.

"To find you a chair. We need to assess your injuries before you try to stand."

What a strangely technical thing for him to say. Not at all the warm, charming words she'd hoped to come out of his lips. "Are you a paramedic?"

"Nope. But I am certified in advanced first aid. I just don't want you to sue me."

"What?" Ivy craned her neck around to meet his eyes. "You're being nice to me to sidestep litigation?" And with that, her personal ocean of humiliation snaked out a riptide, sucking her even deeper. Prince Charmless was more like it. "Put me down right now," she demanded.

"As soon as I find a damn chair!" He turned left into the Great Hall. Early afternoon sunlight beamed in through the wide windows, casting a golden haze across the top of the enormous room.

Ivy waved her hand at two hundred gilt Chivari chairs framing the round banquet tables in perfect arcs. "Take your pick."

He toed out the nearest chair, dumped her on it, then planted his hands on his hips. "Well? You hurt anywhere?"

"Pretty much everywhere." Like black ink from an enraged octopus, the sexy stranger oozed with annoyance and attitude. Ivy just couldn't figure out why her tripping down the stairs had set him off. At the most he looked to be in his mid thirties. Far too young for a case of terminal crankiness.

"I meant did you break anything?" The man knelt on the floor and looked at her with expectant eyes.

"I only fell the last few…hey!" He'd pushed the hem of her dress to her knees and rotated her left ankle. She jerked in response and tried to pull her foot out of his grasp.

"Like I said, I'm certified in first aid. Stop wriggling around and let me check you out."

His touch was surprisingly gentle, and the warmth

of his hands soothing. Wonderfully big, deft hands.
She wondered how many other of her body parts he
planned to handle in a similar fashion. Whoops. Far
too long since her last date if her body responded this
quickly to someone so disagreeable. "Usually I get at
least a cocktail before someone gropes under my skirt."

He ignored her quip. "Good movement on this side."
In short order he checked her other ankle, and per-
formed an equally thorough examination of her knees
and wrists. She hissed in a breath when he found the
cut on her arm. "Doesn't look too bad. More like a
deep scrape."

"Yeah, well, you're not the one wearing it." Irritated
equally by his demeanor and the stinging pain in her
arm, she shook him off. "Who are you?"

"Here we go." He let out a long sigh and pushed to
his feet. "Bennett Westcott, True Life Productions."
After a quick rummage in his lapel pocket he produced
a business card. "Obviously you're a bit shaken up,
but overall I'd say you are fine. However, if you feel it
necessary to contact a lawyer regarding this incident,
I understand."

Confused, Ivy took the card, glanced at the bold
red and black lettering. "Did I miss something? I fell
down a couple of stairs. Unless you totaled my car in
the parking lot or plan to kneecap me later, it's safe to
say litigation isn't even a remote possibility."

"Look, I'm trying to step up and do the right thing
by not denying responsibility for your fall."

A few wisps of hair brushed her cheek when she
slowly shook her head. "Still not a clue where you're
coming from."

"You must've tripped over our tripod bag. Ollie kicked it in front of the stairs right before you landed."

Aha! Now it made sense. In this crazy world where people sued over coffee being too hot, she understood at least a little of his paranoia. "Bennett, I slipped on an ice cube. The caterers dropped a bag of ice earlier, and missed a few when they cleaned up. Your duffel bag didn't help me stick my landing, but it didn't cause the problem, either."

The scowl dropped off his face and everything in his body relaxed. "You have no idea how relieved I am to hear you say that. Ollie!" he bellowed. "Get your butt in here and apologize."

A thin, wiry man who barely looked strong enough to support the video camera propped on his shoulder shuffled slowly through the entryway. His eyes were downcast, his entire demeanor that of a beaten puppy. "I'm really sorry," he mumbled.

"We're in the clear. She's not going to sue," her rescuer announced, relief pinging in every word. His speech pattern also changed. The witness-on-trial formality of his speech pattern relaxed into a normal, conversational tone.

"I promise. Truly, I don't blame you at all. Do you need me to sign an affidavit to that effect?" Ivy asked, at this point only half joking.

Ollie swung the camera to the floor and rushed forward to pump Ivy's hand. "Thank you so much. It was an accident, you know. I kicked the bag behind me without looking, and when I turned around you were on the floor, so I started filming. Reflex, you know?"

"You can make it up to me by erasing that footage." No response. Ivy watched Bennett and Ollie exchange a glance loaded with subtext. Too bad she couldn't translate it. "The wedding hasn't even started yet, so you won't need to edit much," she continued, letting a pleading tone slip into her voice. Their persistent silence was a bad sign. Petty though it might be, there was no way she'd allow her ungraceful tumble to be saved on some random cousin of the bride's wedding video. "Come on, guys, this is ridiculous. I'm not even a guest at this wedding."

In a blur of unexpected speed, Ollie retrieved his camera from the floor and aimed it at her. The record light glowed red. "Can you say that again, and look straight into the camera for me?"

"What? I will not," she fumed. "Bennett, what's with your friend?" Enough was enough! As the wedding coordinator, it was her job to handle crazy relatives. A deft mix of courtesy, charm and humor usually did the trick. But there were times a line had to be drawn, and this was it. No way could she do her job with this nut shoving a camera in her face every two minutes.

To her surprise, Bennett gestured to Ollie to keep recording. "Are you confirming you did not receive an invitation to this wedding? And you got all dressed up and came anyway? That you are, in fact, a wedding crasher?"

Ivy lifted a hand to her mouth to halt an onslaught of giggles. She couldn't wait to tell her assistant, who would laugh her ass off at the accusation. "Oh, my God. Is that what you think?" No wonder the two acted so weird. And really, who could blame them? Catching an unwanted guest in the act could've guaranteed their footage ending up on the local news. Plus, they'd be touted as heroes for "saving" the wedding. The truth would be a huge letdown.

"Didn't you admit as much?" Bennett countered.

Ivy vigorously shook her head from side to side. "Hardly! I'm not a guest, but I'm certainly not crashing, either. My name is Ivy Rhodes. I'm doing day-of coordination for Tracy and Seth."

"You're the wedding planner?" Ollie turned on his heel without another word and left the hall, head down and shoulders rounded in disappointment.

Bennett's reaction was the complete opposite. He pulled out another chair and straddled it, arms crossed over the back. "Sorry. The kid's young, and is sure every gig we do has the potential for major drama. Instead of paying his dues, he plans to catapult to stardom on a clip of the bride falling off a chair during the Hora. Anyway, it's a huge relief to know you're one of us. No wonder you took the whole thing in stride. Now we can relax and get to know each other before all the craziness starts." He flashed a killer grin. It revealed the matched set of dimples bracketing his lips.

It was the kind of grin certain to charm a woman, and Ivy was no exception. Absolved of the threat of pending litigation, his personality had done a complete turnaround. Standoffish, irritable guy now exuded warmth and friendliness from his sky-blue eyes. If she read the signs correctly, he was trying to hit on her. Temptation and harmless flirtation beckoned.

Then her mind caught up to her hormones and told her something was off. He spoke as if they were in this together, but she'd reviewed all the vendor contracts just this morning in preparation. She'd stake her entire paycheck for this event on not having one for a videographer. "Back up a minute. Now I need to turn the question back to you. Aren't you a wedding guest?"

"Nope. I told you, we're with True Life Productions." He reached forward and tucked a stray lock of hair behind her ear. His glancing touch sent a shiver down her spine. Ivy wanted to dismiss it as an unwelcome distraction. Oh, who was she kidding? There was nothing unwelcome about his fingers trailing softly from her ear down the side of her neck. Irritated at her body's betrayal, she swatted his hand away.

"But the bride and groom didn't hire a videographer." Ivy took a deep breath and smoothed her hair to make sure the triple layer of hairspray still held the majority of her French twist in place. "Look, I didn't plan this whole wedding. Day-of coordination means I only show up to run the rehearsal and actual wedding day. But Tracy and I met last month to discuss all the details. We went over every vendor contract. You must have your dates or venue wrong," she insisted.

"Chicago. Great Hall of Café Brauer. Sunset. Third weekend in April." Bennett ticked the points off on his fingers. "It all adds up to me. Why do you care, anyway? Got something against videographers? Cause if that's it, you can relax. I'm also the director, and as a rule, we're much more suave and exciting." He waggled his eyebrows at her.

Ivy bit back a smile at his antics and mustered a stern glare. "I care because this wedding cost a fortune, and I'm sure your services run into the thousands." Then she remembered a seminar on con artists from her last association meeting, and another possible angle flashed through her mind. "Are you the ambulance chasers of the wedding world? Do you follow catering trucks around to find the hot weddings? Is this a scam, where you show up and tape everything, and then strong arm the bride and groom into paying?"

"Oh, they aren't paying for us. We're paying them."

Utter confusion swamped her. They were talking in circles. The clink of glassware filtered in from the hallway. It was a timely reminder the caterers had yet to place the wineglasses and water goblets on the tables. Once they finished, she would set the place cards in their Star of David–shaped holders and hand-written menus. In other words, lots to do and the clock was ticking. A glance at her watch confirmed less than two hours before the wedding march began. Her to-the-minute itinerary didn't include a time slot to solve the mystery of the uninvited, albeit borderline irresistible video guy! "Bennett—"

"Call me Ben." He rose from the chair, and Ivy was forced to tip her head back a little to maintain eye contact. Easily several inches over six feet, most of it was in his legs. The satin stripe on his tuxedo pants only emphasized his height. "I can see what happened. Tracy didn't tell you she won the contest. Probably thought you'd flip out or something. Most wedding coordinators aren't wild about us interfering with the big day."

"What contest?"

"Our show holds a contest every year. Whoever wins not only gets featured on the show, but we pay for their honeymoon. The only catch is that if they do win, we have to tag along and film the whole thing."

"What show?" Suspicion reared inside her. Reality wedding shows were a dime a dozen, and Ivy loathed most of them. Her profession tended to be portrayed in an unflattering light.

He ran a hand back and forth along the ladder-back chair. Carefully pushed it back into place at the table, tucking it neatly under the bright yellow tablecloth. "*WWS*. You know, *Wild Wedding Smackdown*." Ben, anticipating her reaction, at least had the grace to wince.

It took a concerted effort not to let her jaw drop to the floor. Without a doubt his show was the worst of the lot. It featured two couples, each trying to upstage the other with lavish ceremonies and over-the-top receptions. The brides invariably sniped at each other on Twitter, made horrible catty remarks in behind-the-scenes video diaries, or stole a great band right out from under the other's nose. Really, it was like watching high school students fight to have the best prom.

"Please tell me you're joking." Her head reeled. How could one of her weddings be featured on that classless catfight? The millions of people who watched wouldn't know she was hired at the last minute to only do day-of coordination. They might even assume she pushed the bride and groom into participating. This broadcast could ruin her reputation in Chicago, the reputation she'd carefully honed and polished over the past six years. It was a nightmare, pure and simple.

"Wish I was." He looked over both shoulders, then whispered in her ear. "Just between you and me, I hate it too."

"Oh, well, that fixes everything!" Sarcasm weighed down her words.

"I mean it." Ben came around to crouch in front of her and took her hands. The surprisingly intimate gesture from a man she'd just met startled her. Of course, between carrying her and checking for injuries, he'd already run his hands over most of her body. Still, this moment felt different somehow. Very personal, very connected.

"Ivy, I can tell you're upset. You turned white as a ghost the minute I said *WWS*. Trust me, I've worked on the show long enough to know it's a piece of crap. I've been trying to get off of it since day one. As a matter of fact, I just got promoted at True Life. Tonight's my last gig."

His thumb brushed in a soothing pattern over her knuckles. It took a huge effort to split her focus between his words and the tingles he sent zinging up her arm. "Well, goody for you. So glad you're moving up in the world while I'm about to crash and burn."

"It won't be that bad."

She rolled her eyes. The blatant understatement didn't deserve a response.

"I know you hate the show, and I hate the show, but millions of people out there love it."

"Millions of people watch NASCAR just for the crashes," she shot back. Who knew it was possible to be this depressed while a tall blond hunk caressed her?

"Listen to me. Don't look at the glass as half empty. Everyone knows it's impossible to control a bride. They won't blame you for the bad stuff, but you'll get credit for all the good stuff."

The only good side that immediately sprang to mind was meeting Ben. Unfortunately, it was a purely personal perk, and in no way could help save her career. And for all she knew, he might disappear the moment she calmed down. Meanwhile, in a matter of weeks her face would be in high definition on television screens handing out the tacky favors; water bottles plastered with a picture of the happy couple chugging beer at the bar where they met. The smothering weight of despair began to settle over her when his voice caught her attention.

"Think of it as advertising, unparalleled nationwide exposure. It may be hard to believe, but we get a ton of calls after each episode."

"Oh, I believe it!"

Ben squeezed her hands. "Not complaints. People want to hire the vendors we feature, like the planner and the florist."

The thick fog of panic clouding her brain receded a little. "Really?"

"Yes. Trust me, tonight could wind up to be the biggest opportunity you ever get." His blue eyes, mere inches away from hers, radiated sincerity. She wanted to believe him, because frankly the alternative was unthinkable and ulcer inducing. And really, since Tracy and Seth signed a contract, what choice did she have?

Ivy closed her eyes, took a second to regroup. "I'll make you a deal."

"Sounds interesting. Always a good sign when a beautiful woman propositions me." Ben doled out a slow, suggestive smile while at the same time his lids drooped to create the effect of bedroom eyes. It was undoubtedly a practiced look, and potent enough to bring any unsuspecting woman to her knees. Ivy saw the smile for what it was: a sucking vortex of charisma and sex appeal. One she would resist. Or at least would resist until he agreed to her terms.

"I won't hold up a giant sign saying 'Wild Wedding Smackdown Sucks!' during the ceremony if you agree to erase the footage of my fall. Honestly, Tracy and

Seth have enough planned for tonight to give you lots of crazy outtakes. You don't need me."

"Prove it. What could beat a beautiful woman somersaulting down the stairs?" Now his eyes sparked with the hint of a challenge.

Ivy crossed her arms, accepting the challenge. "Okay. You probably know this from whatever they told you to win the stupid contest, but it's an interfaith marriage. We've got both a rabbi and a priest, and if last night's rehearsal is any indication, they can't stand each other. Same goes for the families. It was like being caught in the middle of a turf war."

"Come on, how bad could it be?"

"The rehearsal lasted three hours." Ivy shook her head as she remembered the endless bickering. "They fought over everything. Where to stand. What order to stand in. Who goes first. The parents cursed, the grandparents yelled, a couple cousins got into a shoving match, and finally the happy couple joined in. Tracy actually threw her ribbon bouquet from the bridal shower at one of the readers and knocked his glasses off. It took me an hour to negotiate a truce about which side of the aisle to seat the bride's family."

Ben gave a long, low whistle. "Sounds like a fun group. Would've been great to get on film. Doesn't do me any good now. Maybe they got it all out of their systems. With my luck, they'll be on their best behavior. I need a guarantee of something really big, something our viewers will talk about for days."

She realized he truly had no idea of what was in store for tonight. As hard as it was to believe, Tracy must've kept a lid on her big secret. Delighted, Ivy stifled a grin and tried to look thoughtful. "Bagpiper in a kilt?"

"Run of the mill."

"Bride and groom in a paddleboat?"

"Decent, but not as good as you doing a header down the stairs." He surged to his feet. "Sorry, but if you can't bring anything better to the table, something with real shock value, we don't have a deal."

She pursed her lips, took a beat. "How do you feel about a skydiver?"

His mouth dropped open, then he shook his head slowly and raised a warning hand. "Don't toy with me."

"Wouldn't dream of it." His reaction was everything she'd hoped. And their quick back and forth was the most fun she'd had all week. Now the tables were turned. She was once more in control of the situation.

"Seriously? A skydiver? What the hell for?" He sounded incredulous.

"He's bringing the rings." An array of emotions washed across his face; excitement, amusement and disbelief. Giggling at his reaction, she jumped up. Her bruised knees sent up a protest, but after a quick wince she pushed the discomfort aside. Grabbing his hand, she pulled Ben over to the window. The majestic stone hall sat at the edge of a pond that bordered the Lincoln Park Zoo. "Do you see the dock for the paddleboats? If everything goes according to plan, he'll land there."

"As landing strips go, this one doesn't leave much room for error. What happens if he misses?"

"Funny, that's exactly what I wondered. I consulted a map of the zoo, and my best guess for an accidental landing is the zebra or kangaroo exhibit."

"Which means no chance of life-threatening injuries, but a damn good chance of a kangaroo chasing a parachute?" Ben grabbed Ivy by the shoulders and kissed her hard and fast on the lips. The kiss was more than a peck. She'd classify it as a smooch. Just long and firm enough to tell her this man knew how to kiss. Not quite long enough to make her head spin, but it did wake up every nerve ending between her pale pink toenails and the pearl studs in her ears. Of course above all else, it made her want more. To her dismay, he released her and spun back to the window, probably plotting camera angles.

"It's like Christmas and my birthday all wrapped up in one gigantic present." The words tumbled out of him in a rush. "The skydiver's enough to make my boss dance a jig. But the chances of something going wrong are huge, and if it does, the show's fans will go crazy. I can't believe this is happening on my last shoot!"

His level of excitement surprised her. "Tracy must've told you she'd planned something exciting in order to win your contest and get on *WWS*."

"Had no idea. She didn't have to qualify or anything. We pick the names out of a hat. What makes this show different is the couple lets us follow them on the honeymoon. You'd be amazed the way couples fall apart on their honeymoon, and we're there to capture every tear, every thrown drink, and every night the groom winds up on the sofa of the bridal suite."

So much for happily ever after. "It sounds depressing."

Ben shrugged. "Can't let it get to you. I mean, these people would get into it with or without the cameras. The divorce rate is still over fifty percent in this country."

Ivy swatted his arm. "Don't use that word!" Did the man have no sense at all?

His head snapped around. "What word?"

"The D word." He still looked mystified. "Divorce," she said in a pointed whisper.

"Why not? It's a statistic, not an omen."

"Even if you aren't superstitious, it seems flat-out rude to mention that word on a wedding day. This is the one day when the whole world revolves around their love. One beautiful, untarnished day when everyone puts their petty arguments to the side and concentrates on the magic of love." Ben looked at her like she'd just sprouted wings.

"You can't really believe that load of crap," he said flatly.

Ivy was used to this reaction, but it still stung every time. "First of all, I believe it with every fiber of my being."

"Do you believe in the Tooth Fairy, too?"

"Secondly," she pressed on, despite his interruption, "it doesn't matter if you or I believe it. It's my job to give clients the perfect day. They have to feel the cartoon hearts floating overhead and doves carrying a happily-ever-after banner. Whether it's an illusion or reality, they get to live that fantasy for eight hours."

Hands shoved deep in pockets, he held her steady gaze, considering. After a minute he nodded. "You've got a point. I bet you're really good at your job."

"I try." Ten years of hard work scrabbling her way up the competitive Chicago wedding ladder were wrapped up in those two words.

"Well, for you, I'll give it a shot. As of this moment, I'll officially table my cynicism, my completely realistic view of relationships, and years of experience."

Wow. It was both surprising and sad how many

pounds of emotional baggage weighed down that single sentence. His past must be littered with heartbreak and disappointment. And to Ivy, there was almost nothing sadder than a person who didn't believe in true love. But this time her pity was overshadowed by annoyance at his condescending tone. "Don't put yourself out on my account."

"No, I mean it. You've made quite the impression. I don't want to be the big dark cloud on your perfect day."

She squinted up at him. "Really? No mocking? No snide comments behind my back to your camera guy? No barely veiled hostility aimed at the groom?"

He spread his hands wide, the picture of innocence. "What can I say, Ms. Rhodes? You turned my day around with the possibility of an utter train wreck, then capped it off with a kiss. In my book, that means I owe you a favor. I figure a sunny disposition is the nicest way to repay you."

"You know you stole that kiss," she grumbled. It still rankled how quickly he'd ended it.

"Fair enough." Ben edged closer, and Ivy automatically countered, which brought her flush against the window niche. He caged her in by resting his hands on the deep window sill. She was forced to arch her back in order to meet his eyes. The position thrust her breasts against the stiff lapels of his tux jacket. All the air in the room vanished, and her heart thudded. Without a doubt, Ben was back in charge, and she was merely along for the ride.

"Next time will be different."

"How do you know? I mean," she hastily corrected herself, "what makes you think there will be a next time?"

He chuckled, and kept that sea-blue gaze locked on her. "Certain things in life are inevitable. Sunrise. Hunger. And my kissing you again. Something ignited between us the minute I picked you up. Don't try to deny it."

Heat suffused Ivy's face. Ben lifted his left hand to stroke the spot on her neck where her pulse fluttered rapidly. It was a light touch, and he used only a single finger to trace the path of her vein. It was one of the most erotic moments of Ivy's life. The room, the wedding, the people banging glasses in the hallway disappeared. Her world shrank to a single patch of skin. And yet at the same time, she registered chills racing through her entire body. With a flutter of lashes her eyes closed.

"Are you the wedding planner?" A harsh, accusing voice bellowed across the hall. Ivy's eyes flew open. Ben's expression was unreadable as he stepped back and turned to face the interloper. She pushed off the window sill with a deep breath.

"Yes, I am. What can I do for you, sir?"

A man resplendent in full Scottish dress hustled toward her. The chain on his sporran clattered with every step. His kilt swished in a very unmasculine fashion, tartan plaid trailing behind him. "You can give me my money. The wedding's in less than two hours and I haven't been paid yet. There'll be no bagpipes down the aisle unless you pay me what I'm rightfully owed. Five hundred dollars. In cash."

The last vestige of delicious romance left her system. In its place, Ivy donned a practiced, calming smile. A threat to halt the wedding, a demand for an exorbitant amount of cash she didn't have—it was another average day at work.

CHAPTER TWO

Meticulous planning will enable everything a
man does to appear spontaneous.

—Mark Caine

OLLIE RAN IN, camera at the ready on his shoulder. Ben
waved his hand to indicate he should keep rolling and
received a nod of acknowledgement. It didn't surprise
him that Ollie was hot on the trail of the unhappy bagpiper. The kid had great instincts, and could sniff out
trouble brewing a mile away.

"No stalling, now. You can't treat me like this. I demand full payment immediately." The man causing the
ruckus was short, bald and full of righteous anger. He
slipped in and out of a weak attempt at a Scottish accent every couple of words. The bagpipe cradled like
a baby in his left arm was covered in a bright orange
plaid. It clashed painfully with the red tartan over his
shoulder. Ben wondered how obvious it would be if he
slipped on his sunglasses to mute the effect.

"Don't worry, sir. I'm sure we'll get everything
straightened out." Ivy's tone was polite and soothing,
her expression placid. Her calm under such an attack
was amazing to behold. Ben had seen other wedding
planners crumble under far less. She looked so unas-

suming in her pink dress, but the petite brunette clearly had a spine of steel.

"There's nothing to straighten out. I want my money. Period."

"If I could get your name…" Ivy's voice dropped off as she led the man to a table in the center of the hall. Ben trailed behind, staying out of the shot but still close enough to hear everything. He didn't want to miss a second of the show.

"Robert Bruce."

Ben snorted. He couldn't help himself. As producer, he was supposed to be objective and most of all, stay out of everything. But none of the wedding party was around, and it just slipped out. Unfortunately, it caught the attention of the already riled piper.

"What's your problem?" The man gently settled his bagpipe on a chair and turned to confront Ben, hands on hips.

"Struck me funny, is all."

"You wouldn't be making fun of my name, would you, laddie?"

Another snort escaped him, this time of disbelief. "No way is that really your name."

Ivy's eyes shot daggers at him as she rifled through her stack of contracts in a leather portfolio. "Please don't exacerbate the situation, Bennett."

"Hey, it's a good marketing ploy. Robert Bruce happened to be the biggest hero in Scottish history. Takes a big pair to borrow the name of the guy who freed his country from England." Ben stroked his chin. "A lot to live up to—some might even say disrespectful." Although unprofessional and plain wrong to goad the man, he still found it irresistible. This made his fourth wedding in three weeks, and he was fed up with self-important jerks. He simply didn't give a damn about this crap show anymore. Thanks to his promotion, to-day's event hummed with a last day of school sensation of impending freedom.

"Are ye casting aspersions on my lineage?" Robert Bruce bristled like an over-furled rooster.

"Come on! Using the word *laddie* doesn't make you Scottish. I peg your real accent as pure Long Island, not Loch Ness."

Bruce's shoulders slumped. And with his next words, the burr disappeared completely. "Alright, you got me. I'm just trying to make a buck. People like to think they've hired the real McCoy. What's the big deal? It's not a crime."

"No, but extortion is." Ivy charged forward, bran-dishing a sheaf of papers. "My clients paid you in good faith, and you storm in here demanding more? How dare you?"

"All they gave me was a deposit. I don't care about their good faith. I want my five hundred dollars." His tone was surly.

"Then you'd better check your bank account, be-cause that's where it is." Ivy thrust the papers under his nose. "Isn't this a receipt, signed by you, acknowl-edging that Tracy paid you in full over a month ago?"

The seconds ticked by in silence as Bruce skimmed the paper. Then he crumpled the receipt into a tiny ball and tossed it over his shoulder. "Like I said, just trying to make a buck. Works most of the time." He picked up his bagpipe.

"I won't tell anyone about this if you agree to stay and play for the entire cocktail hour," she bargained.

"Hey, I'm only supposed to play the ceremony."

"True. But if you don't stay, I'll get on every wedding website and blacklist you. Then I'll contact the Better Business Bureau and have them investigate. Wouldn't it be much less trouble for both of us if you stay an extra hour?" Her tone was sweet and beguiling, in stark contrast to the down and dirty nature of her threat. It was beautiful to watch.

"Now you've got me over a barrel. Guess I'll stay." Bruce scooped up his bagpipe. "This job used to be easy. Damned interfering wedding planners ruin everything," he grumbled as he stomped out of the hall.

"Did you get all of that?" Ben asked Ollie.

"You bet. Great stuff!"

"Miss Rhodes, you sure know how to deliver the goods. We haven't even seen the bride and groom yet and we already have some great footage." Ben bounced on the balls of his feet in excitement. Talk about ending with a bang. He might not care about the show, but he still loved a great piece of film. "This is going to be one humdinger of a wedding."

"You're lucky I don't throw you out on your ass!" Ivy hissed. Her glossy lips thinned in anger. "Pull another stunt like that and both of you will be on the sidewalk before you can blink."

Hmm. So a bit of hellcat hid under the elegant pink dress. Every few minutes she revealed a new side. It sure wasn't boring to hang out with her. "Don't have a clue what you're talking about. But whatever Ollie did, I'll make sure he apologizes."

"Not him, you idiot. You're the one who screwed up!" Her voice rose to a near screech by the last word. And of course, Ollie kept rolling.

"Turn off the camera and give us a few minutes," Ben ordered. No way would he allow raw footage of him being scolded by someone who looked like a bridesmaid.

"You don't have long," Ollie warned. "I saw some limos pull into the lot right before I came in. This place is about to be flooded with happy wedding people."

"Go get some best wishes interviews. I'll be right behind you." Ben grabbed Ivy's hand and dragged her back to the window and a shred of privacy. "Was it really necessary to yell at me in front of my assistant?"

"Maybe not," she conceded after a moment. "But I don't have time to play nice. We're about to be overrun with guests."

He had a watch, didn't he? Why did everyone keep drumming that into his head? "Yeah, I get that. Mind telling me why you're so pissed off?"

Ivy huffed out a breath. "I was handling the bagpiper. Or at least, I was until you barged in and made fun of him. You escalated the situation unnecessarily."

She had a point. Worse, she had a really good point. The kind of mistake even the greenest rookie wouldn't make. Part of him was big enough to admit that. But the other part, the *this is my last day and I don't give a damn* part wasn't ready to roll over. Perversely, the need to defend himself reared its ugly head.

"Come on, the guy was a jerk. He tried to scam you for five hundred bucks!"

His rebuttal fell on deaf ears. Her scowl didn't change. Ivy crossed her arms. She looked like a stern pre-school teacher. It was adorable and intimidating at the same time. "And by following my standard procedures, I caught him and put an end to it. All you did was enrage him."

Deflection hadn't worked. Maybe a change of subject would take the edge off her anger. "Before everyone gets here, we should go over the itinerary for tonight." He reached into his back pocket for his crumpled copy of the schedule.

"It's your job to record the action, not take part in it." Guess she wanted to linger on his mistake like a tongue poking a sore tooth.

He flattened the schedule onto the windowsill. "Ouch! The truth really does hurt."

"So you agree your actions were ill advised?"

Her relentless badgering wore him down. Time to give in. "It was stupid. My head's not really in the game today. Sorry." To his complete surprise, a smile broke across her face.

"See? Now I can trust that you won't let it happen again. Every wedding comes with one stumbling block, and hopefully this was it." She stuck out her hand. "Let's aim for a drama-free day."

"Where's the fun in that?" Ben took her hand, but didn't shake. Instead, he rolled it over and traced the inner length of each finger with a feather-light touch. When she responded with a full body shiver, he finished by dropping a kiss on the inside of her wrist where her pulse throbbed furiously. "Am I forgiven now?"

"For what?" Ivy asked on a breathy sigh.

Ben knew enough about women to keep his chuckle all to himself. Still, it felt damn good to fluster the seemingly unflappable planner. "You know, waving a red cape in front of our pseudo-Scottish piper."

"Oh. Oh!" Ivy's eyes snapped back into focus, and

she jerked her hand out of his. "Fine. Just behave your-self the rest of the day. I'll be keeping an eye on you."

I just bet you will, he thought, enjoying the view of her tight ass twitching beneath the satin skirt as she all but ran out of the room.

BEN'S TRAINED EYE took in the scene spread out before him like a postcard. Guests clustered on the flagstone patio behind the brick building. The florist had an-chored the long runner bisecting rows of white wooden folding chairs with pots bursting with some kind of red and yellow blooms that echoed those in the bride's bouquet. Wildflowers clumped together in a serpentine border fronting the wide expanse of a clear blue pond. No doubt it'd make for a beautiful shot. He lowered his video camera and called over his shoulder to Ivy pick-ing her way across the moss-covered paving stones.

"Fifty bucks says the skydiver lands in the kanga-roo pen."

Ollie gave his lens a final wipe with the polishing cloth. "I want in on that action. Fifty from me on a pond splashdown."

"Oh, for goodness sake!" Ivy stopped dead in her tracks. Her head swiveled from one man to the other, then back again. "I don't wager against my client's per-fect day. Since that's why they hire me, it strikes me as a bit counterintuitive."

Ben shrugged with one shoulder, the other cur-rently weighted down beneath his camera. "Well, you could put your money on him sticking the landing, but frankly, it's a sucker bet."

"No betting." She waggled a finger in front of his face, the nail painted the same toe-shoe pink as her dress. "You'll jinx the whole thing. Brides are highly superstitious."

"So we won't tell her." Ollie caught the cautionary look of death glared his way, and turned tail. Coward. "I'll be in position over by the guests if you need me."

"We're a go in three minutes. Exactly," Ivy called after him.

Funny joke, seeing as how she had no way of knowing when this guy would plummet from the sky. Except that she didn't crack a smile. Ben scratched behind his ear, trying to appear nonchalant. Wedding planners could be very territorial. Treading lightly didn't begin to describe the caution he'd use for fear of being seen as questioning her judgment. The only thing worse than a bossy planner was a ticked off, bossy planner.

"Don't you want to wait until you at least have a visual of the skydiver?"

Ivy loosened her death grip on her leather portfolio to grab her skirt before it brushed the tall, weedy-looking things lining the path. "Oh, I'm not worried about Alan. He swears he can adjust his descent and land on the proverbial dime. Besides, all my weddings start on time."

Ben had rolled tape professionally on almost one hundred weddings. Add to that the dozen he'd attended personally, it made him, if not an expert, at least well versed. Which meant he could count on one hand—scratch that. He couldn't think of a single time a wedding began at the appointed hour. She must've fallen back on her standard convince-the-rubes-five-thousand-dollars-is-reasonable-for-a-wedding-planner spiel by spitting out that empty promise. But they were both vendors. Comrades in arms, for the day, anyway. He wanted to hear her real stats.

"No need to over-inflate your success rate for me. I'm not in the market for a planner."

"Did I not enunciate?" She slowed her speech and over-pronounced each word. "Every wedding I run starts on time. Ask anyone."

His jaw dropped. Literally unhinged like a cobra getting ready to swallow an entire wombat. "In that case, you're more than a mere planner. You're a freaking miracle worker. How do you do it?"

"I find that people tend to rise to whatever expectations are set for them."

Ben mirrored her smug, single eyebrow raise and tossed her words back at her. "Really? I find that, given the opportunity, people tend to disappoint on a global scale." The woman didn't just wear rose-colored glasses. She lived in a fluffy, cotton candy bubble. One day reality was bound to fly through her air space and crap all over it.

They rounded the copse of trees hiding the bride. Or rather, the trees that almost managed to hide the super-puffy satin skirt. A red and yellow tartan draped from one shoulder to a belt at her waist. The identically colored bouquet cascaded down to where Ben guessed her knees must be. Her face, though, shone with all the incandescence of his best flash. A light meter couldn't begin to capture the beams of joy radiating from her eyes.

"Tracy, you are a vision." With an exaggerated bow, Ben dropped to one knee and kissed her hand. But he also carefully anchored the camera with his other hand, rolling every second. You never knew what would be worth keeping until the editors hacked away at hours and hours of footage to find the cringe-worthy moments that brought the viewers back every week.

"Usually I'd disagree, but today I truly feel beautiful. Good weather, good hair day, great dress. It's everything I'd hoped." A tiny, vertical line appeared between her brows. "Or am I so excited I overlooked something? Something obvious and important. Do I have a long string of toilet paper stuck to my shoe?" Like a dog chasing its tail, she turned in a slow circle, looking back over her shoulder.

Ivy smoothed a light hand down the veil, then reached down to twitch Tracy's skirts even fuller. "No toilet paper, I promise. You shouldn't worry about those things. It's why you hired me, remember? To take away all the stress and details of today so you could sit back and bask in starting your new life with Seth."

"You're right. I've spent the last fourteen months obsessing over every tiny detail. To say it's hard to let go, relinquish control, is an understatement." Tracy's self-deprecating grin quirked up the corners of her glossy lips. "But I knew I wouldn't be able to enjoy today if I tried to do it all myself. And my friend Brittney said you were wonderful. You made sure she had fun while you ran the wedding like a Swiss clock. Knowing that makes it a little easier to relax."

"I'll make sure there's a glass of champagne in your hand as soon as you and Seth finish recessing down the aisle," Ivy promised. "Bubbles tend to jump start the relaxation process."

Ben marveled at her calm. In his experience, the term wedding planner was synonymous with four-star general. Someone who barked orders into a headset. Bullied the wedding party into order. Ran circles around the bride, fussing and twittering. But not Ivy. She acted as more of a sounding board for the bride, almost like the foam covers around microphones that filter out ambient noise. Even more surprising, she seemed genuinely happy for Tracy. Hard to believe, since an hour before she'd been filled with resentment at being blindsided into appearing on *WWS*, all courtesy of the bride.

A breathtaking smile washed across Ivy's face. The power of it rocked Ben to his core. Just a smile, right? People smiled a dozen times a day. Half the time it was an involuntary reaction, at best. So why couldn't he resist zooming in, right past Tracy to fill the screen with her twinkling hazel eyes?

"Tracy, are you ready to marry the man of your dreams?" she asked.

The bride took a deep breath, held it, then nodded. Ivy stepped out from the cover of the trees and raised her arms. Ben trailed her, seizing the opportunity to be the lone voice of reason.

"You're really not going to wait for the skydiver?"

"No need. He'll drop down right on time."

Maybe with her head so firmly in the clouds, she imagined she could see the parachute unfurling already. All Ben knew was that the clear April sky above didn't hold a plane for as far as he could see in any direction. "Sure, in a perfect world. But this world of ours is light years from perfect."

"Your lack of faith is astounding, and more than a little insulting." She moved her arms up and down in wide gestures, out to the sides.

"What are you doing? Trying to flag down the next

plane that soars by and hope it's got a spare set of wedding rings and a guy willing to jump down with them?"

"Semaphores."

Ben blinked. "You lost me."

"A signaling system, usually with flags. Of vital importance to the British Navy during the Napoleonic Wars. Lets me communicate with my assistant Julianna silently, to let her know we're ready to begin. I picked up the basic alphabet years ago as a lifeguard."

He craned his head to see a short woman with a sleek brunette pixie cut signaling in their direction from the open second floor porches where the guests congregated. Ben hadn't noticed Ivy even *had* an assistant. Talk about working smoothly behind the scenes! His admiration for her skill kicked up another few notches. With her running the show, his last official event for *WWS* might just come off without a hitch. And wouldn't that drive his producers nuts!

"So no headsets or walkie talkies for you two?"

Ivy snorted. "It's a wedding, not a space shuttle launch. They're a measure of last resort for oversized events."

Ben pressed on. Maybe the viewers would be interested in the behind-the-scenes minutiae. Of course, he really wanted to see if she'd throw off her own vaunted schedule by talking with him. "Such as?"

"Filipino weddings, for example, utilize sponsors in the ceremony. Their typical bridal parties are over fifty people. Imagine that many people squeezed up the stairs, into a choir loft to line up for the processional. If I'm at the back with the bride, there's no way to see or hear the front of the line. Times like that, Julianna and I utilize electronics out of necessity. But for a wedding this size, I'd call it sheer pretention." She walked to the edge of the pond and waved at the first bridesmaid and groomsman. Each of the four pairs floated in their own swan boat. Ben hoped none of the groomsmen's legs gave out midway. Paddleboats could be a real workout.

With perfect synchronicity, the ear-splitting drone of the bagpipe rent the air as the first boat began to move. Ben made sure to get a close up, past the giant curved fiberglass swan neck to the red and yellow tartan yarmulke atop the groomsman's head. It matched the pattern in the sash around the bridesmaid's waist. By the time this wedding ended, his eyes would be bleeding red and yellow. One by one, the boats slowly glided across the pond. Ben kept one eye fixed on the cloudless sky.

To his surprise, a small biplane sputtered into the airspace directly overhead. As the first boat docked, a dark speck dropped from the wing of the plane. Seconds later, a red and yellow plaid parachute ballooned open, slowing the fast free fall. Ivy might've actually pulled off this crazy, complicated plan. Deep down, though, Ben still hoped the guy would land in the kangaroo pen.

"Tracy, as soon as Alan lands you'll start up the path," Ivy reminded her. Both women stood, riveted, eyes trained on the now visible man waving a small pillow. Down he gently plummeted.

Even though he'd told Ollie to get the skydiver, Ben couldn't resist tracking the descent with his own camera. At this point, a landing on the kangaroos or antelope didn't appear likely. Alan used his free arm to tug on ropes that corrected his course. By the time the last boat docked, he floated directly over the pond. The *center* of the pond. Zooming in, Ben could see lines of grim determination around his mouth as he yanked at the cords, but it was too late. With a mighty splash, Alan landed in the water, his parachute a bright spreading splotch on the serene blue surface.

He switched his focus to the open mouthed bride. Surprisingly, next to her Ivy still looked the picture of calm. Only her clenched fists gave any indication of alarm at the turn of events. Ben checked his watch and didn't bother to stifle the belly laugh surging out of him. He poked her in the arm.

"Gotta hand it to you. He's right on time."

CHAPTER THREE

> Marriage is popular because it combines the maximum of temptation with the maximum of opportunity.
>
> —George Bernard Shaw

BEN THOUGHT ABOUT muting the sound, but then remembered it wasn't his job to be sensitive. From day one, the directive had been crystal clear—keep rolling no matter what, especially if things get ugly. The weirder and more embarrassing, the better. His producers weren't fans of simple, beautiful events. They craved tears, hair pulling, name calling and objects hurled across the room. Not the most caring mission statement to follow, but it paid the bills.

So he stood by and recorded Tracy's shrill squeals for posterity. The nearby zoo animals were probably going crazy from the noise. And it was a sure bet the guests, even all the way on the opposite side of the pond, could hear, too.

"My wedding is ruined. Ruined! How are we supposed to get married without rings? I knew Alan would screw this up. He's Seth's most useless friend." The serene bride had vanished, replaced by a foot-stomping, hand-shaking virago. "It took the idiot an extra year to finish college because he slept through four of his final exams, two semesters in a row. He's failed the CPA exam twice, so he does the books for his father's company. At the bachelor party in Vegas, he got everyone thrown out of the casino. But this—this is too much to believe, even for Alan."

Her face an implacable mask, Ben watched Ivy's eyes slowly track the waterlogged man wade out of the pond, his sodden parachute dragging behind him. He gave a weak wave at the guests, indicating the landing left him in one piece. When Tracy finally paused for a breath, Ivy leapt into the breach.

"Don't say another word," she ordered. It amused him the way she channeled the firmness of a school teacher. "Alan didn't ruin your wedding. There's no question that he made himself look like an idiot. But as long as you and Seth promise to love each other forever, this wedding is perfect."

Tracy sucked in a breath, then another. Ben could see the physical effort she put into smoothing out the crease between her eyebrows. The white knuckle grip on her bouquet eased up a little. But then her eyes narrowed. "I don't see the ring pillow. Bad enough I'm going to have to follow his trail of water and pond scum down the aisle. Where is the ring pillow?"

Ivy swung her gaze over to Alan, using both his hands to shrug out of the harness. Yards of yellow and red fabric puddled around his feet, but there was no sign of a puffy satin square sporting a set of rings. "In the pond, I imagine," she said, matter-of-factly.

Ben bit back a guffaw at the last second, turning it into a cough. She cracked him up. One minute acting like love solved all the problems of the universe, and the next blithely laying out the cold, hard reality of the situation. How could someone simultaneously be so practical and yet so mushy? Like a candy bar, her gooey center wore a hard outer shell of crunchy sensibility.

All the color leeched from Tracy's face. Ben braced himself, one foot ahead of the other. It wouldn't be the first time he'd had to leap to catch a fainting bride. He had two cracked camera lenses and a faint scar on his left knee to prove it. In the mother of all mood swings, Tracy's shock wore off in a second, replaced by anger. Heat raced up from her chest, turning everything above her lacy neckline the same bright crimson as her flowers.

"Do you know how much those rings cost? More than shitheaded Alan makes in a year. Seth's band is titanium, and mine is platinum with *twenty-seven* channel-set diamonds. All fucking flawless. How are we supposed to get married without rings?"

Yup, he could see why the producers chose her for *Wild Wedding Smackdown.* When the price tag became more important than the priceless memories, then a couple was considered good fodder for the show. Their viewers favored lowbrow, impolite and downright uncouth antics. Nothing like playing to the lowest common denominator.

Ivy dug into the bag she'd propped against the far side of their sheltering tree. A moment later she produced a white pillow, complete with rings. Spring sunlight glinted off the band of diamonds? No, they couldn't be real. No way did she carry around a spare set of actual rings. But if they were Seth and Tracy's, why weren't they at the bottom of the pond? Ivy hitched up her skirt with one hand, and presented the pillow to Tracy with the other.

"Breathe and count to ten." Using her elbow, she bumped up Tracy's bouquet so the flowers surrounded the bride's nose. Not missing a step, she hurried forward to stop Alan from coming any closer. Too bad. Ben would've paid good money to watch Alan try to blunder his way through an apology. The bride looked like a scratcher.

Ivy handed over the pillow and with a shove in the small of his back, sent Alan on his way toward the Great Hall. As predicted, each squishy step left a wet mark on the cement and a few globs of mud and greenish muck, souvenirs from the bottom of the pond. A few more of those flashy arm signals at her assistant, and the piper switched to the wedding march.

"Time to start your new life with Seth." With a beaming smile, she pulled Tracy out from behind the tree. After a quick assessment, she then moved her over a few steps to the right so the spotlessly white dress wouldn't drag through Alan's slime trail. She gave a final floofing of the long train as Tracy began the walk down the path.

Once she was out of earshot, Ben couldn't hold in his question another second. He swung the camera to face Ivy. "What was that bait and switch you pulled on her? Are those rings a couple of great fakes you dug out of a Cracker Jack box?"

"Of course not. Those are the real rings, and the real ring pillow, for that matter. Didn't you notice the red and yellow tartan ribbon tied around the bands?"

"Then what did Alan risk his life carrying down thousands of feet through the ozone layer?"

Ivy's lips upturned in a slow, sly smile. "A cheap imitation."

Ben almost bobbled the camera. "Did the bride and groom know?"

She shook her head from side to side. "They only needed to know that when it was time, the rings would be there. Why worry them with logistics? Wedding rings are an integral part of a sacred ritual." Her stern, all-business expression settled like a mask onto her face. "I don't trust them to a four-year-old, no matter how cute his first tuxedo is. I don't trust them to a dog wearing an adorable bow tie. There wasn't a chance in the world I'd risk them on a skydive. Last night at the rehearsal I gave Alan the stunt pillow."

"You may talk a good game about romance and true love, but behind it all you've got a ruthless core of practicality."

And then she sniffed. By the third sniff, Ben figured it out.

"You're crying, aren't you?"

A quivering finger pointed at Tracy, entering the building. "Every bride, every time. I can't help it. The shiny promise of a lifetime of love always tears me up."

Ben lowered the camera to the ground and shook the pins and needles out of his arm. He used his other to dig in his back pocket for a handkerchief. "Here. Blot away."

"You're quite the well-prepared gentleman. Thank you." Ivy dabbed below each eye. They must teach that to girls the same time they learn how to put on makeup. *How to whisk away tears smudge free, in three easy steps.* "I don't know how anyone can stay dry eyed at a wedding."

"Easy. Know the divorce stats."

"What a horrible thing to say." She froze in the act

of refolding his handkerchief, her eyes round circles of wounded naiveté. "You can't really be that cynical."

"Wanna bet?" Ben picked up the camera and took off for the Great Hall. No reason to stick around and listen to her attempt to defend the mythical sanctity of marriage. Too many women had already tried to flog that dead horse in front of him. Didn't work. He was immune.

Not to say he didn't like women. All it took was a single, sassy glance—kind of like the one Ivy leveled at him a few hours ago—and he'd be in pursuit. Chasing women was fun. Flirting even more fun, and a sweaty round between the sheets ranked right up there with an island vacation home. Great while you were there, but just a financial and emotional drain once out of sight.

"The divorce rate is actually in decline in the United States. Some studies put it as low as 41percent. And 81percent of college graduates stay married. It's all how you mix and sift the numbers." Ivy popped up at his elbow-spewing statistics like a twisted version of a jack-in-the-box. He'd heard it all before. Seen the same sleight of hand employed by guys running street games on hapless tourists in Battery Park.

"You know how to avoid losing at a shell game? Don't play."

"Marriage isn't a con. It's a miracle."

"Right up there with walking on water, huh? Too bad we didn't see any of that today."

"In a world filled with billions of people, it is a miracle," Ivy repeated stubbornly, "when two people find their soul mate. Once paired up, they take a leap and pledge themselves to each other for the rest of their lives."

Ben lowered his voice as they entered the building, stopping at the steps where they met. "You're right. It's a miracle anyone is that gullible. Or stupid. Take your pick."

Cocking her head, she tapped a single, slim finger against her chin. Gave him a thoughtful look, which he assumed could only mean trouble. "Oh, I see. You're messing with me. Trying to get my goat, as it were. All so you can run a promo with a thirty-second hook to reel viewers into the next episode. Something like *watch the crazy wedding planner lose her cool*."

He refrained from pointing out that the camera currently hung from his hand at knee height. Lens cap on, power off. If her misconception meant her saccharine tirade might wind down, he'd keep his mouth shut. Why stir the pot? Although she did look even prettier with the glint of battle in her hazel eyes and a pink flush in her cheeks. The kiss he'd grabbed earlier put the taste of her on his mouth. Not long enough to qualify as an appetizer, the peck had been barely an amuse bouche. Now he wanted to go back for a full, seven-course meal of her lips and the tight little package that went with them.

Ivy barreled on. "Well, it won't work. The key to being a successful wedding consultant is to remain calm, no matter what problems an irate mother or drunken groomsmen may toss at you. Not to toot my own horn, but I'm quite successful. My serene disposition is a thing of wonder."

Oh yeah, she gave him lots to wonder about. How long her hair would be once he pulled the pins out of its tight twist on the back of her head. If her underwear—and her nipples—were the same pale pink as her dress and shoes. How many licks it would take to turn her serenity into breathless pants of pleasure.

Then Ben remembered there were over one hundred people on the other side of the door, and he had a job to do. "We should catch the end of the ceremony, your serene highness."

Ivy surprised him with a giggle. "Wait and see. You may mock me now, but by the end of the night, it'll ring true when you call me the Queen of Calm. The Princess of Peace."

"The Dispassionate Duchess?"

"Don't use that one." She tossed him a saucy wink over her shoulder as she ran up the stairs to watch from the balcony. "I'm plenty passionate."

Ben hefted his camera back up, using her well-shaped calves to check the focus. This could turn out to be the best last-day-on-the-job ever.

Ivy TOED OFF one shoe, then the other. The cool stone of the portico soothed her aching feet. Eight hours of countless trips up and down the stairs, tromping around part of the zoo for pictures and basically running herself ragged to always stay one step ahead of the bride and groom took its toll, even in flats.

The four-tiered cake (red velvet and lemon, once more mirroring the wedding colors) was cut. She'd convinced a few of the burlier groomsmen to help her move the presents to the parents' cars. A white stretch limo idled, ready to whisk the happy couple to a swanky hotel with a view of Lake Michigan. Although why a couple embarking on their honeymoon needed a view escaped her. If it was her wedding night, she sure wouldn't spend it gazing out the window.

The persistent bass throb from the dance floor below pulsed in time to the low throb at the base of her skull. A few more songs and she could call it a night. Sighing, Ivy rested her elbows on the wide, rough-hewn stone window ledge.

"Care for a drink?" asked a low, male voice.

The stock answer popped out before she slipped back into her shoes and turned around. "Thank you for the offer, but I don't drink on the job."

"Scared you'll get wasted and flash all the overweight spinsters doing the Electric Slide?"

That spun her around fast. "Bennett Westcott. Why am I not surprised? You don't have even a modicum of respect for this wedding, do you?"

"Sure I do." He brought out a bottle from behind his back and slowly waggled it back and forth. "They served Veuve Clicquot champagne. I very much respect the good taste of whoever paid for a dozen cases of the stuff."

Ivy kicked her shoes off again, relieved she didn't have to put her game face back on quite yet. "Tracy's father bought the bubbly to celebrate his daughter's happiness. If you don't share his sentiment, you'd better have a darn good excuse for drinking it."

"*Au contraire*, thou sweet champion of love. You've got me all wrong." Ben sidled closer, leaning his hip next to hers on the wall. The sweating bottle he sat on the ledge, using it for leverage while he pulled out the cork. It slid free of the neck with a muted pop, followed by a quiet hiss of bubbles pushing for freedom. He hefted the bottle in the air as if lifting a glass for a toast.

"I, Ben Westcott, do solemnly vow that I believe

today is the happiest day of Tracy's life." He took a quick swig, straight from the bottle.

"Aha!" She knew he'd see the light. No one could resist the magic of a wedding. Love became tangible, frothing the air as effervescent as the bubbles he'd just swallowed.

"So far," he slowly intoned. "To be specific, she's happy today. No guarantees about tomorrow, or a month from now, or even a year."

No camera in sight, and yet still he baited her? Didn't he get that she was quite simply classier, not to mention far more tactful, than the wedding coordinators usually profiled on *WWS*? He could keep trying to push her buttons, but she refused to give him any more fodder for the show. There'd be no getting a rise out of her tonight.

"How about we meet in the middle, and agree the bride and groom had a wonderful day?"

"I can stipulate to that condition." Ben took another drink, then set the bottle down right next to her hand. "Thanks to you. It's really impressive, the knack you have for being in three places at once. Ollie and I could barely frame you in a shot before you'd dart off again. Never broke a sweat, and your smile never wavered. I know, because I watched for it."

"You smile stalked me?" Ivy didn't know how to feel about that. She tugged at the idea from all sides, like trying on a new dress in front of the mirror. A few reactions popped right up; a little intrigued, a little embarrassed—and a lot flirty.

"Catalogued you," Ben corrected. With one blunt-tipped finger, he traced slowly from her ear to her chin, electrifying every pore he passed over.

"The beaming, full-of-pride smile you shared with

all the parents. The joyful smile you used with Tracy and Seth. The indulgent yet chastising smile you bestowed on the groomsmen when you took tequila shots away from a couple of teenagers. Oh, and the worn out but satisfied smile you gave Julianna when you told her to go home."

Now his finger moved along her lower lip. Ivy couldn't resist when he pushed the corners up into a smile. It took all her energy not to let her mouth fall open and her tongue roll out.

"Why did you send Julianna home? Wedding's not over. You're still here, the DJ's still rocking out the crowd. You've got to be just as worn out as her."

So true. No matter how many hundreds of weddings Ivy did, the exhaustion never lessened. Hardened planners simply learned how to ignore it and work through it. And sleep in the next day. No client darkened their doors the day after an event before eleven. "There isn't much left to do. At this point in a wedding, I'm just killing time until the bride and groom leave. Present in body, in case there's a crisis, but in all honesty, not doing anything. No reason for two of us to stand around doing nothing."

Ben lifted his finger to tuck a stray wisp of hair behind her ear. The resulting goose bumps had absolutely nothing to do with the lake breeze rustling the nearby branches. "Which is exactly why most planners shove the end of the night close out onto their assistants."

"Aisle Bound is my company. I won't make my employees do a task solely because I don't want to." Hmm. Sounded very holier than thou. Nobody likes to hang out with a martyr. "We do trade off who gets stuck with it. Might I point out I don't see Ollie dogging your footsteps. You cut him loose too, didn't you?"

"About two songs ago. Kid's never been to Chicago before. He wanted to hit a few bars, and one of the groomsmen steered him toward Rush Street."

"Nice of you to give him a chance to live it up a little. He'll have a blast. And probably a killer hangover tomorrow morning. Will you be joining him later?"

Ben snorted out his obvious distaste at the idea. "My clubbing days are behind me. Besides, Ollie hasn't yet learned that the best place to pick up beautiful women is at a wedding. It just so happens that the prettiest one in the whole place is standing right in front of me." He kicked her shoes out of the way and moved in front of her, his hard body lined up flush against hers. "According to my information, we have two songs left until we can call it a night. Dance with me."

It was a command, not a request. Still, Ivy knew she had to offer at least token resistance. She excelled at brushing off polite and/or drunken requests to drink, to dance, to sit. Men really did view every woman at a wedding as an all-you-can-grab buffet. Everyone from the caterers to gangly teenagers acting on a dare to the ubiquitous groomsmen saw her as fair game. Even, in one extremely awkward situation, the newly divorced father of the bride who'd offered a hefty tip with a wink and a corresponding pinch on her ass. Ivy took random hook-up attempts in stride as just another odd quirk of her job. Sort of like having to wear cocktail dresses and ball gowns to work.

But this time, with Ben's rangy build pressed against her from shoulder to ankle, for the first time, the polite, automatic rebuff didn't feel like the right choice.

Despite her staunch professional ethics, which she'd always used as the foundation for turning away male attention (after all, you wouldn't ask a surgeon to dance right after he took out your father's gall bladder, would you?), Ivy did want to dance with Ben. "We're both still on the clock," she protested weakly.

"The guests are a floor below us. Nobody's been up here since the ceremony ended five hours ago." His right eyebrow streaked up. "Just a dance, Ms. Rhodes. I promise to leave what I'm sure is your squeaky-clean reputation intact. For now."

On the dance floor below, the music changed to something slow and romantic. After ten years in the business, Ivy knew almost every song in the standard DJ wedding rotation by heart. And this one was a classic, but for the life of her, she couldn't remember the name. Or make out the words. A saxophone's sultry wail acted like a magnet. Ivy lifted her head to meet Ben's eyes, turned almost black in the shadows. The thrumming beat hovered, vibrating between their bodies.

Ben didn't wait for her to make up her mind. He grabbed one hand, and moved her other to rest on his shoulder. His strong hand rested in the small of her back. Its weight, its heat commanded the entirety of her attention. Her whole being focused on the five or so inches of skin beneath his palm. A minute change of pressure urged her closer still. They began to sway to the rhythm. The movement brushed the stiff lapels of his tuxedo against her breasts. The satin of her dress wasn't nearly thick enough to prevent her from feeling it—and thereby switching from exhausted and dreamy to wide awake and very turned on in the blink of an eye.

Clothes on, hands not near any overtly erogenous zones, Ben somehow managed to tingle her from the inside out. Oh, this guy was dangerous. Walking-a-tightrope-drunk dangerous. Bomb-squad-technician-with-epilepsy dangerous. Discussing-religion-with-the-in-laws dangerous.

"We fit well together. Makes it easy to...dance," said Ben, a suggestive huskiness in his voice. Was it a line or was he serious? Ivy studied his face, but he stared back, unflinching and unreadable.

"I love to dance." Lame, horrible response. Ivy pictured herself taking a pop quiz in Flirting 101 and getting back a paper topped with a gigantic red F. Belle talked to the Beast while dancing. Cinderella entranced a prince in a single dance. Why couldn't she pull it together and flirt with the very handsome man whose pecs rippled beneath her touch?

"You're very good at this. Dancing, I mean. Smooth, not jerky." As opposed to her conversation style, which had all the smoothness of a fifteen-year-old grinding gears in driver's ed. Ivy never let lust cloud her brain. Romance was what normally spiraled her into speechlessness. Some candles, a bouquet of divine-smelling flowers, and a man could have her in one fell swoop. Ben, with his oddly grating manner, didn't cause any spikes on her romance-ometer. His hotness, on the other hand, speared off the charts.

"This?" He moved them a few steps away from the low stone wall, deeper into the darkness. "I mastered the eighth grade shuffle sway in...well...eighth grade."

Emboldened by she didn't know what, Ivy moved her hand up to curve around his neck. Her fingers raked through the thick, soft hair she'd itched to touch all day. Its longer than average shagginess gave her more to play with. The sun-streaked color brought to mind a lion's mane, especially since this dance felt almost as dangerous as tripping the light fantastic with a wild beast. Ben was slick and moved fast. No question that, out of the two of them, he was the ringmaster. However, she didn't intend to blindly follow his lead like a trained bear.

Ivy tugged out of his grasp to join her hands at the nape of his neck. Everything lined up so that every interesting part of him rubbed against the corresponding part on her. "*Now* it's the eighth-grade version. The only thing missing is the pervasive smell of old socks that always lingered in our gym." Great. Sweaty socks? That was how she stepped up her game? She closed her eyes in mortification. She really needed to stop talking. About five sentences ago.

Ben nuzzled the side of her neck. "You smell like springtime and sunshine."

Oh, he was good. If she hadn't been working, that remark would've puddled Ivy at his feet. Made her whip out a marker and write Take Me Now on her forehead. But professionalism (or the tattered shreds of it she stubbornly clung to) prevailed. Her tired legs rallied enough to keep her vertical. "It's Clinique Happy."

"Hmm. Must be working. I sure feel happy right now." He centered both hands in the small of her back, letting their weight nudge her even closer.

Ivy scribbled a mental Post-it. Tomorrow she'd hit the Macy's in Water Tower Place and stock up on a few bottles. And the bodywash and lotion in the same scent. Who knew this perfume had such a strong effect on men? Well, she'd bathe in the stuff from now on.

"What about you?" asked Ben. "Having a good time, or are you too worn out to follow your own perfume's advice?"

What to say? Admit he'd charmed his way past her defenses? Gush about the intrinsic romance of their moonlight dance? Confess her fingers literally itched to rip open his shirt and feel his skin? No. A combination of nagging professionalism and her nagging conscience (which sounded eerily similar to her best friend, Daphne) prevented her from taking the next step. Stick to cool politeness.

"I'll give credit where credit is due. Dancing with you is a very nice way to end the evening."

If his hands drifted even half an inch lower, they'd cross the line from seductive to groping. Ben didn't give off a lecherous vibe. Interested, sure, but not grabby. What a shame. The last time Ivy had even the chance of a man's hands anywhere near her ass was exactly one hundred eighteen days ago. Her disastrous New Year's Eve date. Which, to put a point on it, did not include any actual touching. Hard to get so much as a kiss and a squeeze out of a man who walked out on her halfway through dinner, leaving her with undrunk champagne and an unpaid bill.

Ivy had sulked and licked her wounds through January and half of February. But the pervasive spirit of love swirling around Valentine's Day buoyed her spirits. Unfortunately, readiness to date again rarely coincided with the availability and attention of a decent guy. In a nutshell, Ivy had developed a powerful itch over the last few months. One that Ben Westcott appeared more than capable of scratching. She could only hope for a geologically unlikely earthquake to shift his hands.

"Tell me, Ms. Rhodes, what's your favorite drink?" Ben pressed her head into the hollow below his collarbone, gently trailing his fingertips back and forth across the nape of her neck.

The answer required no thought whatsoever. Good thing, since her thoughts were centered on the flutters of sensation he raised, like dandelion seeds floating outward on a warm breeze. Bubbly and romantic, she named the first cocktail she'd legally ordered eight years ago and could never resist. "Kir royale."

"No surprise there. It's classy, old school and sweet. Just like you. See, you can tell a lot about a person by their drink."

"Really? What's yours?" she countered.

"Scotch. Johnnie Walker Green. I got hooked on their Pure Malt when I worked in London for a while. When they finally started selling it here as the Green label, I knew I could safely return to the States."

Ivy pondered for a minute. "I'm not sure it gives me any great insight. Maybe that you like to travel?"

"You get a point for trying. What sets this scotch apart is the flavor. As a blend, it's the sum of all its parts. The taste is creamy and complex, just like a woman."

Her heart thudded a triple time beat. Ben oozed sensuality, his words spinning a web of desire. "Guess I should be careful before I ask about your favorite food. Our conversation might need to come with an R rating."

"Get your mind out of the gutter," he teased. "I asked what you like to drink because I'd like to buy you one. The wedding will be wrapped up in less than half an hour. I'm staying at the Cavendish Grand. Pretty sure

I saw a bar right off the lobby swanky enough to mix up a kir royale for you."

"It's late." Even as she said it, the music switched to the last song of the night. Ordinarily she hated the ubiquitous Donna Summer song. Her first year as a wedding planner, she'd heard "Last Dance" close out twenty weddings before she stopped counting. Familiarity certainly breeds contempt when it came to repetition of a cheesy song that truly wasn't so great to begin with. On the bright side, the despised song did signal the end of her long day. Ivy thought of it as her own personal recess bell. But tonight she clung a little tighter to Ben, for once not wanting the song to end.

"True. I don't buy it as an excuse, though. You need time to unwind after an event. Now, you can either go home and watch bad television, surf the web, or come sip champagne across from a man who thinks you're beautiful."

"So you're saving me from my weakness for infomercials? The invitation is strictly out of the goodness of your heart?"

"Quite the opposite. The invitation is strictly selfish. I want to taste you, Ivy." The scrape of his feet against the stones came to a halt. A gentle nudge with his forehead tipped her head back. Their eyes locked. "Why don't we get a jump on the inevitable? Because I don't want to wait another moment."

Ivy had a split second to decide. Stick to her guns—and her professional ethics—and slip out of his arms? Or stay and lock lips with a super sexy man in the moonlight? Really, it was easiest to not decide at all. Her eyelids drifted shut as she waited for Ben to make his move. And waited. Nothing happened. She peeked out from beneath her lashes to see the merest hint of a smirk lifting the edges of Ben's mouth. Her eyes flew open the rest of the way.

"What? What happened to the tasting and the moment?"

"The moment's not right until you decide to commit to it. I promised earlier I wouldn't steal any more kisses from you. Kissing is interactive. A two-way street. You've got to choose to slide behind the wheel and turn the key."

Why did men turn everything in life into a car metaphor? Well, she could play along. Despite showing every sign of being something of a player, Ben had shown her, with that one little pause, that he also had bucket loads of integrity. No sane, single woman could turn down an honest to goodness gentleman. They were a rare breed, and she didn't intend to waste this particular chance sighting. Time to seize the day...or at least what was left of the night.

"Oh, my motor's fully revved. You'd better buckle your seatbelt, Mr. Westcott."

Ivy tightened her grip around his neck and went up on her tiptoes to reach his mouth. The mouth she'd stared at off and on all day, remembering the firm albeit brief feel of his lips against hers. He wasn't the only one who wanted a taste. She puckered up and planted a soft kiss. And then Ben quite expertly elbowed his way back into the driver's seat.

His lips slanted hard across hers, instantly ratcheting the level of heat up from tender to full on sizzle. This was no getting-to-know-you smooch. Ben claimed her mouth with possessive pressure. His teeth nibbled open her lips, allowing his tongue to sweep inside. Her moan of pleasure was all the urging he needed to slide his hands down to not only cup her ass, but lift her off the ground.

Ivy's world spun. Under the spell of the spring night, she'd yearned for nothing more than a touch, a quiet kiss. She'd wanted a sip of water to slake her lustful thirst. Instead, Ben's kisses drowned her in a downpour of passion and heat. The arch of her foot curved around his calf, looking for something to ground her. Each stroke of his tongue ignited an array of sparks behind her closed eyes. He tore his mouth away but hovered his lips a breath away from hers. Eyes heavy lidded, he moved not at all, aside from the pounding of his heart thumping through his tuxedo shirt. Suddenly, she realized what he waited to hear.

"Okay, Ben. You've convinced me to have a drink with you."

A hum of approval sounded low in his throat. He buried his face in the curve of her neck. And then from somewhere behind them, a short high gasp, and the unmistakable crash of glass breaking on the stone floor. Ben's grip bobbled, but he didn't drop her.

"Get your hands off my friend's ass right now, or I'll call in someone a lot bigger than me to make you."

Mortified, Ivy wriggled down until her feet touched the ground. Bad enough if they'd been caught literally necking by a client or another vendor. That alone would have been reminder enough why she never randomly hooked up with men, and especially not on the job. At least then she could've walked away with bruised dignity, but able to bury the memory in a very deep hole. But now, discovered like this, Ivy knew she was in for a solid week of lectures, followed by months of teasing. She peeked around Ben's wide chest to meet the worried gaze of her best friend.

"You can hold off on the imaginary security, Daphne. I'm fine."

Ben rebuttoned the tux jacket she didn't even remember undoing, then turned around. "I assure you, my hands had nothing but good intentions toward your friend's ass." He strode to the doorway, skirting around the shattered remains of a vase, and held out his hand. "Bennett Westcott, True Life Productions."

Daphne wiped her hands on the lavender apron covering her end-of-the-night uniform of jeans and a tee. "Daphne Lovell. Sorry about the mess."

"Daphne's my best friend and business partner at Aisle Bound. She's an amazing florist." Ivy talked as fast as possible while slipping back into her shoes. The more she talked, the less chance Daphne would be able to ask what the hell was going on. "She did today's flowers. I completely forgot you were coming back to get all the vases tonight."

Daphne brought her hands together over her heart in feigned shock. "You forgot? *You* forgot a logistical detail about an event?" Her blue eyes narrowed, swept from the top of Ben's sun-streaked mop of hair, all the way down his more than six feet of handsomeness. "Normally I'd assume the only explanation is a sudden onset brain tumor. But looking at what distracted you, I guess I can understand."

"You can?" Ivy was floored. Where were the recriminations? The scolding at her stupidity and risking the company's reputation?

"God, Ivy, look at him! Who wouldn't want a nibble?

He's hot, built, and apparently you've already hooked him. I say go for it."

"Ladies, I'm standing right here. Could you maybe not talk about me like I'm sex on a stick?"

"Nope. Now you've permanently implanted that imagery in my brain. But I will leave the two of you alone. Have a good time. Oh, and I'll send someone up here to clean up the vase, so you might want to relocate your frolicking." Daphne backed away, putting her hand to her ear in a call-me gesture.

A heavy silence thickened the air. The music downstairs had ended. Ivy wasn't sure what to do with Daphne's surprising nod of approval. Daphne's appearance had splashed cold water all over the magical moment. All the reasons why not to go along with Ben flooded back in a rush. And then he took her hand, planting a kiss in her palm and closing her fingers over it like a promise.

Ben locked inky blue eyes with her, deep dimples ratcheting his smile from sexy to irresistible. "So, how about that drink?"

CHAPTER FOUR

Marriage has many pains, but celibacy has no
pleasures.

—Samuel Johnson

"I FEEL LIKE I'm starring in a madcap thirties movie.
Rushing into a hotel in the wee hours of the morning
dressed in formalwear. If only you wore a top hat,"
Ivy mused as she and Ben crowded together into the
revolving door.

"Decadent, isn't it? Until you remember that we've
been in these clothes since noon, and worked our butts
off all day. Kind of takes the shine off the image."
Ben pushed them through into the refined grey and
black elegance of the Cavendish Grand lobby. A soar-
ing atrium rose three stories, with one entire wall of
windows overlooking the hustle and bustle of Michigan Avenue. The walls were covered in dove grey satin
echoed in the chairs and sofas grouped around a cas-
cade of water streaming from the ceiling into a mound
of shiny black river stones. Sheets of glass formed the
check-in desk, supported by columns of dark granite.

"Miss Rhodes, welcome to the Cavendish. I wasn't
aware any members of your bridal party were staying
with us this evening." Cool as the cucumber slices Ivy
used to de-puff her eyes, the starched British accent

caused her to snatch her hands off Ben's arm as though it were suddenly aflame. Yep, she'd been caught. At this rate, she might as well take out an ad in the *Chicago Tribune* announcing her intention to let Ben keep kissing her.

"Don't worry, Gib. Your crack staff hasn't let you down. Mr. Westcott is one of us. Well, if you only count his actual work as a videographer, and overlook his slimy employer." No use beating around the bush. Gib would ferret out Ben's job whether she mentioned it or not. Better to bring it up now and control the spin. She put a hand on each man's arm. "Gibson Moore is the manager of this lovely facility and one of my dearest friends. Gib, meet Bennett Westcott, who as of about fifteen minutes ago, can proudly state that he no longer works for *Wild Wedding Smackdown*."

Gib's hand was outstretched, ready to shake until she uttered the name of the vile show. Smoothly, he reversed direction to adjust his pinstriped grey pocket square as though it had been his intention all along, and not an evasion. "Are you a guest here at the Cavendish?"

"I am. But you can relax—I don't have any screaming, hair-pulling brides with me. The bridal party is all staying at the Park Hyatt. We try to maintain a buffer zone from the people we film when not actually at the wedding. Learned that the hard way when a pissed-off maid of honor stole all our equipment one time in Denver. I promise your hotel will remain classy and quiet, exactly like every Cavendish Grand around the world."

"Then it's a pleasure to meet you, Mr. Westcott." Gib thawed his icily professional smile by a few degrees and shook the offered hand.

"Call me Ben. Any friend of Ivy's, right?"

"Indeed." That assessing grey gaze that so eerily matched his surroundings swung back and forth between Ivy and Ben. "So what brings you two here in the shank of the evening?"

"Ivy's had a long day. Thought I'd get her off her feet and relax her with a little bubbly."

"Off her feet? I see." Gib shot his cuffs. He often used the gesture to give him a minute to assess. His eyes slid down to take in Ben's fingers intertwining with Ivy's despite her attempts to hide their hands behind the folds of her gown. For she knew Gib's reserve to be, at best, a complete sham. By breakfast he would've used his considerable network of connections in town to spread the word far and wide about her date with Ben. Mocking would ensue, followed by merciless teasing and lots of searching on YouTube for the most reviled, most embarrassing quotes from *WWS* to rub in her face.

"We can certainly accommodate you in the Ascot Lounge. Please enjoy a drink with my compliments." A flick of the wrist produced a card he slid into Ben's lapel pocket. "As you say, any friend of Ivy's…" He trailed off, full lips twisting into the restrained, British version of a smirk.

"Thanks, Gib." Ben gave him a hearty man-clap on the shoulder. "This is a great way to let off some steam, put the day behind us."

Her oh-so-polite friend inclined his head an inch, the picture of a perfect gentleman, as opposed to the virulent gossipmonger he'd turn into the second they crossed the lobby. "I'll be in touch, Miss Rhodes."

"I have no doubt." As Ben led her away, she craned her neck around so she could stick out her tongue. Sure enough, Gib's calm façade had crumbled, and his mouth gaped open. He held one hand at his ear in the gesture used by teenaged girls everywhere indicating that she should call him. Fat chance he'd get any details out of her. At least, not without serious bribery, something on the level of dinner at Vinci on their next wine night.

The Ascot Lounge featured lots of burgundy leather with gold accents, from the deep couches, to the wall of matching books, to the ottomans in front of the fireplace. The only people in the room were the bartender and a tired-looking waitress rolling a stack of silverware into napkins at a table. Ivy sat on a barstool, relieved beyond words to be off her feet. But her physical relief quickly disappeared beneath the weight of anxiety as she watched Ben place their order with the bartender. The intimate bubble in which they'd danced had held up pretty well during their banter on the cab ride to the hotel. Seeing Gib, however, had burst that bubble with all the delicacy of a SCUD missile, and she felt awkward in a dozen different ways.

Self-conscious, Ivy ran her hand over her still somewhat tidy French twist. Undoubtedly a few limp strands had escaped, and most of her makeup had probably faded. How on earth to pick up where they left off and start flirting again? She knew almost nothing about him. Oh, and how to smother her yawns as the after-midnight, post-event exhaustion caught up with her? Drinks with the handsome stranger had been a bad idea. Far too much pressure. For heaven's sake, she wasn't even wearing her date staple, the pink lace push-up bra! Ivy felt the distinct sense of its loss akin to that of an artist who'd left his favorite brush and paints at home, staring at a blank canvas.

Ben pushed a stool aside and leaned sideways on the bar beside her, one elbow propping him up. He'd stuffed his bow tie in a pocket and undone the top three buttons of his shirt. The effect was very debonair. Like George Clooney in *Ocean's Eleven*. And no red-blooded woman could resist anyone remotely resembling Clooney. In a rush, Ivy's anxiety disappeared as quickly as it came, replaced by basic lust. Astounding how Ben put her through an emotional roller coaster without uttering a single word!

"Your kir royale will be ready in a minute. What were you thinking about just now?" He traced the smile brackets around her mouth with a slow, teasing finger. "You've got an odd look on your face."

Crap. Not just a handsome man, but a perceptive one. Ivy scraped the recesses of her mind to come up with a crumb of something, anything but the truth. "When we were talking to Gib, you made it sound as if you'd stayed at a Cavendish Grand before. I wondered where else you've been." Her attempt at misdirection would be great at a church picnic or a quilting club, but it in no way classified as flirting. When would her drink come so she'd at least have something to do with her hands…besides fighting the urge to reach out and toy with the golden hairs cutting across the vee of his unbuttoned shirt?

Now an odd expression crossed Ben's face. "Where I've been is a much longer question than I'm prepared to answer. I will tell you that I've stayed in a Cavendish Grand in Berlin, London, Rome, Sydney and Los Angeles."

Gorgeous, globetrotting guy. It definitely pumped up his sex appeal another few notches. Lent him a worldly rakishness. Except for the utter boredom dripping like sludge off every mention of a far-flung locale. "You tick off those cities like you're naming mundane freeway exits between Madison and Milwaukee. Where's your sense of awe, your sense of excitement?"

"A Cavendish hotel is always elegant, always has a fitness center on the seventh floor, a great restaurant, and a concierge that can score tickets to anything for the right price. The view outside the window doesn't matter so much."

Was he kidding? "You can't mean that," Ivy stated flatly. "I don't accept it. You've stayed in hotels where the view is of ancient palaces, instead of the high-end shopper's paradise we've got here in Chicago. You've opened balcony doors to the swirl of exotic accents, and brushed your teeth in another hemisphere where the water actually swirls down the drain in a different direction."

"Come on, that's just an old wives' tale." Ben punctuated his opinion with a roll of his eyes.

Huh. Nothing disturbed a good rant like a fact check. She'd have to Google it tomorrow and see if he was right. "Maybe so. But still, you've walked down the same streets as kings and popes, trod in history's very path."

"Did I miss the hidden cameras?" In an exaggerated motion, Ben twisted, looking back over both his shoulders. "Are you filming a commercial for the Cavendish, or are we having drinks?"

"Sorry. When I'm enthusiastic, I tend to get effusive. And since I've never had the opportunity to stick a toe outside the United States, you could call me more than a little enthusiastic about travel."

"If you're so worked up about it, why don't you?"

"Why don't I what?"

Ben waved his hand in expanding circles. "Go. Travel. Stick your toe someplace where they call it a *punta*."

"Excuse me? Did you just call me a whore?"

He barked out a surprised laugh. "No. That's *puta*. Why do nice girls always know the dirty words in foreign languages?"

Whoops. "I had the flu last month. I spent three days in bed watching two seasons of *The Sopranos*. Felt like I picked up a little Italian." Probably not smart to mention the twenty-episode marathon of *Love Boat* she'd recently raced through. He didn't seem the type to appreciate the romantic nuances of one of her favorite classic shows. On the upside, if drinks didn't go well, she could rush home and knock off another episode. She'd left off at the pivotal change in cruise directors, and couldn't wait to see how the new one fit in.

"*Molto poco*. Very little."

"Maybe, but at least I do feel I learned three surefire ways to dispose of a body."

"And people say television isn't educational." The bartender delivered their drinks, then immediately backed away to the other end of the bar. Ben picked up his rocks glass filled with dark liquid and clinked it against hers. "Here's to *WWS*."

Ivy halted her glass halfway to her mouth. "No. Absolutely not. I won't drink to that show. And you certainly made no secret of the fact you didn't like it either. Why would you toast to it?"

"Just trying to be succinct. But if you prefer the long version…" he clinked her glass again, "…here's to *WWS*, for dropping me smack into the path of a be-witching, beautiful woman."

Eyes closed, Ivy savored the cool, foaming rush of bubbles against her lips as the black current and champagne concoction burst across her taste buds. Crisp yet sweet, she liked to imagine this was what the distilled essence of pure romance tasted like. "You could've just toasted to Fate. Even more succinct."

"Fate's a two-timing bitch who doesn't pull her punches."

Ivy's eyes flew open. Ben was staring into his drink, swirling the ice cubes with a practiced twist of his wrist. "Good thing you're not bitter at all."

"Sorry. Fate and I aren't exactly tight."

It had to be closing in on one in the morning. Should she press him for the level of information men only revealed with whiskey-roughened voices in the middle of the night? Or, since she probably knew less about him than the TSA screener at the airport who waved him through security, should she overlook the oddly caustic remark and move on? Ivy took another, bigger swallow of her cocktail while she considered.

Standard dating protocol would be to push, to pry open every conversational oyster shell in search of that pearl of personality which could reveal the inner man. But did she really need to delve that deep? Ivy knew his generous lips were talented, his blue eyes bottomless, and his wide chest a vast, uncharted territory she yearned to explore. Tonight was about letting off steam at the end of a trying day with an attentive man. Oh, and hoping to get a few more kisses out of him before she called it a night. Perhaps it served her purpose better to smooth his frown away, rather than seek the cause. She downed the rest of her drink in a nervous gulp. Pushing the glass away, she traced the back of his hand with a TuTuPink-tipped fingernail.

"Would you overlook your journalistic integrity and tell me how we stack up?"

Ben's eyes narrowed, but stayed pinned on the swirling sea of his drink. "Against what?"

"The other *Wild Wedding Smackdown* bride, of course. Now that I'm part of an episode, my competitive spirit's kicked in. I want to come out on top."

He lifted his gaze to lock onto hers. Blue fire burned in the depths, and Ivy felt pinned like a hapless butterfly on a Victorian insect collector's board. The breadth of his shoulders loomed closer, legs pressing against her thigh. It forced her to tilt her head back, and he caught it, cradling a warm palm at the base of her skull. The bartender, the entire bar, no the entire hotel disappeared in the intimacy of their partial embrace. Ben was all she could see, all she could feel, his eyes sending trails of warmth along the same paths the champagne bubbles recently awoke.

"There's nothing I'd like better than for you to be on top. I like a woman who takes the initiative."

Chest tight, lungs cramping in protest, Ivy finally remembered to breathe. If a kir royale embodied romance, then Ben Westcott was the personification of sensuality. And both of them were equally intoxicating. Or maybe she needed one in order to handle the other. "I'd like another drink."

"No." His grip tightened, and his other arm snaked around her waist to pull her flush against him. "I'm cutting you off."

"Chicagoans don't react well to Prohibition. Take

Al Capone, for example. I'm a consenting adult, and if you won't order me another, then I will."

"Your consent is exactly what I've got in mind." Warm breath fluttered at her ear, his lips whispering against the edges. "We could tiptoe around for another hour, throw back a few more drinks. Give us both a chance to relax…and realize how exhausted we are. Instead of wasting that time, let me say that I want you. I want us to go upstairs to my room, right now. I want to take you, fast and hard. While you're still coming down, I want to lick every inch and spiral you right back up to the stars. Then, if you're still game, I really do want you on top." Ben let go, eased back a good foot, leaning both elbows back on the bar. The move stretched his shirt taut against pecs that bulged against the cotton. "But I don't want your brain clouded with booze when you decide to come with me."

Wow. So much more than the stolen kisses and hand slipped between his tux shirt studs she'd planned on. Aside from a forgettable one night stand in college she blamed entirely on her weakness for piña coladas and too much sun, Ivy didn't hook up. She dated. She had relationships. Every man was a stepping stone on the path to marriage.

But Ben talked a good game. If his words alone sped up her pulse this much, imagine what would happen when he applied those lips to her body. Stalling sounded like a good tactic while her brain caught up with her vibrating nerves. "You're so sure I'll just hop in the elevator?"

A smug smile crawled across his lips. "Pretty sure."

"Really? With a man I barely know? For all I know, you could be a serial killer!"

"Then a hotel's the safest place. Tell your buddy Gib to post hotel security on my floor, to be sure I don't try and smuggle a body down the stairs."

"Sweet talker."

"Tell me you're not interested. Tell me you don't want to slide between the sheets, skin to skin with me, and I'll order you that drink. We'll chat about whatever you want, and go our separate ways." Her mouth opened slowly, but before she could form words, he continued in the same, matter of fact tone. "Or I could make your panties—which I'm betting match your dress—damp in less than five minutes."

God. How could he talk like that in the middle of a bar? Where people could hear? How could he be so comfortable propositioning her in the dirtiest way possible while they both wore formal attire? And how could she ever live with herself if she passed up this opportunity?

"Quite a promise." Ivy hopped off her stool, digging her fingernails into her palms in an effort to keep the excitement out of her voice. Matching his blasé approach to what promised to be a white-hot night was sensible. Far less embarrassing than succumbing to the urge to run to the bathroom, call Daphne, and squeal like a teenager anticipating her first hickey. She put a little extra swing in her hips as she headed to the door. "You know you're going to lose at least a minute while we walk to the elevator?"

"You've got to learn to think outside the box, Ms. Rhodes." Arms like steel caught her behind the knees and cradled her effortlessly. No huffing and puffing, no hitch in his step. Ben's long legs kept up a brisk pace across the interlocking grey and black circles stamped into the carpet. Ivy crossed her ankles and looped her arms around Ben's neck, more for the sheer pleasure of it than necessity. She felt as secure in his arms as if back home in her overstuffed purple chair. All those hours he racked up shouldering a video camera were definitely working to her advantage.

Ben's tongue traced the rim of her ear. Tiny shivers cascaded down her neck with each swipe. A quick tickle of the inside, and then he lightly bit her lobe with his teeth. The contrast of the soft touch with the sharp nip amped the shivers up to full-fledged zings.

"That's cheating. You can't start before we even get to the elevator."

"I call it efficient time management. Thought you of all people would appreciate it." Ben pressed the button with his elbow and turned the full force of his raffish grin onto her. Good thing he was carrying her, because that grin alone could melt her knees in one second flat. Ivy's senses spun on overload. Concentrate on the confident swagger in his voice, promising all sorts of R-rated fun? The way his thick bangs drooped over his forehead, just begging for her fingers to comb through? Or…oh…the faint taste of aged scotch flavoring the kiss he began while she was still taking stock of the bank of muscles pressed against her breasts?

Their lips merged. Slow and dreamy, soft and tender. As romantic as any woman could ever hope for. Ivy knew this to be fact, as she spent quite a bit of down time thinking about the perfect kiss. The key ingredients were just the right amount of pressure, the right amount of heat, delivered by a handsome man. Ben hit the bull's eye on every qualification. Plus, he got extra points for swooping her into his arms and Prince

Charming-ed her down the hallway. Her eyes drifted shut at the sheer pleasure. It had been so long since the last time she'd had the opportunity to lock lips with a man. Even longer since she'd been kissed by someone as talented as Ben.

No doubt about it—he'd seduced her into a puddle with nothing more than a kiss. It gave her high expectations for the rest of the night.

Ben set her down and whipped off his jacket. Ivy hadn't even noticed when they boarded the elevator, and now the doors whisked shut behind them. "What's the matter? Did I get you all hot and bothered?" she asked. Regret set in as the words left her mouth. Why did some things sound so good in your head, and sound so much like a seventies porn spoof when said out loud?

"It's for you." He settled the jacket over her shoulders. "Have to keep you decent. Never know when someone might actually be manning the security camera." He nodded at the small, black dome in the corner of the ceiling.

"My dress is perfectly decent," she huffed. Why on earth did he care about this now? "I just worked in it for eight hours in front of more than one hundred people. In front of your video camera, might I remind you. How am I not decent?"

"Like this." Ben backed her against the mirrored panel, captured her mouth with his, and slid both hands down the front of her dress. With a smoothness undoubtedly borne of practice, he lifted her breasts out of the pink satin. The bodice formed a shelf, pushing them up high. Ivy looked in the mirror on the opposite wall to see her eyes dark and wide with shock. And excitement. He'd dropped to his knees in front of her. Ben's golden head filled the space between the lapels of his coat. It obscured her view of her lacy pink bra as he nuzzled along the edge of it. His hand traced the same route on the other side. And then her eyes rolled back in her head from the feel of his tongue swirling around her nipple through the fabric, and she stopped looking.

Oh. My. God. Everywhere he used his mouth, his hand duplicated. His heavy thumb rasped the fabric against her suddenly oh-so-sensitive nipple. It drew circles; lazy, slow circles that spiraled need straight to the hot, pulsing place between her thighs.

"You really are like cotton candy. Every layer I find is pink and soft and melts in my mouth."

Ivy moaned. It was all she could manage. Words required too much thought. She was beyond thought, existing on a plane of pure sensation. Whatever ridiculous fantasy she'd had of keeping up with him, even leading him on, evaporated. All she could do was hang on for the ride. She fisted one hand in his thick hair, wordlessly encouraging him to keep going. Do more, longer, harder. Her hips rolled in response, a seeking gesture. For all he gave, it wasn't enough.

Ben stood, never breaking contact. "Put your legs around me, sweets." Ivy jumped, latching on around his waist. She crossed her ankles for support, but needn't have bothered. He held her, a rock-solid arm under her ass and one around her back. Ben walked them out of the elevator. Smug with the power of her sexuality, Ivy noticed his steps weren't quite so steady. He might have been doing all the work, but she definitely wasn't the only one weak in the knees. Still, the dexterity he showed in navigating the hallway with his lips buried in her neck deserved recognition. Leaning her head to the side to give him better access, her cheek brushed the satin strap of her dress. Not the wool and poly blend of a tuxedo across her shoulders.

"Oh, no. Ben, I think your jacket's still in the elevator."

"Hope it enjoys the ride."

Ivy laughed, giddy with desire and the joy of the moment. She'd dated men, far less spontaneous men, who would've immediately turned around and gone back for the coat. The fact Ben didn't, and in fact hastened his steps to his room, proved how turned on he must be. And she'd caused it!

"Grab my key. Left side. *My* left," he amended hoarsely, as her hand delved down, patting through the wrong pocket. Lingering when she ran up against something far larger and more solid than a keycard. "For the love of God, find the key!"

"Working on it," she trilled. Nice to turn the tables, to be the one putting the slightly wild look in his unfocused eyes, the color of an angry ocean. But she wanted in as badly as he did, and concentrated on finessing the plastic rectangle into the slot. Once through the door she dropped the key. Inside, outside, who could tell. Who cared? Her hands ripped at his shirt, studs pinging as they flew across the room and hit something metallic. Finally, *finally* she could feel him. A light mat of hair springing beneath her fingers, she reveled in finally touching his skin. Warm skin stretched taut over muscles that rippled at her touch.

Ben toed out a chair in the darkness from what she imagined to be a desk, or maybe a table. Didn't matter. All that mattered was that when he sat down, everything lined up perfectly. His hardness rubbed against just the right spot, even through her voluminous layers of skirt and slip. The sound of her zipper lowering was the only sound in the room. Then, a frenzy of rustling as he pushed her dress above her hips, and she unzipped his pants. Unfortunately, the cummerbund had to stay. No time to get it off, and no room with him pressed against the back of the chair. Didn't matter. Ivy could feel his chest, and soon she'd feel even more.

His hands now lifted her breasts out of her bra, the straps snapping from the pressure. His mouth closed over a nipple, the sensation a thousand times more and better than when he'd done the same over her bra. The warm wetness combined with the swirling pressure from his tongue almost sent her over the edge.

"Ben, do you have a condom?"

He chuckled, a dark, sexy noise low in his throat. "You don't? Little Miss Plans-For-Everything?"

"Of course I do. I'm no fool. Desperate groomsmen pay up to fifty dollars a pop for one in a clinch. But it's in my purse, which might be still at the bar, or in the elevator, or across the room. I simply don't know at this point."

"No worries." He reached for his back pocket, palming his wallet. In the time honored tradition of every man past puberty, he pulled one out from behind a credit card.

"Let me." Ivy snatched it away, hoping he'd take the hint and return his attention to her breasts. Smart man that he was, his head dipped once more. She fumbled to push past his waistband, and then he sprang free into her hands. Pulsing, hot steel with a life and a mind of its own. With lightning speed, she unrolled the rubber down his length. He responded by ripping her panties off in one swift tug.

"I promise to pull out all the stops on round two. But I'll go crazy if I don't get inside you right now. Please tell me you're ready?"

This wasn't him pulling out all the stops? He'd rocketed her from zero to have mercy in the space of an elevator ride, and he hadn't even used his good moves? "Oh, I am so ready."

"Knew we were on the same page. You're about to burn me up, sweets." Ben lifted her, impaled her. Thrust all the way inside to places she'd forgotten had feeling. Filled her. Filled her until she didn't think she could take more, didn't think she could move. And then couldn't resist moving against him, an unconscious rhythm they fell into as easily as breathing. Warmth filled her. Heat suffused her from the inside out. Fire lashed at every tiny nerve, licking in time with her heartbeat. There was nothing but the rough sound of Ben's breathing harsh in her ear, the strong feel of his hands cupping her ass, moving her with exquisite timing and tenderness.

"This is amazing. You're amazing," she panted.

"Right back at you. But I can't get enough of you like this." Ben tipped forward, out of the chair onto his knees. Buried deep inside, he lowered her to the floor. His slow slide became more frantic, more animalistic. Ivy crooked her knees, pulling him closer. The weight of his body covering her was all male and stirred her up even more. He thrust harder, faster, with a singular purpose. It was more than she could take. It was everything she needed all at once. A series of small earthquakes began to shatter her world. Ivy shuddered, everything exploding from the top of her head to the tips of her toes in a velvet-sheathed sunburst that pulsed through her without end. She screamed, nails clawing down Ben's back as she bowed up, melting up and into him. A second later, a guttural cry burst from his throat and they met in a kiss that sealed the imploding sensations between them.

Ben's kiss gentled, softened the primal beast into a tender lover. He rolled onto his side, bringing her with him still in a tight embrace. His lips worshiped her face, moving across the cheekbone, up to her forehead, and back down to her lips. A quick tryst in the middle of the night with any other man could've left her feeling used, but Ivy felt treasured by his soft caresses.

"What time is it?"

"Are you kidding me?" Ben propped up on one elbow, leaned over to nip at her neck. "Got another hot date lined up?"

"Of course not. But I did want to know if you hit your goal of under five minutes."

A long belly laugh rolled out. Ben smoothed his hand across her hair. Nimble fingers worked at the fortification of bobby pins still holding her updo. "We're both very goal-oriented people, aren't we? Well, I can respect that. But since I forgot to look at my watch when I started, let's set a new challenge. Go the opposite direction."

Ivy couldn't see him in the heavy darkness, but could bet he wore his devil-may-care grin that broke through her defenses in the first place. Which meant she'd fall in line with whatever he suggested. "I might be open to giving you a second chance. What do you have in mind?"

"That I can hold you on the edge of orgasm for an hour."

He made the most extraordinary statements, and yet made them sound perfectly plausible. Ivy was no prude, but still thrilled at his earthy, shameless approach to sex.

He fanned his fingers through her loosened hair and sucked in a short, tight breath. "Might be more of a challenge for me, because everything about you pushes my control to the breaking point." Ben lifted her in his arms—*wow, she could get used to that!*—and carried her into the bedroom. "This way we can see the clock. And it should prevent any more rug burn. Sorry about that, by the way. I'll have to check you later for it. All over. Probably in a bubble bath, just to be thorough."

This was turning into the best night ever. "On your mark, get set, go!"

CHAPTER FIVE

Though marriage makes man and wife one flesh,
it leaves 'em still two fools.

—William Congreve

IVY PULLED THE sheet over her head against the painful brightness, but it was no use. Resigned to being awake, she opened her eyes and threw back the covers. Then promptly pulled them back up tight beneath her chin, very aware of her nakedness in an unfamiliar room. Grey damask stripes covered the walls. She huddled beneath grey satin sheets topped with a fluffy duvet. Comfortable as could be, but definitely not hers. Her gaze swung to the tall man standing next to the window, backlit by the morning sun. Each bulge of his muscles, from prominent biceps to toned quads, stood out in silhouette. And every second of the previous night flooded back into her consciousness, lusty quicksand pulling her back into a state of semi-arousal from the memory.

Ben looked amazing. Her vocabulary had dwindled to that single word ever since he'd shed his clothes. One hand braced him against the glass, stretching the muscles of his long, lean back into taut definition. Ivy drank him in. She'd explored his body repeatedly during their…encounter? No. Didn't come close to describing the toe-curling, earth-moving night they'd shared.

Tryst? Too old-fashioned. Made her think of virgins and unicorns. Sexual marathon? Yup, that about summed it up. Getting to see everything she'd touched woke her up faster than a triple espresso shot. But why had he left the bed? Usually men had one thing on their minds in the morning, and it wasn't staring at the Chicago skyline.

"Good morning." Not exactly an invitation back to bed, but she needed to find her footing. When Ivy woke up in a man's bed, it was usually after many dates—or at least more than a gulped drink in a bar. Fantastic sex aside, she didn't know enough about Ben to figure out if he wanted her to grab her clothes and disappear, or hang around for another round. Heck, she didn't know enough about Ben to figure out what state issued his driver's license. But she wanted to. Boy oh boy, did she want to find out more.

"Sorry. I didn't mean to wake you up. But since we're on the thirtieth floor, I wanted to take a peek." Ben leaned against the floor-to-ceiling black drapes, twisting to face her.

"Enjoying the view?" she asked. Because God knows she was. Full-frontal Ben Westcott was something she could stare at for days. All the muscles he'd used to carry her so effortlessly were sculpted and sexy. Firm pecs covered with a light mat of golden hair led to a set of abs underwear models would kill for. His body looked sculpted by hard work, rather than the overdeveloped bulges of a gym rat. Afraid that if she looked any lower she might drool, Ivy forced her eyes back up to the glorious mess of his thick hair.

The corner of his mouth tugged up. "I am now." His eyes left a trail of steam in their wake as they swept from her toes to what she assumed to be an epic case of bedhead. But a certain part of his anatomy didn't seem put off by her messy mop of hair.

Emboldened, she propped herself up on her elbows, letting the sheet slither just south of respectability. "So what do you think of Chicago?"

"I think the welcoming committee is very friendly. I'm amazed people ever leave."

Ivy bit back a giggle, tried to look wholesome and solemn. "It's our famous Midwestern hospitality."

"Oh, you've been quite hospitable." Ben stalked forward, stopped at the foot of the bed and planted his hands on his hips, feet spread wide. "The mayor should give you a medal."

"Your appreciation will more than suffice." She enjoyed his playful mood, and decided to push her luck. "I would, however, be willing to accept a gratuity. Perhaps pancakes?"

The half smile slid from his lips. "No. It's too late."

Okay, then! Apparently she'd misread him. On the one hand, she'd come to his room without any expectations. On the other hand, they'd shared an incredible night. Ben's fun and tenderness layered over white hot passion made a potent combination. He not only rooted tiny seeds of intimacy for Ivy, but sprouted them, too. Why was it too much to ask that his reaction be the same?

No time to process the disappointment. Or, worse yet, let him see it. However, they might as well be adult about this awkward situation. Ivy's gaze darted about the room, trying to locate her clothes. Damned if she'd give him a free show. She'd grab her dress, make a run for the bathroom, and get out before he kicked her out. "Thanks for a nice time. I'll be out of here in five minutes."

"Whoa! Where are you going?" Ben lunged forward, trapping her beneath his body. He circled her wrists with one hand, holding them against the upholstered headboard. His other hand traced a slow line down her side, then caressed the swell of her breast. The shivers of desire he induced made it remarkably hard to process an answer.

"Like you said, it's late. I'm sure you have places to be, and I have a million things to do today." Number one on the list? Try to ignore how drop-dead sexy he felt pressed against her. Reminding her of every spectacular moment their bodies were joined. Number two? Try not to wriggle shamelessly.

"Ivy, I don't want you to leave. It's just that it's too late to order pancakes, because room service will be here any second with French toast."

He didn't want her to leave *and* ordered breakfast for both of them? Ivy didn't know which point made her happier. Emotional whiplash kicked in from the U-turn he'd spun her into. No complaints, though. Not when her go-for-one-cocktail date had morphed into something far better. Now for the bonus round question. "Any chance you ordered bacon?"

Ben dropped her hands and rolled off her, flopping onto his back. "You insult me. What's the point of room service without bacon?"

"I'm sold. I'll stay for breakfast." It kept getting better. Hot sex and bacon? Could there be a more perfect end to a perfect date?

Still staring at the ceiling, Ben asked, "What about after?"

Good question. Ivy yawned and stretched, buying time to come up with a suitably leading response. His ordering breakfast for her, coupled with his obvious physical interest, pointed to him feeling the same… more…that she did. Although if Daphne were here, she'd point out that when you jumped to conclusions, it often resulted in a long and painful fall. For all her good intentions, Daphne could be a real killjoy.

"Have something specific in mind?" That's right. Play it coy. Don't burst out with the fact that she'd willingly give up all her breakfast—coffee included—to roll around in bed with him one more time.

Shifting to prop himself on an elbow, Ben stared down at her. "My flight doesn't leave until tonight. For all the dozens of times I've been to Chicago, I've never done the tourist thing."

"You're a frequent visitor to my favorite town? Do you come that often because you've got family here?"

"Nope. Work."

She waited a few beats for him to expound. And then another few. Weird. After all, brides didn't normally fly in their own videographer. There had to be a story behind it. Or was the real story the fact Ben obviously wasn't willing to divulge any more on the topic? He couldn't even meet her eyes. Kind of a feat in and of itself, since a mere six inches separated their faces. "My, aren't you loquacious in the morning."

"Not before coffee."

Funny. He'd been able to string together a full sentence two minutes ago. *Before* the subject of his work came up. Ivy wanted playful, sexy Ben to return. Might be hard, though, to nudge a moody, tired man she barely knew. But what did she have to lose? "I know the feel-

ing. Once I ran out of beans and left the house so coma-
tose I had to go back three separate times for my coat,
my keys and my purse. Now I keep a stash of choco-
late-covered espresso beans in my nightstand. Enter-
tained serious thoughts about putting them behind a
glass door. You know, to break in case of emergency?"

Her silly, albeit both embarrassing and true, story
teased his dimples out of hiding. Heavy-lidded eyes the
color of an early spring iris captured hers, then winked.
"What a coincidence. I keep chocolate syrup to cover
things *with* in my nightstand. Except I don't wait for
an emergency to break it out."

"Oh. Oh my." If she squeezed her eyes shut and
concentrated, could she teleport his nightstand here?
Ivy never put much faith in psychic powers, but now
seemed a really great time to become a believer.

"So if you aren't too busy today, I thought maybe
you'd be willing to show me your city."

Yippee! Ben wanted to spend the day with her.
Which meant this interlude was about more than sex to
him. Maybe they'd started this relationship backward,
but they could still go back and cover all the steps they'd
skipped. With her odd hours, a long-distance relationship might be the best solution. She could get to know
him over the phone, really discover each other. With,
of course, an occasional, torrid mid-week rendezvous.

Daphne always accused her of leaping into love. Ivy
didn't see anything wrong with her system. When seeking your soul mate, the search needed to be serious. So
many people wasted time casually dating, spending too
long with the wrong person because they didn't throw
themselves into dating. Maybe Ivy did jump in with
both feet at every potential true love prospect. But she

believed if something was worth doing, be it running a business or looking for love, it demanded one hundred and ten percent effort, every time. Besides, *Ben* was the one who initiated their fling, and *Ben* was the one who voiced his wish to continue.

Ivy blinked slowly. Trailed one finger down the valley between his pecs to the dark line of hair bisecting his belly. Sliding her hand beneath the whisper-soft sheet, she kept moving south to wrap her whole hand around the blatant evidence of his interest. Despite catching only four hours of sleep, one part of him was unmistakably wide awake and raring to go.

"That could probably be arranged," she purred. Ben's prowess between the sheets had vaulted him to the top of the heap, teetering on the edge of being named the best sex she'd ever had. Exhaustion had dulled her senses by their third round. Ivy wanted the chance to judge his expertise with clear eyes. And with bright sunlight illuminating every one of his sexy muscle ripples. When his stamina gave out, then they'd worry about sightseeing. "I can clear my schedule for the day. Given the right incentive."

"Good to hear." Ben shifted back on top of her, using his weight to nudge her legs even farther apart. White teeth flashed as a wide grin split his face. "Because I ordered an extra side of maple syrup. I've got an interesting idea of how to use it. And oddly enough, it doesn't involve French toast at all."

BEN EXECUTED A quick sidestep off the curb to avoid a mound of gum. Then he jumped back onto the sidewalk to avoid being run over by a taxi. Chicago cabs rivaled

New York's for their utter lack of regard for pedestrians. "Ivy, I need to make a confession."

She groaned. "Gee, that ties with *we need to talk* as the worst conversation starter of all time. Why confess anything on a first date—even if this is part three of said date? Unless you've got a transvestite twin waiting to make a threesome. That, I would need to know immediately."

Funny girl. He enjoyed yanking her chain. Especially the way she sassed him right back. Ben shook his head, wrenched off his sunglasses. Eyes downcast, he said, "I sold you short."

"What, now that you've had your way with me, the sweet talk goes right out the window? What an odd thing to say."

"Hey, I'm trying to give you a compliment. When I asked you to show me the sights, I figured you'd jam a couple of museums down my throat. Maybe an architecturally significant building or two, followed by shopping."

"A fate worse than death?" Ivy shuffled forward a few steps, Ben coming along thanks to his hand jammed into the back pocket of her jean shorts. The very tight pocket gave him an excuse to cup her really great ass. Tight, but still enough there for him to grab onto. Perfectly rounded for squeezing.

People crowded against them from all sides, slowing their progress. The first hint of summer flirted through the air on a warm breeze. Last week he'd been on assignment in Buffalo, and ended up stuck for an extra two days due to a late spring blizzard. The sun beating directly down on his arms without being filtered through layers of coats felt great. Ben remembered

April in Chicago as capricious weather-wise, but today was picture perfect. Blue sky, a few puffy white clouds, and warm enough to be out in a tee shirt. A faded cap from the Athens Olympics was his only protection from the elements.

He gave a quick squeeze, just to enjoy the feel of her beneath his hands. "Let's say my expectations were pretty low on the fun scale."

"So why didn't you ditch the tour and hole up at O'Hare for a few hours?"

Ben readjusted the bill of his cap. It surprised him to uncover a core of insecurity in Ivy. "Come on, stop fishing. A woman as beautiful as you should never stoop so low."

"I have no idea what you're talking about."

"Do I have to spell it out?" To his dismay, Ivy nodded. Why did all women insist on being told emotional junk that should be perfectly obvious? "I wanted to spend time with you. We've really hit it off. You were a pleasure to work with, one of the best planners I've ever encountered. You've got this saucy streak that kind of glints out from behind all your professionalism."

"I appreciate the compliment. May I quote you on my web site? Use you as a referral?"

"Only if you include the second part of the compliment, which would be how much fun I had once the wedding ended. You're one hell of a good time, Ms. Rhodes."

A smile brighter than a halogen light uptilted her kissable lips. "Right back at you, Mr. Westcott."

A few more steps put them through the turnstile. Now Ben pulled her along, urging her forward. Ivy grabbed his arm to redirect him up the concrete ramp.

Laughter echoed off the walls. Peanut shells crunched underfoot, and the heady scent of brats and fries undulated through the air.

"Never, in a million tries, would I have guessed we'd end up here."

Ivy led him to the edge of the tunnel and stopped so he could take in the view of Wrigley Field, in all its ivy-covered glory. The tickets she'd wheedled from Gib put them behind third base, just high enough to glimpse Lake Michigan beyond the roof decks full of partiers. Huh. Not only did those lucky bastards on neighboring roofs have prime viewing, but the beer probably cost a lot less than the concession stands here in the park charged. The vast blue expanse of water almost blended into the bright sky until you noticed all the boats, colorful sails unfurled.

"This is magnificent." Ben's arm swooped around her waist to hug her close.

"For the record, we've got some terrific museums. Impossible for you to be bored at any of them. Next time you're here, a trip to the Shedd Aquarium is a must. But there's nothing like bringing someone to the Friendly Confines for the first time."

"Hmm. A beautiful woman who follows baseball. You sure know the way to a man's heart. Nobody's this perfect. What's your Kryptonite?"

"I can't ride a motorcycle," she offered.

He'd heard that before. Yet he always managed to coax trepidatious women onto the back of his beloved Harley. Every one became a convert after a single ride. "Then this is a match made in heaven. I love to break in motorcycle virgins."

"Give me a break. A man like you avoids virgins

like the plague." She dropped into a seat, thoughtfully leaving him the aisle seat so he could stretch his legs.

"Really? You think you've got me pegged? This should be good."

"You're too experienced to dally with virgins. They'd bore you."

Hit the nail right on the head. But why'd she have to make it sound like an insult? "So I prefer an enthusiastic bed partner over a scared girl. Keeps me away from jailbait. I don't see the problem."

"A character assessment, not a problem." She tilted her head, clearly pondering for a beat before continuing. "I see you as a man who abhors wasted time. Every movement yesterday, every direction you gave Ollie optimized efficiency. Your hotel room looked uninhabited it was so spotless."

"Easy to be neat when all I've got is a tux and the clothes on my back."

"No jammies?"

"I didn't see you whip a flannel nightgown out of your emergency pack last night. Your girlish modesty offended?" He sure didn't remember her being bashful once their clothes came off. Especially not the third time perched on the bathroom sink in front of the mirror.

"Not modesty." Ivy shuddered. "My love of hygiene. Hotel room beds are a sanitation nightmare. Or so the local news tells us every sweeps week."

"I travel too much to worry about that stuff." Ben swung his attention back to the field as the announcer introduced the players. Ivy stuck two fingers in her mouth and let out an impressively piercing whistle.

"You're going to have to cheer for the Cubs." She

held up a hand to forestall any comments. "Not just because they're my team. It's a safety issue. I don't want any fans tossing drinks at us if you clap for the other team. We're a pretty hard core bunch here in Chicago. So I hope you're not a Dodgers fan," she said as the opposing team took the field. "You're not from Los Angeles, are you?"

"Nope."

"That's a relief. What team do you follow?"

"I like to watch whatever game's on when I've got a beer in my hand." Ben signaled to the guy with a crate of beer bottles on his shoulder. Old enough to be his father, the man probably trudged up and down the stadium steps a hundred times during a game. Ben slipped the guy an extra ten in exchange for two bottles. Made him feel less embarrassed to sit on his ass for nine innings while the beer vendor slowly destroyed what was left of his knee cartilage.

"Nice evasion. But it doesn't exactly require X-ray vision to see through you. Why won't you tell me where you're from?"

Ben liked to chat up women. Flirt with them, find out what made them tick. What made them light up from the inside out like an outdoor Christmas display. He did not, as a rule, like to talk about himself. "Why can't you take a hint?"

"If you tell me where you live, I won't worry that you're evading the question because you're on the FBI's most wanted list. Although a real criminal would probably have a good cover story in place."

She had a point. Opening up about his address didn't require spilling his whole, sordid life story. "I'm based in New York. But I'm never there. *WWS* keeps me on the road more weeks than not. Before that I lived in D.C. Caught a few Nats games, unfortunately before they built their snazzy new stadium."

"Look at that. You revealed personal details without bursting into flames." Ivy dropped a smooch on his cheek. Liked it enough to come back for seconds, with a long, soft kiss right on the lips. "There's hope for you yet."

"Smart ass." He ran his hand down her smooth thigh in a quick caress. "Nice of your friend Daphne to drop off a change of clothes. Especially driving downtown on her day off."

"Daphne's my best friend. She'd never make me do the morning-after walk of shame." Not that she'd told Daphne any details. To avoid the inevitable lecture, she'd fuzzed the truth. Said they'd stayed up all night talking. Ivy didn't like lying to her best friend, but she hadn't wanted to waste any precious moments with Ben stuck in an argument with Daphne. "Plus, she was motivated by more than friendship. Her delivery fee will cost me a dinner at Reza's, our favorite Persian restaurant."

"Totally worth it. In case you haven't noticed, these shorts are a lot more conducive to me touching you than the acres of skirt in your gown. Don't get me wrong. I have fond memories of that gown. The way it looked pooled around your waist in the elevator. The way it looked lying on the floor while you were naked on top of me." Fired up by the pictures in his brain, Ben leaned in for some real time action. Instead, he got broadsided in the forehead by the bill of her Cubs cap.

"Why'd you leave D.C.?"

Damn it. The fatal question. If he answered with the

truth, she'd drop him faster than the shortstop bobbled that ground ball a minute ago. If he handed her some made-up line, she seemed the type to cry foul. And all Ben wanted was to watch a ball game in this iconic setting, with his hand on the thigh of a pretty girl who kept him on his toes. While he appreciated Ivy being both whip-smart and perceptive, he just wished she didn't aim those talents in his direction.

"Thought this was a baseball game, not twenty questions." He followed up the deflection with a kiss, this time tugging her head back by her ponytail to slide in beneath her hat. Until she started the third degree, Ivy had given him the perfect day. Her kiss tasted of all of it; breakfast in bed, a stroll along the lake, and the surprise visit to Wrigley. It was fun and bright, exactly like Ivy herself. And then it turned. Ben went deeper, demanded more. The cheering fans, the crack of the bat and the crackle of the loudspeaker faded away. His tongue twined with hers, joining in an inner caress that shocked him with its shot-to-the-gut power. She answered his need, thrust for thrust with breathy little moans that made him want to toss her over his shoulder and run all the way back to the Cavendish.

Satisfied with his method of distraction, he resettled his cap. Then let out a whoop as what could've been a fly ball turned into a home run for the home team. Ivy surged to her feet before he could let out the first clap. Whistling and screaming, she celebrated along with the other thirty thousand people in the stands. The timing couldn't have been better. Talk about a distraction! He planned to point the conversation firmly toward her for the rest of the day to prevent any more games of dodgeball with revealing the truth. Starting now.

"A play like that should be capped off with a hot dog or two. Give us a base for these beers. You got the tickets, so the snacks are on me."

Ivy bit her lip. "The tickets were free."

"I'm not a client demanding an itemization." He refused to let her innate sense of fair play ruin the gesture. "How about you relax and let me treat you. We've done this whole date thing ass backward. You deserve candles and a fancy restaurant with flowers on the table. At least let me spring for a damn pretzel."

"When you put it so nicely, how could I refuse?" Ivy giggled.

BEN BLINKED AGAINST the onslaught of light as they emerged from the darkness beneath the thick maze of El tracks. Donning sunglasses, he loped along beside Ivy, her determined stride eating up the sidewalk. She walked with purpose. He wanted to walk to the nearest patch of grass and take a nap.

"After sitting for nine innings, I thought it'd be nice to stretch our legs," said Ivy.

The woman had a boundless supply of energy. Whereas Ben was very much aware of how little shut eye they'd grabbed last night. He couldn't wait to collapse into his airplane seat and sleep the whole way home. On the other hand, he wanted to hang with Ivy for as long as possible. She brought a sparkle to the day, like a flashlight pushing past the dusty cobwebs of moodiness that hit him after each assignment.

"Are we going far? Should we load up with water and provisions?"

Patting her stomach, Ivy groaned. "I won't be eating

again for quite a while. Why'd you talk me into splitting that tray of nachos with you?"

"Couldn't finish it by myself. It'd be a shame to let good nachos go to waste." Oughtta be a rule about that sort of heinous crime. It should include pizza, wings, fries—all the basic bar foods.

"We're almost there."

"Because you're trucking along at a hundred miles an hour. Flames are coming off the backs of your shoes."

"Whiner. Do you need a taxi to go one more block?"

"You just can't let an opportunity slip to push at me, can you?"

"Why would I? It's fun to watch your eyes crinkle at the corners while you try to figure out a slick way to razz me right back."

Uncanny. A little scary, truth be told. "Remind me never to play poker with you. Sharp as you are, you'd pick up all my tells."

"I minored in psychology. I like to think of myself as a perpetual student of human behavior. In my business, it helps to be able to know what makes people tick. Figure out how they might respond before they even know."

"Interesting hobby." Insightful and beautiful. If only he had a couple more days to burn. For too long now, he'd stuck to women who were only good between the sheets, but bored him stiff in daylight. Easier to avoid any hint of a relationship that way. But Ivy tempted him to break his own rule.

"I have others. Yoga, for example. I'm very bendy."

"I noticed."

"With all the air miles you log, it'd be great for you

to pick up. Nothing like stretching after a long plane ride. Speaking of, where are you off to next?"

"No idea. I'm going to be grounded for at least a few weeks dealing with my promotion."

"If it gets too hard for you to stay in one place, you could always nip back here for a weekend. Pretty short plane ride from New York."

Wait a minute. She knew this was nothing more than a lost weekend, right? A really great one, sure. Looked forward to repeating it any time work swung him through Chicago. But they weren't dating or anything.

Ivy took off her sunglasses, hooking them in the neck of her tee shirt. Throwing her arms open wide, she said, "Here we are. Make a mental postcard. Buckingham Fountain is a Chicago landmark."

For good reason. The massive plume of water looked as high as the city's skyscrapers arrayed behind it. In the surrounding pool, stone seahorses shot water at three pink marble basins. Ben spun in a slow circle, taking in the view of dazzling architecture and endless lake iconic to the city. He'd seen it in photos before, but they couldn't properly encapsulate the majestic sight. Ben laced his fingers with Ivy's, gave a quick squeeze.

"No wonder you like it. Kind of looks like a big, wet wedding cake with all those tiers," he teased. "Did you always want to be a wedding planner?"

"Well, I've always wanted to be a bride."

Whoa. Danger ahead. Ben dropped her hand, and had to force himself not to back away. With a single sentence, Ivy transformed from perfect paramour to a toxic cliché. The kind he avoided at all cost. Women who focused on the white dress and spending daddy's money on flower arrangements taller than an NBA forward, rather than finding the right partner. Could she really be one of those? Nah. No reason to jump to conclusions. Yet. What did it matter, anyway? He'd be gone in a matter of hours. Still, Ben decided to toss out a test balloon, see how she responded.

"You're only a bride for a day. Then you're stuck in a marriage for years."

"Don't you mean forever and ever?" She laughed.

"Hell, no. Show me a lasting marriage, and I'll show you a pre-nup somebody's waiting out."

Ivy tried to laugh again, but it sounded forced. "You can't really be that cynical."

"Wanna bet?" Frustrated, he whipped off his cap and shoved his hands through his hair. Ivy stood there, gaping like he'd run over her puppy, backed up, and done it again.

"Ben, be serious."

Why wouldn't she believe him? "Oh, I'm as serious as a heart attack on this subject. Marriage doesn't work. I've got an entire family tree full of proof. High school graduation is synonymous with parents divorcing. If they even last that long."

"It sounds like your family has had an unfortunate string of bad luck. But you can't discount the institution." He could tell she chose her words carefully. Not that she, or anyone for that matter, would change his mind. "Everything in life is better when you share it with a partner. A loving relationship is the foundation for a happy life."

"You can't really be that naïve," he shot back. "Opening yourself up to the level required in a marriage opens you up to heartbreak. Your great love, the person who knows you best, is the person who can hurt you the most."

"True."

Amazing she conceded that much. He watched her pace back and forth on the grass moat surrounding the fountain. Looked like she was winding up for one heck of a pitch. Ivy stopped right in front of him, clasping her hands over her heart like an operatic ingénue.

"But only if you aren't with the right person," she continued. "You can fall in love over and over again with wonderful people who enrich your life. And yes, may cause pain. It's all a part of the journey to find your soul mate."

Unbelievable. Ridiculous. Ben barely knew where to start. "I can't believe I'm still standing here listening to this. In your world, the clouds are heart shaped. Bird crap comes out with a pastel, candy coating. You don't have a grasp on reality."

"Reality is what you make it; what you form for yourself. I choose to form mine around love. And it is a lot happier place than the dark, bitter reality you cling to."

Christ. It was like arguing with a freaking cartoon character. Kind of looked like one too, with the perfectly perky ponytail swaying in the breeze. Her adorable figure showcased by a snug tee and those very short shorts. Damn it. He should've known that with a total package of smarts, common sense and a smoking body, a serious imperfection lurked beneath the surface. Should've been on his guard from the start. And he'd pay for that mistake by nipping in the bud whatever romantic fantasy she'd no doubt already concocted about him.

Ben jammed his hat back on. "Hardly. Out of the two of us, I'd put money on you getting far more hurt. So let me do you a favor and forestall any mixed messages before you start text-stalking me. I am not boyfriend material. I don't do relationships. Of any kind."

"Why are you having such a bad reaction to a simple comment about marriage?"

"Consider me allergic to your particular brand of wide-eyed idiocy."

Ivy laid a soft palm on his cheek. "You're either scarred or scared. I'm guessing both. Who tainted love for you?"

"Life. And I'm no more tainted than that guy. Or that one over there." Ben jabbed his finger at a lone man staring at the lake, and another sweeping trash off the pebbled path. "I get it. You have to wear rose-colored glasses to do your job. But one of these days, you should scratch the surface of the gilded frame you've put around marriage. Because a fancy frame can't compensate for faded ideals that simply can't survive in today's society."

Ivy snatched back her hand as if his skin had superheated. "I understand if you don't want to see me again. However, there's no call to attack a belief system I've built my entire life around."

Obviously they wouldn't be meeting in the middle on this issue. Right about now, the bar at O'Hare looked pretty inviting compared to continuing this conversation. "Look, I'm sorry we got off on this tangent. I'm a straight shooter. So I'll tell you I enjoyed our time together the past two days. You're a special woman. But I think I should get to the airport." He dug a crumpled twenty out of his pocket and handed it to her. "Here's cab fare for you to get home. Nice meeting you, Ms. Rhodes."

Because he couldn't help himself, couldn't resist those glossy pink lips even after all the nonsense she'd spouted from them, he pressed a firm, fast kiss on their softness, fighting the urge to take it deeper. The woman had a mouth built for pleasing a man, and she knew how to use it. Seemed a shame to walk away from the first woman to really challenge him in as long as he could remember. No. Didn't matter. A Grand Canyon-sized cavern gaped between them, and it wouldn't get any better no matter how much time they spent together. Better to call it quits before things got ugly.

Ben walked away as fast as possible, not daring to look back. He'd done the right thing by giving her cab fare. Hadn't abandoned her on a deserted highway or anything. So why did it feel so very wrong?

CHAPTER SIX

Make no little plans; they have no magic to stir
men's blood.
                                              —Daniel H. Burnham

IVY COULD SWEAR that love swirled in the air along with
the delicious aroma from the box of strawberry muffins
under her arm as she walked down the sidewalk. The
tangible breeze of romance blew out the last of winter's gloom and put a smile in everyone's heart. This
week alone, Aisle Bound had two bridal showers, five
consults, and three weddings and their accompanying
rehearsals on the books. Business boomed in mid-May,
and it would only increase its frenetic pace all the way
through to Halloween.

She paused beneath Aisle Bound's lilac awning for
a minute to admire the window display of pale pink
satin draping from floor to ceiling. It set off hot pink
vases bursting with white apple blossoms, stacked on
white cubes of varying heights. Daphne's work, impeccable as always. Simple yet dreamy. Ivy used her new
wedge sandals to nudge open the door to Aisle Bound.

Milo lifted his nose from the appointment book with
the unerring accuracy of a bird dog. "I smell treats.
Yum! What are we celebrating this time?" He twirled
his chair around in glee. Twice. Milo had a gift for

wringing every morsel of fun out of a situation. His buffed, manicured, and occasionally polished little finger held more *joie de vivre* than the rest of the company put together. Today's stylish ensemble consisted of a black-and-white-checked vest over a black shirt, white pants, and old-school oxfords. And the obligatory diamond stud in his ear. Milo swore he'd gotten it from a leftover gift bag at one of Oprah's staff parties.

"This is National Strawberry Month," said Ivy.

"Of course it is." Daphne stepped out of the refrigerator case at the back of the reception area which held display bouquets as well as the completed table arrangements for today's bridal shower. "Honey, I know you like to turn every day into a special occasion, but it's getting out of hand. Last week it was ribs for lunch for BBQ Month, and peanut butter cookies on Bake Sale Day. Pretty soon they'll be able to float us in the Macy's Thanksgiving Day parade."

"Don't worry. I thought you might object, and timed this accordingly. It just so happens to be Eat What You Want Day." Ivy winked at her best friend and deposited her box on the glass coffee table next to the single peony floating in a crystal bowl. "You know you can't resist anything from Lyons Bakery."

Daphne poked open the top of the box. "We've been stopping there at least twice a week for years. How come I've never seen strawberry muffins on their menu?"

"Oh, I might have mentioned strawberry month to Sam when he dropped off the Taggart-Chang cake on Sunday. He promised to talk his mother into whipping up something special."

"Sam's a sweetie. And his ass is absolutely delecta-

ble." Milo draped himself artfully across the oversized
wing chair closest to the muffins. Ivy thought of it as
a throne chair. Like something out of *Alice in Wonder-
land*, the seatback rose to almost five feet. Covered in
white brocade, it enveloped a bride, putting distance
between her and the matching sofa where Ivy relegated
however many well-meaning but overbearing relatives
accompanied her.

Julianna hip checked Milo right onto the floor as
she walked by. "If I've told you once, I've told you
nine thousand times. Unless you're paying our exorbitant fees, no eating on the stain-attracting furniture."

"Do you see any food in my hands?" He waved his
hands in the air. Ivy saw the gesture for what it really
was; an excuse to show off the checkerboard-patterned
cuff links.

"You were about to make a move on those muffins.
Don't pretend otherwise." Julianna and Milo bickered
constantly yet managed to work together flawlessly.
The pretense of animosity kept them sharp at all times.
Deep down, Ivy knew they'd go to the mat for each
other without a moment's hesitation. It made for a lively
workplace.

Daphne twisted her almost waist-length hair into a
bun, and stabbed it into submission with what looked
like a leftover rose stem. "Let's get this meeting rolling. I have to finish six bridesmaid bouquets by lunch.
And two flower girl pomanders. Ideally, their floral
headpieces as well."

"No whining. We pledged that when we started, remember?" Ivy darted down the long hallway into her
office to grab her notes, but kept talking. "When we

only had two clients booked for an endless six weeks after we opened? A busy day is a good day."

"Sorry. You're right. I had to get up an hour early this morning for a special delivery. Then I spent two hours stripping thorns off a massive order of roses. I won't speak again until I've front loaded more caffeine and sugar." Daphne bit into a muffin and stalked over to the insulated coffee carafe Milo kept filled at all times.

Ivy carried out a plastic shopping bag and perched on the edge of the sofa. "While everyone gets settled, I want to show off a little something I picked up last night. Potential merchandise."

"No, no more shopping for you," groaned Julianna. "You've gotten completely out of control. Our storeroom only has a finite amount of space."

Milo nodded his head with the speed of a wind-up toy. "She's right. Buying things for an imaginary store you may or may not open at an unforeseeable point in the future? Nutty. Pretty soon they'll feature you on one of those reality shows about hoarders."

Party poopers. Joy suckers. No matter how valid their points, Ivy didn't think they should rain on her parade. With enough planning, her idea for a store celebrating all things romantic could viably become a reality. And Ivy happened to be a stellar planner.

"My store may only be a dream right now, but that doesn't mean it won't happen. Men and women are overstressed and under-romanced in today's world. They need a place where they can get a spontaneous, *I love you just because* present. Or fixings for a romantic picnic lunch. Or the perfect chocolate truffle to leave on a pillowcase." A little skepticism wouldn't tarnish her dream. Love made life worth living. And sometimes people needed a little help in that department. "Daphne and I opened this place on a wing and a prayer. I'll find a way to raise the capital to open A Fine Romance, and I'll do it in less than five years. You're welcome to place bets on that."

If only she could convince a bank to bet on her. Ivy's last two loan applications had been turned down. Her project had been officially classified as too-risky-for-this-economy. But the banks knew business—not the business of *romance*. She knew the industry inside and out, and had no doubt her store would not only survive, but flourish. If only they had vision to look beyond their spreadsheets. So none of her friends knew she'd been quietly trying to find a way to open the store this year. Safer to work in stealth mode. Then she didn't have to deal with the pitying, albeit comforting looks when things went wrong. Far better to present it as a fait accompli once all the loose ends were tied up.

Unfortunately, she'd turned over most available rocks in her search for funding an initial start-up. Every lender looked at the mortgage on her condo and monthly expenses for Aisle Bound (running in the black since year one, thank you very much) and declared her finances were spread too thin to sustain a third. The unspoken goal had always been to open A Fine Romance before she turned thirty. Luckily unspoken, since the fateful birthday loomed in less than a year.

Daphne held up a finger sporting two bandages, probably courtesy of the morning's rose strip-a-thon. Belle rode above the knuckle, and Ariel below. She always went for the Disney Princesses first in her vast collection of cartoon-themed first aid supplies. "First, show us what you've got. I might be talked into investing, but only if you convince me that you've really got your finger on the pulse of what the romance-deprived public truly needs."

"Then call me a human stethoscope. Get a load of this." Ivy pulled her prize out of the bag beside the sofa and unfurled all its glory.

"A fleece blanket?" Milo grabbed another muffin, shaking his head. "Did you open a new checking account and get it as a freebie?"

"You're all worked up about a blanket carried everywhere from Macy's to Walgreens to truck stops along I-94?" Daphne slurped her coffee. Began to sit on the blindingly white sofa, then looked at her coffee mug. Ivy could see the thought flash behind Daphne's eyes of how much it cost to spot clean, reconsidered, then crossed her legs and sank onto the floor.

Ever cognizant of her role as *associate* wedding planner, Julianna judiciously kept her mouth shut. The sudden arch to her right eyebrow, however, spoke volumes.

"You all lack vision." Ivy looked down at the pumpkin-and-yellow-striped square in her hands. Square. Whoops. In all the excitement, she'd left out the best part. "Well, that and I forgot to explain the hook, the whiz-bang twist."

Milo sniffed. "That blanket could fart daisy petals and it still wouldn't make me blink twice."

"Picture it big enough for two, a picnic blanket…" Ivy drew out the suspense while she traced an outline in the air with one hand, "…and heart shaped."

"Oh. Oh, that's brilliant," Julianna gushed. "People would buy them for tailgating at Bears games, or just for snuggling on the couch. They would fly out of the store."

"The thus far imaginary store," Milo corrected. But he softened the comment with an approving nod and grin.

"See, this is why I went into partnership with you in the first place. You know your stuff." Daphne leaned over to give Ivy an awkward, one-armed hug around her calves. "How'd the brainstorm hit you this time?"

"If I give away all my secrets, you won't continue to bow down before my genius."

"Is the oxygen thin way up there on your pedestal?" Daphne snarked back.

"Fine." Ivy refolded the blanket. Even she couldn't look at the jarring color combo much longer. "Grandma Rhodes is leaving on an Alaskan cruise next month. Even though it'll be summer, she's convinced her state-room will be as cold as the surrounding icebergs. I thought this would be small and light enough for her to stuff in a carry-on. Then I remembered she'd told me about a shore excursion she scheduled: a picnic on a glacier. The idea just hit me."

Jazzed, she'd stayed up late surfing the web for companies to produce the unusual shape. Ivy found two conglomerates which looked promising. Even bet-ter, a little past midnight she'd tracked down a family of third-generation hand crafters in Indiana, no more than an hour away. Her enthusiasm had flattened as she saved her notes, tempered by the realization she had no place to sell her new item. Yet. But she still got up at the crack of dawn to drive out there for a sample of their work.

Julianna cleared her throat and discreetly tapped her

CHRISTI BARTH

109

watch. "We're a few minutes behind. We should really begin the run down of this week's events."

"You are an automated, synchronistic treasure. Thank you for keeping us on track." Ivy enjoyed it when someone else stepped in to be the schedule police. She stuffed the blanket back in its bag, then sat on the sofa. Opening her portfolio, she rifled through a stack of color-coded schedules. Pink tabs for showers, lilac for engagement parties and deep purple for weddings. A small perk of owning her own business was being able to jump on any excuse to use her favorite color purple in all its shades.

"We'll start with the Lambert shower. Evanston Woman's Club, thanks to membership by, as far as I can tell, every woman in her family, his family, and several coworkers. You all know the venue. Old school, charming, sweet and the pinkish beige color scheme matches well with the bride's."

Daphne opened the display case and removed a cluster of tiny sweetheart roses twisted into a corsage. "Ashley wants all her guests to feel special today, so she's ordered corsages for everyone. Guests in ivory, bridesmaids and moms in pale pink, and bride in a variegated pink. Cranking out sixty of them wasn't exactly a creative challenge, but I know they'll be a huge hit. We're using teapots as the base of the centerpieces. I had Milo go nuts one night on eBay and pick up dozens of them for a song. Most are cracked, which kept our price low, but doesn't keep us from a decent profit margin. The flowers will cover the imperfections, and each table's bouquet will be unique."

"Resourceful and creative. Sounds like today should

be pat-the-whole-team-on-the-back day. Nice job, Daph."

"We've already coordinated with the maid of honor. Each centerpiece will be given to the winner of a game." Julianna consulted her copious notes. "We're doing ten tables of six, and yes, if you do the math that means they'll be playing about eight too many games. I talked myself blue in the face, but couldn't convince her that one round of designing a dress out of toilet paper is more than enough."

"Which brings me to the reminder to hit Costco for an entire carload of toilet paper. The people behind are going to think someone has serious health issues when we buy fifteen packs. Not it," Ivy quickly shouted.

Daphne placed her corsage back in the cooler. "I'm out. Too much still on my petal covered to-do list to run to the store."

Julianna and Milo stared at each other with the intensity of gunslingers at high noon, both waiting for the other to flinch. Before either could move, the door swung open, and in walked an earnest-looking woman in her late forties. She listed a little to the left, weighed down by a briefcase big enough to anchor a yacht. A sensible brown suit did little to enhance her stocky frame.

Walk-ins weren't unheard of, but they were rare. An unscheduled visit by a lone woman without an entourage of family and friends definitely fell in the atypical column. But every potential client deserved the same royal treatment, planned for or not. Hopefully, she didn't feel awkward or unwelcome for walking into the middle of an obvious breakfast staff meeting. To prevent her from turning right back around, Ivy jumped up.

"Welcome to Aisle Bound. Won't you join us for coffee and a muffin?"

"Thank you." The woman tucked a limp strand of her asymmetrical bob behind one ear. "You have no idea how badly I need coffee. My plane landed an hour ago. I got up before dawn this morning, and I'm only in Chicago on a long layover. Houston this afternoon, then back on a plane to Vegas, and if I'm lucky, catch the red eye back across country tonight."

Milo rushed to pour her a cup, and handed it to her while ushering her to the wing chair. He whisked back a minute later with a tray of cream and sugar in delicate china, patterned with trailing violets.

"My name is Milo. The moment you need a refill, you let me know." He finished off with a wink. Milo loved to flirt. Man or woman, young or old made no difference to him.

"Dripping it directly into my veins might not even get me through the day, but I appreciate your kindness. Especially since I barged in without an appointment. Checked my email in the cab on the way here, and found a mea culpa from my secretary about forgetting to set a time up with you. Not at all the way I prefer to do business. I'm Ruth Moder, by the way." She took a long sip of coffee, closed her eyes and sighed deeply.

Ivy pushed the muffin basket closer to Ruth while she did a quick round of introductions. "Your day sounds challenging, to say the least. I hope we can help ease your stress a little. It's our job to remove the worries and endless lists. All that's left is for you to enjoy being engaged."

"Ha! This is my typical Wednesday. Mondays are

ten times worse. Does it sound like I have time to fawn over a man long enough to get a ring on my finger?"

Ivy bit back a grin. The woman squeezed wedding planning into a four-airport day, and it wasn't even her wedding? Talk about dedication. Ruth didn't look quite old enough to be mapping out the big day for a daughter. Maybe a sister? Or just here to order some of Daphne's fabulous arrangements for a corporate event?

"Honestly, I'm amazed you have time to blink. So how can we assist you? Are you here on behalf of a friend?"

"I'm here for you, Miss Rhodes. I'd like to offer you a job."

Random. Weird. Plus, Ivy already had the best job in the world. "Thank you, but I'm going to stop you before you go any further. I'm not interested in changing jobs."

"We don't want you to." Ruth set down her cup and leaned forward, elbows propped on knees. "You remember filming an episode of *Wild Wedding Smackdown* three weeks ago?"

"Yes," Ivy said cautiously. A flurry of other words threatened to tumble out. Things like she'd never forget the twenty-four hours surrounding that wedding. That she thought about it every day. Well, every other day she worried about what sort of an impact the show would have on their business. Had she come off as competent and approachable? A good commercial for Aisle Bound? Thanks to ruthless self control, she only allowed memories of Ben to drift into her consciousness at night. Every night, when darkness filled her bedroom and nothing could distract her from the constant replay of their brief time together. A bad habit she'd give anything to break.

"The episode was fantastic," Ruth said. "We all loved you at the network."

Milo started a round of applause, and the others joined in. "Proud of you, boss."

"I can't take all the credit," Ivy said. "Aside from the excitement before the ceremony, everything ran according to plan." Yes, *aside* from rolling around naked with the videographer after the wedding ended. Because really, no matter how ruthlessly a wedding coordinator organized the day's itinerary, it never included three orgasms before dawn. Ivy pinched her subconscious for drifting back Ben-ward. Bad enough to do it in the privacy of her own bedroom. Far, far worse to think lusty thoughts in front of her coworkers about a man who'd called her a naïve, unrealistic idiot. A man who didn't know the first thing about love. A man she was glad to wash her hands of—and if repeated like a mantra, she might actually start to believe.

"Hands down, you're the best wedding planner we've ever seen in action. Which is why RealTV wants to feature you on a brand new series we're rolling out. *Planning for Love*. It'll follow wedding planners for two months, really capture what they do, how they interact with brides, what really goes on behind the scenes at a wedding. But," Ruth hastened to add, "without any of the negativity or backstabbing *WWS* is known for. We want this to be a feel-good show. The goal is to make every woman who watches it want to rush out and get married."

"Somebody better warn all the single men," quipped Daphne.

Milo snorted back a giggle. Julianna stabbed him with an evil glare that backed him away from the table to start a fresh pot of coffee. Ivy watched as her friends stilled and turned, one by one, to catch her response. The weight of their expectation and interest circled above her head, like the layer of humidity that blanketed the city on hot summer days. If only she could hit a pause button to get two spare minutes to focus. Since rewriting the laws of physics didn't seem likely, she went with the first thing that came to mind.

"No. I'm flattered, but my answer is no."

Ruth squinted. Drained her cup, and waved a finger at Milo to indicate a refill. "Don't you want to be on television? Be famous?"

Interesting question. Ivy didn't think Ruth would let her leave it at a simple "no" this time. "I want to be successful. Notoriety could as easily work *against* as *for* our business. If anything goes wrong at a wedding, it's my job to fix it so the bride isn't worried, and hopefully she never even finds out that Great Uncle Peter ripped the seam of his pants, or that her cousin's child stuck her entire face in the back of the wedding cake. Your cameras would capture all of it—the good and the bad. You'd take away the bubble of peace my clients pay us to ensure."

"Pay." Ruth smacked the heel of her palm against her forehead. "Of course. My mistake entirely. I didn't mention the terms. Unlike *WWS*, our contract would be with you, not the bride and groom." She leaned forward and grabbed Ivy's portfolio and her pen. After scribbling on the top page, she handed it back. "We're willing to pay you the amount you see *per wedding*. Over the eight weeks we'll shadow you, that comes to about twenty events? We'll need at least that for a season."

"More, in the summer," murmured Daphne.

"We could start right away. This weekend, in fact. We've got a crew on standby."

Although she wanted to resist, Ivy's eyes succumbed to the magnetic pull of the scrawled number. Twelve thousand dollars. Enough to rent the Shedd Aquarium twice. Or enough for a six-piece band and a really spectacular cake. A Vera Wang couture wedding dress. She ripped the paper off the pad and handed it to Daphne. Whose eyebrows promptly shot straight up to her hairline.

Daphne grabbed Ivy's hand and yanked her off the sofa. "Excuse us, won't you? We need to have a quick pow wow. Won't be a moment. Have another muffin." Daphne practically frog marched Ivy all the way to the storeroom at the back of the office. Once the door was firmly shut she leaned back, palms flat against the wood. "Wow."

Ivy nodded. "I know. The nerve, right? To barge in here, no appointment, and try to sweet talk me into making a fool of myself on national television. Again!"

"Okay, a very different wow. Want to explain why my perennially perky partner only sees this glass as half empty, while I see it as filled to the brim with vintage champagne?"

Um, experience? She'd watched a slew of the wedding shows, and the planner ended up looking like a harpy. Bossy, overbearing and selfish. Ivy had to believe the editing process created the monsters. There couldn't be that many horrible planners out there. What if they cut and pasted everything she said until Aisle Bound looked just as unprofessional?

"It could backfire. One thing goes wrong, the press makes a field day of it, and our reputation is shot. Or what if we don't get our clients to sign off on it? What if they don't want to be reality stars?"

Daphne inhaled deeply, held it for a beat before exhaling. "You're scared. I get that. But remember, she pointed out this isn't supposed to be a drama-centric disaster. Sounds like this show will be all hearts and flowers and happy endings. And you said having the cameras around for Tracy and Seth's wedding ended up being much easier than you expected. Most of the time you hardly noticed they were there."

Ivy straightened the row of identical back-up ring pillows. Lined up the stack of emergency tissue packs on the shelf below. Squared the corners of three boxes of bandages. Tidying with her hands helped her tidy her thoughts. Plus, it gave her an excuse not to face Daphne. To avoid the logical, clear gaze of her best friend that all too often saw right through Ivy to things she wanted to keep under lock and key. Who could absolutely not learn the reason Ivy had been so scattered of late all stemmed from the aftermath of her last stint in front of the camera. Over margaritas that Sunday night with her best friend, she'd dismissed the incident as no more than a sexually satisfying mistake. Back when she assumed if she didn't talk about Ben, she wouldn't think about him. Endlessly.

"Of course I'm scared, Daph. Even if filming goes well, we don't need national exposure. We're not going to franchise Aisle Bound like a hot dog stand."

"True. But we *do* need money fast. Lots of money. I did the math, being far better at it than you. If you don't negotiate and simply accept their offer as is— even though I'm sure you could negotiate a sweeter deal—you stand to make $240,000. In two months."

Daphne poked her head over Ivy's shoulder to whisper in her ear. "I wonder what you could buy with that much money. Seems to me it would be enough to put a down payment on a space, stock some shelves, decorate, and voila—you've got yourself your dream store."

Turning around, Ivy saw the gentle humor in Daphne's eyes. "I didn't think of that angle." Probably because she'd been too busy thinking about Ben and his stupidly sexy lips. Damn it, no more. No more thinking about him or dreaming about him. Daphne had a point. It would take an enormous amount of work, during their busiest time of year, but this influx of cash could make A Fine Romance a reality in a matter of months. Two months of being constantly followed by cameras was a small price to pay.

Daphne snapped her fingers in front of Ivy's nose. "Your eyes just glazed over. You're decorating and stocking inventory already, aren't you?"

"Maybe. But only if you're on board, too. With that kind of money we could make an offer on this building, own instead of rent. Shore up what we have before launching a new venture. Are you sure you're willing to take the leap with me?"

"I've got faith in you. It turned out pretty great last time. Why break a winning streak? And if it goes badly, you'll feel so guilty I'm sure you'll pretty much do my laundry and cook me dinner for the rest of my life." Daphne toyed with the loose end of a bandage, then looked up with a wicked glint in her eyes. "Maybe we should write that into the contract, just to be on the safe side."

"Gee, that much faith and five dollars still wouldn't be enough to buy me a latte." But Ivy enveloped Daphne in a tight hug. She knew the money didn't matter; deep down Daphne's willingness to expand their partnership had everything to do with friendship and their love for each other. And with love in the mix, what could possibly go wrong?

The storeroom door flew open. "My only daughter's going to be on television and didn't bother to tell me?" Samantha Rhodes stood backlit for a moment, no doubt pausing for effect. Her mother never did or said anything without a well thought out reason behind it. Thanks to a career as a marriage counselor, Mom knew the value of measuring each word and gesture. This time Ivy figured it to be a way to force her audience to fully appreciate the pink peau de soie stilettos, a single shade darker than her St. Johns suit. Another beat, and Samantha burst in, glomming onto their hug. Her signature heart-shaped ruby brooch bit into Ivy's shoulder. At least it provided distraction from the rose-scented perfume quickly rising to toxic levels in the closetlike space.

Ivy stifled a cough. "Mom, this isn't a great time. Plus, you're about two hours early for our lunch date."

"My eleven o'clock patients canceled. Declared themselves cured and called me from the airport. They're on their way to Bermuda for a second honeymoon. Sometimes I amaze even myself with my prowess. So, I decided lunch wouldn't be enough to make up for you skipping Mother's Day this weekend. You owe me the whole morning."

Here we go. The guilt bombs she'd been dropping ever since Ivy broke the news Aisle Bound had an event on one of her mother's favorite holidays. "You know we have a wedding. Booked over a year ago. It's not as if I'm choosing to run off to Vegas to avoid spending Mother's Day with you."

"Darling, I support your career. Truly, I do. But couldn't you make an exception this one day? Put family first?" To really drive the wheedling tone home like an ice pick to the heart, Samantha tucked Ivy's bob behind one ear and pinched her cheek. Astounding what a drop-dead imitation of a Jewish grandmother she could do, despite being raised the daughter of a Lutheran minister.

"I'd love to. But you ask me that on every birthday, anniversary and pseudo holiday. Last month you wanted me to skip a wedding to go with you to your hairdresser's daughter's sweet sixteen. And I've never even met the girl." Although she adored her mother, being the sole recipient of all her parental attention could be tiring. The curse of being an only child. Smothering versus mothering.

"Exactly why you should've come with me. You should meet Brittney. She's delightful. She taught me how to tweet. I adore the rigid simplicity of fitting an entire thought into one hundred and forty characters. Like a modern day haiku."

"Mrs. Rhodes, we've got strawberry muffins from Lyons Bakery. Probably still warm and definitely delicious. Why don't you have Milo set you up with a plate? Ivy and I will be right behind you." Daphne hustled her out and shut the door behind her. "Your mother is a little nutty. Especially for a shrink. Does she really think you'll cancel your entire morning to hang out with her?"

"Yes." Ivy sifted through her schedule in her head, trying to create a gap large enough to satisfy her mother. "But it's impossible. This week is already jam packed. Distraction is our only hope. Have you finished sketching the centerpieces for their anniversary party?"

"Yes. I came up with four choices, one for each decade of marriage. But I thought you wanted the party to be a surprise?"

"Desperate times call for desperate measures. With the added bonus of giving her the pleasure of deciding on cake flavors and buying a new dress." Samantha's love of shopping and sweets ran second only to her love of Ivy and her husband. After office hours, if she wasn't with David, you could put money on finding her at Marshall Field's, a chocolate store, or hanging around Ivy's shop. "Hopefully if I tell her about the party, she'll run straight to Michigan Avenue to try on every size-four cocktail dress she sees. With only seven shopping weeks until the party, she'll be in emergency mode. Then we can get back to work."

"You realize you'll have to let your dad in on it, too. Before Samantha spills the beans."

"Good point. Ask Julianna to get him on the phone while I walk Mom out." Her parents each wanted to be the one to hear from her first with any news. Ivy knew there were worse things than being lavished with love by one's parents. But staring down thirty, she felt far too old to deal with the loving rivalry.

This time a brisk knock came before the door flew open. Ruth leaned in, tapping her fingers against the doorjamb. "Sorry to interrupt, but I've got three more planes to catch. As much as I enjoyed breakfast with all of you, I need an answer. I've got two other wedding consultants to line up by day's end. We're offering you unparalleled exposure and a hefty chunk of change. If you're the savvy businesswoman you appear to be, you'd be flat-out crazy to let me walk out of here with an unsigned contract in my briefcase."

The moment of truth. In her peripheral vision, Ivy caught Daphne's tiny go-for-it nod. The offer seemed too good to be true, and yet thoroughly legitimate. After slamming into brick walls for months, here was a wide-open doorway to realizing her dream. A way to infuse hum drum days with romance for everyone.

"I need time to study the contract and run it past my lawyer. If everything checks out, I'll sign and scan it to you first thing tomorrow. There needs to be a clause about only portraying the positive side of our business and our events," Ivy tossed in, not for a minute thinking they'd go for it.

Ruth shrugged. "No problem. Given our network's track record, I completely understand. We'll send you an amended draft this afternoon."

That was easy. Proof they were willing to work with her, be reasonable. Maybe the next two months would turn out to be hassle free. Ivy grinned, excitement bubbling through her with the momentum of an overdue geyser. "Then I'll give you a conditional yes. If you bump up the offer by ten percent?" She held out a hand to see if Ruth would seal the deal.

"Done." Ruth pumped her hand vigorously. "You won't regret this, Miss Rhodes. Partnering with RealTV will give you two months you'll never forget, captured on film for a lifetime."

Daphne giggled. "Sounds like a bad jewelry store ad."

"Oh, we're always looking for sponsors, if you have a good relationship with any jewelers," said Ruth.

Ivy's finely honed coordinator sense went into full

red alert on her tacky-ometer. Reading every inch of the fine print on that contract jumped to the top of her list. "No. I won't let you force any of my clients to plaster advertising all over the wedding. No sponsors."

Ruth shrugged again as all three of them headed down the hallway. "Only an idea. Whatever you say, goes. It's your show. RealTV will bend over backward to do whatever we can to make you happy."

"Wow. If you were a man instead of a production company making a promise like that, we'd have to propose to you on the spot," joked Daphne. "Sounds perfect."

Uh oh. After putting on literally hundreds of events, Ivy could promise her clients exactly one thing: nothing was ever perfect. The trick lay in planning for the worst, which allowed her to preserve the illusion of perfection. Now a shadow of worry underscored her elation at lining up funding. How to plan for the worst, when she didn't have *any* idea at all of what to expect from this experience?

CHAPTER SEVEN

Many people spend more time planning the wedding than they do in planning the marriage.
—Zig Ziglar

THE SHEDD AQUARIUM topped the list of Ivy's favorite hometown attractions. It bore the unique distinction of also being at the top of her list of least favorite wedding sites, due to its vast size. After the tenth time she'd crossed the wide pebbled floor of the Oceanarium's amphitheatre, gone down the steps to the edge of the dolphin exhibit where Daphne beflowered a makeshift altar, Ivy stopped counting. Her feet already throbbed in anticipation of the miles yet to cover. Zipping between the dolphins, the ornately columned main lobby and the galleries surrounding the Caribbean Reef rotunda would take a physical toll as the evening progressed. Ivy always crossed her fingers at a Shedd event—just surviving the night with a problem-free event was hard enough.

"Are they here yet? The television crew that'll turn you into the next reality star?"

"Hardly a star. Remember, you'll be on camera, too. All that long, flowing blond hair and kewpie doll blue eyes should make you an instant hit. Maybe you'll get an offer for a centerfold spread out of this," teased Ivy.

After all, she didn't want to be the only one uncomfortably in the spotlight. Share and share alike with her partner, especially when it came to potential embarrassment on a nationwide level.

"Bite your tongue!" Daphne tightened the purple bow around her messy ponytail, then tugged on her lavender apron. "I'm as far from glamorous as it gets. Couldn't even pass for farmgirl chic in my jeans and sneakers. Ideally my floral creations will get in the spotlight, not me. Not at all. But you look snazzy." She whistled at Ivy's teal A-line dress, pouffed out like something a fifties movie star would wear.

"I always wear this dress at Shedd events. The color helps me blend in with the water in all the exhibits." While true, it didn't hurt that the cinched waist of the dress made her feel super skinny. She'd been haunted since Ruth left by the old saying *the camera adds ten pounds*. Must've been invented by a man. A relative of the guy who made dressing room mirrors add fifteen pounds and bags under your eyes.

Daphne paused, a clump of blue and green hydrangeas in one hand and a stalk of deep blue sweet peas in the other. "A man is waving at you from the top of the amphitheatre. It's too early for guests. Must be your crew. Are you ready for your close up?"

"Not really. But, it gives me courage to picture how great it'll feel to open A Fine Romance in a few months." Though maybe not enough. When Ivy had signed the contract with RealTV, she hadn't stopped to consider how it would feel to constantly have cameras trained on her. The episode she'd taped of *Wild Wedding Smackdown* focused on the bride and groom, but *Planning for Love* would keep its lens squarely on her much of the time. Like a restless flamenco dancer, nerves tapped out a rhythm insistently just beneath the surface of her skin.

Taking a deep breath, Ivy turned around. And immediately felt as though a thousand-pound hippo stomped all that air right back out of her. The one man she'd spent weeks trying to banish from her thoughts currently leaned, ankles crossed, on the entrance wall to the Oceanarium, devilishly debonair in a tux. And why did her first reaction have to be noticing how damn handsome he looked? Because Ben Westcott—whether clothed or stark naked—was nothing if not drop-dead good looking.

"Uh oh," whispered Daphne. "Isn't that—"

"Yes."

"Are you freaking out?"

"Little bit," Ivy admitted. Daphne didn't know the half of it. Holy crap. Blown away was more like it. Reeling from shock. Heck, if this was Victorian England, she'd probably fall into an old-fashioned swoon. Not that she intended to betray even a hint of her emotional uproar to Ben. She'd be as cool as the air in the penguin exhibit a floor below.

"Bet you're surprised to see us, aren't you?" Ollie hollered as he skittered down the steps, taking two at a time.

"Careful," warned Ben. "We don't want to recreate our first meeting with Ms. Rhodes. No reason for one of us to end up with a skinned knee every time we work together." Pushing off the doorway, he shoved his hands in his pockets and descended the steps. He looked like a model. Make that a spokesmodel for very expensive sports cars. Or yachts. Or he could pass for a jet-setting prince in a Hollywood blockbuster, ready to gamble the night away in a Cote d'Azur casino.

Ivy blinked away the comparisons. She'd wasted enough time dreaming about Ben. Doing it with him right in front of her approached a pathetic level of absurdity. Plus, she didn't want Daphne to realize just how shaken she was to see him again. She fisted her hands in the fluffy folds of her skirt, digging her nails into her palms. The sharp pain reminded her of the stinging words he'd hurled at her heart. When everything went so horribly wrong. Ivy smoothed on a smile for his gangly assistant.

"Ollie, it's nice to see you again. Hope you've recovered by now from what I expect was an epic hangover from your first trip through the debauchery of Rush Street."

He plopped onto the row of stone benches right in front of her. "It did take a few days. The plane ride back to LaGuardia—brutal." Like an aspen in a blizzard, Ollie's whole body shivered in remembrance. "Good thing my man Ben here was just as bad off. I swear there weren't two more miserable people on that entire flight."

"Really?" She took a tiny shard of comfort in his misery, although finding it strange. No, incomprehensible. The way Ben left things with her, Ivy thought he would've two-stepped the whole way home in delight at his narrow escape from her evil, romantic clutches.

"Oh, yeah. Had to drag ourselves in for a staff meeting the next morning. Everyone said they'd never seen him in such a pathetic state. I don't think Ben cracked a smile for three days straight. He wouldn't tell me what messed him up so bad, but I'm guessing Jagermeister. Nothing else makes you feel so lousy."

Ivy supposed she should feel grateful he hadn't blabbed far and wide about the details of their night together. Good that nobody else knew exactly how torn and tattered he'd left her self-esteem.

"Cheap champagne," offered Daphne. "All that sugar will make you wish you'd never been born. Learn from the mistakes of your elders, kid, and stay far, far away from it." She wiped her hands on her apron, then extended one to Ollie. "Daphne Lovell. Welcome to our little corner of the wedding market. You picked a great event to dive into. Look at these flowers. Eight different shades of blue. Be sure to get a close up. The reception centerpieces will knock your socks off."

"Why are you here, Ben?" Ivy blurted in a rush. Immediately she regretted that loss of control. Dealing with Bennett Westcott demanded a cool head and dispassionate manner. "It seems as if Ruth would've mentioned you two would be my crew. Especially since I'm quite sure she told me to expect a team by the names of Randall and Maria." She checked her watch. "Ten minutes ago, as a matter of fact. Care to explain?"

Ben made his way to the edge of the dolphin enclosure. Squatting, he peered through the glass at an inquisitively squirming dolphin. "Sorry we're late. Must've thrown a kink in your perfect schedule." He straightened and looked her square in the eyes for the first time. His steady blue gaze gave away nothing, but a single eyebrow speared up into a mocking arch. "Or did you build in an extra deal-with-meeting-the-TV-crew cushion?"

"Naturally." She looked down her nose at him. Or

tried to, before realizing the six inches in height he had on her made it impossible. Ivy settled for slitting her eyes and hoped the intended derision came through in her tone. "But it was ten minutes ago. And forgive me for being hung up on a technicality, but I'm forced to ask again, what are you doing here?"

With a jerk of his thumb to indicate Ollie as well, Ben shrugged. "We're a last-minute substitution. Randall's in the hospital with a pin in his shoulder. Souvenir from Friday night's event at Union Station in D.C. Supposed to be his last gig with *WWS* before he jumped ship with me to RealTV."

"He filmed the groom getting down and dirty with a bridesmaid. *After* the ceremony. Before they even cut the cake." Ollie related the story with a morbid glee. "Groom and a few of his buddies demanded Randall hand over the camera. Of course Randall said no. He knew he had the best episode of the season in the can. Threats turned into shoving which turned into pushing him into an iron balustrade. Knocked his shoulder so out of whack he ended up in surgery that night."

"What an appalling story," Ivy said. The only contact sport at a wedding was supposed to be hugging.

Ben pressed his lips together into a thin line. Nodded his agreement with a hangdog expression. "On several levels. I'll bet nobody used those honeymoon tickets. To an all inclusive resort in Bora Bora. What a waste. Their happily ever after lasted about an hour and a half."

An expected response from a man who believed romance guttered out the moment the wedding unity candle was lit. "Of course. Who cares if two lives were ruined in the process? The real tragedy is the line of endless mai tais that will go undrunk on a white

sand beach halfway across the world." Ivy threw up
her hands. "It amazes me you can repeatedly subject
yourself to weddings when you clearly hold them in
such disdain. Isn't there anything else you'd rather be
doing?"

Eyes frosting to the frigid blue of Lake Michigan
in January, Ben's voice dropped to a husky whisper.
"You have no idea."

What? He was the one trashing the centuries old,
noble institution of marriage. Why give her a look that
said she'd just trampled over his hopes and dreams like
hapless dandelions on a soccer field?

"*Wild Wedding Smackdown* is on immediate hia-
tus. They've suspended production of the whole show.
Too many injuries in the line of duty." Ollie shrugged.
"Anyway, with Randall out of the picture, we were the
only available crew to film *Planning for Love*. We're
the ones who'll make you famous."

Daphne waggled a remonstrative handful of feathery
greens in Ollie's face. "Hopefully not. Apparently Ivy
had them remove the glitz, glamour and fame section of
her contract. Which is really a shame. I was hoping to
walk a few red carpets as the faithful sidekick. Maybe
have one of the castoffs from *The Bachelor* hit on me.
All the perks of stardom without my pores being broadcast to America's living rooms in high-def."

"So this is your big promotion?" asked Ivy with an
intentional sneer in her voice. Might as well make it
clear she knew that Ben standing in front of her had to
be the last place he wanted to be. Given his disparag-
ing attitude toward romance, it must gall him to be on
assignment for a show celebrating love. "Stuck following me around?"

"Hardly," he drawled. "RealTV snatched me away from True Life Productions. I'm the executive producer of *Planning for Love*. Artistic freedom, at long last. We've got five crews shooting around the country, overlapping. My job is to craft the finished product, put the spin on each and every episode."

"Be careful. Your God complex is showing." Smug, self-important jerk. Ivy surged forward till she stood nose to nose with him—well, his nose to the top of her head. What a crappy day to be caught in shoes without heels. He might be taller, but she fully intended to bring him down a notch or two. With the grace of a game show hostess, she swept her arm in an arc at the dolphin pool. "Plan to part the waters anytime soon?"

Ben stepped in, flattening the front of her dress against the sharp pleats of his trousers. The tips of their shoes touched. Their arms, legs and torsos almost did, separated by nothing more than the thick miasma of two flaring tempers. Ivy had to tip her head back to maintain her indignant squint. She refused to let him back her down. Not on her turf, not at her event.

He shushed her by placing his palm across her lips. "Only after you hop down from your pedestal and finish walking across."

Daphne dropped her bucket of flowers. The sound echoed through the Oceanarium like the bell signaling the end of a boxing match. "Whoa. We just went from zero to sixty in about five seconds, and I'm not wearing a seatbelt. Or padding, which is beginning to look like an oversight on my part. How about we all take a step back? Actually step back," she encouraged, putting a palm each on Ben's and Ivy's chest and shoving them apart.

So much for keeping a cool head. Mortified, Ivy spun away. Ben got under her skin faster than a blood-sucking tick. Daphne probably thought she'd lost her mind. And Ben—well, she didn't care what Ben thought. After all, he started it. Provoked her. No self-respecting wedding consultant could've stood literally at what would become (after about two more buckets of blue and white blooms) a wedding altar and listen to him ridicule the disintegration of a marriage. Even one that barely lasted past the cocktail hour.

"Tonight is a big deal to the bride, the groom and two hundred and fifty of their nearest and dearest," Daphne reminded them, parsing her words in an exaggeratedly slow fashion. "You two need to work seamlessly to make sure it is nothing less than magical for them. And you need to work together. So whatever's going on between you two? Knock it off. Bennett, why don't you start by walking it off? You and Ollie should go find Julianna. She's in the lobby setting up the place cards. Ivy will join you in a few minutes."

Ben didn't move. Not an inch. Was he—yes, he was waiting to see if Ivy flinched first. Juvenile. Utterly laughable. Especially since he could stand there for months. Years. Decades. Until that tux turned to dust, leaving him clad in nothing but his truly superb muscles, and still she wouldn't yield first.

"Ivy." Daphne spat out her name and grabbed her arm, yanking her toward the exit. "I left the aisle runner in the van. Help me carry it in."

Glancing back over her shoulder, Ivy saw Ollie pulling Ben up the steps in a similarly forceful manner. "He would've buckled under my righteous wrath in another minute. Damn it, Daphne, why did you interrupt?"

"Because this isn't the O.K. Corral at high noon. It is a wedding that cost upward of seventy thousand dollars. And even if this event barely hit four figures, the amount the bride and groom have invested in it is invaluable. As you well know." She stopped in the dark hallway leading to the back of the Oceanarium. It ran parallel to the whale and dolphin tanks. The faint slap of water against the walls coupled with dim blue and green pulsing lights created the illusion of being underwater. "While this isn't an appropriate time or place, I feel the need to convene an emergency partners' meeting, and point out your unprofessional behavior. It's probably a bad idea to antagonize representatives of the network that owns you body and soul for the next two months. Honestly, I've never seen you come so close to losing it. So tell me, what the hell just happened?"

Ivy bit her lip. Wished they were anywhere but in a hallway so she'd have an excuse to look somewhere besides straight at Daphne. "Nothing. A slight difference of opinion."

"Really? Do you remember last week when you wanted pad thai for lunch and I wanted gyros? *That* was a slight difference of opinion." Daphne crossed her arms over her chest and shook her head. Disapproval rolled off her as thick as the humid salt tang in the air. "After barely exchanging five sentences, you and Ben looked ready to go at it for nine rounds. Either in a mud pit or in bed, I'm not sure which."

Great. Now the image of Ben with sticky, wet mud clinging to his legs popped into her mind. Sort of an Indiana Jones look, like he'd escaped from a tribe of restless jungle natives and slogged through quicksand just to get to her. Her mind added a battered felt fedora to the image. Nothing else—just Ben, the slick mud, and the hat. So he could whip it off and send it sailing into the trees once he spotted her, reclining in a hammock, naked, waiting for him. Ivy shook her head the tiniest bit. Nope, the image refused to pop back out. He lingered there, larger than life, dripping and toned and ready.

"Ohhh." Daphne drew the word out like sticky taffy being pulled by a master candymaker. "Oh, no. I was just kidding when I said in bed. But now your eyes are all glazed over, and, eww, you're licking your lips. God, Ivy, you're not mad at him, are you? You *want* him?"

Who wouldn't? From the tips of his golden hair down to his strong, well-shaped calves, Ben was the ultimate eye candy. A man morsel capable of making any woman want to pop him in her mouth and suck, long and hard. Ivy was only human. But she also lusted after chili cheese fries and meatballs dipped in fondue. All of which, including Ben, were equally bad for her. Clogged arteries were a lot less painful than the clogged heart Ben carried beneath those well-formed pecs.

"As it so happens, I am quite peeved with Mr. Westcott. His complete lack of respect for the institution of marriage is an insult to me, my profession and the profusion of love-struck couples everywhere."

Daphne rolled her eyes. "Whatever. You want him."

So not the point. In fact, not at all pertinent to their current discussion. "He can't effectively deal with our clients with such a negative attitude. I refuse to let him taint Diana and Niko's special day."

"He baited you, not the clients. Let's backtrack for a minute. At Tracy and Seth's wedding, did he do anything untoward? Anything at all to ruin their magical day of bliss?"

Although it pained her, Ivy knew she had to be honest. In truth, Ben's ability to stay in the background and not be noticed had impressed her quite a bit that day. "No."

Daphne smiled knowingly. Nodded her head. "Like I said, you want him."

"Stop saying that."

"Stop thinking it. Anger and passion are divided by a very thin line. If you ask me, the line looks pretty blurry between the two of you. Is it possible you didn't fill me in completely on exactly what went down back in April? Have you been holding out on me?"

Well, of course. Ivy's pathetic, emotional longing for Ben, followed by his disastrous attack on everything she believed in, didn't need to be shared. She enjoyed being half of a couple. Loved the feeling of being in love. Of course, despite what her friends thought, Ivy didn't fall like a ton of bricks every time a guy smiled at her. She'd kicked her share of losers to the curb. But she'd also moved a bit too quickly in her last few serious relationships. And she learned from her mistakes.

Ivy now parsed out information carefully to her friends. They'd developed a combination grimace of pursed lips and a head tilt which communicated their pity all too well. Sure, they meant well. But she didn't think her enthusiasm for the possibility of a long-lasting relationship deserved to be treated with the same tragic consolation as if she'd announced that all her hair fell out overnight. Love happened, and Ivy refused to miss her shot at it by being too cautious.

Given their current situation, with a steady diet of

Ben on the horizon, it seemed even more prudent to not elaborate. Filling in the sordid details right now of what happened in April would only give Daphne reason to worry. Ivy figured one of them in the partnership worrying was enough. Clear away all the personal stuff, and Ben was nothing more than a conduit to fulfilling her contract with RealTV. Dodging Daphne's question didn't make her a bad friend, but rather a good businesswoman.

Ivy bobbed her head in apology. "I'm edgy today. Stayed up far too late working on plans for the new store. To compensate, I overdosed on caffeine. Then I couldn't find my shoes. Not only was I running late, but traffic was the usual nightmare getting to Lake Shore Drive. You know how much I hate not being on schedule. I think I took out my frustration on Ben. He took me by surprise, and I didn't handle it well. End of story."

"Really?" Daphne didn't sound convinced. "Because I've seen you handle much bigger surprises. What if I'm not there to play referee the next time Ben surprises you? Julianna's far too much in awe of you to break up another tussle. Forget about the show for a minute. Run through a couple of rounds of that breathing stuff you do in yoga class. Or whatever it takes to calm you down. Our job is to remove the hassles for our clients, not create them."

Ivy flashed a smile, hoping it came off as confident and cheerful. "Diana and Niko will have a perfect wedding today, thanks to the efforts of everyone on the Aisle Bound team. Which, for the next two months,

includes Ben and Ollie. No more trouble, I promise."
Thankfully the pouf of her skirt hid her crossed fingers. On both hands.

CHAPTER EIGHT

The most dangerous food is wedding cake.

—American Proverb

"THE MEAT IS wrong." Ione Kosta looked like a blue dandelion quivering in the breeze. She tapped her left foot insistently, which set the multiple layers of fringe on her dowdy mother-of-the-bride dress at a constant shimmy. From the top of her gravity-defying mass of teased hair to the feathered mules Ivy had whispered she'd custom dyed to match the color of the aquarium water, the woman personified outrage.

Ben swallowed a sigh. He'd had a good run of probably a dozen weddings since his last outraged MOB. They were a standard hazard of the job, and usually resulted in gigantic headaches for everyone in a ten-foot radius.

"Mrs. Kosta, I checked the plates before they left the kitchen." Ivy whipped out the banquet order form and pointed out the line in question. "Filet mignon with Madeira rosemary sauce and a grilled lobster tail. Let me assure you, the menu is exactly what you and your daughter ordered six months ago."

"Of course it is."

Taking a few steps back, Ben widened his shot to encompass what he pegged at more than two hundred pounds of irate Greek mother as well as Ivy's fixed, patient smile. He knew it had to be merely a mask. Nobody liked dealing with pissed-off moms. Not even a wedding planner with a heart as big and squishy as Ivy's.

"Then how is the meat wrong? Not cooked enough, perhaps? We can fix that for you in a jiffy," Ivy offered, her toothpaste ad smile guileless. Definitely phony.

"My piece is too small." The irate woman held up two pudgy fingers pinched together, with a whisper of space between them. "They're all too small. I'll be ridiculed by everyone in St. Konstantine's parish."

"We were both at the tasting. This plate is identical to what you tried and approved back in March."

Yup, Ivy's patience was melting away faster than a scoop of rocky road in the Sahara. Her smile was a few clicks wider, milk chocolate eyes saucered in sympathy, but he saw a telltale sign in the interlaced fingers behind her back. She wiggled each one up and down the row, then back again, over and over, as if channeling all her inner irritation into that small, repeated motion.

Mrs. Kosta brandished her iPhone. "Look at this. I took a picture of everything that day. In this picture, the meat comes to the fifth scale thingy on the lobster shell. My piece tonight stops at the fourth one. Those caterers are cheating me out of at least a quarter inch of meat."

Ivy didn't need to lean forward to see the photo. Mrs. Kosta zoomed in and enlarged the shot, then held it practically under Ivy's nose. Ben wondered if she'd gone around and snapped every plate at her table for comparison. And now, instead of holding court at the head family table while enjoying what looked like a damn tasty dinner, she was out here blowing off steam about the freakin' filet. Which Ben would happily scarf down in a second.

He and Ivy both stood by the rule that vendors don't eat until every guest is served. Since the first tray of appetizers had paraded past him close to two hours ago, his mouth had set itself to permanent drool. It all looked good and smelled even better. The guests had gorged themselves on mini lamb chops and gyros, shaved to order. Ben's tongue almost rolled out of his mouth when he caught a whiff of barbequed pork in a pastry shell. In his opinion, the raw seafood bar was kind of in bad taste at an event in the middle of an aquarium, but the guy shucking oysters could barely stay ahead of demand.

"Ooh." Ivy pursed her lips, then gave a minute head shake. "I can see why you're disappointed. Each and every detail of today should not just meet your expectations, but exceed them. Now, there's nothing we can do about the filets. At this point all your guests have been served. But I hear your point about the caterers not delivering all they promised. So here's how we can make it right." She cocked her head and looked up at the ceiling for a minute. Classic lost-in-thought stall tactic. "I will get the catering company to completely waive their entire cake cutting fee for tonight."

The older woman's face crinkled into happiness. "Well. That is very accommodating of you. Yes, if they agree to it, I will consider it a satisfactory compensation."

"I'll insist they do. There are no compromises when it comes to a client's happiness."

"You are a miracle worker." She gave Ivy's cheek a hard pinch. "Thank you for handling this. I simply don't have the energy to fight with the caterer. It is my

Diana's wedding. Tonight, we dance!" Her weirdly blue shoes shuffled away to an unheard rhythm.

"Congrats," said Ben. "Looks like you've racked up another happy customer."

"They happen to be our specialty."

Ben had no trouble believing it. Ivy smoothed those seriously ruffled feathers in record time. It was a treat to watch her in action, her deft and seemingly effortless steering across turbulent, emotion-drenched waters. Kind of like watching Kobe Bryant sink dunk shots or Tiger Woods swing a club.

"Tell me the truth. Did some chef go knife happy in the kitchen and scam her out of an extra ounce of beef?"

Ivy leaned closer to the thick aquarium glass, following the antics of the yellow and black fish as they schooled and unschooled in giant semi circles. "I'm sure the minute size difference was unintentional. Silver Platter Catering is one of the best in Chicagoland. Their food and their service are always impeccable."

It didn't gel. Her confidence in the caterer belied the assumption of guilt she'd fed Mrs. Kosta. Years of training and instinct kicked in, and Ben pressed to find the real story. He zoomed in, catching the play of light from the exhibit rippling down the side of her hair with a blue and white halo. "What makes you so sure you can get the caterer to waive that fee?"

"Nobody wants a disgruntled customer. It can be hard, if not impossible to recover from the damage done by a single nasty rant on a few different wedding blogs. Reputation is everything. Chef Paul and I have worked together on enough events. I'm quite certain the final invoice will not include a cake slicing fee."

The hint of a smile gave her away. Score. He might

be rusty, but he knew when there was more to a story. But he also knew Ivy would never make her clients look less than angelic on camera. Good or bad, her brides, grooms and their families always paid, and that kept Aisle Bound up and running. Discretion could be as important as organization in the wedding business, and she intended to always represent them in a good light. She'd spent a good ten minutes explaining this principle to Ruth before greenlighting *Planning for Love*. Ivy's impassioned speech so surprised the hardened saleswoman that she'd repeated it almost verbatim at the last staff meeting. Everyone else's jaws had hit the floor, but Ben hadn't been surprised. Ivy truly cared, and it showed in everything she did. Damn it, why'd she have to care so much?

Ben stopped taping, and lowered the camera to the floor. Even slid on the lens cap to give her an additional feeling of security. "Okay, we're off the record. What's the real story?"

Still, she peered around the curved glass walls of colorful parrot fish as if checking for spies. Rose up on tiptoe to whisper in his ear. "Silver Platter doesn't charge for cutting the cake. Different venues, different vendors do much of the time, so it seemed a safe thing to promise her. It calmed her down, and kept her from insulting the caterer who's worked like a dog tonight."

"No hurt feelings, nobody loses."

"I prefer to say that everybody wins. My glass is always half full."

Ben tried not to breathe too deeply. The slight swing of her hair sent a hit of grapefruit topped by a layer of tropical flowers right to his nose. From his nose it ran straight to his dick. Why did a simple whiff of perfume turn back the clock until he was once again the thirteen-year-old idiot who sported wood every time he smelled Mary Sunderbrook's grape lip gloss?

But he'd learned his lesson over the past twenty years. Mary got him sent to detention for doing her homework in the hope of earning a taste of those slick grape-flavored lips. And the twenty-four hours he'd overindulged in Ivy left him with a serious case of emotional indigestion. No matter how good a woman smelled, the fetid stench of disaster could be discerned with a trained noise.

"Half full or half empty, you can still get dysentery if the water in the glass is tainted."

Ivy wrinkled her nose. "My, aren't you a puddle of joy?"

"Can't help it. I've seen dozens of women like her in the past year. How can she muster the energy to be so unhappy over something so small? Shouldn't she be dabbing away tears and soaking up every moment of this once-in-a-lifetime event? The day she's dreamt of since the doctor first laid the pink-wrapped screaming bundle in her arms? She's missing it obsessing over meat. There's enough food here to feed the whole crowd for three days, and she wants an extra bite of steak? Crazy."

Maybe working on a show as negative as *WWS* had pushed him too far. Not a believer in romance to begin with, Ben's experiences taping the worst in people on their supposed happiest of days made it impossible for him not to focus on the bad behavior. Not that he'd had a choice. It took him months to scrape together that job, and beggars couldn't be choosy.

"Look at you, cheering for the side of sentiment."

She put a hand on his chest, the heat searing through his thin tuxedo shirt. "There is a heart throbbing under there after all."

Clearly Ivy misunderstood his position. Instead of rooting for love, he was just rooting against stupidity. Ben stepped back, away from her touch. Away from the memory it yanked to the forefront of his mind. The curse of having a visually oriented career meant he often saw things as still images. Her gentle touch triggered a snapshot of Ivy astride him, both hands on his chest for balance. Beautiful. Sexy. And everything he needed to avoid.

Ben reshouldered his camera. He led them back toward Diana and Niko's sweetheart table, sticking to the edges of the tightly packed rows of tables. "I hope she missed something really big, like the cake cutting or a toast."

"Not much chance of that. I'm running this show, remember? Nothing goes down unless both you and I are there. We're a team."

Yeah, right. About as likely as his hotel room turning into a gingerbread castle, with marshmallow pillows and a Guinness-filled bathtub. "Is that so? A few hours ago, you looked ready to push me into the shark tank."

"I signed a contract. I intend to abide by it. Everyone at Aisle Bound will bend over backward to work with you and Ollie. RealTV won't be disappointed in their decision to hire us, I promise."

Interesting turn around. Fast, too. Too fast. "What's the catch?"

"No catch. I overreacted earlier. Daphne quite rightly pointed out this is a business arrangement. Whatever

happened personally between you and I should have
no bearing on how we conduct ourselves at events."

Ben halted at one of the twelve foot high ridged columns at the entryway to the Caribbean Reef exhibit.
Close enough to keep an eye on the major players, but
back far enough that he could finish this conversation
with Ivy, buffered by the din of hundreds of people
talking while eating their puny pieces of filet. God,
he'd do anything for just a bite of one of those runtish
pieces of meat. Afternoon weddings were the worst.
He'd grabbed a plastic-wrapped muffin on his way out
of the hotel about eight. Closing in on half past two
now, his stomach was sending out a constant stream of
distress signals. Like if it didn't get fed soon, it'd start
eating itself. The freaking Donner party was about to
be reenacted in his belly. Maybe needling Ivy would
distract him a little while longer.

"Ah. So it's the money. You don't want to miss the
big payout. What, are you worried I'm going to run
back to the network and tattle on you? Complain you
don't play nice?"

"No. Not at all." Ivy leaned against the column, eyes
glued to the smiling bride. "Well, maybe. A little."

"You think I'm that petty? Unprofessional? You
think I'll run to the guy behind the big desk like I
can't fight my own battles?" His gnawing hunger disappeared beneath a portion of righteous anger. After
they'd connected so fast and so well the first time
around, how could she treat him like just another bean
counter? Sure, it ended badly, and he'd take more than
a fair share of the blame for that. But he thought if nothing else, she respected him as much as he did her. As

people, and as two driven toilers in the same salt mine. "Christ, I'd never pull such an underhanded move."

"Of course not. I'd never accuse you of it."

"You just did, babe. Trying to back your way out of the truth doesn't change it."

"No. Ben, you misunderstand. Of course you'd never rat me out. My waffling isn't about you at all." Ivy pushed off the column and closed the short gap. Her proximity forced Ben to lower the camera. For all the times he'd stopped filming her today, he'd be lucky to get an hour of usable footage. Not a great way to start.

"I'm worried I won't be able to live up to the expectations of RealTV. The amount I know about filming a reality show could fit on the tip of a boutonnière pin. What if I'm not interesting enough? What if they change their minds and say I didn't live up to the terms of the contract?"

Oh. Deep-seated insecurity, not distrust. Made sense. He'd seen a lot of insecure women cross in front of his camera. None as pulled together as Ivy, though. Ben never would've guessed her self-confidence tank occasionally dipped toward empty. "Guess I jumped the gun this time. Sorry."

"Well, that makes us even. No harm, no foul."

Ben knew he could let the whole thing drop. Get back on the clock and start rolling tape again. Ignore the frantic thrumming of her pulse he watched flutter in her neck. The tremor in her voice and the fists crumpling handfuls of her swooshy skirt. He also knew walking away, trading off with Ollie for a bit and getting some air, would be the smart move. Number one rule? Never get involved with the people on the other side of the lens. Record the action; don't become part of it.

Damn it, how he could walk away when she still worried those perfect lips with her two front teeth? How could he look anywhere but at the lips he'd feasted on? Tonight they were a deep purple, like she'd slicked them with a well-aged Merlot. Did she do it just to torture him—and any other man with a pulse in the vicinity?

"Ivy, you shouldn't beat yourself up. There isn't an uninteresting bone in your body." Ben ran a quick, reassuring hand down her arm from shoulder to elbow. Immediately regretted it once he registered the silkiness of her skin. *Pull it together, Westcott*, he ordered. *She's as off limits, and as volatile, as a munitions factory.* "Worrying about it will only stiffen you up, make you come across as unnatural. Which then *would* be a problem."

"Interesting advice. Did you know that the more you tell someone not to think of a topic, the more they're unable to do anything but think about it? I'll probably morph into a female version of the Tin Man any second now."

"If I remember right, the Tin Man didn't have a heart. You couldn't pull that off on your worst day." He hefted the camera back into position and resumed filming. With any luck, it could act as an invisible forcefield between them. Kind of like in *Star Trek*. Talk about a great movie franchise. If he thought about sexy green female aliens, he might be able to resist the temptation to give Ivy a reassuring hug.

"Thank you. I think."

An odd, easy peace descended. Maybe they could work together, after all. As long as Ben remembered not to touch her. Or remember the way she'd looked in the shower, with soap suds sliding over the slope of her creamy breast. Or never, ever looked at her. Might make filming dicey, but at least he'd keep his sanity and his libido in check.

Ivy's stomach growled. With a rueful laugh, she pressed a hand against the pouf of her blue skirt. The one that made her look like a very cute extra in a Doris Day film. Ben had always been a sucker for those old comedies. They reduced this whole big, complicated world to a small place, with black and white issues. Doris Day was always goofy and pretty, and Cary Grant or Gordon MacRae could always solve her simple problem. Happiness attained in ninety minutes or less. Talk about the power of film. Whereas for the last handful of years, everything Ben filmed only served to complicate the world, or document the worst of the human condition.

"I'm starving, in case you couldn't tell," she said.

Grateful to have his train of thought interrupted, Ben patted his own belly. "I passed starving about an hour ago. Didn't have much breakfast, so I'm running on fumes."

"That's what I call a critical strategic error. Weddings aren't for the weak. At the beginning of each season I let a novice wedding consultant shadow me at a wedding. I like to choose a really huge, elaborate affair. Once they walk in my shoes for ten hours, it's easy to tell if they have the endurance needed for this profession. Want to know the three secrets to surviving a big wedding?"

"Uh, yeah. Our viewers will eat it up. Always good to get tips from a pro."

"First of all, you need two pairs of shoes. Cushy, comfortable sneakers to run around in during setup, and fancy flats once people show up. Anything with a heel more than half an inch is a rookie mistake. And let me tell you, that is a mistake no one repeats."

Ben looked down at his shiny dress loafers. Couldn't begin to imagine the torture women inflicted on themselves with pointy shoes balanced on a three-inch heel the width of a nail. "I'm kind of stuck with what I'm wearing. What else?"

"Sit whenever possible. Grab a pew for the ceremony, perch on anything with a seat during cocktails. The few minutes of relief will make all the difference."

"So why aren't we sitting right now?"

"No extra chairs here at the Aquarium. Everything is trucked in on an exact count. We're stuck on our feet until after dinner. Once they start dancing, I plan to make a mad dash to a bench in the Amazon Rising exhibit. I'll still be able to monitor the event, but I won't want to chop my feet off at the ankles."

"I filmed a few tables set up in that exhibit. Scary, wild stuff. Won't sitting in front of anacondas and piranhas freak you out?"

Letting her head thunk against the column, Ivy closed her eyes. "It will now. Thanks a lot."

"Hey, I go where you go, remember? The thought of a twenty-foot snake slithering around behind me, even behind glass, doesn't sit right."

"I thought all boys were fascinated by reptiles."

"Boys like to play with garter snakes and frogs. I'm a grown man." He paused, noticing her fast, triple blink. Did it mean Ivy shared his problem with flashbacks to their night together? If there was any justice in the world, she did. Why should he have to suffer alone? After all, if it wasn't for her stupid nosedive into meaningful commitment-land, they could be looking forward to scratching their respective sex itches tonight. Well, nothing cured blue-balled horniness like thinking about man-eating snakes.

"I've seen those things in the wild. Without any protective glass between us. Trust me when I say the experience would give most people a healthy dose of caution, if not downright fear."

Ivy's hands fisted around the bright blue of her skirt, making a rasping noise. "You saw an anaconda? Up close and in person?"

"Yep. Waaay too close for my taste. I'm in no hurry to get a second look." Ever. When he'd almost stepped on what he thought to be a tree branch, his guide Nestor grabbed him by the collar and dragged him backward off his feet. Next thing he knew, the massive, mottled branch began to move sinuously, with a speed that scared the spit out of Ben. As wide as a man, it looked big enough to swallow him in one gulp. Along with Nestor and the other three people in his production crew. It took weeks before the nightmares about the giant snake subsided. Damned if he'd let a wedding, of all things, dredge them up again.

"God, Ben. It sounds terrifying. What on earth were you doing traipsing through an anaconda's habitat?"

Another memory he didn't want to relive. "Taking an after-dinner stroll."

She shook her head, shimmying her sleek bob against her jaw. "Nobody in their right mind strolls within five miles of an anaconda. You probably weren't supposed to be there. Admit it, you were lost, weren't you? Men hate to admit when they're lost."

Lost? Sure. Because when blindly running for their

lives through the jungle from a crazed gang of drug runners, it can be hard to follow a path. "It's not as if the damn thing had *No Trespassing* signs posted around its feeding ground. Now can we please move on?"

"See what happens when you don't eat? You get testy. Next time we do a midday wedding, please be sure to have a big breakfast. Remind Ollie, too. That's another one of my survival secrets."

He hated that she was right. Hated that he knew better. Hated that a little thing like imminent starvation coupled with near constant arousal in Ivy's presence took him off his game. Ben checked the shot again. Not because Ivy had moved even an inch, but because it gave him a reason to hide behind the camera. And a way to legitimately stare at her, drinking in her face. The way the dim blue lighting cast a waterlike halo behind her head and deepened her changeable eyes to a mermaid green. Made a man think about finding the nearest pool and diving in. Tangling her long legs with his, slip-sliding together while he kissed droplets off her neck. Damn, but she distracted him easily. Better get this over with and get Ollie to cover for him. Fast.

"What's your final secret to surviving a wedding?" Ben asked.

"Hydration. Super easy to get caught up and not drink anything from the minute you greet the bride until the reception's halfway over. Always carry a bottle of water, and grab it on the fly whenever possible." Ivy shook an emphatic finger. "Dehydration saps your stamina."

"Words to live by."

"My go-to is tonic water. The bubbles cut your thirst quickly. Tasty, too."

A bitter shudder roiled across his taste buds. "Sure. Once you top it off with a hefty splash of gin. Big wedge of lime. Stick a beach chair under my ass and color me happy."

"Nope, no drinking on the job." Ivy pointed across the room at the bar. "Go on, give the straight stuff a try tonight. Satisfaction guaranteed."

"Really? What sort of satisfaction will you deliver if I don't like it?" Damn it. From the moment Ben had taken this gig, he swore up and down not to flirt with Ivy. Not to let her get under his skin with her star-bright smile and whip-smart wit. Now here he was, day one, tossing a sexually loaded grenade into the conversation. Into the relationship minefield that was Ivy Rhodes. Idiot!

Two front teeth that would make an orthodontist weep with joy toyed with her bottom lip. Second time he'd seen her do it tonight, and again, he couldn't tear his eyes away from the sight. It should be his teeth nipping at her. God, why did someone so sexually perfect for him come with an entire wagon train of relationship expectations? Might as well give a jewel thief the keys to the Tower of London, drive him to it, park, and then wait to see what happened.

"Whatever it takes to put a smile on your face," she promised with a saucy wink.

"I can think of seven things without even trying. You've even got clothes on in five of them."

A pilot light of answering heat flared brightly behind her mermaid eyes, then shuttered so fast he almost thought he'd imagined it. So much for good intentions. The filter between his dick and his mouth kept short circuiting around Ivy.

"Ben, you seem to be good at your job, and you're excellent with the clients. But you need to drop the suggestive comments. Immediately."

She wasn't saying anything he didn't already know. "I'm sorry. Truly. No rebuttal."

"Good."

Might as well go for broke. How much more pissed could she get? "Look, there's all this weird tension between us. I know you can feel it, too."

A curt nod, coupled with a tiny jerk of one shoulder. Well, at least she hadn't bitten his head off. Or walked away. "Obviously the middle of a wedding isn't the time or place to delve into it," he said.

"You think?"

"Why don't you come out for a drink with me when we finish? If we don't smooth things out, this will be a painful two-month stint for both of us. I bet if we talk through it, we can reach a level playing field." Cliché alert. Like he'd tried to distill an entire season of *Oprah* into three sentences. This is why guys didn't talk about their feelings. Because they sucked at it.

"Welllll…" Ivy drew the word out, probably making a pros and cons list in her head. She seemed the type who'd make a list before deciding which parking spot to take. A little push should do it.

"I'm staying at the Cavendish again. Five-minute taxi ride, tops. We can have a drink in the bar."

The light in her eyes flared again, then disappeared behind a cold, heavy-lidded squint. "No. No way, no how. I know where drinks at the Cavendish can lead. I'm not sleeping with you again. It's more likely that the Cubs will win the World Series. Or that Lake Michigan will freeze solid in the middle of July. You're a player, Ben Westcott, and I refuse to be played."

Ivy lifted her chin and flounced away, skirts frothing around her. Every twitch of her hips spoke of her righteous wrath. If she was a cat, her fur would be standing on end. In other words, that couldn't have gone worse if Ben had whipped out a condom and suggested a quickie on the dance floor before the garter toss. On the other hand a real player wouldn't have screwed things up quite so royally. Small comfort. And he bet his chances of getting dinner anytime soon evaporated the moment she walked off. So much for episode one of *Planning for Love*.

CHAPTER NINE

Marriage is a great institution, but I'm not ready
for an institution.

—Mae West

POWERING THROUGH A full circuit of weight machines
didn't put a dent in Ben's frustration. Half an hour in
the pool shriveled everything *except* his still white hot
lust. Maybe he could sweat out his problems on the
treadmill. He hated the machine—always made him
feel like a hamster—but desperate times called for desperate measures. Some might say living in a hotel had
its drawbacks (although he couldn't think of any—Ben
saw no downside in room service, maid service and
travel-sized free shampoo) but no one could dispute
the huge plus of access to the extensive gym facilities
at the Cavendish with no monthly fee.

He hopped on next to a guy with his face buried in
a towel. Fine by him. Ben couldn't stand gym chatters.
Idiots who spent more time posing with their mouths
flapping than pumping iron. On the other hand, he liked
the energy of having people around him. To push yourself to the limit, it helped to be able to nod at someone
in a similar amount of pain and exhaustion.

Focused on working the whole day with Ivy out of
his system, Ben blew right past jog and run to a full

out sprint in minute one. The machine shook as his shoes thudded in a frenzied pace. Arms pumping, sweat dripped down his forehead at minute three. Five minutes in, he wheezed like an asthmatic. Veins he didn't know existed threatened to throb right out of his thighs.

"You alright, mate?"

Grateful for an excuse to quit the self torture, Ben slammed his palm against the red stop button. "Not really." He suspended himself by his arms while the treadmill wound down, on the very strong chance his leg muscles were now the consistency of overcooked angel hair pasta.

"It's Ben, isn't it?"

"That's right." Unable to see past the river of sweat stinging tears from his eyes, Ben registered the British accent and took a guess. "You're the hotel manager? Gib?"

"That I am. As manager, I have to inform you that our guests prefer not to have their stays interrupted by the wail of ambulance sirens. You, sir, appear to be moments away from a heart attack. Bad for all our guests, bad PR for the hotel and very bad for you. Why don't you step off the treadmill and let me get you some water?"

"Great idea." As long as his ankle bones didn't disintegrate as soon as he put pressure back on them. Keeping a death grip on the machine, he gingerly lowered himself to a sitting position. At least now if he fell, he wouldn't have far to go. Sitting helped. The weird black dots in front of his eyes disappeared. Encouraged, he rested his forehead against his knees. It only slightly diminished the possibility of throwing up and/ or passing out.

"You're not a runner, are you?"

Ben heard the rubbery suction of a refrigerator door opening. Wondered if he'd look like a total wuss if he asked Gib for a straw to use in his much anticipated water. No way could he straighten up enough to take a slug from the bottle. "Not even a little. I swim, I hike, and when I get the chance, I bike. No running, though. I hate it. I hate the idea of it. Hate the way it turns my knees to custard and how it makes all the oxygen in the room disappear."

"Then why, if you don't mind me asking a personal question, were you just running as if pursued by an angry mob out for blood?"

"Nice imagery."

"Thank you." Gib handed over an icy bottle. "I wanted to spin something about an enraged, shotgun-wielding father and a recently defiled virgin, but I didn't want to cast any aspersions."

"Well, you British are famous for your restraint." Summoning his last shard of manly dignity, Ben forced himself to sit up. He propped an elbow on the cross brace and took his first glug of water. Decided a few, life-affirming sips later that he might actually be able to pull it together and not pass out. "I lift weights, but my go-to exercise is tai chi."

"The ancient Asian thing? Isn't it a hybrid of stretching and martial arts?"

"Exactly. Fits well into my traveling lifestyle. You actually get to stand in one spot for most of it. Pretty much the antithesis of running."

"So why put yourself through an unsupervised cardiac stress test here on my watch?"

"I guess I thought I could outrun my problem. Try,

anyway. My brain is kind of stuck in a groove right now, like a record player needle."

"Ah, you're dating yourself."

"Hey, vinyl is classic. We wouldn't have rock and roll without it. And what good would life be without Elvis Presley?"

"I'm more of a Kinks fan, myself."

"I've got a collection of about a hundred records stored in my sister's hall closet. She gripes every time she moves about hauling around my obsolete shit, but I can't let go." Great. Now, on top of feeling like dog puke, he'd remembered being about three months overdue on his monthly call to Belinda. She'd spend half the call guilting him into feeling lower than dirt, and the other half bitching about their perennially absentee parents. Putting a reminder on his calendar for the call usually coincided with a few fingers of scotch. Recovery from the call itself required an entire bottle.

"Tai chi is a great stress reliever, but you should try to add in a cardiovascular routine. Slowly," Gib hastened to add, "and try not to cram a lifetime's worth of running into five minutes. Next time I might not be here to save you."

"Duly noted. Although it'd be easier to avoid my problem entirely by avoiding women for the rest of my life."

"You've got woman trouble? No wonder you look so miserable. I've got just the thing to set you to rights."

"I doubt it." Even in his blue Under Armour shirt and matching workout shorts, Gib looked very capable. After all, you didn't get to manage a world famous hotel like the Cavendish without some pretty powerful brains under the jarring note of his ratty sweat band.

Still, Ben doubted the man could make a few phone calls and make Ivy understand the situation. Or give him his old life back—which would then build the foundation for his currently non-existent future. Pity party, table for one.

Gib squatted in front of him and rubbed his hands together. "Tonight is poker night."

"On a Sunday? Interesting break with tradition."

"Hey, it's the wedding business equivalent of Friday night. We work all weekend, so Sunday night is our best chance to let loose. Thought we'd have to cancel tonight. One of our regular chaps is down with food poisoning. You'd be doing us a favor if you took his place. I can promise you an obscenely immense spread of chips and pizza."

It sounded too good to be true. Then Ben remembered he was in the city where Al Capone gunned down a racketeer, where gambling raids occurred with regularity throughout the last century. A city where dirty money flowed like water. Better to ask a stupid question now, defenseless and sprawled on the floor. Gib certainly couldn't think any less of him. "Are you guys high rollers? Is there a low-down hustler hiding behind that stiff English upper lip?"

"Hardly. No trust fund idlers in our group. We all work in the wedding industry. A baker, a DJ, a photographer. For the most part self-employed, which translates to low antes. Merely a chance to shoot the breeze. And no shop talk. I promise you, nothing cancels out the annoyance of women like the clink of poker chips."

True. In fact, the night sounded like just what the doctor ordered. "Throw in a beer and I'm all yours."

"There's the rub. Carl—the unlucky recipient of food

poisoning? It was his turn to supply the beer. If you take his seat at the table, you also assume his responsibilities."

Hauling himself to his feet, Ben let out a long, low whistle. "I am being hustled."

"Maybe just a bit." Gib laughed, and Ben couldn't help but join in.

"Fair enough." It was worth the price of a couple of six packs *not* to think about Ivy for the rest of the night.

"COME IN. I'VE been dying to meet you. I'm Milo, the office manager at Aisle Bound. You have simply got to be Bennett." Before Ben could react, a skinny blond man enfolded him in a hug.

"Uh, hi." Ben pushed his way out of the hug immediately. He wasn't a hugger. Especially not with guys. Especially not with guys he'd never met before. With an elaborate sweep of his arm, Milo ushered him into Gib's townhouse. A quick scan as he crossed the threshold revealed green velvet drapes, green-and-white-striped wallpaper, and a couch big enough to hold the starting line of the Chicago Bears. Comfortable and flamboyant at the same time. Maybe he'd read Gibson wrong, and he played for the other team. Pretty obvious that the hugger did. Not that it mattered at all to Ben. Not when his eyes were magnetically drawn straight to a five-foot-long sub sandwich bisecting the dining room table like a human sacrifice.

"Well? How did your first official event with Ivy go? Did you capture her brilliance and poise?"

"I didn't expect to see anyone from Aisle Bound here." Not a great way to kick off his not-thinking-about-Ivy night.

"Why not? Did Gib forget to tell you he's got a room-mate? Moi?" Milo twirled like a ballerina.

That certainly explained the velvet draperies. And why Milo wore a matching green velvet smoking jacket that would do Hugh Hefner proud. "He didn't mention it."

"How naughty of him."

Huh uh. *Naughty* didn't come close to the word Ben wanted to use. "The wedding went great."

"Details, if you please."

Ben shrugged. "No bloodshed and it ended on time. That makes it a winner in my book."

"Milo, ease off a bit. Remember the rule: no shop talk on poker night." Gib handed Ben a tumbler. "Jack and Coke to tide you over until the beer chills a bit?"

"Perfect."

Three loud, laughing men spilled through the front door. While two were in jeans, the shortest man with a crooked nose that spoke of a long history of breaks sported a full tuxedo.

"Miguel, how many times have I told you: poker is semi-formal. We only go black tie for craps and rou-lette." Milo pulled off the bow tie with a quick yank.

"Very funny. I came straight from a gig. Trust me, I'm itching to get out of this penguin suit." He barreled up the stairs with a quick wave in the general direction of Gib and Ben.

"Miguel's a reformed boxer turned DJ," Milo explained. "After spending so many years wearing only shorts to work, he still chafes about dressing up for events. I've tried to teach him to appreciate the finer points of style, but it doesn't seem to sink in at all."

"Give it up already, it's a losing battle. But you've

got enough panache for all of us." A lanky man in an Aquaman tee shook Ben's hand. "Hi, I'm Lewis. Gib texted us that you'd take Carl's place. As long as you brought the beer, you're welcome here."

"It's in the fridge." Ben returned the shake. Lewis had his priorities straight. And he held a sack in one arm brimming with bags of potato chips. The night was looking up.

"Good man."

The last of the trio deposited a large white bakery box on the dining room table. "Sam Lyons," he said as he turned, hand outstretched for introductions. When his eyes met Ben's, he paused. His other hand rose to brush a wave of dark hair off his forehead in surprise.

"You're Bennett Westcott."

Here we go, Ben thought. His anonymity in Chicago had lasted all of nine hours. "Yup," he said curtly, hoping his unfriendly tone would head off the inevitable questions.

"Do you know who this is?" Sam asked his friends.

"I'm gonna go with…Bennett Westcott?" said Lewis. He dropped onto the sofa and propped one foot on the coffee table, despite Milo's violent hiss of disapproval.

"Are you famous, Ben? Do we have a celebrity in our midst?" Gib asked.

No reason not to answer. If Sam recognized him, it was pointless to try and hide the facts. "More like infamous." Ben took a long, bracing gulp, taking comfort in the distraction of the searing hit at the back of his throat. Too edgy to sit down, he paced the length of the room.

"Wow, I'm sorry. You took me by surprise. Should've kept my big mouth shut." Sam clapped him on the shoulder. "I'm guessing you don't want to relive the whole thing, do you?"

"Nah. Why should I mind going over the excruciating details of the biggest mistake of my life?" Nothing like getting an emotional root canal to start off a night of cards.

"This is Bennett Westcott," Sam repeated. "Doesn't the name ring a bell?"

"Not really sure." Gib cocked his head. "Why don't you say it a few dozen more times, see if anything shakes loose?"

"I just can't believe you don't recognize him. The man's face was plastered all over the news for like a week straight. How do you not recognize him?"

Miguel loped down the stairs. "Recognize who?" Without using even one hand for leverage, he leapt over the back of the sofa and landed next to Lewis. Impressive move.

"Bennett Westcott." Sam slowly over-enunciated the name.

"For Christ's sake, if you promise to stop saying my name I'll tell the story." Ben drained his glass. "I used to be a documentary journalist. My team traveled all over the world doing exposes. The last one I worked on, we shadowed a presidential candidate. Unprecedented access. Hell of a long shot, because we didn't know if our guy would survive the first primary, let alone go all the way."

"Oh. My. God. You're the guy who dropped the camera!" squealed Milo. He hopped from one foot to the other as if crossing a bed of hot coals. "During the assassination attempt on President Calhoun in Alaska. You were on the dais, right behind him. Twenty other news cameras caught the whole thing on tape. The first shot rang out, you panned the camera toward the crowd. Then you dropped it and ducked for cover. Missed Calhoun shaking off the Secret Service, grabbing his rifle and tagging the shooter himself. Most people say that day won him the election. It gave him a new slogan for the last six weeks of the race. *A man strong enough to protect himself can protect the whole country.*"

Ben looked at the guys. All wore some variation of slack-jawed astonishment on their faces. Nothing he hadn't seen a hundred or so times in the past two years. "Yes. That is the official story. I'm the lily-livered coward. The scaredy cat who ignored the biggest story of the decade unfolding in front of him and curled up in a ball on the floor. Film at eleven." He bent into a mocking half-bow.

"What do you mean, the *official* story?" Gib asked. Without any prompting, he'd prepared a fresh drink and handed it to Ben.

"Doesn't matter. Calhoun's a hero, and I'm a laughingstock. Career down the drain."

Sam shook his head and crossed his arms, his eyebrows drawing together into a thick, dark row. "Suddenly, I'm not buying that line. Look, I feel awful about bringing this up."

"You should. Usually it takes a trailer hitch and a two-ton tractor to pull so much as the weather forecast out of Mr. Taciturn over there. You picked a hell of a moment to get chatty," Miguel remonstrated. He pulled out a bag of chips and smacked it open with a loud pop.

"Hey, it's not every day one of my personal heroes shows up for poker."

Ben sipped his drink, reminded himself it was num-

ber two. Time to pace. He had no intentions of revis-
iting the drunken island of forgetfulness he'd parked
himself on for a month after losing his job. No matter
how tempting. "I'm no hero. If polled, I'm pretty sure
a whopping, let's see...*all* of America would agree."

"Then they'd be wrong. I've seen every one of your
documentaries. Brilliant work. You deserved those five
awards. And you were robbed last year when you didn't
win for your piece on the families of drug gangsters
in Rio. Can't believe they gave it to a film on shark
preservation instead. Come on, they're sharks. Natural
predator, right? Where's the story there?"

Lewis rolled his eyes. Speaking around a mouthful
of chips, he said, "You'll have to excuse Sam's babbling.
He's a bit of a news junkie. Since he spends most of his
waking hours playing with chocolate and frosting, he's
a little bit scared of turning into a girl. He overdoses
on news to compensate. Even made his parents install
TiVo in the bakery."

"There's no shame in staying abreast of the news of
the day," said Gib. "You can't rib Sam for being well
informed."

Miguel scowled and opened another bag of chips.
"Well, make him stop fawning over our new poker
player like he's a friggin' movie star. Ask for Ben's
autograph and be done with it already, man. I'm ready
to play."

"Go divvy up the chips if you're so ready." Sam
pointed to the dining table without taking his eyes off
Ben. "Shuffle the cards. Grab plates for the sandwich.
But I'm not laying out an ante until we hear the rest
of Ben's story. If there's more to it, you've got to spill.
Don't leave us hanging."

Funny. Ben had spent the past eighteen months either being ignored, or treated like dirt once people recognized him. Now he'd found the one person in the country who respected his body of work. At least, the work he used to do. Doubtful Sam was a hardcore fan of *Wild Wedding Smackdown.* It felt kind of good. Reminded him who he used to be. The man he was proud to be. Too bad that sense of pride came as a package deal along with a double scoop of bitterness and pain at losing it all. Why not tell them what really went down? At this point, his day couldn't get any worse. Ben took one final sip then set the glass on a bookcase and stepped away.

"Here's the deal. I didn't actually drop the camera and hide from the bullets. It was the kind of once in a lifetime moment you yearn for. Never, in a million years would I have dropped the camera." Sucking in a breath and squinching his eyes shut, Ben paused before letting everything go. The shrink he'd blown off after two visits would be so proud.

"I passed out. Right before the first bullet. I was already halfway to the floor when all hell broke loose. The timing is so split second that it's hard to tell unless you know what you're looking for on the video. One of the Secret Service kicked my legs out of the way when he ran to protect Calhoun, which is why it looks like I'm curled in a ball."

Miguel jerked his chin. "Healthy guys like you don't just pass out."

"Not too healthy. You should've seen him on the treadmill at the gym this afternoon, sucking wind." Gib clutched at his chest and loudly gasped for air.

"That was after I'd swum laps for half an hour."

Irritation sharpened his tone. Ben had a feeling Gib wouldn't let him live the episode down for the rest of his stay in Chicago. "Regardless of my current fitness level, Miguel's right. A super-high fever made me pass out. Conveniently, none of the news organizations rolled tape of me being loaded onto a stretcher and taken away in an ambulance, still unconscious. They preferred to run with the sensational story of a hardened journalist dropping his camera."

Silently, Lewis offered his bag of chips. Ben interpreted the gesture as an attempt at commiseration. Grateful for an excuse to step away from the heavy weight of their stares, he took it to the kitchen and dumped the contents into a bowl. Only a handful of people had heard his version of the worst day of his life. It didn't exactly roll off his tongue. He needed a minute to brace himself for the next step, the inevitable, manhood-shriveling looks of pity.

Miguel and the others crowded into the kitchen almost immediately. Right. Now that they knew who he was, they probably didn't want him at their poker game. He'd been kidding himself. After all, every one of his buddies in New York and D.C. dropped him. Practically overnight they'd frozen him out, both as friends and professionally. He couldn't get another job for six months after being let go. Doors slammed in his face time and time again. Why would total strangers want the guy known around the world as "the Cowering Cameraman" sitting at their table? To his surprise, Miguel was the first to speak. He jammed beefy fists into the pockets of his cargo shorts.

"Finish the story."

"Yeah. We can't concentrate on the game if we're

worried you're gonna give all of us Ebola or some-thing," added Lewis with a wink.

Ben snorted out a half laugh. Teasing he could han-dle "You're not far off the mark. The week before, I took a couple days off and flew down to Brazil. My team helped expose a major player in a drug cartel. We wanted to film him being sentenced, to cap off the story. Felt good, watching his face as it sank in he'd spend the rest of his life in jail. The courtroom was filled with family members of his victims. Drug mules who died when balloons of heroin burst in their stom-ach. Innocent children caught in machine gun crossfire. Strung-out addicts who sacrificed their entire lives to feed their habit. Each family got to speak, to explain why this scum shouldn't see the light of day again his entire life."

"You were at the Perez trial?" Sam's hushed whis-per approached hero worship. "The man's a monster. I heard it was an American news team that finally man-aged to catch him in a web of lies."

"You heard wrong. We were with a multi-national team of drug enforcement agents from five different countries. They'd been trying to nail him for a couple of years. We just happened to be around when it all came together." An understatement of gigantic proportion, but they'd all signed about fifty different confidential-ity agreements. Chances were slim these Chicago wed-ding vendors would even know how to rat him out to the Bolivian government, but why risk it?

"Because I'd been to Brazil, the doctors had a list as long as my arm of funky tropical diseases my body could've been hosting. Ebola was about the only thing not on the table. For a while the contender was dengue fever. Nobody wanted to start a panic, so they locked down all information. Even my family didn't find out I'd been in the hospital for a week until after they released me. Turned out the culprit wasn't Brazil, but the senator's recent trip to Colorado. I was the proud owner of a case of Rocky Mountain Spotted Fever."

"Sounds itchy." Lewis wrinkled his nose.

"Don't remember much of it, to be honest. By the time I fully surfaced, it was too late for damage control. I'd been branded the Cowering Cameraman. Got fired before I even regained consciousness." That probably stung the most. Out of all the indignities, the name calling, the derision, he'd been astonished his producer hadn't fought for him. Had bowed to public opinion even though he knew damn well Ben lay in a hospital bed covered in icepacks to bring down the stubborn fever. Fucking gutless wonder.

Gib's jaw dropped to the floor, followed a second later by his butt dropping onto a white, wooden stool at the breakfast counter. "They sacked you? For being deathly ill?"

"More for looking like an idiot. It took me a month to recover, two months to stop being pissed at the world, and three more months to find anyone willing to hire me to hold a camera in any capacity." Ben held his hands out, palms up, at his waist. "So ends my sad saga."

Would they believe him? Or would they see it as a trumped up, stupid attempt at an excuse? Ben's parents and sister believed him. Hard to argue with the facts presented when Ben showed up on his sister's doorstep, so weak the doorman had to help him from the cab to the elevator. Or the hospital bills his parents helped pay because he'd been dropped from his insurance carrier. But when he'd tried to explain what really happened to a so-called friend at CNN, the guy laughed in his still hospital-pale face. Tried again two more times with worse results.

Didn't matter, in the end. Ben knew better than to expect people to stick by him. *Nobody looks out for you but you.* Might as well be his family's motto. Generations of divorces and betrayal seared that little saying into the Westcott family DNA. Why the hell had he even bothered trotting out the truth one last time? Ben figured he should leave now before they tossed him out. He turned sideways to slip between Miguel and Milo, but never made it to the kitchen door. Miguel straight armed him, fist out. It took Ben a second to adjust his perception and realize he was being offered the highest male accolade—the fist bump. Almost in slow motion, he bumped back.

"Dude, you got screwed. Proves you're not from here. It never would've happened in Chicago."

Milo nodded. "You'll show them. When *Planning for Love* rockets to the top of the ratings and you get to go on Letterman and talk about your miraculous comeback, vengeance will be yours."

Sam squished in between Milo and the refrigerator to clap his hand in a staccato salute on Ben's back. "You can't let the general ignorance of people get to you. You stood strong against adversity. Hell, maybe someday they'll shoot a documentary based on your life. Reveal the truth to the world. Wouldn't that be ironic?"

After rattling in the cupboard, Lewis slammed down a handful of shot glasses. "Bring it in, guys. We'll do a shot for Ben. For getting a new job, and giving all those douchebags the finger." Milo produced a bottle of Maker's Mark and poured a round.

"Really? Is that truly necessary? You know I prefer to show my enthusiasm by a firm *jolly well done*. British reserve isn't a cliché. It is an emotional chasm that cannot be overcome simply by living in America for five years." But while Gibson rambled, he picked up a glass.

Lewis handed the shots out, then raised his in the air. "To Ben, and his comeback from one hell of a shitstorm."

"To Ben." Everyone else clinked their glasses and threw back their shots.

Ben couldn't breathe. The small amount of air he managed to suck in made it abundantly clear that the wedding Miguel worked today lacked air conditioning of any sort. Lewis's chip breath blasted in a straight line past his ear right to his nose. Sam's weird adulation made his skin feel two sizes too tight. And when he woke up this morning, Ben certainly hadn't anticipated doing shots with a man so flamingly gay that self-combustion at any moment was a real possibility. In the spirit of public safety, Milo really ought to keep a fire extinguisher in a waist holster at all times.

The show of emotional support weighted him down almost as much as gravity. Over the past year and a half, people had shown Ben their backs and slammed the door in his face. He almost didn't know how to respond. Girls would cry and hug and swear eternal friendship. Talk the whole thing over twenty more times. Thank God none of them had ovaries. Knowing these men—strangers only half an hour ago—were all on his side? The equivalent of emotional jumper cables to his scarred psyche. There could be only one appropriate response. One way to break them out of this huddle before Ben gave in to the moist pressure behind his tightly clenched eyelids.

"Who's ready to lose some money? I'm dealing first, and nothing's wild. You've got to have the cards, or balls big enough to convince us otherwise. Ante up, gentlemen."

CHAPTER TEN

Life is what happens to us while we're busy making other plans.

—John Lennon

WHENEVER THE DISCUSSION turned to glass half full versus half empty, Ben always came down on the side of half empty. War, famine, cancer, terrorism, cheaters, liars, burnt coffee, burnt popcorn, jammed copiers, lookie-loo traffic jams, middle-of-the-night leg cramps...no matter how big or how small the issue, it was always easy to find a reason why life sucked. A rainbow in the sky translated to Ben as thousands of people who had just sat through an endless, rainy commute. Pregnancy spelled no sex, no sanity and no money for the next eighteen years. Four leaf clover in the lawn? Just a weed, and dandelions couldn't be far behind.

Despite his life-long cynicism, Ben couldn't complain too much about his new job. Juggling taping and his production duties over the other four teams out shooting meant crazy hours. But it was kind of a blast editing the rough cuts every day, honing each story down to its powerful core. Being based at Aisle Bound didn't exactly suck, either. Over the past two weeks, Ivy trumped up some ridiculous thing to celebrate on a daily basis. He'd never heard of Blueberry Cheese-cake Day, but it didn't stop him from scarfing down three slices from Sam's bakery. So far this office tradition had netted him half a box of saltwater taffy, a giant pickle the size of his forearm, and best of all, a sidewalk grilled burger to celebrate National Beef *and* National Barbeque Month.

Where was the woman with the daily picnic basket full of treats? Already hooked on Aisle Bound's endless Kona coffee and ever-present snacks, Ben's stomach growled. "Did the world start spinning backward? A thin sheet of frost settle over the gates of Hell?"

Julianna stepped out of the display window and spiked a brow at him. "I know I'm going to regret asking, but what are you talking about?"

The sleek brunette had proved a hard nut to crack. His usual surefire combo of lazy charm and calculated flirtation failed when it came to Ivy's assistant. She remained polite, verging on cool and distant, verging on impossible to read and impervious to every one of his conversational sorties. Ben didn't want to hit on her, for God's sake. He just didn't want to wonder every time they crossed paths if she planned to drive an ice pick between his shoulder blades. Julianna's loyalty to Ivy ran fathoms deep. Although she might not know the whole story of what transpired that fateful April weekend, she'd at least picked up on the layers of tension between him and her boss.

"Ms. Rhodes worships at the altar of punctuality. Practically breaks out in hives when anything veers her off schedule. So," Ben glanced down at the display on his laptop, "since she's half an hour late, I need to assume that we're either in a parallel universe, or she's been kidnapped by a white slavery ring and is even now in a cargo container on her way to Indochina."

"While, as owner of the company, Ivy is not required to punch a time clock, she mentioned the possibility of a later start this morning. I'm sure she'll be here in plenty of time for our first appointment of the day."

"Stayed up too late color coding her closet?"

"Ivy had a hot date last night!" Milo blurted the news in a rush, stumbling over himself as he leapt from behind his desk. Or maybe he wasn't yet used to the high heels on his tight leather boots. "A cutie patootie, according to the buzz. Tall, dark and rolling in cashola. The kind of man every mother dreams about her daughter landing. Which is why Samantha set up this blind date for Ivy. The guy's her lawyer. Well connected and well toned. The complete package."

Milo sounded ready to jump the guy if Ivy passed on him. Ben didn't like the idea of her going on a blind date. Was she that desperate to wash the taste of him out of her mouth? Then it occurred to him she might've been dating this whole time. It didn't sit well. The idea weighed heavily in his gut. Kind of like the time he ate three Philly cheese steaks on a dare.

"You've certainly got the goods on the mystery date. What else do you know?"

Toying with what he'd haughtily informed the office was a cravat (although to Ben it looked like a skinny scarf in a knot), Milo continued. "Andrew Wolkoff went to Northwestern, then somewhere big back East for law school. Toyed with some headhunters for a while, but ended up back here in his hometown. Doesn't practice splashy law. Contracts or titles or some such boring thing. But it must pay well, because the plan was to take Ivy out on his boat last night for a moonlight cruise."

"It sounds dreamy." Daphne appeared at the end of the hallway leading to her work area. One hand cradled her oversized mug painted with bright flowers. "A perfect first date. Romantic and intimate."

Yeah, Ben had a date last night, too. Except his was a couple of hours with Sam. They talked back to the idiots on CSPAN over takeout burgers. Nice to have someone to hang with who got as riled up about politics as he did. But the thought of Ivy being intimate with a perfect stranger clenched Ben's teeth together. "How intimate do you want her to get with someone she's never met?"

She uptilted her unglossed lips into a slow, knowing smile. "We researched him on the web, silly. Found quite a few pictures. He looks great in tennis whites, but my fave was a shot of him on his boat wearing only trunks. Andy's got great…potential."

No wonder she and Milo were collectively licking their chops. He sounded like a Jewish matchmaker's wet dream. A law degree, all the attendant cash that went with it, *and* looks good half naked? No matter. Ivy wouldn't be taken in by shallow, outward trappings. It took more than a nice set of pecs to entice her. Probably. Not that he cared.

"Hotness is no measure of character."

"You ought to know," Julianna shot back.

Ha! A tiny crack in the armor, but big enough to squeeze through a retort. "So, you think I'm hot? The truth finally comes out." Ben tipped an imaginary hat and swept into a bow. "Wait until Memorial Day passes and I break out *my* white shorts. You may be forced to physically restrain yourself to keep from throwing yourself at me."

"Oh, I'm tempted every day to throw something at you."

"Play nice, kiddos," Daphne cautioned. "We've got a holiday weekend to survive, which means four straight days of events starting in, oh, half an hour. If you get snarky now, there's no room to grow as we get more and more exhausted."

Milo eagerly glommed onto the change in topic. "You'll be running on fumes by Sunday night. I can't believe you have to do an event on Monday, too. What kind of person throws a picnic on a national holiday for a wedding?"

"The kind of person who pays us double for pulling it together on said holiday. This is a good thing, Milo, not a punishment." She filled her cup halfway, and filled it the rest of the way with milk. Four sugar cubes, a towering squirt of whipped cream, along with a sprinkle of cinnamon and two liberal shakes of cocoa powder later, she stepped back.

"Can you still taste the coffee underneath all that dessert you've loaded into it?" asked Ben. He didn't actually consider it coffee anymore—more like tiramisu in a cup. All it lacked was a shot of rum.

Daphne delicately licked off a curl of whipped cream. "My sweet tooth is legendary. Don't even try to keep up. I've been here since five checking in deliveries, and it's shaping up to be a sixteen-hour day. Something's got to fuel my engine."

Ben understood. The only thing that got him through college was a serious Mountain Dew habit. Now he couldn't look at the stuff without feeling nauseous.

"Now, are we ready to take bets? Usual stakes?"

Julianna and Milo each handed Daphne a five dollar bill. She produced one of her own from a pocket, and then stuck all three beneath a paperweight.

"Hey, I want in on the action." Ben whipped out five dollars and waved it high in the air. After winning at this week's poker game, he felt lucky. "What are we betting on?"

"Ivy. Every time she has a first date, she bursts in, full of enthusiasm, telling us how 'he might actually be the one'." Daphne crooked her fingers into quotation marks. "We're sick of it. The woman could go out with Daffy Duck and she'd still see him as a possible husband. She's hopeless."

Milo sat in the wing chair across from the sofa Ben had appropriated as his temporary office space. "It's our take on a swear jar. You know, a punishment to help her break a bad habit. And instant infatuation at Ivy's age is a seriously bad habit. We're trying to cure an incurable romantic, before she scares away every eligible man in the state. So we all bet. Any mention of The One, and she owes us lunch."

"How do you know she'll spill any details?"

Daphne almost did a spit take, but recovered in time to choke down her mouthful of coffee. "How do you know the sun will rise tomorrow? I love her like a sister, but when it comes to love, Ivy's an open book. Even when you're dying to slam the cover shut."

"She can't help it." Julianna leapt to Ivy's defense. No surprise there. "Her whole family perpetuates this ridiculous romance myth. Do you realize that everyone in her family has gotten engaged or married on Valentine's Day? For over a hundred years? And not a one of them has ever divorced. In the Rhodes family, perfect, true love isn't just attainable. It's expected. Can you imagine how hard it must be to live under that kind of pressure?"

Ben dug his fingers into the upholstery to prevent a full body shudder of distaste. No wonder she'd acted so weird at Buckingham Fountain. If he dated every woman in the country, he probably wouldn't find someone less suited to him than Ivy Rhodes. Her life might be all about love, but his single goal was to avoid that particular condition like the plague. Talk about a narrow escape.

"Bottom line is that Ivy has two focuses in life—her business and her search for the perfect mate. And she'll happily talk your ear off on either subject. No prompting needed." Milo leaned forward, dropping his voice to a gossipy whisper. "Don't get me wrong. I enjoy a good gabfest as much as any girl or gay, but Ivy doesn't have an off button on this topic."

Ha! Milo wasn't exactly the soul of discretion. When Ben filled in for a second week straight at the poker game, he'd gone on in excruciating detail about his ingrown toenail removal. Gib had offered him five dollars to stop talking, but Milo refused to wind down until they all knew exactly which of his shoes caused the problem, how much the procedure hurt, and how he still refused to give up the offending pair of Italian loafers.

"Alright, you've given him full disclosure," said Daphne. She nudged Milo with her hip. "Now add his money to the pot."

Milo reached for the bill now lying on the coffee table, but Ben snatched it up, lifting it out of reach.

"Huh uh. Ask anyone in Vegas. The stupidest thing

you can do is bet against the house." Smart Ivy, who caught the bagpiper trying to double dip with her client, wouldn't have any trouble seeing through a slick, self-important lawyer. Nope, no way would she fall for Attorney Andy. "I'm sure you all know the Shakespeare quote *The first thing we do, let's kill all the lawyers*. The man had an excellent point. So I'm putting my money on Ms. Rhodes. Hope you all enjoy buying us lunch." He opened his fist and let his five dollars float back down to the table.

"Really, Ben, you're new to our little group. Trust me when I say you'll regret this." Milo tried to hand him back the money. Julianna was quicker, though. She grabbed it and stuck it under the coffee pot.

"A fool and his money are soon parted. There's a quote for you," she said with a gleeful grin. Not Shakespeare, but not bad.

"Good morning, all. Ready for the official kickoff to the summer wedding season?" Ivy entered in a flurry of movement. A wide sash swung from the waist of her pink sundress, bobbing along in time to the sparkly pink drops hanging from her ears. From the pale bow around her ponytail to matching sandals, she looked as fresh and inviting as a scoop of strawberry ice cream. Tossing her sweater onto the coat rack, she dropped three bags at Milo's desk and handed Daphne a white bakery box.

"I looked at your schedule and figured you'd need a boost in a few hours, so I swung by Lyons Bakery. You've got a jelly donut for now, a triple chocolate éclair for lunch, and a piña colada cupcake for an afternoon pick me up. Just don't eat them all at once."

"This is why we're best friends." Daphne circled

Ivy's waist with one arm and gave a quick squeeze. "You look after me so well."

"Merely good business acumen. With six events in four days, we can't afford to have you at anything less than your best." Ivy hotfooted it down the hall, talking over her shoulder. "I have about twenty calls to make in the next hour, so try to hold down the fort. We'll bump the staff meeting to after lunch, if that's alright with everyone."

"Hold it." Ben stood, hefting the camera to his shoulder. The viewers would eat up this behind-the scenes type of action with a spoon. The more it degenerated into a personal soap pera, the better. "You're late, Ms. Rhodes. Want to explain this deviation from schedule?" Ivy stopped dead in her tracks. If Ben hadn't been watching so closely, he'd have missed the way she squared her shoulders before turning around. She marched back to the sitting area and faced him across the coffee table.

"I'm not late. Before leaving yesterday, I updated the schedule. Which is beside the point, as I do not report to you. Your job is to film what happens when I'm here. Period."

"Defensive, hmm? Got something to hide?" he goaded, hoping to flare her temper and push her into revealing some dirt. Plus, he enjoyed the way her eyes snapped and her cheeks pinked up when she got in a snit.

"My preference is not to air my dirty laundry to the nation in prime time."

You could frost a bottle of vodka with the chill in her voice. But in Ben's world, a signed contract meant nothing was sacred or off limits. Compelling reality television could only be produced by shining a bright light on every aspect of the subject. He could pick and choose later what to keep or toss. "Too late for that. Your colleagues here are more than happy to chat about what goes down when the office lights go off. I'm magnanimously giving you the opportunity to comment."

Working together like a single-celled organism, Daphne, Milo and Julianna all melted toward the hall. Ivy flicked her eyes in their direction, then back to Ben. Spinning on one foot, she flounced over to the coffeepot. With her back to everyone—and especially the camera—she poured herself a cup.

"Yes, I had a date last night. The world didn't stop turning. Nobody took out a radio ad, and we didn't phone in with hourly updates. A nice man took me for dinner. Sorry there's no banner headline. Single, available women date. No big deal."

Still moving as one, her friends oozed back up the hall. Milo spoke first. "But Andrew was hot, right? Even better in person?"

"Yes. He's a very attractive man. And although it may burst your bubble, he's decidedly not your type. Andy is a ladies' man, through and through." Ivy methodically stirred in a single packet of sugar, the spoon clinking against the china rim.

Daphne's eyebrows pulled into a tight line, and she lifted her shoulder in a questioning shrug. "Did you enjoy dinner?"

"Very much. He picked up takeout from Renaldi's. We started with a dozen oysters, then moved on to lemon chicken with angel hair pasta, asparagus, and finished with a chocolate ganache tart with Grand Marnier sauce. Exquisite."

"Oysters, huh? Gee, his plan's as transparent as the champagne I'm sure he served." Ben got up, circled over to Milo's desk to capture Ivy's profile. "Am I right?"

"Yes, we had champagne. A perfect complement to the oysters. So?" Still absorbed in her coffee, she dribbled in a scant amount of cream. And the rhythmic stirring began again.

Skirt-chasing jackass. The man didn't deserve a woman as complex and nuanced as Ivy. What the hell had her mother been thinking when she fixed them up? "Sooo, your pal Andy didn't want to line up a second date. He laid out this big seduction scene, with aphrodisiacs and holing you up in the middle of Lake Michigan all alone on his boat to, well, get laid."

"Wow. A leap that big should come with a parachute." Daphne pinched Ben on the tender inside of his elbow. Hard. "Samantha Rhodes would never set her daughter up with the sleazeball you just described. If you ask me, the date sounds utterly romantic. He obviously put quite a bit of thought into setting the right mood."

"Sure he did. Fastest way to seal the deal." That earned him another dirty look from both Daphne and Julianna. Milo, however, gave the impression of at least considering Ben's argument. He stepped away from the women, over to his usual perch on the arm of the sofa. After a short, loud sigh, Daphne harrumphed to Ivy's side and snatched the cup and saucer out of her hands.

"Ivy, for goodness sake, we don't have time to dawdle over details all morning. We all know the drill. Tell us how terrific Andy was. Tell us he's truly special and just might be the one. Most of all, tell us how wrong

Ben is, and we can get on with the day. Those sixteen buckets of tangerine roses can't arrange themselves."

"Fine." Ivy snapped out the word with the strength of a crocodile chomping into its prey. "I'm not blind. I see the money for your bet piled next to the teapot. I'd hoped to keep our personal lives off the show, but I realize that goal was improbable, at best."

"I would've used the word naïve, but improbable works, too," ventured Ben.

"The twilight cruise, the dinner, the iPod loaded with Sinatra—it all added up to an obvious routine." Ivy began to pace the length of the room. "Any woman would've been interchangeable. Andrew talked about himself on the way to the dock, all the way through dinner, and up until the very moment he dropped me at my door. At best, he asked me a handful of questions, all of which were softballs leading right back to information about him. Did I like sailing? Had I ever watched one of his tennis matches at the club?"

She stared at the floor, and her face appeared implacable. Her pacing quickened, however, sending her ponytail into a sideways bobbing frenzy. "He moved a few inches closer in between every course, and tried to make me lick chocolate sauce off his finger. Ugh. Smarmy and cheesy, simultaneously. Appeared mortally offended when I wouldn't follow him into the cabin filled with a black satin-sheeted bed. Given a choice, I'd rather knit a scarf out of dryer lint than go out with him again."

"He's scum," Milo said hotly.

"He doesn't deserve you," Julianna added.

Daphne took Ivy's clenched fists in her hands. "I'll break it to your mom that she missed by a wide margin.

You don't need to sit through her endless questions and rehashing. I'll call her right after lunch."

"Thanks." Ivy picked up her coffee and headed past a phalanx of hugs in the direction of her office.

Every rigid inch of her body indicated her reluctance to continue the conversation. Didn't anyone else see she was too wound up to work? The sympathetic approach only gave her license to hunker deeper into her misery. Good thing Ben had a different strategy. He turned off the camera and set it on Milo's desk. Creeping softly in well-worn deck shoes, he caught up and nipped into her office right behind her, shutting the door. Ivy whirled around, defenses up and a question in those big hazel eyes. Today sadness drowned out any green hints, replaced by almost solid pools of golden brown. Casually, he leaned back against the door and crossed his ankles.

"Want me to deck him?" Because by God, Ben's fingers itched to ball up and let loose into his face. He'd never felt the urge to defend someone's honor before, but now seemed as good a time as any to start.

Nothing happened for a very long minute. Maybe he'd misjudged her capacity for humor in this situation. Their first few days of shooting had been strained, but things evened out soon. They'd fallen into a groove. And now he'd very possibly wrecked it with one careless comment. Certainly wouldn't be the first time.

"Do you mean it?"

He shrugged, shoved his hands deep into the cargo pockets of his shorts. "Sure. You say the word."

Ivy giggled. The giggles quickly turned to full out guffaws. She doubled over and slid to the floor, back pressed against a tall file cabinet. Holding her stomach, laughter rolled out in waves.

"Thank you. Sincerely. Don't worry, I won't hold you to it. As a lawyer, he'd probably sue you before you finished cocking your arm back to clock him. But I'm really, really glad you offered."

Without lifting a finger, he'd restored the equanimity of the entire office. Ben called that a good day's work. He slid right back out the door before he said anything else that could screw it up.

FROM THE FAR corner, Ben watched Ivy light up the massive white tent like a firefly. She sparkled, completely in her element. Running hot on adrenaline, her marathon of six events in four days certainly didn't show. Speedy and silent as a jaguar on the hunt, she buzzed around smoothing every wrinkle in the event. Sullen, overtired children were soothed, bows straightened, glasses refilled and the sound system volume adjusted. A single lifted eyebrow brought the catering staff running. And the guests never noticed anything besides what a phenomenal time they were having. Keeping his camera trained on her all weekend was—on paper—the easiest gig ever.

Especially in comparison to the endless months he'd spent taping *Wild Wedding Smackdown*, Ivy's events were a cornucopia of joy. She got people to talk about their happiness, from grandmothers to best friends to the bride and groom. Under her gentle prompting, they gushed about their delight in the day and the couple, elation about the future and the quiet thrill of their own stories. It couldn't be better for the show if he'd scripted it himself. But he'd seen enough to know Ivy didn't ask people to share their hearts for the camera. She did it to remind every single person celebrating of their own connection to the special day. To put an extra layer of emotional glue around the often disparate groups at a wedding.

The reality of focusing all day, every day, on her shining eyes and tight little body had become a living purgatory. Beautiful, warm, able to juggle a shocking number of details seemingly without effort, she flat out entranced him. Which flat out sucked, since Ivy believed in forever and Ben believed in a good three-day weekend. They were oil and water. Fire and ice. As good an idea as putting together the Pope and a hooker with Tourettes.

"Hey." Ollie slid into position next to him. "I didn't think they'd be able to make a Memorial Day picnic fancy enough for a wedding. I mean, what's exciting about potato salad and ribs, right? But then one of the caterers passed me these caviar-topped deviled eggs. Wow."

Ben nodded. Even the vendors tended to eat well at upscale affairs. Especially since all the caterers adored Ivy and saved her staff the good stuff, rather than the box lunches he'd suffered through at some events. Since walking in the door of Aisle Bound he'd gained three pounds. The flat Illinois prairie didn't present any options for hiking, so Gib now met him every other morning to run along the lakeshore. The sweating and gasping for air was more tolerable when he could watch hot women in spandex pounding the pavement in front of him.

"Did you try the wedding cake yet? The best strawberry shortcake I've had in years."

"Ivy turns out pretty swanky weddings. The people are nice and the food's great." Ollie pumped his hand twice, hard. "I've gotta say thank you for rescuing me from *Wild Wedding Smackdown*. This is a much better job."

Ben clapped him on the back, oddly touched. "We're a good team." The kid more than pulled his weight. His youthful exuberance and eagerness to learn made him easy to work with. "After I'd already spent all that time breaking you in, no way could I let them partner me with someone new."

"I got some good footage today. The grandmother of the bride did the chicken dance with the five-year-old ring bearer."

"That'll play well in promos." Good to know the kid was learning to think beyond the moment to the finished product. "Nice catch."

"Oh, and while you were finishing dinner, I caught the best man making a move on Ivy. I made sure to stay tight and get good audio, in case they end up on a date this week."

"What?" Ben grabbed Ollie's camera. Would Ms. Rhodes really sully her untarnished ethics and hook up with a wedding guest? Nah. Couldn't be. "Show me."

"No can do. I switched data cards."

Swinging around, Ben scanned for the bright red bow topping Ivy's ponytail. Sure enough, it bobbed next to the best man. No neck and huge shoulders proclaimed Jerry to be an ex-football player. He'd swaggered around the gardens before the ceremony as if he owned the place, or at least every woman in it. Coat and vest long discarded, he'd wrapped his red, white and blue-striped bow tie around his bicep. Ben could spot his type a mile away. Relied on muscles instead of brains. He knew without a doubt Jerry to be the one responsible for the lineup of shot glasses in the groom's changing room. And the bra Ivy spotted about an hour ago flying from the top of the flag pole.

"Ollie, it's almost time to wrap up this shindig. I'll start to pack up the equipment. Why don't you check with Julianna and get in position at the end of the driveway? I saw the bridesmaids tying about five hundred cans to the back of the getaway car."

"You're right. The groom's upstairs getting their suitcases right now." Ollie took back his camera, then paused. "Are you getting me out of the way so you can score another piece of shortcake?"

Ben tried to manufacture an easy grin. It felt more like cracking through rigor mortis. "You see right through me. Go ahead and call it a day once you wrap the big exit."

"Thanks, boss."

Hefting his camera off the ground to his shoulder, Ben wove through the rows of white picnic tables. The merest pressure of his finger zoomed in on Ivy. Her wide smile radiated the sheer joy of loving her job. Ben knew that feeling. Had even started to recapture a little of it for himself over the past few weeks. Then he noticed Jerry the Jock holding Ivy's hand. Twenty steps, two clusters of overtired children on the ground and five tables closer, he refocused to find that massive paw still engulfed her from fingertip to wrist. Ben forced himself to a halt right beside them. He remembered the tongue lashing Ivy gave him when he'd inserted himself into the bagpiper situation at their first wedding together. If he tried to break up this conversation, she'd kick his ass.

"Did you know all the bridesmaids are engaged?

Every single one." Jerry shook his head with a hangdog expression. A half-empty mug of beer dangled from his other hand.

"Isn't it wonderful? All six of them are going to be in each other's weddings. They're even going to share the same veil. A big circle of love," Ivy gushed.

"At first me and the guys felt gypped. I mean, what's the point of wearing a stupid bow tie if you don't bag a bridesmaid? But then I spotted you. You're way prettier than any of those skanks."

Ivy bit her lip. An eyebrow started to rise, but she tamped it in place and worked up a half smile instead. "Thank you."

"You know how you won't give me your phone number?"

Her smile tightened at the edges. Kind of like an over-pumped balloon about to pop. "Jerry, I told you it's a simple matter of policy. I don't date anyone involved in one of my weddings. Please don't take it personally."

"Doesn't matter." He swatted away her response with his entire arm, almost hitting both of them in the face and dropping his mug onto the grass. "I asked Steve why he'd been holding out about the hot wedding planner. Said he'd make it up to me by giving me your number off his and Patty's contract." Tarzan-like, he thumped his chest. "See, I always win. 'Cause of me we won the title against Notre Dame. Best damn day of my life. Now I'm gonna win by getting a date with you."

"I'm flattered, but I simply can't go out with you. Now why don't you head to the entrance? Steve and Cheryl will be leaving for their honeymoon any minute."

"Rather stay here and dance with you." The big ape

yanked Ivy in close, so fast that she stumbled against his chest. Then he held her there with an arm low around her hips.

Ben battled back the red tide of an emotion he chose not to name. But he sure as hell wouldn't stand there and let Ivy be manhandled. He turned, set his camera on the table to have both hands free. When he turned back around a split second later, Jerry was halfway to the ground in an awkward crouch. Ivy held his thumb and pinkie at a visibly unnatural angle.

"If I push any harder, you're going to be a very unhappy man." She spoke in a soft, calm voice. "On the other hand, if you promise to leave me alone and walk away, I'll let go. No harm done. Your choice, Jerry."

Could that be a tear oozing out the corner of his tightly clenched eyes? Ben bit back a laugh, and resisted the years of ingrained habit that sent his hand groping for his camera. God help him, but some things were just too good to share with the viewing public. Plus, he didn't want to leave Ivy open to a stupid nuisance lawsuit by embarrassing this guy on national television. It would, however, be indelibly imprinted on his mental playback reel.

"Steve made me promise to say goodbye," Jerry mumbled sullenly.

"Of course he did. You're the best man, after all." Ivy released his fingers and stepped back. "He's probably waiting for you right now."

Without another word, Jerry slunk off. Ben slowly clapped his admiration. "Kudos, Ms. Rhodes."

Her cheeks flushed to almost the same shade as the bow in her hair. "Don't make a big deal out of it."

"Why not? You brought a grown man the size of a Buick to his knees. Where'd you learn those moves?"

"Self defense class. Weddings don't have bouncers, and with the free-flowing open bars, situations arise. Daphne and I both took the course when we opened Aisle Bound."

"You really are prepared for anything, aren't you?"

"It's my job," she said simply. Then a dancing light sparked in her eyes. "And I happen to be great at it."

That touch of arrogance diluted her too-good-to-be-true perfection just enough, like a shot of rum blunting the sweetness of a strawberry daiquiri. And it pushed her from annoyingly desirable into the dangerous, must-have column. He'd tried for two weeks to ignore the undimmed spark between them, the desire he couldn't shake. Ben knew it was seventeen kinds of wrong. She'd drive him straight up a wall with expectations he just couldn't meet. But he couldn't ignore the compulsion to touch her again. Sidling closer, he bumped her hip.

"Why don't we go out tonight?" Maybe now that she knew upfront where he stood on the subject of dating, she'd be willing to deal with her emotions on her own time and just live a little.

Ivy didn't say anything, but lifted a well-arched eyebrow.

"Don't worry, I'm not suggesting a drink," he snapped. Couldn't she cut him a little slack? "I sure as hell don't want to send you off the deep end again. Dinner between colleagues. You and me."

"Why?"

"It's been a stressful weekend. The rest of the country spent it relaxing and barbequing while we worked our asses off for four days straight." It'd been a long time since a woman didn't immediately fall prey to his well-practiced charm. Decades, probably. Practically a law of nature. Dimples made him irresistible. Ben Westcott could get any woman he wanted, without effort. How could the one girl he didn't want to want resist him? Hands buried wrist deep in his pockets to keep from stroking the curve of her cheek, he hip checked her once more. "I think we deserve a nice night out."

"Your stance on dating kind of seared its way into my memory in April. You're not a boyfriend kind of guy. You don't do relationships. So why on earth would I spend an evening with you?"

No surprise it took the blink of an eye for that to come back and bite him in the ass. "I didn't like watching Jerry the Jerk draped all over you."

She dipped her head. "Believe me, I appreciate you not inflaming the situation and letting me handle it."

Good thing she didn't know how close he'd come to throwing a right hook. "Point is, he rubbed me the wrong way. Next time I can't promise the same outcome. You've got to go out with me."

Her eyebrow shot up again. Damn thing was doing jumping jacks. "Or else what? Or else you'll threaten to start a rumble with every guy who looks at me sideways?"

Pretty much. Except that tactic didn't seem to be working. Ben regrouped, and gently tugged her hand off her waist. "I'm persistent. I'll keep asking until I wear you down. Come on, Ivy," he wheedled, "we have fun together. Why not share a few laughs and some good food?"

It rankled him, waiting for an answer. Made him feel like all kinds of a fool. Now, on top of wanting to be with her, his pride kept him nailed to the spot, proverbial hat in hand. This better be the best damn date of his life. A hair's breadth away from second guessing the whole thing, her hand squeezed him back. Ivy quirked those lush lips to the side.

"One dinner. We'll go out tonight if you promise to drop the issue for the entire rest of the shooting schedule. It'll be up to me after that. I may choose to walk away without a backward glance, or I may choose to see you again. But I make the decision, not you."

First she ran him like a marlin on a hook, and now she held the tip of the sword to his throat. Why hadn't he felt the earthquake that so shifted the balance between them? There should be jagged spears of earth surrounded by rubble. Instead, when he looked around the rapidly emptying tent, all he saw were a few hardcore dancers and an elderly woman scooping leftover favors into her purse. Ben wondered what she intended to do with forty star-shaped, inch-high picture frames. Maybe sell them on eBay?

"Sounds good. We should be wrapped up here soon, so how about I pick you up in two hours?"

"Two and a *half* hours," she corrected.

"Oh, is that how it's going to be?"

"Depends on how good a time you show me."

"Hey, I only offered dinner. We're not taking some whirlwind fantasy trip to Paris or anything."

"Good. I'm too tired already to deal with jet lag."

So Ivy expected a kick-ass but low-key date. Ben knew she'd hated the moonlight lake cruise. And he was painfully aware of his scant-at-best knowledge of Chicago and its nightlife scene. Now what?

CHAPTER ELEVEN

Energy and persistence conquer all things.
—Benjamin Franklin

IVY HEARD A sound not unlike elephants shod in fleece racing down the hallway. Her bedroom door slammed open to reveal a panting, pajama-clad Daphne.

"Ben's coming up the stairs."

"Already? He's ten minutes early." Ivy spun to the mirror, hands shifting to autopilot to fluff a sexy tousle into her loose curls. "Why on earth did you let him up?"

"He buzzed. What else am I supposed to do, leave him standing on the curb like a hobo?"

"Well, yes."

Daphne threw herself into a prone position on the bed. "I still think you're crazy. After the hours we've put in the past few days, wouldn't you rather be in your jammies eating pizza on the couch with me?"

"Tempting, yes. But you should've seen him. The man all but begged. And threatened to keep begging until I caved. If I get it out of the way tonight, he won't bother me any more the rest of the time he's here."

"I don't buy it." Daphne toyed with the drawstring on her pink-and-white-striped bottoms. "You don't cave. You don't let yourself be boxed into a corner. There's some other reason you said yes, isn't there?"

"Am I that transparent?"

"To me. Probably not to Ben. So hurry and tell me. With legs that long, he'll cover those two flights of stairs in a heartbeat."

"I'm going to be the best date he's ever had. Fun, flirty, sexy. He'll ache with wanting me. And then I'll cut him loose. See how he likes being the one left wanting." Ivy sat on the edge of the bed. "Does that make me a terrible, vindictive person?"

"Oh, yeah. But if you were perfect, I couldn't be friends with you. Everyone needs a flaw or two."

Three hard knocks echoed through the apartment. Ivy smoothed the straps of her sin-red sundress, chosen to set Ben to drooling the minute he saw her. "Don't save me any ice cream. I plan to eat my way through Ben's credit card limit tonight."

"Go get him, tiger."

Ivy's needle-thin stilettos tapped against the hardwood floors. She opened the door to catch Ben midknock. His hand froze, upraised, as his eyes inched down in a slow slide past the cotton lace-up bustier, past the skirt so short she couldn't bend over and stay decent, then back up to hover at her glossy, vixen-red lips.

"Va va va voom, Ms. Rhodes. You look incredible."

"You look early," she replied, gratified by the stupefied expression slackening his jaw. Of course, she had to remember to keep hers from dropping as well. At this point, she'd almost gotten used to how rakishly sexy Ben looked in his wedding uniform of a tuxedo. She thought she did a pretty good job of not *openly* staring at his muscled thighs when he wore cargo shorts to the office. But tonight he displayed a whole new sartorial side. The summer linen suit over a pale blue shirt un-

buttoned at the neck made him look relaxed and suave.
Sort of like James Bond on a Caribbean island.

"Better than late, right? Besides, I had an inkling
you'd try to keep me out of here. Half expected you to
be waiting out front."

Well, that *had* been her plan. There was an inher-
ent intimacy to letting him into their place. He hadn't
earned that privilege. She didn't like him being one
step ahead of her. "Don't be silly. We love to show off
our place. Daphne and I spent two solid months painting and sprucing when we first moved in."

She stepped back and swept her arm to the side in invitation. The pale lavender walls covered with close-up
photographs of individual flowers didn't exactly measure up to the grandeur and elegance Ben was used to
at the Cavendish. Extra wide chairs covered in a wa-
tercolory print of lilac sprays were super comfortable
for reading away an afternoon. She and Daphne had
chosen the deep purple velvet sofa for its make-out potential: had to be long enough for a tall man to stretch
out full length. Although it hadn't seen much of that
type of action, she loved the dramatic flair it brought
to the room.

Ben, however, bypassed the comfort of the couch
and ambled straight to the fireplace. Flanked by built-
in bookcases, it was Ivy's favorite part of the room. The
wide white mantel held a whimsically mismatched collection of picture frames.

"Looks like you've got your own gallery up here."
Ben ran a finger along the edge of several frames in
a row.

"We call it Ivy's heart on display." Daphne sprawled
on the couch, a pizza box balanced on her stomach.

"Everyone she cares about is up there. Kind of a place of honor. If you make it onto the mantel, you're in the inner circle."

"Good for people to know where they stand," he said absently. His finger lingered on a shot of her family in Adirondack chairs at their lake cabin in Wisconsin. Then he jammed his hands in his pockets, which raised his jacket high enough to show off a very fine ass. "Don't want to be late for our reservations. We should go."

Like a cloud passing overhead, his mood had shifted for a moment, darkened. Or maybe she imagined it. The tight roundness of his ass certainly qualified as a distraction. Ivy collected her bag and a white pashmina from the mirrored armoire by the door.

"I'm going to wait up, so don't expect any post-date nookie, Westcott," Daphne warned.

"Actions have consequences, Lovell. Cock blocking me means I nix my plans to bring you back a dessert." He closed the door behind Ivy before Daphne could splutter out more than a few angry syllables.

"Interesting choice of words," said Ivy, picking her way down the stairs.

Ben laughed. "Daphne and I enjoy shooting the shit. We both dish it out as well as we take it. Neither one of us means anything by it."

"Does that mean you'll still bring her dessert? You can't toy with her when it comes to her sweet tooth. Because, and let me be clear on this, Daphne's presence at the apartment is not what's stopping you from getting laid tonight."

"No kidding. I live at a hotel. She could camp out

in your living room for a month while we run through every condom in the city."

Ivy overshot a step and almost lost her footing. Obviously they weren't on the same page about the agenda for the evening. "I think you're missing my point. Allow me to strip you of any illusions you might have, there will be no sex tonight. Not in your hotel, not in my apartment."

"What about on the desk in your office?" Ben opened the front door and led her through with one hand cupped beneath her elbow.

Was he being deliberately obtuse? Obstinate? Idiotic? Suddenly involved in a body swap with a sex-crazed fifteen year old? "No." His mouth started to open, and she held up an index finger to shush him. "Oh, and before you ask, also not on the observation deck of the Hancock Tower or the end zone at Soldier Field."

His open palm moved to the small of her back, guiding her down the tree-lined street. "Ivy, relax. I'm just poking at you."

"That's the only poking you'll be doing."

"For God's sake, I don't expect you to put out for a glass of wine and a meal. Is that really what you think of me?" Legs braced wide, Ben stopped walking. He skewered her with a laser-sharp gaze. Dusk crept in from shadowy corners, darkening the sidewalk even as the sky morphed into an abstract painting with thick streaks of apricot and periwinkle. Mockingbirds twittered from behind clusters of vivid green leaves. The first crickets of the night began their rasping song. A warm breeze carried the scent of honeysuckle. The moment couldn't be more romantic if she'd orchestrated it herself. Not to mention the thoroughly handsome, albeit annoyed man waiting for an answer.

"No. No, I'm sorry, Ben. I guess I'm more exhausted than I realized. I should've known you were kidding." After all, the hard freeze punctuating their first few days together had thawed all the way to occasional friendly, if not warm, banter. She'd watched Ben jovially joke with everyone in her office, although to a far lesser extent with Julianna. Her assistant refused to drop her guard around him. "You *were* just kidding, right?"

Ben opened the door of a sporty silver convertible and helped her in with old world manners. She rubbed her hands over the butter soft leather of the seats while he walked around to his side. With an ease she'd always assumed required stuntmen and wires, he planted his hand and vaulted over the door into the seat.

"Yes." Smoothly manipulating the gear shift, he pulled out into traffic. "Unless you offer up a quickie at the Art Institute. I've always been a sucker for Monet."

This time he had to be kidding. Probably. Ivy snickered. "I'm not interested in getting horizontal anyplace with a marble floor. I bruise too easily."

"Duly noted." Ben drummed his fingers on the steering wheel while they idled at a light. His wind-tousled hair drooped into his eyes, giving him a boyish, innocent look. As if!

Ivy trailed her arm over the edge of the door and thought about how the last few minutes had played out. For all intents and purposes, Ben gave every indication of being a decent guy. In hindsight, sure, he'd hurt her. But only by being upfront and completely honest about his feelings. He didn't deserve her doling out this ongoing punishment for such sterling qualities.

"Look, I've obviously got a hair-trigger response to you. Which seems kind of ridiculous, since I'm the one that offered up the peace pipe. Starting tonight, I truly promise to let bygones be bygones. A guaranteed fresh start."

"Sounds good to me."

She worried about how quickly his response popped out. Had he truly heard what she said, tuned out to deal with traffic, or possibly not trust her to follow through? "Really? It's that easy?"

"Don't go looking for trouble under every single rock. Life's too short to hold grudges. I take people at their word." Ben slid a quick look her way before swinging onto Lake Shore Drive. "You tell me we've got a clean slate, I believe you."

Ivy looked at the beautiful expanse of Lake Michigan, shimmering on her left. Due to the holiday, the blue water sported more sailboats and speedboats than usual. The park edging it overflowed with families crowded around tables groaning with food, and the acrid charcoal scent of portable grills made her mouth water. A patchwork quilt of music with a Latin beat pumped out of dozens of boomboxes. She'd worked all the summer barbeque holidays for years, always going home to crash at the end of the four day slog. It was nice to be out in the middle of the festivities for once, sharing the holiday with millions of other Americans. Even nicer to experience it with an easy-going, yummilicious man.

IF IVY COULD'VE chosen any place in Chicago to be on a warm almost-summer night, the rooftop deck at Pegasus would be it. Located in the heart of Greektown, the view from their candlelit table encompassed the entire downtown skyline. The casual, fun atmosphere was exactly what she needed to relax and let go of the accumulated stress from the last four days. How had Ben done it? In a city with literally thousands of restaurants, how had he so perfectly gauged her mood?

"You did well, Mr. Westcott. A spectacular view, great food, epitome-of-summer atmosphere, not to mention the convertible ride down Lake Shore Drive. Less than half an hour in, this night is already about as perfect as it can get."

Crossing his hands behind his head, Ben kicked back to balance his chair on two legs. The position exposed a vee of golden chest hair, and spread his shirt tautly across his pecs. All stretched out, he kind of looked like an actor in a really sexy cologne commercial.

"I realize it's no satin sheets on a sailboat—"

"And for that I thank you," she interrupted, with a mental shudder. Never again would she let her mom set up a blind date. Ever.

Ben chuckled, deep in his throat. "Let's call it my own brand of romance."

Where could she sign up to be the spokesperson for his brand? "Wow. Look at that. You used the R word without breaking out in hives or gagging."

"Very funny. All kidding aside, I don't believe romance is evil."

"Really? 'Cause you do a pretty convincing impression. You see a guy walking down the street with a dozen roses, and you all but whip out the holy water, garlic and crosses."

His chair clattered to the floor. "I'll admit it has a

place in the world. In measured doses. Too many people become addicted, or worse, wield it like a weapon. Let me tweak a line from Spider-Man, one of the greatest comic heroes of all time: with great romance comes great responsibility."

Cute. She could picture the pre-teen comic book nerd hiding behind all those muscles and self-assured smile. "I bet you've got an ancient, faded shirt with Spidey plastered across the front."

"Used to. I'm not much of a hoarder."

"I don't mean a packed storage locker. You must have a dresser drawer or two full of keepsakes."

"Nope. Mostly because I don't have a dresser."

He might as well be speaking Croatian. The words coming out of his mouth didn't make any sense. "No dresser in your apartment? Where do you keep all your clothes?"

"In a steamer trunk. Well, I keep everything in there. A couple of awards, books, photos and some extra clothes."

"You've crammed your entire life into a trunk? I've heard horror stories about the size of New York apartments, but this verges on the ridiculous. How tiny is your apartment?"

Ben nodded his thanks as the waiter deposited a footed wine bucket next to their table and began the process of uncorking. "There's the five-dollar question. I don't actually have an apartment. I keep my trunk at my sister's place."

Hmm. He didn't fit the nerd stereotype—they guy who lived with his sister because no other woman would have him. The perfect cut of his jacket indicated he tailored his clothes, which meant financial constraints didn't force him to bunk there, either. Odd. "Do you have some weird co-dependency thing going on with your sister? Aren't you waaaay too old to live with her?"

The waiter stifled a snort. He quickly poured them two glasses of a crisp viognier and backed away. Ben shook his head, a downward slant to his lips. "Thanks for taking a non-judgmental approach to that question."

"Sorry. When I'm this exhausted, the tact filter on my tongue goes haywire."

"Relax." He reached across the table to pat her hand. Except then it stayed there, his long, thick fingers tracing idle patterns across her skin that skittered a trail of goose bumps all the way up her arm. "I'm pulling your leg. Truth is, I don't live with my sister. She just lets me keep my stuff there. I'm on the road so much I probably spend three weeks total under her roof. No point paying sky-high rent, or even subletting. RealTV keeps a couple of long-term hotel rooms near their headquarters. About a dozen of us cycle through there when we're in town—basically a crash pad. You never know who else will be there, but it's just a place to sleep and shower."

"Sounds sensible. And quite lonely."

"Nah. I like the freedom. Aside from work, I'm not answerable to anyone."

Ivy mustered a good deal of self control to keep from responding. Said control only gained by pressing her tongue against the roof of her mouth (a trick she used when faced with particularly obnoxious brides) and looking away, out over the rooftops of Greektown. His life sounded isolating and sad. Articles popped online every day about the importance of a social network to keep the elderly young at heart. At this rate, Ben's heart had to be aging prematurely. Funny how he gave the impression of being the exact opposite of a loner. What scared him so much about putting down roots?

"I didn't mean to judge you. Honestly. Since I see you every day, I forget that you spent the last few years hopping to a different city every weekend."

He huffed out a breath that stirred the long, streaky strands of golden hair dipping low on his forehead. "Longer than that. My dorm room was the last place I spent any longer than a month."

Wonder of wonders, Ben was opening up. Ivy had bided her time for a week now, waiting for the right time to discuss his past. For all his jovial, open demeanor, she'd noticed that Ben maintained a very private core. This might be her chance to stick a stiletto in that emotional crack and shove it wide open.

She moistened suddenly dry lips and plunged ahead. "Sam told me."

"He told you what? How I skinned him for fifty dollars at poker?"

"No, but I'll be sure to tease him about that the next time I see him." Ivy flipped her hand over, to lace her fingers through his. "Sam told me about your old job. The, uh, incident."

Ben let his head loll to the left, eyes flicking to the shiny cityscape. "You mean my public branding as a coward and subsequent lynching by the nation as a whole via every media outlet known to man?"

A flash of insight almost made Ivy gasp. Had he shifted to avoid looking at her, or because he worried she might not be willing to meet his eyes? How many women had walked away once they realized they were on a date with the infamous Cowering Cameraman? "*Incident* felt like a shorter way to sum that all up."

"Good call."

"I'm surprised you didn't come up with a snappy acronym for it." Success! Poke the bear with a stick long enough, and it'll turn and look at you. Ben didn't move his head, but rather slanted those slits of icy blue back in her direction.

"Now you're sassing me."

"A little." Hopefully not too much. Kind of a gamble, really. Ivy already regretted saying the careless, teasing words.

He rubbed one wide palm across the back of his neck. "Making fun of my abject misery."

"Just to break the tension."

Legs shifting, neck cracking, he squirmed like a toddler in a sandbox. "Well, as long as you've got a good reason to rub salt in the wound."

"Quite the opposite. All kidding aside, it floored me once Sam shared the whole story. I'm talking about the real story, not the one the media manufactured for shock value. The courage it took to not buckle under all that pressure? To fight tooth and nail to maintain some semblance of the career you love in a field that didn't want you?" She let fly the words she'd kept bottled up since Sam shared the story over bagels a week ago. The words which equally scared and compelled her to speak Scared by both the possibility he'd storm off, furious she'd even broach the painful subject, and also petrified by how he managed to stir such strong feelings in her. "Bennett Westcott, you're the bravest man I know."

Ben took a long sip of his wine. Then another. By

the fourth sip, Ivy wondered if she should try matching him drink for drink. Clearly Sam had been right on the money when he begged her not to say anything to Ben. She'd assumed it to be a guy thing, a way to allow him to keep his emotions under lock and key. But Ivy couldn't keep her admiration to herself. Even went so far as to assume Ben would be elated to finally discuss the true version of the day that turned him into a pariah. As the chasm of silence widened, Ivy began to wonder if she'd managed to set a record for quickest ruined date ever.

With the harshness of fingernails down a chalkboard, the scrape of metal chair legs against concrete rent the air. Ben shoved back, tossing his napkin on the table as he stood. He sucked in a deep breath, expanding his already wide chest. Then he scrubbed his hand from his forehead all the way down to the nape of his neck. Still staring out at the lights twinkling on block by block across the city skyline.

"Trust me when I say I'm about as far away from brave as this planet is from Pluto—all I do is make it through the day." Finally, he directed his gaze straight at Ivy. "But I'm honored and humbled you think so. It goes a long way toward mending the tattered shreds left of my so-called pride."

Ben bent from the waist to drop a soft kiss in the middle of her forehead. He pulled back, looked at her with those slice of summer sky eyes. Ivy held her breath, afraid the smallest puff of air would break the cobweb of intensity spinning ever wider between them.

"Damn. I was planning to save this for the fireworks."

"Save what?" She didn't understand, and she almost

didn't care. Who needed the power of cognitive thought when a handsome man held you tight in the unwavering tractor beam of his eyes? "What fireworks?"

"Gib told me there'd be fireworks in about an hour. Because of Memorial Day. It's why I brought you here—for the view."

Her heart flipped. Turned right around in a somersault like she used to do down the grassy slope at her grandparents' house.

"On the other hand, why should I wait for the City of Chicago to light up the sky?" He framed her face with those big, wide palms, tilted her head back. "Let's make our own fireworks."

Before she could savor the sexy promise in his words, Ben kissed her. A gentle touch for the space of a heartbeat—well, three beats at the rate Ivy's heart raced—and then he sank into her mouth, as if it were a feather pillow to cradle him. Firm, deep kisses that somehow contained the richness of melted chocolate, the kick of a strong margarita, and the undeniable allure she'd succumbed to all those months before.

The earth tilted on its axis. No, it was Ben bracing his hand on the back of her chair, tipping it back for a better angle. Her feet dangled in the air. She hooked them around the chair legs in an attempt to anchor herself. Silly, really. The floor had dropped out from under her the minute his tongue slipped in between her lips, tasting, questing. And she knew without a doubt those strong arms wouldn't let her fall.

Her hands reached out to feel them, to caress the tight, corded steel beneath his jacket. A quiver grew deep in her core at discovering she couldn't wrap her hands all the way around his biceps. Muscles like that belonged to a broadsword-wielding knight. One who carried her off on a white horse while the crowd cheered.

The crowd cheered. It wasn't just one of her flights of fancy. Ivy pulled her concentration from where it lay, writhing, somewhere close to the edge of her red lace panties. The roof deck had erupted into applause, catcalls and whistles. Her eyes flew open. She tapped her toe against Ben's calf, wrenching out of the lip lock.

"We've got an audience."

Undeterred, he nuzzled just below her ear. "Put on a good enough show, maybe we'll get a free meal out of it."

Ivy kicked once more, this time aiming the hard point of her sandal against his shin. But she made sure to let the laughter in her throat burble through. "Enough."

With a gentle tap he lowered the chair to the ground. Then he ran the side of his thumb across her lower lip, setting off one last chain of sparklers in her veins. "Nope. Nowhere close."

For a man who eschewed romance, he sure managed to say the right things. While Ben straightened his coat and sat back down, Ivy let her brain catch up to her speeding pulse. What the heck just happened? Hadn't she just spent two endless months trying to get Ben out of her system? To no avail?

It was one thing to accept his invitation to dinner, to try and work through the white hot...whatever that flared through her system every time she looked at him. She'd banked on a couple hours of basic conversation in a noisy restaurant to lay a groundwork of knowledge about what made Bennett Westcott tick. Her master plan for tonight only played out through the end of dinner. A simple dinner between colleagues. With a side order of chemistry sizzling loud enough to drown out the shouts of *Opa* as a waiter walked past with a platter of flaming saganaki cheese held aloft.

She cast about for a safe topic while her brain retook control from her overcharged hormones. "Where'd you get the snazzy convertible? It didn't have the antiseptic smell of a rental."

"It's Gib's."

"I don't believe you." The flat denial popped out automatically. Too late, she realized she'd more or less accused him of lying. How many flirting rules did that break? Why did he so unsettle her composure with just his mere presence?

Ben pushed his wineglass to the side, making room for the waiter to set down their tray of appetizers. "Why not?"

"Because none of us have ever seen his car, let alone touched it. He swears it has a single purpose."

"Yup. To score women."

The feminist side of her broke out in hives at the nonchalant way it rolled off Ben's tongue. Almost as annoying as every single time Gib plumly rolled his accent around those same words. Ridiculous to have that be the sole reason to own a car. Gib refused to use his car except when in pursuit of the fairer sex. Never used it to bring home bags of groceries, or drive to the movies when the thermometer dipped below freezing, or even to pick up family from O'Hare on their rare visits. He swore he only used it on dates, and *only* when close to sealing the deal.

"Said purpose does not include letting any of his friends borrow it or ride in it. Ever."

"I heard the speech. The power of the car can only be used for good. Christ, it was like Obi-Wan Kenobi droning on about The Force."

Hmm. That could be interpreted as a pro or a con for her favorite movie franchise. Better to get it out in the open from the start. "Are you a *Star Wars* fan?"

"Rabid. New, old, recut version, digitally remastered, you name it. I read the books, I read the comics, and I play the video games. You?"

"For ten years running, I dressed up for Halloween as Princess Leia. For the past six years I've been working my way through each of Queen Amidala's costumes. Most people laugh when I tell them I love all six movies."

"Well, sure, there are haters for both trilogies. We could sit here for a week straight debating the merits of each episode."

"Count me in."

"See?" Ben shoved the plate to the side and reached across the table. He waited, palm up, until she laid her hands atop his. Instantly, his grasp tightened as he leaned forward. "It isn't every day I come across a woman willing to not just indulge, but participate in my *Star Wars* obsession. You're fun, Ivy."

"So you said earlier," she sassed back, desperate not to let him know how his firm clasp sent her mind whirling. Ever since they began taping *Planning for Love*, she'd gotten to know and respect Ben. See him as, yes, a fun colleague, one whose easy quips passed the day a little more quickly. Putting to the side the raw pain she still harbored over his using and discarding her like a wet tissue, Ivy genuinely liked Ben as a friend. Tonight, however was no simple dinner between work buddies. He'd morphed back into the flirtatious, downright compelling man she fell head over heels for in April. What did it mean? What turned the tide? And as long as she didn't mention marriage or weddings or true love, would he stay like this?

He scowled, drawing his eyebrows together into a single, bushy blond line. "Thought we were having a conversation, not comparing dictation notes. Next time we go out I'll bring my own stenographer."

"Sorry. But you sounded like you were about to crown me queen of the nerd table. You should know that my sci-fi obsession begins and ends with *Star Wars*. I don't play *World of Warcraft* and I don't read manga. And I loathed every single science class I took in school."

"I don't care." Ben rasped his thumb slowly across the back of her hand. The touch flooded a river of goose bumps up her arm. "Maybe I came about this from the wrong direction. The *Star Wars* thing is just the cherry on top of a well-mixed Manhattan. Point is, we click. We work well together, and we've got this explosive chemistry. Cards on the table. You already know I'm not a long-term kind of guy. But can't we enjoy ourselves for the next six weeks while I'm here?"

If Ivy understood him correctly, Ben had just proposed the longest one-night stand in history. She needed to be crystal clear on the parameters. "Define 'enjoy ourselves' for me."

"Should've known you'd insist on labeling it. This— dinner, drinks, you know." He jerked his right shoulder forward. For somebody so eloquent about what he didn't like about relationships, he sure had trouble verbalizing what he did want out of one. His obvious discomfort made her wonder if Ben really knew what he wanted.

"Is *you know* the latest slang for sex?"

"It is if you say yes." Ben paused, waited for a response. With a final squeeze, he released her hands and sat back. "Otherwise, we'll fall back on the alternate definition of just having a few laughs."

A horrible thought occurred to her. "Did Gib promise if you borrowed his car, I'd agree to anything? Remember, I warned you flat out you're not getting sex tonight. No matter what."

"Nah. Matter of fact, he warned I didn't have a snowball's chance in hell of pulling this off. He loaned me the car out of pity." After loading a pita with hummus and feta, he paused, hand in mid-air. "Question now is, will you take pity on me? Give me something to look forward to besides a muffin made out of whatever June's fruit-of-the-month is?"

Ivy thought about it. She thought while scooping an extra dollop of lemony sauce onto a dolmades. She thought while the waiter topped off her wineglass. She thought while the silence grew into a thick cloud encircling their table. The entire time, it was one, single thought doing laps in her brain: maybe it was time for a new plan.

CHAPTER TWELVE

A plan which succeeds is bold, one which fails
is reckless.

—General Karl von Clausewitz

"THE ONLY ACCEPTABLE reason for being up this early
involves death. Or winning the lottery. And if you did
win and you don't intend to share with me, then I'm
going back to bed." Daphne dropped into the chair next
to Ivy. She wore workout shorts, a thin tee, and a decidedly disgruntled expression. "Either way, if I don't
get coffee soon, something dire will happen. Murder.
Mayhem. Not sure of the details exactly, but I promise
you I will scrape together all my energy to pitch a fit
until there is a full coffee cup in front of me."

"Good morning to you, too." Ivy pushed her own
mug of steaming goodness in front of Daphne. "Here,
I'm happy to share until the waitress swings by." Wordlessly, Daphne lifted and drained the entire cup, slamming it back into the saucer.

Julianna twitched in her ladder-back chair at the
sharp crack of china. "I shouldn't have to remind you
that our next potential bride could be sitting in this very
restaurant. Image is everything."

Despite it being not yet eight o'clock, Julianna
looked bandbox neat in an apricot linen suit and a

pearl choker. It bothered Ivy, since she'd chosen her own scoop-necked sundress through sleep-squinted eyes. Not until she sat down at Ann Sather's did she open her eyes enough to notice the slew of wrinkles pleating the tangerine polka-dotted skirt. Oh, and the strong possibility (she refused to look down to confirm) she'd slipped on clashing pink sandals instead of white. And she knew without looking that her own eyes boasted steamer trunk-sized circles and puffiness. Makeup could hide a lot, but not the exhaustion toll levied by pulling off six weddings in four days. What sort of deal with the devil had her assistant struck to look so disgustingly perfect?

"The image of my *floral creations* is everything," Daphne corrected. "I am strictly a behind-the-scenes girl. Besides, great artists are notorious for frumpy outfits and quirky personal hygiene. Do you think the Pope ever asked da Vinci to smarten up and remove his smock? Did Queen Elizabeth ever demand Shakespeare don a fresh doublet and breeches?"

"Whoa, there." Milo swooshed into place beside the table, one hand outstretched like a crossing guard. "Want to rein in that ego, Michelangelo? Not sure there's room at the table for all of us with that big head of yours."

Ivy swallowed, hard. Then she bit the inside of her cheek in an effort not to break into a huge guffaw. A navy blue kimono covered with pale blue, snarling dragons draped across Milo's shoulders. In the open neck of his white shirt fluffed an ice blue ascot. Below the cheery yellow tablecloth, Daphne's hand clutched at Ivy's thigh like the talons of a hissing cat. Guess she was trying to play it cool, too, rather than roll on the floor laughing. They'd learned years ago Milo took his fashion choices very seriously. And he took criticism of such very poorly.

With perfect aplomb, Julianna leapt into the breach. "Interesting outfit. I don't recall seeing it before."

Although Ivy interpreted *interesting* to mean ridiculous and mockable, Milo preened. "It is a vintage silk smoking jacket. Perfect for lounging through an early breakfast." He slid into the seat across from Daphne. "Back in the good old days, everybody ate breakfast in robes."

Daphne snorted. "We're not back in the day. And we're in public. You look like a gay Hugh Hefner." Ivy sighed. Daphne's depleted reserves of both caffeine and sugar left her tactless and irritable. Not bursting into guffaws the moment she spotted Milo must've used every bit of her self-control.

"Thank you. He did begin his empire right here in Chicago, you know. What better place to emulate one of our town's greatest icons?"

"You think Hef's an icon?" Ivy leaned forward, chin propped on her fists. "I thought your tribe idolized Liza and Bette Midler, not a guy who built his empire on parts of the female anatomy that generally make you break out in hives."

"True. But the man turned loungewear into an acceptable fashion choice. What's not to love?"

Coffeepots in each hand, their waitress appeared. Before she had a chance to fill the empty cups, Daphne pushed hers forward and raised a finger. "Here's what's gotta happen in the next five minutes: you can give me straight coffee now, but then I need you to bring me your biggest mocha latte, extra shot of espresso, double drizzle of chocolate syrup on top, absolutely covered with marshmallows. As soon as you bring it, turn right around and start making a second one. Or feel free to bring two at once. And while we decide on breakfast, we'll need a round of cinnamon rolls for the table."

"You betcha, hon." The middle-aged waitress took the verbal barrage in stride, filling all four cups before hurrying away.

"You've got a take-no-prisoners approach to ordering. Hope that your crankiness doesn't inspire the kitchen to spit on our cinnamon rolls." Ivy tempered her words by slinging an arm around Daphne's shoulders.

"If they do, it's your fault. What on earth possessed you to call an emergency meeting this early? Did the building burn down overnight? Or maybe the White House contacted you to handle the First Daughter's wedding? Because those are the only reasons I can think of after the week we put in to be up so early."

Ivy surveyed the faces of her friends: Daphne's grumpy squint, Julianna's inquisitively arched eyebrow, and Milo not meeting her gaze, but rather stroking the lapels of his kimono. After her big revelation, she expected them to tease for a bit, but end up stalwart supporters as usual. Probably. Hopefully. Should she wait until they all had a gooey, delicious cinnamon roll before breaking the news? Everything sounded better with caramel, nutty sweetness toasting your tummy.

With a shrug, Daphne shook off Ivy's arm. "Spill it, Rhodes, or I'm taking my liter of lattes and scooting straight back to bed. Why couldn't whatever this is wait until we open the office at eleven?"

"Because Ben will be there."

"Ah." Daphne nodded slowly, then folded her arms

over her chest and leaned back. "You've got my attention. As long as I also get an order of Swedish pancakes with lingonberries. Extra syrup. Side of sausage."

"Before Daphne scarfs down half the menu, do you want to bring the rest of us up to speed? What's the deal with Ben? Did he set our building on fire?" asked Milo, a facetious smirk flattening one side of his mouth.

"Not the building. Just me." God, could she sound more like a deluded soap opera virgin? Apparently Daphne wasn't the only one running on fumes. Ivy slurped down half of her coffee at once. "Ben and I went on a date last night."

"After the Sigurski wedding? Where did you find the stamina?" asked Julianna. "I went home and melted into the couch."

"Ben can be...persuasive."

"Did he persuade your panties off?" Milo sniggered.

Fair question. After the frantic phone calls dragging them out of bed, the least her friends deserved was total honesty. "Not *this* time."

Three mouths fell open. She'd struck them all speechless. Then the glances started. Swift, darting looks between Daphne and Milo, Julianna and Milo, then Daphne and Julianna. Ivy could tell they were trying to figure out who should take the lead in the inevitable interrogation. Their imaginary psychic powers must not have been on line yet, since the careening cue ball effect just kept going. Even the arrival of the first platter of cinnamon rolls didn't break the pointed stares, accompanied by truly impressive eyebrow gymnastics.

She'd give them a quick recap of the April weekend. Like peeling off a bandage, right? Their judgment would only hurt for a second before she moved on to the real reason for the meeting. "After the taping of *Wild Wedding Smackdown*, Ben and I shared an…encounter."

"Definition, please?" Milo dipped the tines of his fork in the moat of melted butter and brown sugar surrounding the rolls. "How much does an encounter encompass?"

Maybe they didn't deserve *total* honesty. After all, Ivy wanted them to be able to look Ben in the face without blushing in a few hours. "Enough. Use your imagination."

He licked his lips. "Don't think you want that to happen, boss. Are we talking you dropped your handkerchief and he retrieved it? Or he dropped his trousers and you—"

Julianna clapped her hand over Milo's mouth, stifling the rest of his sentence. "Not at breakfast. I can't take suggestive smut at breakfast."

"Ivy started it."

Oh, for crying out loud! As if this story wasn't hard enough to blurt out without dodging their interruptions. "What level of sordid detail would you like? Or should I see if we can get the elevator's security tapes from Gib?"

Daphne dropped her fork to make a time-out sign with her hands. "You told me when I dropped off clothes for you that you'd stayed up all night talking and fell asleep on the couch. And now I find out not only did something more happen, but Gib knows? I'm your best friend, and I'm kept in the dark, but you tell Gibson Moore?"

The last thing Ivy wanted to do was hurt Daphne's feelings. So far her summit meeting was off to a less than stellar start. "No. Of course not, Daph. I'm sorry

I misled you, but I needed to keep the lid on this one. I haven't told anyone what really happened until right this second. The only thing Gib knows is that we had drinks in the lounge at the Cavendish. Unless he's turned into a flaming pervert and really does review the security tapes looking for skeevy behavior."

Mollified, Daphne took another bite. "Okay. We'll save the story of what happened in the elevator until the next time we're knee deep in margaritas. Let's get back to this encounter. Or should I call it a romantic interlude? How long did it last?"

"We spent the night together. And the next day. Then he left." Then she cried into her pillow for so long she had to change out the damp blob in the middle of the night. "And I couldn't say anything because I didn't want you to tell me how stupid I was, to open up my heart so completely. Trust me when I say I didn't mean to."

"Ivy, the door to your heart doesn't even have hinges. It's permanently welded open. We all love that about you," said Julianna.

Her hands began to clench on the sunny yellow tablecloth dusting the tops of her thighs. "But I knew Ben should be nothing more than a lost weekend. I went into it with every intention of a fun fling. Except we had lots more fun than I expected. Ben lights me up. He's fantastic." Ivy swallowed hard, realizing the person at the table she most needed to be honest with was herself. "I let myself peek into the what-if closet. What if we stole time together every few weeks as he criss-crossed the country? What if the wonderful feelings he brought out in me could last?"

Julianna covered her mouth with both hands. "Oh no. You didn't tell him this, did you?"

"Doesn't matter. To Ben, twenty-four hours together might as well be a long-term relationship. It's about ten hours too close to serious for him. The man's allergic to love. The thought of living happily ever after is so incomprehensible he can't even say the words without laughing. We're oil and water. He told me this, upfront."

"Stand-up guy. Gotta admire him for that." Milo shrugged his shoulders, wide-eyed. "What? We're not talking about a stranger. Ben's been nice to work with these past couple of weeks. Am I supposed to bash on him? I'm still ultimately on Ivy's side."

"And don't forget it for a second," Daphne warned, shaking her loaded fork so hard a bit of flaky pastry flew across the table. She'd demolished an entire cinnamon roll, and was now sneaking bites off of Ivy's.

"Nobody's choosing sides. We're all on the same side. Even Ben and me. He just doesn't know it yet." Ivy turned to the hovering waitress and ordered a round of pancakes for everyone. And a third coffee for Daphne. She didn't want any more interruptions. "That's why I called this meeting."

"I'm confused. If Ben doesn't do relationships, why'd he take you out last night? Scratch that." Daphne shook her head. "First, tell me if you made it home last night, or if you did the dawn walk of shame."

"I was tucked into my pj's listening to the snores from your bedroom before eleven. You know, a good roommate would've fallen asleep on the sofa, at least pretending to wait up."

"True, but a good business partner remembered the twelve centerpieces for the pre-graduation party which have to be made today, and needed to recharge before recreating Evanston High School's wildcat mascot out of orange daisies."

"Good point." Ivy hadn't minded coming home to a quiet house. She'd needed a few hours to marshal her thoughts and solidify her plan. "When it comes to love, Ben and I couldn't be farther apart. I think I repel him on a physical level when I bring up the subject."

Julianna steepled her fingers, her square-tipped French manicure meeting at the top. "Ivy, honey, you're not making any sense. You can't date someone who repulses you. Which, by the way, I don't believe for a minute. Ben can't take his eyes off of you. Both of you click into high gear the moment the other walks into the room."

"Exactly!" Count on Julianna to come through with a weird mixture of perception and logic. "We're drawn to each other. I tried to deny it because I didn't want to get hurt again. Ben tried to deny it because he doesn't want to get involved. But this thing can't be ignored, can't be denied." Ivy took a beat, looked each one of her friends in the eye before dropping her bombshell. "I've been planning for love my whole life. Now it's time to put that plan into action."

Daphne half-coughed, half-gurgled, as though trying to swallow an aborted spit take. "Sure. And while you're at it, why not try to tame a tiger using only gummy bears and hugs?"

"Don't be snide. I'm serious." Although Ivy refused to admit it out loud, Daphne did have a point. The chance of her plan working was slim. On the other hand, slim was better than non-existent. Slim fueled her with hope and motivation. She'd never stepped back from a challenge just because of a lack of guaranteed success.

Fingers clenched around Ivy's wrist, Daphne looked her straight in the eyes. "Are you telling me he's the one?"

"Prince Charming in the flesh?" Milo added.

Maybe. Hopefully. Ivy shook her head. "I don't know. There's no way I could know. But I need to find out, one way or the other. I refuse to walk away and spend my life wondering if I'd just taken the time, made the effort—if I would have found my one true love."

The ever-rational Julianna added her two cents. "But Ivy, he doesn't want to be *anyone's* true love. We've all heard him say it, and you've told us the same thing. It'd be like trying to convince an atheist to become Pope."

"Nope. I don't believe it." Everyone wants to love and be loved. The truth of that statement resonated in Ivy's core. Even Ben. "That's simply his current frame of mind. The more I thought about it, I realized he's scared. Petrified. I'll figure out the root of his phobia, open that dark closet of scary monsters to the light of day. No doubt he's scared off more than his fair share of women with his anti-love bluster. They didn't have the drive, the grit, the focus to break down those titanium walls he's built around his heart. Well, I do."

"No way." Julianna slammed her empty cup onto the table. Ivy's eyebrow twitched. Although close friends, Julianna rarely contradicted Ivy. Her silence, when differences occurred, spoke volumes. She must have strong reservations to be driven to speak up. "We can't let you do this. You're opening yourself up to so much potential pain."

"Or the potential for a lifetime of happiness," Ivy

countered. Why couldn't anyone else see the glass as half-full? They worked in a business full to the brim of happily-ever-afters. This level of cynicism could be expected from divorce lawyers or therapists, but not from people whose paychecks relied entirely on the endurance of love.

Their waitress slid four platters of lingonberry pancakes, heaped with whipped cream and swimming in syrup, onto the table. The discussion hit a momentary lull while everyone dug in. Ivy hoped the break would give everyone time to chew over her rationale. She needed them on her side. After all, what good was a support system if they didn't support her?

Daphne put her elbow on the table and propped her chin on her fist. "This isn't how dating works. Love at first sight is a myth."

"You're right. But I'm not claiming love at first sight. I've worked side by side with Ben for two weeks now—fourteen hours at a time on event days. If you do the math—and trust me, I did—it equates to the same amount of time a normal couple would spend together over nine weeks, factoring in three dates per week. Which means I've experienced more than two months of getting to know Ben, concentrated into a shorter period of time."

"Did you make an algebraic equation to figure that out?" Milo teased.

"I like to pull out my business degree every so often, dust it off and make sure I still remember how to justify the worthiness of a new concept. In Bennett Westcott, I see a treasure cave full of potential, and I won't ignore it."

"Some men just don't have the commitment gene,"

Daphne mumbled around a gigantic bite of pancakes. "Take George Clooney."

"I'd love to," Milo deadpanned back.

She stuck out her tongue, stained blue from the lingonberries. "Henry VIII. Howard Hughes—"

Ivy cut her off before the list could grow any longer. "Henry married six times. I call that mega commitment. And Howard Hughes was a certifiable nut job. He may be leery of love, but I don't think Ben's at any risk of starting to collect his own nail clippings in a jar. If he does, I promise to drop him like a hot potato."

"Good to know you draw the line somewhere," said Milo.

"Let's cut to the chase." Daphne pushed back her plate, leaned back and crossed her arms. She raised her voice a little to be heard over the fork-clattering, plate-scraping din of the breakfast rush. "How can we talk you out of this insanity? You're tilting at windmills. That never ends well. Fact, Ben's going to leave the second filming ends. Then we'll be the ones left picking up the tiny shards of your shattered heart."

Her support team wasn't rising to the occasion. A more apt description of their reaction so far would be raining on her parade. Ivy knew they had her best interest at heart, but would a little *go get him, slugger* be too much to ask? "You don't think I can do it?"

"I think if anyone could, it's you. But the risk is too great. For God's sake, the man is the anti-Cupid."

"The risk/reward ratio is weighted in my favor."

Daphne huffed out a breath. "Stop analyzing this like it's a corporate takeover. Human emotions don't fit neatly into a spreadsheet."

"Plus," Julianna said, meticulously folding her napkin into an elaborate, flapped pocket and sliding in her silverware one at a time. "You can't steal five minutes here and an hour there for a full-out strategic assault in the middle of wedding season."

"And while planning for your new store on top of it," Milo heaped onto the growing stack of verbal cons. Ivy pictured each of their rebuttals as logs on a pyre, with her potential romance on top, about to go up in flames. Well, she refused to let any of them light the fatal match.

"Ben claims not to believe in romance, and yet he took me to the roof deck at Pegasus and kissed me while we watched fireworks. He's already unconsciously partaking in romance, despite his best intentions. He cracked the door open all by himself. I just need to keep showing him all the pluses of being in a relationship." She worried her bottom lip between her teeth, thinking about the hardest part of her plan. "Without, needless to say, letting him know he's in one."

Milo nodded his head, stroking one hand up and down his wide, navy lapel. "Sneaky."

"Strategic," Ivy shot back. Then nibbled a corner off her now lukewarm stack of pancakes. If they were going to continue to shoot her down, she might as well have a full stomach.

Daphne cleared her throat. "Let's get down to brass tacks. What do you need from us? You didn't call us together just to tell us about your dreamy rooftop smooches. How do we figure into your Machiavellian scheme?"

"As little as possible."

"Good. Because, frankly, I'm not entirely on board. I love you like a sister. This plan of yours feels a lot like watching you drive off a cliff with nothing more than a friendly wave."

Better than nothing. At least they weren't flat out refusing to help her anymore. Putting them into a food coma must've helped diminish their resistance. "I'm going into this with my eyes wide open. First of all, I realize there's a chance Ben might end up feeling like he's been played. I don't want any of you implicated. You each have your own existing relationships with Ben, and by extension, RealTV. All I need from you is one thing. And, I might add, the entire plan hinges on it."

"Let me guess, keep our big mouths shut?" asked Milo, miming a zipper pulling across his lips.

"Got it in one. Ben already knows about your running bet about my dates. The last thing I need is for you to tease him." To prevent any possible misunderstanding, she spelled it out for them, ticking off each point on her right hand. "That means no asking him once a week if he's fallen in love yet, or if he's caught me scribbling our names together. No nudges, winks or double entendres. No mention of how I picked out my wedding colors before I picked a college major. Love, lust and Ben are all off limits as conversational topics."

"Which leaves us what, exactly? Politics, weather and religion? Oh, that'll lead to lively discussions over coffee breaks."

Left unchecked, Milo could babble on about his own complicated love life for hours on end. And he once spent fifteen minutes debating the merits of straight leg versus skinny cut jeans. Ivy doubted he'd ever resort to chatting about Democrats or deacons. "I'm sure you'll manage."

"So while we're muzzled, you'll be insinuating yourself into his stone-cold heart how?" Daphne's cocked head, still-crossed arms and overall rigid posture broadcast on all frequencies her ongoing disapproval. Ivy had a strong feeling her roommate would corner her several more times over the next few days to try and change her mind.

"I'm going to coax him into amazing yet subtle dates that will let him experience all the benefits of a real relationship."

"Like what? Sex three times a day?" Milo wiggled his eyebrows and pursed his lips.

Julianna bumped his ribs with her elbow. "She said a *real* relationship, not a *Penthouse Forum* letter."

"No sex," Ivy announced. It killed her, but sometime around four in the morning she'd realized celibacy had to be the linchpin of the entire plan.

Milo's jaw dropped. "What? You might as well try to carve a turkey with an origami knife."

"He's sampled the water, shall we say, and has made it quite clear he wants to make another trip to the well." The raciness—for her—of the euphemism tinged Julianna's cheeks peony pink as she spoke. Ivy thought it might be the most blatantly sexual thing her very uptight assistant had ever said.

Daphne nodded, hard and fast. "You're shooting yourself in the foot. The one thing in the plus column is that Ben's got the raging hot and lustys for you. Why not use your…assets?"

The feeling was mutual. Distracted by his mind-bendingly succulent kisses, Ivy hadn't even noticed when the fireworks display ended. A waitress had finally given Ben a discreet tap on the shoulder to break them up. "Sex messes up the equation. We already know we push all the right buttons in that area. I want to find out what else makes Ben tick. Getting horizontal shifts all the blood south of the belt. In order for this to work, the only organ I need him focused on is his heart."

"In order for this to work, you need a bolt of lightning to strike Ben in the head. A near-death experience is the only way that man will suddenly embrace commitment. But," Daphne unfurled a slow, reluctant smile, "if you get me a hot chocolate to go with extra whipped cream, I promise I'll keep my mouth shut."

"Fair enough." Managing her friends was the easy part. The hard part started in an hour when, on less than two hours sleep, Ivy needed to roll into the office of Aisle Bound and greet Ben with a sparkle and a smile. Not to mention an irresistible date to dangle in front of him. Now to begin learning if he'd rejected *her* on that warm April day, or just relationships in general.

CHAPTER THIRTEEN

It takes as much energy to wish as it does to plan.
                                    —Eleanor Roosevelt

BEN WHISTLED AS he added two more bottles to his iced tea pyramid. It took up the entire coffee table and didn't look anywhere close to stable. But it would surprise the pants off Ivy and her whole team. And a pants-less Ivy, any way he could get her, was exactly what he had in mind.

Ever since they'd kissed on the roof deck two weeks ago, the angry tension between them had disappeared, replaced by an entirely different kind of tension. He wanted her. He craved her. His fingers twitched when-ever she was near, wanting to reach out and touch that satiny skin. Stroke the rounded tops of those sexy breasts she displayed every day in sheer sundresses that drove him wild. Lick the valley between them until her eyes glazed over. Her hands would clutch his head closer, and she'd moan, low and breathy.

Shit. Ben reached down and adjusted his suddenly too-tight cargo shorts. His self control had regressed back to the level of a teenager, getting rock hard at the mere thought of tasting Ivy. And he thought of her all the time. Even at inopportune times, like his early morning racquetball games with Sam and Gib. When her image popped to mind even as he careened off the wall to avoid the slap of Gib's racquet, Ben knew the problem was serious.

She drove him crazy, the way she smelled like sex covered in flower petals, the way she let her silky hair trail over his arm, which made him remember the way it felt trailing down over the rest of his body. If they didn't have sex soon, his insistent cock might rub a hole right through his fly. It leapt to attention the moment she walked into a room. Since they worked together all day and hung out most nights, he lived in a constant state of semi-arousal. He couldn't take it much longer.

"I do so enjoy starting the day with a leisurely ogle of Mr. Tall, Blond and Handsome." Milo swished through the door. Hell, Milo swished more than Ivy and Daphne put together. "It's so nice having eye candy around the office."

"Try not to sexually harass the nice man," Daphne warned. "Or at least not when there's this many witnesses around." Julianna and Ivy entered right behind in a clatter of heels and slapping sandals. This week Ivy's toe nails were painted the same deep red she'd slicked over her lips. They peeked out from under a series of black strips that ended up tying around her ankle like ballet shoes. Which, of course, made him think about untying them, running his hands up her calf, under her floofy black skirt…Damn it. Ben dropped into the wing chair to try and hide his third erection of the morning.

"What's with the coffee table sculpture?" Daphne dropped her bag on the floor and put her hands on her hips. Unlike the other women, whose breezy dresses indicated a full day of consults, her uniform of shorts and a tank top let him know she planned to stay wrists deep in roses and ribbons.

"Ask Ivy," he said with a jerk of his head in her direction.

"I didn't tell you to make…" her voice trailed off. Ivy clapped her hands together and bounced on the balls of her feet. "Oh Ben, it's wonderful! How on earth did you know this is National Iced Tea Month?"

"You're not the only one who knows their way around a search engine." One at a time, he pointed at each row. "There's papaya mango, raspberry, peach, lemon, green, and of course the classic black iced tea. If I missed your favorite flavor, I can get it here by lunch."

"Surprisingly thoughtful," said Julianna, nipping a bottle off the top. "Well done."

He shrugged off the praise. The happiness radiating out of Ivy's golden tinged eyes was thanks enough. "I like working here. Beats being cooped up in my hotel all day with my nose to the grindstone. Just trying to fit in."

Ivy dropped a kiss on the top of his head. Since she'd declared the wacked-out rule that the office had to be a no-make-out zone, Ben assumed his pyramid of plenty was the cause. "You're in a good mood."

"Having a good day. Gib made me run with him at the crack of dawn. Behind all that quiet British politeness, the guy's a hard ass. Says if my shirt isn't wet enough to wring out, haven't gone far enough. Can't wait til we hit July and I sweat through it in half a mile." Ben wasn't at all sure he liked being Gib's personal training mission. Who cared if all this running prevented a heart attack twenty years down the road when his calves ached like a bitch today? "Since I was up, I came in early to edit some scenes from Houston's *Planning for Love*."

Milo stopped checking voice mail, angling the phone away from his ear. "Don't make them more interesting than us," he pleaded with a long, drawn-out whine on the first word.

"Not a chance. Their footage was pretty damn raw. The crew down there put way too many hours in the can. No focal point, no story arc at all."

Julianna sniffed. Actually god-damned sniffed, like he'd farted the words. "Aren't the bride and groom the focal point of each piece?"

One step forward, two steps back. Every time Ben thought he'd thawed the redhead an inch, she slammed right back behind the icy walls of her friggin' fortress of solitude. She'd never forgive him for hurting Ivy. Which meant he had nothing to lose by sniping back at her. "Rookie mistake. People won't tune in week after week to a formulaic, cookie cutter approach to the white dress and the tux. Gotta have a hook."

"You're trying to reduce true love to a sound bite?" Her tone held roughly as much heat as a sun right before it supernovaed. Yet she sat at her desk, outwardly calm, the borderline OCD straightening and restraightening of a stack of contracts the only giveaway of her true feelings.

"Don't give me that knee-jerk negative spin on my job." Ivy laid a hand on his shoulder. She didn't say anything, but the soft touch reminded him it wouldn't further his cause any to go ten rounds with her treasured assistant. Since Julianna made herself invaluable to Ivy on a daily basis, he'd force himself to play nice.

As long as he didn't have to *mean* it. "What if you try and come at it from a different direction?"

One eyebrow the color of cinnamon candy arched high enough to buttress a cathedral. "Such as?"

"I give people a reason to tune in, by making happily ever after accessible to the non hearts and flowers masses."

Milo swiped his finger down an imaginary scoreboard. "Touché. Camera guy one, Aisle Bound nada."

It might be as useful as talking to a turnip, but knowing Julianna wouldn't listen didn't stop Ben from hoisting the flag on his favorite topic. "Documentary filmmaking is all about making people care about real life. Opening a window to a slice of life they might not know about. Or bother to care about. If I do my job right, I'll coerce them into caring. It's heady stuff."

Ivy perched on the coffee table in front of him. "See? You've got this impassive outer shell, but deep down, you're filled with passion. Except that instead of my obsession with love and romance, your passion is wrapped around filmmaking."

He swatted at the finger she waved in a lazy circle in front of his nose. "Cut it out. Makes it sound like I've got some weird sexual fetish."

"I mean it. You're so passionate about capturing life with a camera, you're like a thousand-year-old volcano ready to blow."

"You really think talking about flowing hot lava about to erupt makes your argument sound any less sexual?"

"What happened to the office being a no-foreplay zone?" Daphne's huffy voice preceded her down the hall. She brandished stripping shears in one hand and a bunch of fluffy white things in the other. "All the steam you two are generating is going to prematurely open my entire order of Asiatic lilies. The Yamamoto wedding's not until Saturday, so cool it!"

Ben wiggled his hands in the air. "Nobody's naked, and my hands are empty. To me, that sadly indicates I'm not getting any action. So why don't *you* chill, Lovell."

Milo shoved back from the desk. His chair banged into the wall as he bolted out of his seat. "Excuse me, but I need to interrupt your petty bickering."

"Attitude check for a certain office manager." Ivy crossed her arms and stared him down. His cheeks flushed to match the cherries printed on today's ridiculous vest. A single, tiny red bunch clustered out of his buttonhole. "Milo, why so snarky?"

He ducked his head. "I'm sorry, but we've got a code red on our hands. Emergency extraordinaire. Catastrophic crisis."

"What's wrong, Milo?" Ben leaned around the side of the chair for a better view. Guy probably broke a nail. He actually kept a manicure set in his top desk drawer. "Did ya miss an opportunity to ogle George Clooney in person when he buzzed through town yesterday to visit Oprah?"

"Before we sink deep into the quagmire that is Milo's dating history, I need to update you all on today's appointments." Julianna gingerly settled her phone into the cradle. "We've had two cancellations for this afternoon, both from potential clients. And one more cancellation for Friday."

Daphne cocked her head to the side. "What's going on? We haven't had this many holes in the schedule since the swine flu epidemic a few years ago."

Ivy shuddered, bumped Daphne with her shoulder. "Don't even say those words out loud. We can't afford to get so much as hay fever—this is our busiest season."

"Apparently not this week," said Ben. His comment earned him a trio of glowers from the women. "Geez, lighten up, ladies. You're not going to go under because of three missing appointments." This time he provoked an eye roll from Daphne.

"Obviously you don't know the nail-biting fear of owning a business. Think about it—we don't get a lot of repeat customers in our line of work. We scratch and claw to put every single name in our books."

"And we will continue to do so," said Ivy, a stubborn set to her jaw. "So Julianna, do your best to reschedule the consults. Then check the news to see if there's been an outbreak of food poisoning. There must be some reason behind this rash of cancellations."

"Oh, I know exactly where to point the finger." Milo moved out from behind his desk to claim the floor. "I just listened to seven straight calls from vendors. All royally pissed and using language that would make a sailor blush. Photos by Frank, Swing Time, Essential Sounds, the Bridal Bower. The little old lady who runs Sweet Confections has got some mouth on her. I tried to tell you, we're in the middle of a situation with a capital S. The common theme in all the messages is betrayal."

Uh oh. Ben flashed on a probable cause, and it meant he'd be persona non grata in about two minutes. If right, his chances of getting back into Ivy's panties would be nonexistent.

Ivy crinkled her brows together. "What on earth are they upset about?"

"The first commercial for your episode of *Wild Wed-*

ding Smackdown ran last night. They've got a three-second shot of you standing next to a sopping wet guy in a tux with a pissed-looking bride in the background."

Ivy winced. "The idiot ring bearer who parachuted into the pond."

"He's dressed like a groom, so people assume the worst." Daphne pressed the back of her hand against her forehead, as though trying to press out a headache. "Damn it. That show is a train wreck. Everyone on it comes out looking like an idiot. By association, all the vendors we use are worried about the fallout. What if they stop recommending us? Take our link off their websites? They probably all think you asked to be on that show."

"How many times do we have to go over this?" Ivy began to pace between the front door and the hallway to her office in a slow circle. "I didn't have a choice. By the time I discovered we'd be filmed, the only way out would've been to break our contract with the bride and groom. On their wedding day. Do I really need to spell it out? How much that simply was not an option?"

A beat of silence, electric with simmering tension. "Maybe you do."

Ivy stopped mid-turn, bobbling on her ice-pick heels. "Seriously, Daph? We'd be a sitting duck for potential litigation. There isn't an escape clause in our contract that covers smarmy, trash television taping. Not to mention we don't work that way. Our job is to iron out any wrinkles in the wedding day, not create one."

Another long beat. Then Daphne ran a quick hand of apology down Ivy's arm. "You're right. You were thrust into an untenable position. I'm sorry—I just so badly want to throw heaping shovelfuls of blame on *somebody*."

Ben didn't need to physically see a lynch mob to know one was forming. With his name on the noose. He was nothing more than a living, breathing symbol of the one thing currently threatening Aisle Bound—reality television. Sure enough, before he could beat a hasty retreat out the front door, Milo and Julianna stalked forward. They stopped on the opposite side of the table. Ivy and Daphne flanked his chair.

"What did you do?" Ivy asked, arms akimbo.

As expected, they wanted to make him the fall guy. Well, fat chance. "Nothing, I swear. For God's sake, I didn't edit the piece. I had no input on the finished product—and no idea what it looks like. Don't dump this on my lap. Just because I'm here doesn't mean you can poke me with a stick. Remember, I left True Life Productions. I've got no ties to that crap pile of a show."

Glossy red lips pursed together, then thinned into a straight line. Turning on her heel, Ivy clattered away toward her office. Halfway there, she paused and wordlessly jerked her chin to indicate he should follow. Ben gave a fleeting glance at the front door and the freedom that lay beyond it. But he knew his only chance of getting back in Ivy's good graces relied on not making a break for it.

She waited, arms crossed and sparks all but leaping out of her eyes, until he shut the door behind him. Ben dropped into a chair, slouched with legs crossed at the ankles. No damn way would he stand there and be lectured, metaphorical hat in hand. He'd listen to her grievances, but he wouldn't roll over.

"Did I not tell you from the start that being on that

damn show petrified me? That it could sink my business? Six years of blood, sweat and tears leveled by a single, half-hour reality TV schlockfest!" She raised her arms to the sides in an unspoken plea. "Running a business encompasses more than showing up and doing the work. It is a responsibility. I provide a livelihood for everyone who works at Aisle Bound. I have a partner, full-time employees, the team of part timers that helps Daphne, and our interns all depending on me to put a paycheck in front of them every two weeks."

Ivy dropped her arms to hang limply at her sides. For a moment, Ben thought she might be winding down. No such luck. She sat behind her desk, lining up folders and pencils and paper clips with laser-sharp precision. Without looking up, she plowed ahead.

"Oh, not to mention we currently have more than eighty active contracts." Picking up an old-fashioned fountain pen, she jammed it into her blotter with each sentence. "Contracts which stipulate I am obligated to supply vendors, even *if* I'm blacklisted by every band and bakery and photographer in Chicago. Contracts with brides who need and expect my help. Brides who are counting on me!" The nib broke off under the unforgiving pressure of Ivy's white-knuckled grip. A small puddle of violet ink spread across the blotter.

Ben expected her to be pissy. Bust his balls a little. He hadn't expected her to completely lose her cool. Interesting to watch. Made him a little amused, and, damn it, a little aroused. To top it off, he was very fearful the waterworks would start to flow any second. "Are you done?"

She siphoned a long, slow breath. "Yes. I think I got it all out."

"You sure? I'm not letting you go back out there until you're the uber-annoyingly calm planner I've come to admire."

"Calm enough to fake it, anyway."

"Hmm." Ben uncrossed his legs, braced his palms on the desk and leaned forward. "Are you honestly mad at me, or am I just a handy whipping boy?"

A corner of her mouth tilted up, but her eyes were still a flat, brownish gold. Anger muddied away all the sparkling green flecks. They were almost the same color as the candied ginger he ate by the handful on airplanes to prevent motion sickness. "Do I have to choose?"

"Yes. Forget about your business. Forget about the people who used to sign my paycheck and their stupid editing. It boils down to trust." Ivy didn't get to be the only one on a high horse. Suddenly Ben's gut churned. Where did she get off blaming him? Anger propelled him to his feet. Using his foot, he spun her chair to the side. With one hand planted on the backrest, he used the other to tilt her chin up to look at him. To see him as a person, not a representation of a faceless company.

"In your heart, do you believe I'd do anything to portray you in a negative light? That I'd sacrifice my integrity? Slant my taping to portray anything less than the truth of the moment?"

Ivy's lips parted, like an overripe strawberry falling open, but no zippy retort came out. Ever so slowly, she moved her head side to side. As she shook out the answer he'd hoped for, her eyes brightened with unshed tears. Because of him? Because of what he'd said? The situation? Whatever the reason, he couldn't bear it. Ben dropped to one knee and brought his hands around to cup her face. He wanted to be gentle, to reassure. But the moment he covered those juicy lips, all semblance of restraint disappeared.

Sweet, pliable and oh so supple, Ivy kissed him back with equal fervor. It felt like she channeled all her worry and frustration into pure, physical passion. No hesitation, no lingering coldness. She met his tongue, stroke for stroke. Flinging both arms around his neck, she pressed her tight little body against him, toppling them both to the ground. Even though a corner of the file cabinet bit into the top of his head, Ben forgot they were in her office. Forgot there were three people just down the hall, waiting for the two of them to come back out. Everything slipped away except for the warm, soft weight of Ivy stretched on top of him. The sensation was like having champagne poured directly into his soul.

Ben's eyes flew open. What a fucking horrible, girly, romantic thought. A tiny part of his brain must've gone rogue. His dick might be hard as a drive shaft at the moment, but a few grey cells had gone unaccountably softer than a moldy hot dog. Gently he pushed at Ivy's shoulders to break the kiss. She sat astride him, loose skirt gathered almost to her panty line. Hair mussed, lips puffy and eyes at half mast, she was the poster child for an office quickie. Beautiful and desirable, Ben wanted nothing more than to crab-walk backward to put some distance between them until his romance outbreak passed. Who knew what he'd do or say while under its infectious influence?

"You're right. You were a convenient target, and I shouldn't have directed my anger at you. I'm sorry, Ben."

"Yeah—I got that message loud and clear from your frontal assault."

Ivy wriggled off of him, flashing an impressive amount of creamy thigh in the process. "A singular aberration, trust me. A response to extreme emotional distress. My no-fooling-around-in-the-office rule still stands." She stood and smoothed the creases out of her silky white top. "And don't think you can pick a fight just to get me fired up in the hopes of scoring in the supply closet. You may be wily, but I'm a certified planner. I'll always be one step ahead of you."

"Challenge accepted."

A sharp trio of knocks didn't give Ben any time to get up before Daphne cracked the door and stuck her head through. "Everyone good in here?" A wide smile brightened her face as she took in Ben sprawled across the floor. "Ah. I'd say somebody's been very good."

Slipping inside, she shut the door and circled the opposite end of the desk from Ben. "I didn't realize bedhead was this month's new style trend." Daphne tugged Ivy's crooked black bow all the way off her head, and then fluffed the rest of her disheveled hair. "But if you want my opinion, this look goes better with trampy lingerie than your Talbot's blouse."

Ivy snatched back her ribbon. "Did you have a specific reason to interrupt my...meeting with Ben?"

"Wow. A meeting? Seriously? Is that what you're calling this?" A lazy wave of her hand encompassed Ben and all that his current position implied. "Could you get Milo to put a few of these special 'meetings' on my calendar? As partners, we're supposed to equally shoulder all the burdens of running this place. Too many meetings," she put the word in air quotes, "are bound to wear you out."

"I believe RealTV's contract stipulates my point of contact solely as Ms. Rhodes." Ben got to his feet. He slung an arm around Daphne's shoulder and winked at Ivy. "But I could be amenable to the idea of two beautiful women fighting over me."

"Eww. Only in your dreams, Westcott." Daphne shrugged him off. "Okay, back to business. Believe it or not, today's cancellations may be a blessing in disguise, because you need to drop everything and go meet Sam."

"Does he have a cake emergency?" Ben only allowed himself to sample the fluffy pastries at Sam's bakery on the days he ran. Coupled with the multiple slices of wedding cake he managed to snag every weekend, he figured he'd upped his sugar quotient by about nine zillion percent since coming to Chicago. If he couldn't sink himself into Ivy right now, he could at least sink his teeth into something sweet, rich and covered in icing. "I'm willing to throw myself on the sword if he needs someone to test a new flavor. Or even eat leftovers. The man's a freaking magician with chocolate."

"Ivy, Sam says that movers came this morning to the shop next to Lyons Bakery." Moving behind Ivy, Daphne finger combed her hair and neatly retied the bow. Blouse retucked and hair neat once more, all evidence of Ben's momentary lapse into gooey-heartedness erased. "They cleared the place out and left a For Rent sign in the window. He already called the agent and asked her to give you first dibs. You can go check it out right now."

"Where the tea shop used to be?"

Daphne nodded. "It's the perfect size and perfect location. Go find out if the price is right, and you just might have yourself a storefront by lunch."

Their conversation didn't make a lick of sense to Ben. "Are you moving?"

"Expanding," Ivy said with a mysterious eyebrow waggle.

How could a wedding planner expand? Maybe try the opposite end of the spectrum and plan really snazzy funerals? "I have no idea what that means, but I bet it'll make for a compelling segment. I'll call Ollie and have him meet us over there."

"Great idea. If this pans out, it'll be a historic day for Ivy. She'll want it commemorated."

Ivy *excited* about being followed around by cameras? Ben knew she tolerated their presence, at best—most likely due to the big fat check she'd get in a few months from RealTV—but he couldn't imagine what she'd want filmed. Just when he thought he had a handle on her, another surprising layer metamorphosed. He looked forward to finding out what else motivated her beyond spreading squishy romance around the city like peanut butter on toast.

CHAPTER FOURTEEN

A good marriage is the union of two good forgivers.

—Ruth Bell Graham

"I WANT TO spread romance all across the city of Chicago, into every nook and cranny," said Ivy.

Astonished at the naiveté of Ivy's statement, Ben almost stopped in his tracks in the middle of the street. The only thing that propelled him forward was the certainty that the crazy Chicago drivers wouldn't bother to slow down, or even swerve around him. He hustled across Armitage to confront Ivy from the relative safety of the sidewalk. Traffic had trapped Ollie on the opposite corner, so he jerked his thumb to indicate their direction. "That's your business plan? To ooze romance? Bet it's hard to get banks to back you with that kind of mission statement."

"Not everyone is as cynical and stone-hearted as you. Or rather, as you claim to be."

"What makes you think people even want you oozing all over them?"

"It's not about want, Ben. It's about need. And yes, a lot of people out there need more romance in their lives."

The warm scent of chocolate packed a visceral

punch. Such a rich aroma, Ben imagined it coalescing into a physical being. Using its dark might to lure him across the threshold of Lyons Bakery, where he would willingly surrender for just one bite.

Unbelievable. Now he was ready to make love to a cloud of cocoa powder. If he didn't have sex with Ivy soon, he'd crack up. Go literally insane with need. It reminded him of being back in high school and trying to round the sexual bases. When he'd gotten her stripped down to her bra on a Tuesday, Ben assumed they would progress from there on Wednesday.

No such luck. Generous with her kisses, Ivy made him work for a glimpse of skin. Sure, he enjoyed the long make-out sessions. She kissed like a dream. What little he'd recently seen of her breasts, coupled with Technicolor memories of their marathon night in April, drove him to distraction. Constant distraction. All he could think about was how to overcome her surprising reticence to climb back into his bed. The non-stop desire must be fuzzing his brain, since Ben still had no idea why she wanted a storefront.

"So you're opening—what—a dating service?"

She gasped. "Not in a million years. The fear of not finding true love for every client would keep me awake at night. What a horrible responsibility to shoulder."

"Then explain why we're here, before I throw myself through the window next door onto that German chocolate cake I see." Seriously, how could Sam work all day surrounded by such deliciousness? If it were Ben's bakery, he'd have all the profits eaten by lunchtime.

Ivy cupped her hands to peer through the glass. "Do you see the kitchen area, in the back? With the long counters? Oh, and they left all the shelves on the wall. This is absolutely perfect."

"For what?"

When Ivy turned around, her professional mask of calm slipped once more into place. The excitement dropped out of her voice, replaced by a calm recitation. He could almost see the neat pages of a business plan lined up in her brain. "I'm opening a store. Greeting cards, whimsical tokens of love. One-stop romance. Something for first dates, anniversaries and every occasion in between."

"A romance store?" Was it a euphemism? She couldn't mean a sex toys shop, could she?

"I'm calling it A Fine Romance. Might as well make it easy for customers to know what we're about, right?" Ivy tugged at his shirt to pull him closer to the smeared window. "See the counter?"

"All I see are shadows."

"Doesn't matter. The realtor should be here soon, and I can show you. In the back will be all the ingredients for the perfect spontaneous picnic; wine, cheese, bread. Well, the wine depends on getting the right licenses, but I don't have to worry about that right now. Picnic baskets, blankets, wine glasses, vases, with all the inventory in a range of prices. Best of all, a full line of gourmet truffles. Nothing is as versatile as chocolate. It can say *Be Mine* and *I'm sorry* and *I love you*."

"Can it say *let me strip off all your clothes*?"

"Without a doubt."

Wow. He'd expected to shock her into silence. Instead, she met him toe to toe. He'd gotten a nice dose of sass. Ivy kept surprising him; her whole store concept being yet another example. "This isn't a spontaneous decision, is it? You've put a lot of thought into this concept."

"I've been planning it, in the back of my mind, for years. The store is why I agreed to be filmed for *Planning for Love*. It's providing the seed money I need to get it up and running."

And there was the searchlight-bright, gaping hole in her plan. "You already work crazy hours. How do you expect to run another full-time business? Is cloning yourself next on your agenda?"

Ivy waved to Ollie as he trundled up the sidewalk. "I'm ambitious, not suicidal. The idea is my baby. The execution is somebody else's headache. Hiring the perfect manager is the key to success, and I've already got someone in mind."

Naturally. Ben flicked on the camera. "Is there anything you haven't planned to the nth degree?"

"Nope."

"No stretch to say you and I are on opposite ends of the romance spectrum. Do you really believe there are enough people in the middle to keep you in business?"

"Absolutely. Don't worry, I've got a doozy of a business plan to back up my assertion."

"I should've known."

"Pages and pages of facts and figures. Hopes and dreams encapsulated in pie charts and bar graphs." Ivy worried the ends of a wide sash through her fingers. "If I sign this lease today, there's no turning back. Rent, another business license, inventory. Cross my fingers that my dream pick for a manger is both available and interested. I should call her today. I should really call right now."

"Whoa there. Breathe. Even you can't do everything in the next five minutes."

"I know. Especially with four weddings staring me in the face this weekend."

"You mean you forgot to schedule an extra hour to launch a new business? Talk about an oversight."

A pretty pink flush stained Ivy's cheeks. Bright green sparkled pinwheels in her eyes. A vivid personification of excitement, she also had the look of a woman in the throes of mind-bendingly hot sex. He remembered that look. Craved to see it again while they were both naked, not standing on a sidewalk surrounded by cameras.

His phone rang. He thrust the camera at Ollie. His sister's face flashed across the screen of his smart phone. Hoping the constant drone of traffic would deter a long conversation, he put her on speaker phone. "Hi, Belinda."

"No time for chit chat. Get your crap out of my apartment once and for all."

"So nice to hear your voice." His parents received quarterly duty calls, an arrangement he'd agreed to when he'd been covering war zones. His sister, on the other hand, hadn't spoken to him in almost six months. She'd been so bitchy the last time they spoke, he didn't bother to bunk with her during his last break between shows. Better to sleep on his buddy's couch in Brooklyn than to put up with her attitude souring his cereal milk. Given the craptastic level of her mood, he'd guess her latest guy just kicked her to the curb. Didn't know his name, or the last guy's, for that matter, but he didn't need to. Rich, vapid and willing to parade Belinda through the top echelons of New York society. Each one completely interchangeable.

"Bennett, I've hauled your meager collection of belongings along on eleven moves. I'm sick and tired of moving it in circles around Manhattan."

"Funny, I thought you'd be sick of the stupidity of moving in with every man who blinks at you twice. If you spent the time to get to know these rubes, you might last longer than a month."

Her voice doubled in volume and intensity. Even as he winced, Ben took a second to appreciate the clarity of his phone's speaker. "It took me three months to kick Lars to the curb, thank you very much. And you're the last person on earth—besides our parents—qualified to give any relationship advice. You've been in Chicago for what now, four weeks? How many of those Midwestern farmer's daughters have you bagged and tagged? Six? Or are you up to double digits with the easy pickings of bridesmaids parading in front of you every week?"

Staring straight down at a weed growing up from a crack in the cement, Ben knew Ivy and Ollie had to be looking at him, sharing his embarrassment. He lifted the phone to his ear and moved down several paces. The window display at the bakery just might give him the moral restraint needed not to chuck the phone in the gutter. If he stayed civil and finished the conversation with Belinda, he'd reward himself with a slice of the German chocolate cake. Eight layers of coconut, fudge and booze-soaked cherries would be a good start. A year ago, he'd have started with a fifth of whiskey. Chicago had softened him. But he couldn't let his sister know. In his family, the best defense was a good offense.

"Did this scumbag cheat on you?" he asked. He and Belinda were far from close. Still, her strident assumptions verged on rude, even for her. Given her horrendous history with the opposite sex, he'd put good money on a bad breakup as the cause for her foul mood. "Or worse, refuse to pay your latest bill at Tiffany's? Because you sound pretty riled up, Lindy. Come on, you don't want to pick a fight with me. You want to go give this Lars guy a swift kick in the nuts."

A low, throaty chuckle burbled into his ear. "You see right through me. And I poured an entire bottle of Cristal over his head at Donald Trump's cocktail party last night. The public shaming is punishment enough."

Good. He'd flicked her mood swing switch. Maybe now she wouldn't bite his head off. "I apologize yet again, on behalf of my entire race. Men are pigs."

"On that we will always agree. You and I both stand firmly on the side of happily *never* after. So you can imagine my surprise when Mother mentioned you're working on a show about marriage, of all things?"

"Weddings," he swiftly corrected. Big, loud, fun parties. Not the twenty years to life implied by marriage.

Belinda sucked in a whistled breath. "Even worse. Aren't you worried the Westcott curse will rub off on all those bright-eyed, bushy-tailed couples?"

Only a little bit. The greater fear lay in Ivy's reaction if he breathed a word of it to her. No doubt in his mind that she subscribed to every wedding superstition out there, and took them all as seriously as a heart attack. If she learned her perfectly planned weddings had been tainted by a man genetically cursed to resist lasting relationships, she'd probably kick him off the shoot. Worse yet, then his chances of stealing more kisses would undoubtedly slip to less than the proverbial snowball's chance in hell. "It's a family curse, not smallpox. I don't think it's contagious."

"I suppose we'll find out in six months, give or take. Watch out—you don't want all those disillusioned couples to sue you for cause when their marriages break up one by one."

An icy cold shard of fear speared up his spine and lodged in the very front of his mind. In today's overly litigious society, Lindy's teasing threat had a better than average chance of coming true. After his time spent as a nationwide laughingstock after being branded the Cowering Cameraman, he knew the press would froth at the mouth with excitement if they could plant a new title on him. Something like the Wedding Wrecker. Or the Marriage Miscreant. Nah, too highbrow to make a good headline. "Not funny. Not even a little bit."

"Consider yourself warned. Don't look to me to help pay a lawyer's retainer when it happens. Now, I don't intend to waste space in a very expensive moving truck even one more time. You're a grown up, so act like one, and take responsibility for your own things. Can I ship it all to Chicago?"

Had she lost her mind? "Hell, no. This gig in Chicago is only temporary."

"I thought you were there for two months with this fancy promotion. After ten years of bopping around the entire globe on a daily or weekly basis, it sure sounds permanent enough to me."

Funny. He'd been thinking the same thing recently. Not that he'd done anything crazy like actually unpack. "Slow down. I don't know yet where I'll be based. There's a chance RealTV will force me to stay put in one city, and an almost equal chance they'll let me keep wandering. If I want to, that is."

"Excuse me? You, of all people, don't know what you want?" She let silence thicken the air like a wintery London fog to drive her point home. Unnecessary, of course. Ben knew it sounded ridiculous as soon as the words left his mouth. He might not have always been dealt the ideal cards in life, but he'd always known what to do with them. Until now.

"That's not the Bennett I know. You don't dither about anything. And you hate to be tied down. So pick a city with good restaurants and pretty women, and start there. If you don't like it, move on in a week, a month, whatever. Why are you hung up on something so simple?"

Why did Belinda ignore him for half a year, and suddenly have the urge—and the perception—to psychoanalyze him? While he dripped sweat on a street corner, half-deafened by traffic and half-asphyxiated from exhaust fumes? If he dodged answering, she'd get even more interested and call him daily, hammering away until he finally cracked. Easier to tell her now and get it over with, like ripping off a bandage with a single, swift yank.

"Figuring out a place to hang my hat isn't the problem." Chicago suited him just fine. Good vibe, great food and one woman in particular prettier than all the rest. That is, if somebody put his feet to the fire and made him choose. Which he'd never, ever willingly do. "Look, I've faced reality. I know I'm never going to get my old career back. After everyone in the business laughed in my face, it didn't take long to realize I was done."

"Washed up," Belinda suggested, oh-so-helpfully.

"Sure. Rub salt in my flayed and bleeding emotional wound."

"Reality can be a hard pill to swallow. Best not to candy coat it, because false hope can be toxic."

No worries on that particular point. When it came to his career, he and hope had parted ways awhile ago. "Even though I know it's stupid, I feel like I'm completely shutting the door on my old life if I put down roots. Here or anywhere."

Belinda gave a delicate snort. "Renting an apartment isn't putting down roots. You're not the kind of guy who'll ever settle down. Why worry about changing your spots when you're perfectly happy as is?"

"Am I? I'm not sure anymore." Ben watched a chunky woman in a brown suit extend first her hand, then a business card to Ivy. At the same time, the door next to him clanged open. Sam came out, clapping a cloud of flour from his hands. A round of hugs ensued before what he assumed to be the leasing agent unlocked the empty space. Ollie darted through first, probably hoping to get the money shot of Ivy's face lighting up as she took in the breadth of the potential store. Sam lingered in the doorway, thumb tucked into his half-apron. A sideways jerk of his head indicated Ben should join them. In that instant, Ben hated being on the outside, recording other people's moments. He wanted, no, he needed to be inside with Ivy, sharing in her infectious delight at the platter of possibilities which lay before her.

"Lindy, keep the trunk. Better yet, stick it in a cab

and send it COD to Dad's office. I'm sure his secretary will figure out a place for it. And let's try something crazy, like talking again before the seasons change." He clicked off without giving her a chance to refuse. The slab of cake would have to wait. The celebration of Ivy's new business venture struck him as the perfect opportunity to back her into a corner and kiss her speechless. Why worry about the murky future when his present sparkled with the near certainty of sweet smooches?

"Isn't it hard to eat cake when you're using both hands to text?" Ben asked pointedly. He'd been jonesing for his reward slice for more than two hours now. Ivy had taken forever with the leasing agent, inspecting every nook and cranny, every outlet, and a bump in the floor Ben couldn't even feel.

Great to share her excitement, sure—for about half an hour. After that, the joy got smothered by the oppressive tedium of her, well, to be polite he'd call it attention to detail. But he wanted to call it finickiness. An important quality in a business owner, but boring as hell to watch. The lack of action left him way too much open brain space to think about the conversation with Belinda. Her words had picked at the scabs of one too many tender spots in his psyche. Casting about for anything to distract him, he focused on the multilayered goodness of the German chocolate cake right next door. But he couldn't dive in until Ivy dropped the phone and picked up her fork.

"Sorry, but this is an emergency." She poked at one last button, then raised her hands with a flourish. "Done. Now I'm scheduled to chat with Mira tonight."

"You schedule your girlfriend chats? Would the world stop turning if you waited an extra day to discuss the latest cast-off from *The Bachelor*'s 'most dramatic rose ceremony ever'?"

Her eyebrows drew together into a vee of displeasure. "First of all, I'm only hooked on *The Bachelorette*. Seeing the choices controlled by a woman is much more compelling television. Besides, we keep up with our crucial comments by live-streaming them on Facebook during the show."

Funny. Guess the sexes weren't so opposite when it came to social media. "I do that with baseball games," he admitted. "It's the next best thing to sitting next to your buddies getting rowdy at a game."

"Furthermore, I scheduled a business chat with Mira. If it goes well, I'm going to make her the manager of A Fine Romance."

"Bold move. The ink isn't even dry on the lease, and you're already hiring employees?"

"As you pointed out, this is my busy season. I loved creating the concept of A Fine Romance, but execution is a whole different animal. I need someone I trust to make my dream a reality. With the lease signed and a very large deposit dropped, the whole project has to fast forward. My seed money gets eaten up by the rent every single day. Inventory's got to be collected at the speed of light. The plan is for the store to open in September."

"Wow. Fast."

"Yes. Hard, but doable. I've crunched numbers into more shapes than a protractor, and the most financially viable operating plan hinges on the doors opening within no more than three months."

"This Mira better be tough to survive the gift shop boot camp you've envisioned."

"She's the best. We went to grad school together. Mira's work ethic matched mine. Every once in a while, I have to admit, she'd even put me to shame with the scope of her projects and crazy hours. Stubborn, driven and smart as a whip."

"That description makes her sound like your twin. Well, if you add gorgeous and sexy. Couldn't describe you and leave those words out."

Halfway to her mouth, Ivy's fork stalled. She blinked slowly, twice, shuttering away whatever swirled in her hazel eyes. Then she popped in the bite of cake, and licked the frosting off each tine. "I tend not to think about my friends' sexy quotient. But now that you mention it, she does have amazing breasts. Thanks for reminding me. I'll mention it to her tonight, to give her a little ego boost. A compliment like that is sure to seal the deal."

"Smart ass." She kept surprising him, like complex layers of flavor in a well-aged wine. "Your paragon of virtue isn't the only one who can help get your store open on schedule."

"Trust me, I'll take any help with open arms. What did you have in mind?"

Ben had been waiting for just such an opening to drop this bombshell. Hopefully he could spin it well, before she got the chance to machine gun off an automatic no. "An interview. A live interview, to be exact."

She cut another bite, eyes now focused on the cake. Hiding her well-merited suspicion, perhaps? "For what?"

"A reporter called a few times last week. I told the

big bosses about it, and they were mulling the pros and cons of having you do a sit down with her."

The slow licking of each tine that drove him crazy recommenced. "Why would anyone want to talk to me?"

"Remember that pesky commercial that aired last night? Your *Wild Wedding Smackdown* episode?"

"No. I mean yes, of course I'm aware that damn episode is about to run. But no, I won't do an interview about it. Absolutely not."

"Use good publicity to fight the bad. In an interview, you can tell your version. And if we make it a live interview, they can't mess with your words in editing."

Ivy still wouldn't meet his eyes, fixating on a point somewhere up by a row of antique copper baking molds hanging from the ceiling. "I'm not a fan of the old cliché that all exposure is good. The cancellations this morning prove that bad press is just plain bad. My plan is to let the whole thing blow over as quickly and quietly as possible."

Sometimes, it sucked to be right. He'd warned the RealTV executives her reaction would be, at best, a resounding no. And now the thankless job of forcing her to change her mind fell to Ben. "You can use it to your advantage. The timing couldn't be better. Give them a quick sound bite on *WWS*, and then segue to talk about the amazing store you'll open in a few months. Great publicity. More importantly, free publicity. Who in their right mind could turn that down?"

"Then I guess you should order me a straitjacket in pale pink, because I still say no." Now, finally, she looked him head-on. And there was no mistaking the stubborn jut to her jaw or the glint of battle in

her changeable eyes. Ben would admire her passionate determination—if only it wasn't presently aimed at
him like a World War II howitzer. "I won't talk badly
about my bride. The only way to explain my presence
on *WWS* is to throw Tracy under the bus for not letting me know ahead of time. Which leaves me with
nothing to say."

Damn her moral compass with its permanent setting to true north. The conversation with Belinda had
used up his entire quotient of emotional drama for the
week. He didn't have the stomach for fighting with Ivy.
Especially not about work. Last night Ivy mentioned a
trip to a drive-in movie theater in the offing. A tub of
buttered popcorn, seats that reclined, and the chance
to kiss his way underneath Ivy's top. It sounded like
the perfect night to Ben. But chances were good she
wouldn't be in the mood to park if he pissed her off over
a three-minute sound bite on the local news.

Unfortunately, the people who signed his paycheck—significantly larger now with his new producing duties—cared only about results. Ben's lack of
action between the sheets didn't figure into their reams
of spreadsheets. He looked up, and caught Sam giving
him the fish eye from behind the counter. Ever in protective friend mode, the guy could probably tell Ben
was pissing Ivy off. If they were in a cartoon, there'd be
steam coming out of her ears right about now. Or was
Sam worried their difference of opinion would upset
the other customers? The elderly woman at the table
next to them had raised her copy of the *Tribune* into a
protective shield as Ivy's voice increased in both volume and intensity.

Ben's spine stiffened. Either way, he sure as hell

wouldn't let some apron-clad man rolling out cookie dough intimidate him. Or influence how he did his job. Ivy might want to play hardball, but she clearly didn't realize Ben held all the cards. Or some better cliché that didn't mix metaphors. "Look, we're both pussyfooting around the obvious."

"Which is?"

Her arch tone pushed him too far. "You're doing the interview. Bottom line. You can huff and puff all you want, but you'll put that sweet little butt of yours in a chair across from whatever anchor I say."

She started to stand, then thought better of it and sank back down. Instead, she settled for balling up her napkin tight enough to hurl across home plate. "Perhaps I missed a memo. Who died and made you my keeper?" she hissed.

"You did," he lobbed back. Ben pushed his plate out of the way and leaned forward, elbows on the table. "The moment you signed the contract with RealTV."

Ivy stabbed her index finger into the air. "Exactly. I'm contracted with RealTV, *not* with you. I'm quite sure your job is to record my daily life, not interfere in it."

Why did she have to be so stubborn? Time to play his ace in the hole. "Nice try, but I'm not just a cameraman you can push around anymore. Think of me as the living, breathing manifestation of that multi-page contract you signed. The one where it stipulated you would do any and all press requested to promote *Planning for Love*."

Her lips firmed into a thin red line. He could almost see her mentally flipping through the pages of legalese, looking for a loophole. "But you said the reporter wanted to interview me about *WWS*?"

"Yup. But the same opportunity to garner free publicity for your new store gives us the chance for some free publicity for *Planning for Love*. Once the camera is on, you can steer the interview to hype your new, exciting, happily-ever-after show. No way can we let you turn your back on a lucky break like this." Fingers steepled, he cocked his head. "You did read every line of the contract, didn't you? A savvy businesswoman like yourself?"

"Of course I read it," she huffed. "As did Daphne. As did our lawyers. I'm fully aware of the section you're referencing." Deflating a bit, she hunched her back and hugged her arms. "I simply didn't think it applied in this particular case. Or that you'd be unfeeling enough to put it to the test." Ivy's gaze raked him from head to toe, then back again. "On second thought, I should've known better."

Low blow. Not entirely unfair, but still a hit below the belt. Especially from the saccharine sweet Ms. Rhodes. But if she thought he could be manipulated just because they'd spent twenty minutes making out in the office storage closet after hours yesterday, she'd better think again.

"Don't. Don't make this personal. Whatever we have going on now, whatever happened between us in the past, has nothing to do with the situation at hand. Nothing, do you hear me?" He slammed his hand flat on the table, making the plates jump. Ivy stayed stock still, except for a twitch in her clenched jaw. "This is business. This is my livelihood, or what's left of it, at any rate. Do I like putting the screws to you? Hell, no. Did I fight with our marketing director about it? Damn straight. But am I willing to risk my job over it? Or watch you get sued for breach of contract? No freaking way."

A beat of silence, quiet enough to hear the rhythmic, sticky slap of Sam's rolling pin against dough. Their table neighbor had lowered her paper, now unabashedly watching Ben and Ivy fight it out. Ben white knuckled the edges of the table. When she accused him of being unfeeling, it was nothing he hadn't already turned a deaf ear to from dozens of women over the years.

But this time the words carried a painful sting, and drove him to a rare level of honesty that he already regretted. And he had no idea how Ivy would react. Part of him braced, expecting her glass of water to splash his face in about a nanosecond. Another part envisioned her storming out the door. Guess the next five minutes didn't matter, as long as she agreed to do the interview, right?

Right on cue, Ivy reached for her glass. Ben flinched. But all she did was trace a line through the drops of condensation beading along the bottom edge. "You really fought for me?" she asked in a small, surprised voice.

Really? That's what she took away from a near epic loss of his trademark cool attitude? "You bet." Ben wasn't sure who he astonished more with that revelation—Ivy or himself. Better drive his point home while he had the advantage. "Concentrate on the silver lining of Tracy and Seth's event. You're good at that, right?" The woman could bottle her oddly unquenchable positive attitude and hawk it at natural disaster sites. Or funerals.

"Talk about how your meticulous planning prevented

the rings from taking a dive into the lake, and saved the entire ceremony. Talk about how your job is to make the most wonderful day in someone's life...truly the most wonderful day, and not a massive stress attack. It'll make you come across as caring and capable. Easy segue into your new wedding show, which then leads into your new business venture." Ben reached for her hand and covered her damp fingers with his palm. "No one comes off in a bad light. Your ethics are intact, our marketing department scores a slam dunk, and you'll have people already lining up for opening day of your romance emporium."

"A Fine Romance," she corrected softly. Ivy flipped over her hand, interlaced her fingers with his.

"Good name." Apparently they'd ridden out this particular storm, without any collateral damage. Ben didn't know how it happened, but the electric tension in the air had dissipated. The lack of verbal fireworks must've disappointed their elderly neighbor, because she rattled her paper mightily, sniffed and disappeared behind it once more.

"I'm sorry. I overreacted. It's childish to fault you for the terms of a contract that I knowingly signed. You're absolutely right—you don't deserve to be sucker punched by my frustration with RealTV. I'll do the interview." A single eyebrow shot into a perfect vee. "Not simply to adhere to the letter of the law, but also because it's a smart marketing choice. I appreciate you pointing that out." Her brow smoothed out, and a hint of a smile teased at the corner of her lush mouth. "I'd also appreciate it if you would help me run through some talking points. You seem to have a good handle on how I should spin the interview."

Wait a minute. Ben's head spun. No tears, no shout-
ing, no storming out. And to top it all off, an acknowledgement of the wisdom of his approach? Ivy Rhodes
was unlike any other woman he'd known, in the best
possible way. "How appreciative are we talking?"

Her smile grew bigger, while still close mouthed
and mysterious. "Well, if you're still up for the movies tonight, I know they're playing a double feature
of something I'm really excited to pay no attention to
whatsoever. While lavishing all my attention—and my
kisses—on you. Sound good?"

Ben squeezed her hand in release, then began shoveling in the reward cake he'd now earned twice over.
"Best offer I've ever had."

CHAPTER FIFTEEN

Expect the best, plan for the worst, and prepare
to be surprised.

—Denis Waitley

"I'M NERVOUS," SAID Ivy. She clenched and unclenched
her hands over her belly. "I had butterflies in my stomach, but they got eaten by raccoons. Who then were at-
tacked by bears. Do you hear me, Daphne? I have wild,
rabid bears knotting up my stomach!"

"I was right there with you until you turned the bears
rabid. You need to get a grip." Daphne tugged at the
leg of Ivy's navy cotton pants covered with grinning
cows jumping over the moon. "Besides, nobody can
be nervous in their pajamas. It's why we're having a
pajama party in the first place, remember? You'll feel
so ridiculous sitting around our place with everyone in
their jammies you won't feel nervous about watching
yourself on *Wild Wedding Smackdown*."

"A sound theory, but I'm finding that embarrassment
on a nationwide level trumps my embarrassment about
Ben seeing me in my distinctly non-sexy sleepwear."
Ben was the kind of man who inspired late night Internet shopping for lacy teddies. See-through camisoles
and silky panties. Not the faded pajamas Daphne had
given her five birthdays ago. She'd already refused to

have sex with him. How could she keep him interested once he saw her dressed like an undergrad during finals week? Why hadn't she thought of all this before they invited him to the viewing party?

"Please. He can't keep his hands off of you. And trust me when I say that tank top clings in all the right places. Whereas I look like a linebacker."

"You *are* wearing a Bears jersey," Ivy pointed out. "Besides, why do you care? You aren't trying to impress anyone." She watched Daphne give herself a rigorous once over in the mirrored closet doors. For a night spent hanging out on the couch, she seemed overly interested in her ensemble. Ivy ran down the short list of male attendees. Ben was taken, Milo played for the wrong team, they thought of Sam as a brother, and Gib was a die hard Casanova. So why on earth was Daphne putting on lipstick and belting the oversized jersey? "Or is there a hook-up potential here I don't know about?"

"What?" Daphne abandoned her obsessive preening and whirled to face Ivy. "Of course not. This is our crew, our regular guys. We're all in the trenches together. I wouldn't touch any of them if they came laid out and oiled up on a silver platter."

"Oiled up, huh? Methinks the horny lady doth protest too much."

Daphne threw up her hands. "Of course I'm horny. It's wedding season. Who has the time or energy to date? Oh, wait, that's right—the crazy woman in front of me juggling a full-time job, a start-up company, and six feet of the occasionally charming, dangerously sexy Mr. Westcott."

"Just call me the Energizer bunny."

"Isn't that a coincidence? I've got a few Energizer D cells of my own in my rather overworked rabbit."

"Eww. We are not going to stand in my bedroom and discuss vibrators." Ivy shooed her roommate down the hallway. "I need some good, old-fashioned liquid courage. What are my options?"

"Well, this *is* a premiere, jammies notwithstanding. So I bought many, many bottles of champagne. But it is hard to guzzle, and I think you need to take the edge off, fast."

"Liquid valium would be good, with the bubbly as a chaser?" Ivy suggested, not entirely kidding. Her knotted stomach, along with a racing pulse and the beginnings of a stress headache tickling her temples, made her want to huddle on her bed in the fetal position. Instead, she eased onto a stool at the kitchen counter. "I am not cut out for this, Daph. I'm serious. What if my ass looks fat? What if all of America points and laughs at my gigantic ass?"

"On the bright side, you'll never know what most of America thinks. Ignorance is bliss, right?" Ice rattled into highball glasses.

"You're not helping."

"Well, this should help." Daphne pressed a glass into her hand. "The talk of vibrators inspired me. I made you a screaming orgasm. Or has Ben taken care of that already today?"

Ivy swallowed half her drink in one, fast gulp. The icy liquid did nothing to cool the heat burning in her cheeks. "No. Which is the same answer I gave you when you asked at breakfast, and the same answer you got when I came home from my date last night. No matter how many times you ask, the answer will continue to be no. I told you, I am not going to have sex with Ben. Not unless he falls in love with me."

"Hold on a minute. I believe your original plan rested on exploring *if* you love him, as well. Or have you already made up your mind on that point?" Daphne threw back her drink, slammed the glass onto the granite counter. "Nix that, you don't have to answer. It's written all over the dopey grin on your face. You're in love with Ben, aren't you? Damn it to hell!"

"Why are you swearing at me?"

"Because I'm on the verge of losing my best friend."

Now Ivy's stomach reknotted itself into something complex only a seasoned sailor could produce. Their friendship was a sacred, unbreakable bond, and it cut her to the quick that Daphne might be worried. "Oh. Oh Daph, I'm going to have to go with a plain and simple *no* again. Why would you think that, for even a second?"

A shrug, and then Daphne busied herself refilling their glasses. Fancy, cut crystal highball glasses etched with their college logo. They'd purchased them in celebration of their twenty-first birthdays, only a few weeks apart. A symbol of where their friendship had begun, lined up on the counter next to the glasses they'd had etched with the Aisle Bound logo the day they signed the partnership papers.

"You've wanted to be in love, tried to be in love dozens of times. Maybe even thought you were once or twice. But Ben? I'm pretty sure he's the real deal. The mega-jackpot. Honest to God, I'm happy for you. Nobody I know deserves, or appreciates, true love more than you do."

"Thank you." Ivy sipped her fresh drink slowly.

Probably best not to get wasted before any of their party guests showed up. Plus, it gave her something to do with her hands while trying to figure out why Daphne would assume their friendship was circling the drain.

"On the flip side, however, true love tends to be all-consuming. Natural progression, completely understandable, etc., but things will never be the same between you and me once you and Ben become official."

"Whoa. Slow down. Ben and I are dating. Well, he wouldn't deign to call it that. Would probably rather walk away than put a specific name to what we're doing together. But we're still only dating." Ivy ticked off points on her right hand. "First, I have to convince him dating isn't an evil, soul-sucking tool to rob him of his masculinity and independence. Second, bring him slowly to the realization he's actually been in a committed relationship for all these weeks. However many it turns out to be. Third, figure out a way to deal with him working in another state, once he moves on from Chicago. He doesn't even know yet where he'll be based. Last of all, there's still the big, hairy question of whether or not Ben manages to fall in love with me."

A dismissive raspberry pffted out of Daphne's lips. "Don't be silly. The man built you an iced tea tower. What more do you need—a flashing neon sign? Of course he's in love with you. He doesn't know it yet, but the rest of us sure figured it out."

"Do you really think so?" She hadn't let herself ponder the possibility. Had, in fact, ruthlessly cut off all thought about the depth of Ben's feelings for her. In order to protect her heart, Ivy lived in the moment. Or at least tried with all her might. If and when he declared his love for her, she wanted it to be a complete surprise. What could be more romantic?

"Look at you. Dewy eyes, mouth open just a tad as if waiting for his kiss." Daphne laid her fingers along the crook of Ivy's neck. "Yup, and a racing pulse. You've got it bad."

Ivy batted away the hand. "Maybe I do. You're right. I think I'm falling in love with Ben. There, I've said it. And will wonders never cease? I'm still sitting here talking to you, instead of running out to prostrate myself at his feet. No matter what I feel for him, my feelings for you are inviolate. You're my partner, my roommate, my best friend. And you will always be all those things to me."

Daphne threw her arms around Ivy, almost knocking her off the stool. "Shit. Now you've made me cry."

"*Both* of us cry," Ivy sniffed.

"Even worse. Why would you make us have red noses and puffy eyes when company's coming over?"

"To prove you're my best friend, and best friends do things together?" They both laughed, and grabbed for the tissue box at the end of the counter. "No more tears tonight. Agreed?"

"I'll drink to that." Daphne clinked her glass against Ivy's, and the moment that had turned Ivy's stomach inside out passed.

Back to the first stomach-churning anxiety. "What if the show's edited to make me look like a brainless idiot?"

"Not possible."

"Or one of those bossy consultants brides fear?"

"Running out of patience here. Worrying won't do you any good. All you can do is wait for the show to air, and then figure out if there's any damage control necessary. Now take this." Daphne handed her a platter from the refrigerator. "Drinking isn't doing the trick, so maybe work will distract you. Help me set out the appetizers. Maybe pop a deviled egg in your mouth. At least chewing might shut you up for more than five seconds."

She slid off the stool and carried the platter to the coffee table. Daphne had covered it with red and yellow plaid material identical to what Tracy and Seth had used at their fateful April wedding. Her roommate could be a real stickler for details, even for a pajama party. "I've officially lost it, haven't I?" Too wound up to eat, Ivy fanned the yellow cocktail napkins into a pretty circle.

"Oh, yeah. The infamous Rhodes icy-cool composure hit boiling point by the time we got to work this morning."

Next Ivy moved to the mantel, shifting a dish of mixed nuts from one end to the other. Then back again. "I'm sorry. My insecurity gauge is at full throttle right now. Have I been driving you crazy all day?"

"Yes. Understandably so. It's why I dragged you home an hour early. I didn't want Julianna and Milo to give in to the temptation to either slap you silly, or quit."

"Come on. I wasn't that bad." The front door opened, and Julianna hustled into the foyer. Ivy wiggled her fingers in greeting. "Speak of the devil. Daphne's busy maligning your favorite boss. Tell me, did I really make you want to quit today, J.?"

An elegant figure in white silk men's pajamas, Julianna paused, mid step. She scrunched her eyes shut and fisted a hand in her short, red hair. It spiked up through her fingers from the top of her head. "Better to quit than to be let go," she intoned in a low, ominous voice.

Ivy goggled at her. "What the heck is that supposed to mean?"

"Why don't we sit on the couch? You should definitely be sitting down for this. You both should," she said, with a nod toward Daphne, still transferring copious plates and bowls from the frig to the counter.

"I don't like the sound of this." Ivy dropped to the sofa, and waited for Julianna to explain.

"Milo and I flipped a coin. I lost, so I came over early to tell you."

"Tell me what?" At this point, her stomach knots reached out to ball up with whatever internal organs were closest. While hazy on anatomy, Ivy knew for certain that everything from her neck to her toes clenched in dread of whatever bomb her assistant was about to drop.

"After you left today, the phones rang off the hook. Apparently the news ran a promo about the local angle of tonight's *WWS* episode. Not only did more angry vendors call, but clients, too. We have seven cancellations of already booked weddings. Full weddings and two day-of coordinations. They're strung out from next month to next May." Julianna paced in front of the fireplace. "I ran the numbers, and if we follow our cancellation policy and return the deposits, we'll be out close to thirty thousand dollars."

"Whoa." Daphne sank onto the cushion next to Ivy. "Pretty big chunk of change. You know, the contract doesn't stipulate we return their money if they cancel."

True. But it felt wrong to be greedy in the face of someone's very real emotional pain. "I've only done it three times," said Ivy. "But each time, the bride had so much to worry about with losing her fiancé, on top of what might be her life savings, it didn't feel right to keep the money."

"Yes, but this time the bride isn't the one getting dumped. It's us!" Daphne swiveled around to track Julianna's circuit, now extending the length of the room. "I'm going to go out on a limb and assume all these dissatisfied clients gave only one reason for breaking their contracts? *Wild Wedding Smackdown?*"

"Mmm hmm."

"Fuck."

"I second that." Ivy curled her toes into the carpet. The bottom had just dropped out of her world. She needed a minute to ground herself in the physical. Floor—still solid. Her hand groped out, found Daphne's, and clutched it tightly. She took a quick assessment. Best friend and partner, still rock solid. The condo looked the same as always. The caramel-ly goodness of Ben & Jerry's Phish Food remained the most incredible ice cream in the world. Body intact, still breathing, albeit sucking in air in shallow gasps. It only felt like the earth was spinning out of control on a tip-tilted axis.

"This could be the tip of the iceberg. If running the promo created this sort of response, imagine what will happen once the episode actually airs? By this time tomorrow, we might not have any clients left at all," Julianna wailed. Tears began to blob down her cheeks, and in the unfortunate manner of all redheads, her skin blotched immediately.

Damn it. If she and Daph were alone, Ivy could've fallen apart. Given in to her desperate desire to roll on the floor, kicking and screaming. Instead, she had to get a grip and be a rock for Julianna. Sometimes it sucked to be at the top of the totem pole.

"No tears allowed. Not five minutes ago, Daphne told me not to freak out about what-ifs, what might happen. Let's wait and see. The episode might not be as bad as we fear."

"But we just lost thirty thousand dollars."

"Maybe. Worst case scenario. Daphne and I will need to discuss whether or not to keep the deposits on an individual basis. Damage control is still very possible. Bring people in, let them read a few more glowing testimonials, and reassure them we are the best company to be there on their big day." Ivy heard the words come out of her mouth, but didn't believe a single one. She stood, gave Julianna a one-armed hug. "Why don't you go freshen up in the powder room before the guys get here?"

"Thanks for being such a rock, Ivy. I don't know how you do it." Julianna disappeared down the hall, sniffling.

"I don't know how you do it," Daphne echoed in a fierce whisper. "Shovel such an enormous load of bullshit, that is. We are screwed. Seven cancellations in an hour? It couldn't be worse if we were carriers of the Ebola virus!"

"Well, that would be worse, because we'd be dead," Ivy hissed back.

"Dead would be an improvement. We wouldn't be around to watch the city of Chicago turn us into laughingstocks. We may never work in this town again."

Ivy sat back down on the couch, resting the side of her head against Daphne's. The initial shock and panic had receded, leaving her numb. "What happened to not worrying about what we can't control?"

"The theory only works when it's not personal. Do you really want to pack up everything, slink out of town under cover of darkness and relocate? Where do you go when you're run out of town on a rail? Iowa? Indiana?" She twisted around to face Ivy, blue eyes wide with dread. "I'm telling you right now, I can't live in a place where every morning radio broadcast starts with the farm report."

"Are you planning to move to Iowa, or to the nineteenth century?" Ivy laughed. "Anyway, we're not moving."

"Riiiiight." She drew out the word, clearly skeptical. "But if we do, how about Colorado? Or South Carolina. Think of all the beautiful flowers they have down there: Columbine, coreopsis, gardenias. Have you ever seen a pawpaw? Silly name, but the most beautiful purple flower. We could even incorporate it into our logo."

"Cut it out. The logo stays, and we're staying. Right now, we've got to focus on putting on brave faces and getting through this damn party. As soon as everyone leaves, we'll figure out a game plan. Check in with every single client in the next twenty-four hours."

"You think that'll do it? A verbal pat on the back, and all their faith in us is restored?"

"No." Ivy worried her lip. If only it could be that easy. "I think it's a start. Ben's making me do a live television interview. Hopefully I can turn that to our advantage."

Daphne spread her arms wide, palms up. "Are you nuts? Doesn't there come a point where not all exposure is good? Anything can happen on live television.

Do you really want to open yourself up to making a bad problem potentially worse?"

"Thanks for assuming I'll botch the interview, Daph. Just the ego boost I need right now."

"Don't get all pissy. I meant the reporter could blind-side you, twist your words."

As if that very thought hadn't circled her mind in a Moebius loop ever since Ben first mentioned the interview. "I don't have a choice. Apparently it's in the contract with RealTV you were so hot for me to sign."

"Oh." Daphne's hands dropped back into her lap. "We're in a real shitstorm right now, aren't we?"

Ivy pushed herself up with a deep breath. "Time will tell."

The front door flew open, the knob banging into the wall. Gib, Sam and Ben piled through the doorway. They all wore loose shorts. Ben and Sam wore Cubs tee shirts, while Gib sported a Manchester United soccer jersey. "We come bearing gifts." Ben held up a bottle by its foil-covered neck. "Champagne, to toast your amazing television debut."

Gib raised a clear glass bottle. "Or tequila, to get you royally smashed in case you bomb."

"And in either eventuality, you'll need chocolate. Mom made you a chocolate rum cake. My contribution was decorating it." Sam placed the box on the dining room table and lifted the lid. All six of them crowded around to get a look. The smooth white fondant glittered with gold dust. In the center, a large silver star contained Ivy's name. Beneath it, piped in calligraphy, were the words *a star is born*.

Tears stung the corner of Ivy's eyes. She had the best friends in the world. Any desire she'd harbored of riding this night out in solitude from beneath her comforter fled. Together, they'd all get through it.

Except…another venomous what-if snaked into her brain. What if the fallout from the show spilled over, affected her friends? A big, international corporation like the Cavendish could survive a few cancellations. The family-run Lyons Bakery could not. Her numbness burned off under righteous anger at being suckered into this whole situation in the first place. Since Tracy and Seth weren't handy, Ben would have to do. Ivy punched him in the arm. Hard.

"What the hell is wrong with you?" he demanded, rubbing his arm.

"Turns out I'm really, really mad."

"Sorry. I thought you liked champagne. Not what I'd deem a punching offense, but I get that you're nervous and off-kilter. I can go get something else. How about a bottle of Merlot?"

As quickly as it flared, her temper washed away under Ben's easygoing charm. As he'd pointed out before, lashing out at the guy who manned the camera didn't do any good. Her real beef was with Tracy and Seth, for not notifying her their wedding would be filmed until it was too late to back out. Blame the murderer, not the weapon. All Ben did that day was his job, just like she did. "Champagne is fine."

"Women are weird," said Sam.

Ivy almost choked on a half-sob, half-laugh. "Thanks for the diagnosis. And thank your mother for the cake. I know it'll be sinfully delicious."

"Figured we'd stick with the alcoholic trend of the gifts. Thought you might be in need of a little Dutch courage."

Waving a fistful of tissues, Julianna shuffled to the couch. "You don't know the half of it." She dabbed at visibly red eyes. Ivy had never seen such a huge chink—well, more of a chasm—in her assistant's composure.

"What's wrong with her?" asked Sam, jerking his chin at Julianna.

Ben grabbed Ivy's chin, gave her a good, hard look. "Yeah, what's going on? It looks more like a funeral in here than a party." She turned her cheek into his palm, taking comfort from the small touch. It was all Ivy could allow herself. No hugs, no burrowing into his shoulder, or she'd fall apart. After a glance at the clock on the mantel, she picked up the remote. It was almost time for the show to start.

"You hit the nail on the head. Depending on what happens in the next hour, this may end up as a wake for Aisle Bound." Daphne carried a tray of champagne flutes into the living room. "So let's drink a toast now, while we still have a company *to* toast."

The men burst into a chorus of questions. Ivy waved the remote to get their attention. "Two-minute warning. Everyone grab a seat, some food and a drink."

"Only if you explain Daphne's cryptic comment."

"The news ran a promo for *WWS*, and within an hour we had seven clients cancel their contracts." It physically hurt Ivy to say the words out loud.

Gib let out a whistle. "You took quite a hit."

Julianna raised her hand. "Actually the number could be higher by now. Milo stayed at the office to man the phones, just in case talking to a person instead of voice mail helps dissuade anyone else who calls all worked up."

"Good thinking. Let's remember to save him a piece of cake." If Ivy concentrated on small mundane details like leftover cake, she might be able to ignore the professional disaster about to happen on television. She started a mental to-do list. Cake for Milo. Pick up dry cleaning before Friday. Remind her father to pick out something spectacular from Tiffany's to present to Mom at their anniversary party. At least that event wouldn't fall through, since Ivy was throwing it herself.

"Shrug off the cancellations." Ben handed Ivy a glass, and clinked his softly against it. "So a few people had a knee-jerk reaction. A momentary scheduling blip. It'll blow over. Reality television doesn't have a shelf life."

"Unless it goes viral," Sam pointed out. "Did your couple do anything really out of the ordinary? You-Tube videos get passed around like crazy on the web."

Ben threw him a dark look. "Even if it does, you'll be old news within a week, I guarantee. Somebody will film their Doberman on a bicycle, and you'll be forgotten."

"Great pep talk. Now my competitive spirit's kicked in. I'm sort of motivated to outlast a trick dog," joked Ivy.

A cheesy, Muzak version of the wedding march played as various wedding photos splashed across the screen. The room broke into loud boos when a cardboard cutout of Tracy and Seth cramming cake in each other's mouths slid into place on the set draped with flowing white curtains. A formal shot of another couple rolled to a stop beside them. The host, in a slinky silver cocktail dress, walked in and perched on a stool.

"Welcome to *Wild Wedding Smackdown*, the show

that's a showdown for brides. I'm your host, Tricia Kane. Every week we compare who spends more dollars? Who has more disasters? Who'll win our prize? This week we focus on Tracy and Seth from Chicago, and Karen and Rico in Los Angeles." Tricia slipped off the stool and moved to stand between the life-size portraits of each couple. "No matter which bride blows out their budget the most, I've already chosen my winner. We're doing things a little differently this week, turning our spotlight for the very first time on someone besides the bride and groom."

Trumpet fanfare replaced the wedding march. A screen lowered from the ceiling, a shot of Ivy in her pink gown, a smile on her face with Tracy's shoes in one hand and her ever-present leather binder in the other. Julianna gasped. Ben let out a catcall, while Gib and Sam clapped maniacally. Ivy forgot to breathe.

"I don't know about your ass, but your boobs look terrific in that dress," Daphne whispered.

They really did. Ivy gulped in a breath, and clapped a hand over Daphne's mouth. "Hush. I don't want to miss anything."

With the flair of a game show hostess, Tricia pointed at Ivy's picture. "Tonight we're shining the spotlight on fabulous Chicago wedding planner Ivy Rhodes, who is nothing less than a miracle worker. We've shown you bridezillas, we've shown you toppled cakes, but we've never shown you anyone save a wedding. More than once! Settle in for a very special show, because Ms. Rhodes is about to wow all of you." A commercial for Sandals began, and Ivy realized her fingernails were digging into Ben's wrist almost hard enough to break the skin.

"Did you know about this?" Ivy asked Ben.

"Do you think I would've let you torture yourself if I had?"

"Good point." She turned to Daphne, almost unable to speak through the mile-wide smile stretching across her face. "I think there's a very good chance our company isn't going to fold tonight."

"I think there's a very good chance our business is going to quadruple after tonight." They fell, laughing, into each other's arms. Ivy couldn't believe the roller coaster of emotions she'd ridden in the last half hour. Tears of relief and happiness welled in her eyes.

"Hey, I thought we agreed no more crying tonight," said Daphne.

"You're right." Ivy dashed them away with the back of her hand. Suddenly ravenous, she scooped two deviled eggs, chips and a huge scoop of dip onto a plate. Draining her glass in two long gulps, she held it out to Ben for a refill. Time to kick tonight's celebration into overdrive. She intended to stuff herself, drink at least two glasses more than would be wise, and then get frisky with Ben.

Ivy, Daphne and Julianna's cell phones all began to ring. The house phone also blared. "Nobody answer," warned Daphne. "Let it go to voice mail. We don't want to miss a second of this show. Ben, do I need to set the DVR, or can you get me a copy?"

"I might be able to snag one for you. But remember, I stroke your back, you stroke mine."

Daphne tossed him a wink. "I'll leave the stroking to Ivy."

CHAPTER SIXTEEN

I have always considered marriage as the most interesting event of one's life, the foundation of happiness or misery.

—George Washington

BEN BRACED HIMSELF against a pillar and surreptitiously stretched his left calf behind him, right leg bent deep. Luckily, the Chicago Historical Society was lousy with the ridged, two-story-high pillars, so he took the opportunity every half hour or so to duck behind one and try and relieve his aching muscles.

Pale purple satin swished against his shoe. "What on earth are you doing?" asked Ivy.

"Ultimately? Trying to make it through the night without crying like a little girl." He switched to the other leg.

"Because..." she prompted.

"Gib made me run an extra two miles this morning. Claimed I needed to sweat out all the toxins from the ocean of champagne we put back the other night. The man's a slave driver. I don't understand why he's appointed himself my freaking trainer."

"Can't stand to see good muscles go to waste?" Ivy suggested, her tone saccharine sweet.

He ignored her crack, and grabbed his ankle for a

quad stretch. His leg muscles all felt like they'd shrunk by a good two inches. There would be revenge. Ben didn't know what quite yet, but he'd cook up some form of torture. Milo lived with Gib. Maybe he could be bribed to spill about what drove the Englishman crazy. Skim milk instead of cream in his tea? Start a rumor that his favorite tailor, a wizened little Polish man called Tassilo, was about to retire? That would probably devastate Gib. Because really, what kind of guy had enough tailors to even pick a favorite?

"I told him to go to hell. That I had a wedding tonight and couldn't be expected to stand for ten hours straight if I overdid it. But then he yelled in that starchy, British accent, and my legs just kept pumping."

Ivy ran a sympathetic hand down his arm. "Ollie's got things under control. Once dinner starts, you can find a dark corner and take a load off."

"Or you could rustle up some oil from the catering staff and give me a good rubdown. I scouted out an empty conference room on the second floor, just to be prepared." God, he loved saying outrageous things just to make Ivy's eyes widen, the streaky green-gold of aspen leaves in September. Quick as a wink, her placid, everything-is-and-shall-always-be-perfect wedding mask slipped back into place.

"As intriguing as your suggestion may be, I have to remind you I'm a television star now."

"No reminder necessary. Not since you reminded me of that particular fact at least four times already today." Probably his own fault. He'd snuck back into her apartment at dawn to tape a large gold star to her bedroom door. Thought she'd get a kick out of it.

"When I do cover you in oil and run my hands all

over you," she paused, placing her first finger at the corner of her mouth, "and notice I say when, not if…"

"Oh, I noticed," Ben interjected.

"…I don't want an audience of three million watching. I want you all to myself."

Well. Ben tried to work up some saliva in his suddenly bone-dry mouth. Progress, indeed. Maybe his forced patience and endless blue-balled nights were paying off. At this rate, he'd finally get back into her panties before the Fourth of July. And he'd make damn sure she saw fireworks.

"How did you escape Ollie, anyway? I thought he was stuck to you like a tick. He's been worked up all week about this wedding. Doesn't want you to so much as re-tie the flower girl's sash without getting it on camera." Anthony, the groom, happened to be a senator. Just a state senator, so no big deal to Ben. But it was Ollie's first brush up against a politician, and the kid could barely contain himself, sure he'd hit the big time.

"Even famous TV stars get bathroom breaks. I ditched him so I could do this." Ivy stood on tiptoe to brush her lips against his. Feather soft, her kiss made him instantly ramrod hard.

"Good thing I've got a pillar to hide behind." Ben adjusted his tux pants to ease the tightness around his balls. He loved kissing Ivy. Could do it for hours at a time and not get bored. But a few more of her kisses and he'd be bluer than the hair on the bride's grandmother.

A warning hailstorm of high heels tapped across the marble floor. Ben re-shouldered his camera, flicked it on and aimed it at Ivy. As long as nobody stared directly at his crotch, he looked ready for action.

Julianna poked her head around the column. "I'm so

glad I found you. We have an urgent situation. Everybody's breathing and nobody's bleeding, but it is serious."

"Bride or groom?" asked Ivy.

"It's Sarah. Her dress, to be precise."

Moving at a fast clip, Ivy and Ben followed her across the black-and-white-checkerboard floor and down a hallway. "What happened? Five minutes ago she was making the rounds at the cocktail hour. Dirty martini with four olives in one hand, and Anthony in the other. Perfectly happy."

"One of the groomsmen wanted to recreate the game-winning pass he made in high school that earned him a full-ride scholarship to Notre Dame."

"During cocktails? In a room full of two hundred people in formalwear?" Ivy shook her head.

Sarcasm rolled off Julianna like fog at dawn in San Francisco. "You say that as if there's a better time for acting out football?"

"I would've saved it for the dance floor," Ben suggested.

Julianna narrowed her eyes and scowled at the camera. "And that's why you won't be on the invite list when I get married."

No sense of humor whatsoever. Even though Ivy thought her indispensible, Ben would be thrilled if Julianna quit tomorrow. Or better yet, tonight. She still treated him with the barest of civility. At least her obvious near-loathing made it easy to yank her chain. "Here I thought it was because the sight of me in a tux brings out your inner horny cheerleader, and you wouldn't be able to deny yourself before walking down the aisle."

The redhead barked out a dry laugh. "You've got a rich fantasy life there, Ben."

Ben nudged Ivy with his elbow. "Notice how she doesn't deny it?"

"What I notice is that I'm still waiting to hear the exploits of the Fighting Irish groomsman."

Julianna spun around, and kept walking backward so she could face Ivy. "Long story short, he got meningitis and missed the entire season his senior year."

"How about the long version? You know, the one that includes what happened to Sarah's dress?"

"Oh. He stepped on the back and ripped the bustle out." She stopped in front of a door surrounded by the fancy lintels and carvings of the Georgian architecture. After a tug on the bottom of her deep purple jacket, she rapped sharply on the door. Ivy slid in first while Ben waited outside. They'd implemented the safety precaution after he'd walked in on—camera rolling—a delightful old woman, with her dress peeled down to her waist. Agnes had explained, through peals of laughter, that she'd always wanted to try on a push-up bra, but didn't feel it was proper.

That is, until her granddaughter the bride shared half a bottle of champagne with her in the limo, and then offered up her own miracle bra. Ben thought the sight of the two women, sixty years apart, topless and laughing hysterically, showed their close bond. It was a wedding day memory neither would ever forget. Nevertheless, it scared the hell out of Ivy. Now she wouldn't let him past any closed doors until she gave the all clear.

Julianna opened the door a crack and beckoned him into the makeshift bride's room. Garment bags, clothes and assorted tote bags littered the floor. So many curling irons, steamers and flat irons sagged from outlets it surprised Ben they hadn't shorted out the entire building. Tackle boxes full of makeup balanced on folding chairs. In the middle of the chaos stood Sarah, head craned around like a dog chasing its tail. When she opened her mouth, Ben braced for anything from sobs to screams.

"The bustle's gone. Stupid Mike. He trots out that pass every time there's a party. We've all seen it a hundred times. Now he's ruined my dress. I've got a four-foot train. How am I supposed to have any fun dragging four feet of satin and lace behind me?"

"Your dress isn't ruined. It is still beautiful, and you are breathtaking." While she spoke, Ivy ran her hands all around Sarah's train, lifting and gathering. As her arms rose and fell, so did her words, soothing and distracting. "Did you see Anthony's face as you came down the aisle? We could've lit up the Hancock Building with his smile. You and this dress blew him away."

The memory stopped the tears welling in Sarah's big, brown eyes. Ben caught the moment of transformation. He knew that split second where she flipped from the edge of full blown panic into dreamy remembrance would be the shot of the night.

"I'm so lucky. Anthony's the best man in the world."

"You can tell him to his face in five minutes." Ivy rummaged through her emergency bag. "Julianna, please let the caterers and the band know we're pushing everything back by ten. While you're at it, reassure the groom his bride has not gone AWOL on him."

"What are you going to do?" Ben asked.

Ivy rolled her eyes. "Kind of a stupid question. The girl needs a bustle, so I'm sewing her one. Actually, I could use your help. Hold this." She stuffed an acre of heavy fabric into his free hand.

"It weighs a ton." Ben panned across the length of the train slowly. "What held that up before?"

"A complicated system of buttons and loops. None of which can be fixed at this moment, since two of the buttons are missing and the loops tore away."

Sarah gasped. "Our signature dance is the samba. We've been taking classes for months. I can't do it if we're both tripping over my stupid train."

"Don't worry. I've got something better and faster than buttons. A secret weapon." She threaded her needle and dove into the bunched material.

Ben knew absolutely nothing about sewing. He did, however, know a little bit about fishing. The most important fact being that he hated it. But he did recognize the assorted bits and pieces of the sport. "That looks like fishing line."

"It is. Super duper strong. Stronger than steel, in fact. This particular one is spiderwire fused line. They use it in deep sea fishing." Ivy sat on the floor and tunneled up through the copious layers of the dress.

"Very impressive, Captain Rhodes. Are you going to follow this up by using a cutlass on the cake?" Ben razzed her, since talking was the only way to keep his jaw from hitting the floor. The most ruffled, pink-pouf-loving woman he'd ever met knew about the tensile strength of fishing line? She amazed him. His girl could take any random nugget of information and find a way to apply it to weddings.

Wait. *His girl?* Where the hell did that come from? Did his very own, mutinous brain cells spit out that thought? Ivy was…a challenge. A colleague. A great way to make the weeks fly by while stuck in Chicago. The most exciting woman he'd ever chased. But only for right now. She might be a lot of things, but the single, overarching thing she wasn't—was *his girl*.

"I watched you on television this week," Sarah blurted out.

Right along with the rest of America. The phones at Aisle Bound had rung off the hook for the past two days. All the vendors apologized, calling Ivy a credit to their craft. They even wanted her to speak about her experience on *Wild Wedding Smackdown* at the next Association meeting. Ben thought she should do it. Take the opportunity to make 'em all feel bad for cold-shouldering her in the first place. Ivy, being far less petty and vindictive than him, was still on the fence.

Wannabe clients called in droves; the more aggressive lining up around the block, hoping to snag the hottest planner in Chicagoland for their wedding. Milo even fielded calls from out-of-state; brides who offered to fly her to Miami, Dallas and Los Angeles, respectively to work her magic on their big day. Ben and Ollie captured it all on film. The network was ecstatic.

"It's sweet you took the time to watch," said Ivy, right arm flying up and down with each long stitch. "You had such a busy week with so many of your family flying in from New Mexico."

"It kicked off my bachelorette party. We all had chocolate martinis and watched my awesome wedding planner in action." Sarah lowered her voice to a near-whisper. "I hate to admit it, but I laughed. The girls and I all laughed when that skydiver landed in the pond."

Hell, who could blame her? It had taken all of Ben's years of experience not to lose it himself when that guy cannonballed into the water. If he hadn't been holding a camera, no, getting *paid* to hold a camera still, he'd have laughed his ass off.

Sarah double checked the bobby pins holding her elaborate up-do, pressing each one a millimeter deeper into the mound of sausage curls. "We thought the wedding was ruined. But you saved it."

"All it takes for a perfect wedding is the bride and groom declaring their love. Everything else is icing on the cake." Ivy recited her mantra fervently. Ben had heard her use it at every wedding, many rehearsals, and every single potential client appointment. Yet each time, she managed to infuse the words with an almost worshipful ring of truth. Ben couldn't say the same words with a straight face if offered a million dollars.

After a deep breath, Sarah rolled on in a rush. "Still, I laughed at that poor girl, and smugly thought how lucky I was that nothing like that would possibly happen at my wedding. I hired you to plan my wedding two days after I got engaged because I didn't want to risk anything going wrong. Didn't want to be stressed out by a year of decision making. Didn't want to call fourteen different bakeries to set up tastings, or spend my weekends putting favors together. And you've been terrific. While watching *Wild Wedding Smackdown*, I never imagined I'd have a disaster at my own wedding. Yet here you are, coming to my rescue. Nobody will ever know what a near miss I had."

Ben wiggled his fingers in the soft folds of her dress. With his arm outstretched so he could still film, the ache in his bicep was almost as painful as his overworked calves. He'd take Ivy up on her sexy massage talk—except tonight, he actually wanted the massage

more than the sex. Not that it mattered. He'd pulled out
every well-honed trick in the book, and still couldn't get
back into Ivy's bed. Every date ended the same way—
him going back to the Cavendish. He either swam off
his frustration or headed straight for a cold shower.
Had the messy end to their April weekend caused her
to re-virginize? Take a vow of celibacy? Because that's
the kind of information that really ought to be shared,
upfront. Of course, Julianna would leap at the chance
to point out he had no one to blame but himself, if that
were the case.

"Nobody tonight needs to know about your near-
catastrophe, Sarah. But in about three months, we kind
of hope most of America will be watching *Planning for
Love*. The secret's going to come out." Ben often reminded couples of the release forms they'd signed for
the show. The network's lawyers encouraged it.

"Well, it'll make for a funny story. You can try it out
when you check in for your flight to Bermuda. Maybe
the gate agent will feel for you and upgrade you to first
class. Right now, though, you're back in business and
ready to samba." Ivy stood, and waved her hand in an
unspoken order for the bride to twirl.

Sarah complied, spinning around three times, laughing giddily. The train had disappeared, transformed
into a poufy, drapey sweep of satin. Ben swore it was
the identical bustle she'd worn at the start of the cocktail hour. Ivy had just pulled off another amazing save.
He'd be willing to bet there wasn't a single messed-up
situation she couldn't handle without so much as bat-
ting a hazel eye. On top of that, she still looked camera
ready, even after crawling on the floor under Sarah's
dress. Truth be told, she looked damn near edible. Ben

clamped his other hand on the camera, realizing it wobbled because he literally shook with need. He had to get his mouth on Ivy tonight. *All* over her.

"Go tell your handsome husband to get ready for the introductions." Ivy checked her watch. "We're a go for them in five minutes." Sarah gave her a big hug, then swooshed out the door.

"You're Batman," said Ben. "You've got this crazy, whiz-bang, souped-up tool kit and a costume that shows off that rocking body. You're constantly helping the innocent out of jams. Seriously. Tell me one way you're different than Batman."

"He wears a codpiece."

"I'M JOHN RIDLEY. I've known the groom my whole life. He helped me hide a garter snake in the teacher's desk our first day of kindergarten. I've had his back ever since."

As a rule, Ben enjoyed wedding toasts. Fifty percent of the time, the toasts rocked. Amazing personal stories came out, stories of family and friendship, celebration and love. Under cover of midnight, when sleep eluded him, Ben could admit to himself that he'd been known to feel a dampness in his eyes more than once during a kick-ass toast. Twenty-eight percent of them were average. Go to enough weddings, and you heard the recycled jokes and best wishes any lazy sap could pull right off the Internet. He pegged today's toast as average. The best man, more than slightly drunk, had already back slapped the groom three times during the speech, and leered at the bride's sister once.

The temptation to let Ollie do single camera coverage was strong. Mostly because Ben was standing by the door, and saw the mounds of shrimp left over from the cocktail hour. He could nip out, scarf down a handful of shrimp and be back before the guy made the never-funny joke about who had the upper hand in the shiny new marriage. But even though his job may have downgraded, his mile-wide streak of professionalism hadn't slipped a single notch. He braced his back on the door frame and took a slow pan of the room, catching a decided lack of reaction to the ho-hum toast.

"You all know Anthony's a decorated veteran. He doesn't brag about his medals. Guess being modest helped him snag the pretty girl in the big, white dress. But I think all of you deserve to know just how great a guy, how big a hero he is. Our boy was part of the very first unit in Afghanistan."

Whoa. This toast just catapulted from lackluster to lively. Juicy war stories weren't usually on the menu. Ben zoomed in on the groom, caught the tic working in his jaw. His fist opened and closed on top of the table. The bride looked tense, but not surprised. Whatever the big story, she already knew it.

John used a napkin to mop sweat from the top of his receding hairline, then raised his glass high in the air. "Anthony doesn't like to talk about it, but he did more than his fair share of keeping the world safe for democracy. He—well, his unit—ambushed a terrorist training camp."

Holy shit. If John thought this topic made for an appropriate wedding toast, imagine what got said at the bachelor party! Ben tracked the direction of Ollie's camera to discover Ivy in a nearby alcove. She practically vibrated her displeasure. He crossed past two columns to join her. Then he muted the record feed on his camera.

"What are you going to do?"

"I don't know. This is a nightmare. Today is supposed to be about love and celebration, not blood and violence." Her hands clenched in the folds of her dress, much as the groom's still did on the table. "It breaks my heart to see him pollute their wedding day with such ugliness. Look at Anthony and Sarah. You can tell how upset they are."

They weren't the only ones. No silverware scraping against china, no ice clinking in glasses. Two hundred people sat stock still, frozen in surprise by the unfolding story. Ben hated that months of Ivy's careful planning and hard work could be undone, ruined by a single thoughtless, drunken man. "You've got to stop him."

Ivy bit her lip. "I can't stop him, if the bride and groom won't. I can't make the call to muzzle his oldest friend." She pressed a hand to her stomach. Ben guessed the debacle of the toast not only hurt her heart and her passion for producing a day of unparalleled happiness, but churned her up so much she might be physically sick. He wrapped his free arm around her waist, snugged her close and hoped it would comfort her.

Ben turned his attention back to the increasingly awkward speech. John had wandered away from the head table as he paced back and forth on each sentence. "Once the RPG took out his Humvee, Anthony got pissed. All by himself, he took down twenty of those stinking Afghans. Just really let loose with the old machine gun. Take no prisoners, huh, buddy?"

The groom had turned as pale as the bride's dress. The bride's face matched the blood-red roses in the centerpieces. Somebody was either going to stroke out, or get punched out. Worse yet, Ivy would no doubt beat herself up about not being able to fix a horrible situation, impossible to predict or prevent.

In his previous life, Ben always obeyed the golden rule of journalism—don't get involved. Record the facts, and don't do anything to change them. Keeping himself apart from the subjects he taped had sometimes been hard, but he'd never been tempted to break the rule. Until tonight. This time, he couldn't stand by and let events unspool around him. Not with Ivy quietly hyperventilating beside him. He felt the rapid rise and fall of her chest against his own ribs. Ben turned off his camera and set it on the ground.

"What are you doing?" Ivy dug her fingers into his arm.

"You can't shut him down. I get that. Since the bride and groom pay you, it's a line you can't cross. But I can. Professionally speaking, I don't answer to anyone in this room. I'll take the heat if they get mad." Ben shook her off, then ran along the perimeter of the room to the DJ's table. With a why-the-fuck-haven't-you-done-anything look, he shouldered him out of the way and cut off the power to the microphone. Confused, John stopped mid-sentence. He tapped the top of the mic a few times. When nothing happened, he took a few steps toward the DJ, hand extended, gesturing for another microphone.

Ivy snatched a champagne flute from a tray stand and rushed forward. She lifted John's hand, clinked his glass, and the roomful of guests eagerly followed her lead, effectively ending the least romantic toast ever given in the history of weddings. Ben flicked the speakers back on.

"For the love of all that's holy, spin some music," he ordered the DJ. A few seconds of near silence while people muttered a half-hearted "cheers". Prince's "Kiss" roared out of the speakers. Anthony pulled Sarah up, dipped her and kissed her while enthusiastic cheers and applause rang out. The wedding was back in its groove. Ivy escorted John back to his seat.

Ben tossed the DJ a salute for his excellent music programming, then ambled back to his camera. Ivy caught up and slid her arm through his. Ollie came at him from the opposite direction.

Looking straight at the camera, Ben bowed from the waist with a flourish. "Crisis averted."

"Nice going, boss," said Ollie. "It was touch and go there for a few minutes. Can't believe you stepped in and saved the day."

"That makes two of us." If word of this got out to his friends in the news business, he'd be a laughingstock. Thankfully, Ben would put big money on the fact none of them watched reality wedding television. "Do you think I've earned a five-minute break to snag some leftover appetizers? I'm starving."

"Are you kidding? Right about now, I bet Anthony and Sarah would give you the filet off of their own dinner plates. They'd let you dive face first into the cake. You saved the wedding, Bennett. You flipped one little switch and saved the whole darn thing. You're my hero."

"Well, I'm no Batman. No tool belt. But I could be a halfway decent Green Arrow. He didn't have superpowers, but he knew how to get things done." Ben looked down at Ivy. She seemed pretty darn grateful. Capitalizing on it might be his best chance to reclaim his spot in her bed. "We make a pretty good team. How about we celebrate a little later?"

CHAPTER SEVENTEEN

Love is an ideal thing, marriage a real thing.
                                              —Goethe

ARMS AROUND HIS neck, Ivy burrowed her face against Ben's pleated tux shirt. One minute she'd been complaining about her aching feet, and the next she was in his arms, like Snow White or Scarlett O'Hara. He'd carried her this way the day they met. Tonight, it gave her the same romantic thrill as the first time. Maybe more so, now that she and Ben had a connection. A connection he refused to name, but she still had a little time to get him over that hump.

"Open your eyes, tired girl. The night's not over yet." Ben stopped walking and set her on her feet. "That is, if you're up for a little romance. I figure you're such an addict, you must be jonesing for a hit."

Did she hear correctly? The man who couldn't utter the word *romance* without getting heartburn planned to actively engage in it? This could only mean one thing— her plan had finally worked. Ivy wanted to run in circles, pumping her fist in the air. But she tamped down the joy fluttering in her heart. Better to play it cool and be sure before performing a victory dance.

"Guilty as charged," she said. "Even though I just

spent ten hours at a wedding, I can always do with a little extra."

Ben took her shoulders and turned her around. "Then your carriage awaits."

In front of them sat the red and green trolley the bridal party had used earlier in the day. A pat on her ass propelled her up the polished wooden steps. Ben prodded Ivy all the way to the back. They both sank onto the wide bench seat.

Confusion muddied Ivy's tired brain. "The trolley contract ended four hours ago. Why is it still here?"

"Don't worry, nobody deviated from the sacred contract. Billy," Ben pointed at the driver, big enough to be a strip club bouncer, "agreed to come back after his last run and give us a moonlight tour."

Not a good idea. Ivy might be worn out, but her business sense never checked out completely. "Anthony and Sarah aren't paying overtime for this," she warned. "The trolley company's very strict with their timekeeping. I won't let my clients get charged extra because you had a yen to take a joyride."

Ben shrugged out of his jacket. "Oh, for Christ's sake, I'm paying for it. Working hours are over, Ms. Rhodes. You've clocked out. Now can I do something nice for you without the third degree?"

Oh. Trolleys didn't rent by the mile, or by the hour. Ben must've done some fancy talking to convince the driver to stick around at the end of the night. Trolleys also weren't cheap. They were old-fashioned, romantic and extravagant. It was official. Ben was—finally— making a grand gesture. To think she'd almost ruined the moment by being practical!

"I'm sorry. This is a delightful idea. I've never ridden on the trolley for fun—or with less than a dozen other people."

Ben pulled a cord to ring the loud bell, and they took off toward the lights of the Magnificent Mile. He folded his jacket into a tidy bundle. "Scooch over against the window." Ivy turned sideways, and he stuck his jacket between her back and the paneling as a cushion. Then he lifted both of her legs across his lap.

"Comfortable?" he asked.

"Very."

"Brace yourself, because it's about to get even better." His thumbs pressed firmly into the arch of her right foot. Ivy bit back a groan.

"There is nothing better, at the end of a wedding, than a foot rub."

"Nothing? You think the bride and groom are tucked up in their fancy honeymoon suite giving each other foot rubs?"

"If he's smart, absolutely." Ivy curled and uncurled her toes with each of Ben's long, sure strokes. "She'd love it, and thus feel compelled to express her gratitude. Trust me, everybody wins with a foot rub."

Lights in the trees twinkled as they passed. Music spilling from the clubs on Rush Street created a faint wash of background noise, the muted but still vibrant soundtrack to the city. Store windows lit up like a series of jewel boxes. A warm breeze flapped the plastic, roll-down windows. Ivy loved taking the time to appreciate the glamour of downtown the glowing buildings and the happy clumps of people partying away the night.

Ben switched his ministrations to the other foot. "I don't expect you to express any gratitude. I just want to pamper you a little. Make you feel as special as you make your clients feel."

The bungee cords strapping down her eager heart snapped. Love swelled it to twice its size, then burst it like an overfilled water balloon. The entire puddle of love flowed straight to Ben, with the inevitability of the mighty Mississippi to the Gulf of Mexico. Ivy couldn't overlook it any longer. She loved Ben. It might not be safe, or smart, but she had no choice.

"Good point. Gratitude would be the wrong reaction entirely. Lust, on the other hand, big, burgeoning lust would be a very appropriate reaction." Ivy anchored her feet on the other side of his thighs and pulled herself close. "You fill me with lust, Mr. Westcott."

"Sounds like a dangerous buildup. We'd better provide some outlet for it." When carrying her from the History Museum to the trolley, Ben had used such care, such tenderness. His foot rub, soothing. Well, her words must've snapped something in him, too, for that gentleness vanished. He pulled her to his chest, flattening her breasts against him. One hand dove down to cup her ass, and the other drove into her hair. Bobby pins tinkled to the floor as his mouth claimed hers.

It was heat; circling, spiking flames that seared her with each swipe of his tongue. Her lips tingled beneath the onslaught. Her nipples tingled against his rock-hard pecs. Who was she kidding—everything tingled, inside and out. Over and over again she ran her fingers through his thick, silky hair. She wanted him to rub that mop of hair all over her body. Softness against her softness. Wanted to feel him unleash his desire. Wanted to lie naked with him, tasting and touching and becoming one.

"Want more," Ben muttered. "Need more." He tilted her backward until she lay on the bench. Bracing one knee on the floor, he covered her body with his own. The onslaught of kisses moved down her neck, setting off shivers of delight, down to flutter the lightest of licks across the swell of her breasts. Like butterfly wings beating against her skin. The delicate touch contrasted with his right hand diving under her skirt to stroke the length of her thigh.

Ivy wanted to concentrate on each sensation, but there were too many. She could only revel in the circling layers of desire he built, one atop the next until all she knew was a throbbing hunger. Her hand yanked his shirt out of his pants, desperate to touch skin. Instead, she hit the pleated layers of his cummerbund. Lacking Ben's one-handed dexterity at clothing removal, Ivy thrust her hand underneath, scraping her wrist on the metal clasp. The sting of pain broke through the haze of lust.

"Ben, we should stop," she murmured into his ear.

His hands stilled, then his head dropped heavily onto her shoulder. "Fucking curse," he grumbled.

Weird. Not your standard pillow talk. "What on earth do you mean? What curse?"

He jolted upright, eyes a little wild. "Did I say that out loud?"

"Yes. Care to explain?"

Ben knelt again, both hands framing her face while he looked at her intently. "I didn't plan to tell you, but maybe it's time."

"Time?" Her mind flew in a dozen directions, but none of them made sense. "Time for your curse to reveal itself? What are you, a werewolf?" she joked. Because really, who talked about curses in this day and age except in horror movies?

"Worse. The Westcott family curse stretches back to my great-great-grandfather Arthur. He worked for James Garfield, helped get him elected president." Ben leaned against the seat back behind him, but kept both hands curled loosely around Ivy's.

"Impressive."

"Nope. It started the curse. You see, he married the beautiful and fiery Zelda a few years earlier. Then, just like politicians today, once he hit the campaign trail he forgot to keep his pants zipped. Soon after the inauguration, a woman showed up at the house carrying the baby she claimed Arthur had fathered."

His voice had fallen into an almost sing-song pattern. It blended in nicely with the rocking motion of the trolley. Ivy imagined it passed down through the years, almost as a salacious bedtime story.

"Zelda, who was part-gypsy, flew into a rage. She cursed Arthur and the entire Westcott line to never be able to find or keep love. And we haven't. Relationships don't stick. My sister's never had one last more than four months. Westcott marriages, made for convenience, not love, always end in divorce in three years or less. Churn out a couple of kids, then call it quits."

Leveraging herself up onto her elbows, Ivy blinked at him. "You're pulling my leg."

His hands tensed. "I could not be more serious. Generations of unhappiness are no laughing matter."

"But, a family curse? You don't believe in vampires or ghosts or wizards, do you?"

The side of his mouth shot downward into a sneer.

"Of course not. I don't believe in the Easter Bunny, either."

"Then why can't you be pragmatic and recognize this for what it is?"

"Now you're going to explain away the curse that's struck each and every blood relation for more than one hundred years?" Ben stood, grabbing hold of the floor to ceiling pole in the middle of the car for balance. "This ought to be good."

It didn't surprise her that he'd backed away on every level. Ben didn't talk about his family or his feelings. Ivy could almost hear titanium shields slamming into place around his heart. For that matter, she was shocked he'd been able to spit out the word *relationship* without foaming at the mouth. Progress, indeed. Proved she was getting to him, at least on some level.

"Let's set aside, for the moment, the ridiculous notion that curses even exist. Ben, this problem in your family isn't a curse. It's a choice. A series of choices."

"Riiiiight. We chose to be miserable and alone."

Subconsciously. But she couldn't tell him that. The belief in this supposed curse sure explained a lot about Ben. And it gave her hope that she could debunk this idiotic family legend and get him to believe in happily ever after. Believe that he deserved one, and could sustain it.

"Loving someone is hard, and people have to work at it with all their might. Your family fell into a bad habit, like smoking, of giving up too easily when push came to shove. Not believing in themselves, their ability to sustain a commitment. My mother sees it all the time."

"Your mom the marriage counselor? Great, now I'm

in vicarious therapy. Switch places with me—I should be the one lying down."

Ivy knew he lashed out from fear. But she pressed on, convinced this might just be the most important conversation they ever had. The turning point that led to their long-term happiness. And short term, enable him to declare his love so they could finally have sex!

"I bet your father looked at this decades-long string of failed relationships and thought, well if my dad couldn't do it, and his dad couldn't do it, how can I be expected to make something this complicated work? So nobody tried. Laziness kept them from fighting for what they most wanted, or what could very well have been the right relationship." She swung her legs around, off the seat, and fired her last shot, staring him straight in those ice-cold blue eyes. "Be honest with yourself, Ben. Brutally honest. How hard have *you* ever tried?"

Seconds ticked by. The trolley bell rang its warning at a crowded crosswalk. Two more blocks passed in silence, and it rang again. Then Ben let loose a stream of curses. He raked both hands through his hair until it stood on end, finishing by grinding his palms over his eyes.

"I don't know. If I dig deep, I don't think I can say I've ever put everything toward making a relationship last. I always assumed they were doomed to fail, so why waste time to make the effort?"

Ivy's heart broke a little for him. Being right didn't always feel good. "Have you ever heard the saying, *it's the journey, not the destination*?"

He shrugged. "Sure. Clearly thought up by some poor sap who couldn't afford to vacation at a kick-ass resort. Scuba diving in Belize is way better than the five cramped hours in the plane to get there."

If he could make jokes again, they were back on level ground. Ivy bit back a smile, and scowled at him instead. "Pretend to be obtuse all you want, but I know you get my point."

"Maybe." He sat next to her, draping an arm around her shoulder to pull her close. "What if you're wrong? What if I stop believing in the curse and it pisses off the spirit of my gypsy great-great-granny?"

"If you really made her mad? She'd probably turn you impotent. I imagine that's the go-to revenge for not respecting the family curse."

"Mock me all you want. You'll be the one who suffers if she un-mans me."

"Hmm. Better hedge our bets. I'll put Milo on research tomorrow, see if he can find a way to break the curse. I'm sure something will happen if we get our hands on a gallon of chicken blood and mix it up with a strand of your hair and maybe a photo of Zelda."

Ben chuckled, knowing she probably wasn't joking. "See? That's what I like about you. You always have a plan."

CHAPTER EIGHTEEN

Always plan ahead. It wasn't raining when Noah
built the ark.

—Richard C. Cushing

"LADIES AND GENTLEMEN, we appreciate you joining us
here at News Midday. Thanks to Ivy Rhodes of Aisle
Bound for coming in to talk weddings. Don't forget to
tune in to her new show, *Planning for Love,* coming
in September on RealTV. We'll see you back here at
four on WXCH." Maggie Shea nodded at Ivy, nodded
at the camera, then froze with a practiced smile until
the director yelled cut.

Ivy's head immediately swiveled to seek out Ben in
the shadows. "Did I talk too fast? Did I talk too much?
Was I dull? Was I too perky?"

"All things considered, this being your very first live
interview..." Ben walked through the glare of stage
lights and joined her on the set.

"Uh oh. You're stalling. You're stalling and quali-
fying. Did I suck?"

Aww. Pretty adorable in her hot pink suit, nervously
tapping a matching sandal against the rung of her stool.
Ben wanted to lap her up like a dish of strawberry ice
cream. One of the most poised people he'd ever met, he
got a kick out of Ivy's self-consciousness about being

on camera. Made about as much sense as a giraffe worrying about having a long neck.

"I give your interview a solid B plus. The joke you made about being afraid to use the bathroom while miked went over well." He leaned down and gave her a quick peck on the cheek.

"Oh, it's not a joke. There is nothing funny about Ollie possibly listening to me pee because I forgot to turn off the mic pack."

"I don't think Ollie's any more excited about the prospect than you are."

Ivy's lush lower lip pushed out into a pout. "Have to say, I'm not really comfortable with a B plus. I've always been a straight A kind of girl."

"A few more private coaching sessions, and we can get you bumped up to an A before your next interview."

"The only thing I learned in your last private coaching session was how good you are at unhooking a bra with one hand."

Oh, Ben remembered. A black bra with red lace that if he hadn't managed to unhook on the first try, he would've ripped off her with his teeth. The mere sight of Ivy got him firing on all four cylinders, but the minute she removed a layer of clothing, his lust took over and clouded every brain cell until he operated solely on his basest instincts. He ached for her. He ached to touch her, to taste her, and more than anything to be in her.

She'd packed a powerful punch in that bra. His cock throbbed right now with the memory. His balls ached with the further memory of being sent home soon after he'd dispatched the bra. If Ivy didn't sleep with him soon, internal combustion might be a real possibility. For the life of him, he couldn't figure out why the holdup. Why she slammed the brakes on every damn time his fingers wandered anywhere south of her belly button. Or, what he was starting to call the Undiscovered Country.

"Good point. I'll take the blame. Our—ah—departure from the syllabus is probably what held you back today. If you promise to keep your clothes on and not distract the teacher, we can get you up to speed."

"Oh, so many things wrong with that sentence. The Bennett Westcott I know would never encourage me to keep my clothes on—"

"True."

"—and for the record, you're the one who told me I'd be less nervous if I took my clothes off while we practiced."

"Did I say that? I think you misunderstood me. Classic theater trick to calm nerves is to imagine the audience naked, not get naked yourself. Sorry if I wasn't clear."

"Trust me, your intent was crystal clear. More importantly, what do you mean, the next interview? I've been a wreck for a week dreading these lousy ten minutes. You're going to force me to go through this again?"

"No. Not me. I wouldn't dream of putting you through that kind of stress. RealTV, on the other hand, will absolutely force you to do more interviews. Your episode of *WWS* was a huge hit, and you're beautiful, you're passionate about weddings, eloquent, and you're not crazy. In the world of reality television, that makes you a quintuple threat."

"Which translates to how many interviews, exactly?"

"The network's trying to get you on a nationwide

morning show, to ride the wave right now. Probably next week. Then in late August they'll start hyping *Planning for Love*, and you'll do a few more local spots—tv and radio, as well as at least two national interviews. Maybe a wedding magazine, or even *People*. I'd say ten, tops."

Ivy's mouth dropped open. "Seriously?"

The anchor scooted her chair forward to join the conversation. "My producer just told me that you're already on our schedule right after Labor Day. And don't listen to your boyfriend—you did great. You were a natural. It was a pleasure chatting with you."

The words popped out of Ivy's mouth faster than a sneeze at the peak of allergy season. "He's not my boyfriend."

It stung a little, how she fast she rejected the idea. "Wow. Kind of quick on the draw, aren't you? I'm not Attila the Hun over here."

"I just don't want you to feel pressured by a label." She swiveled back around to face Maggie. "We're colleagues."

"My colleagues don't usually kiss me after a segment."

"Friendly colleagues," she amended.

"Well, if you're truly not dating, I wouldn't mind getting friendly with your colleague myself." With a smoothness Ben admired, Maggie slid her card into the front pocket of his khakis. "Feel free to call me. Anytime."

Ben's mental scoreboard was upside down. The woman he wanted had just definitively stated they weren't dating, and a woman he had no interest in at all wanted him, and still had her fingers at his groin, deep in his pocket. "While you get unhooked, I'll run to the bathroom." He backpedaled off the set, down the hall. The studio had emptied out for lunch the moment the show stopped taping. His footsteps echoed in the marble-floored corridor.

The network affiliate took up two floors of a gorgeous old building downtown, and didn't look like any studio he'd been in before. It did look like a set for a Tracy/Hepburn movie. Art deco touches everywhere, black veined marble on the floors and stairs. If it had been a traditional news studio, lined with posters of current shows and anchors, Ben would've been twitchy. He didn't care to bump into any reminders of his old life.

Pausing at the bathroom door, he jammed his hands into his pockets. Who was he kidding? Being back in a news studio made him more than twitchy. Awareness marched under his skin like an army of fire ants. The vicious roller coaster of what-ifs and might-have-beens churned through his gut. It surprised him how much he liked his new job producing, liked carving out a spot and routine of his own here in Chicago. But being back in a news studio today, without being a part of the daily news cycle, put him off balance. Edgy.

He toed open the door, then froze, one foot in, one foot out. A man bent over the stainless steel counter beneath the mirror, sniffing…something through a rolled-up bill. Ben guessed the substance to be cocaine. He knew, however, without a shadow of a doubt that the man was Senator Lawrence Newsome. Senior Senator from Wisconsin, chairman of the Appropriations Committee. A proponent of the three strikes law in his state, and he cited drug abusers as a main reason for the harsher sentencing guidelines.

The man jerked at Ben's appearance. Rubbed his nose, and whisked the bill into his pocket in a quick, practiced gesture. "How's it going?" he asked in an overly jocular tone.

"Sorry to barge in," Ben said. Above all else, he didn't want to spook the guy. Didn't want to give him any reason to think he'd been recognized. For that matter, Ben hoped the senator didn't recognize him as the Cowering Cameraman. "Everyone deserves a little private time in the john."

Senator Newsome pointed at the remaining thin, white line on the counter. "Care to join the party?"

Surreal enough that he'd walked in on the uber-conservative lawmaker doping up. Far weirder to be invited to get high with him. How many lines had the guy already sniffed to be so openly offering drugs to a perfect stranger? Without any apparent care for possible reprisals? The Senator had to be higher than the proverbial kite. "Thanks for the offer, but I'm good." Ben forced himself to walk to the sink and wash his hands, pretending to scrub at an ink spot. Normal, everyday trip to the bathroom. Nothing to see here.

To his amazement, Lawrence shrugged, then did the last line right in front of him. A few sniffs, then a swipe at his nose with a balled-up paper towel. "Have a good day."

"You, too," Ben said as the older man left the room. Ben continued through the motions, drying his hands, taking his time in case Newsome returned for any reason. When he couldn't come up with a way to stall, he left the room and returned to the set, checking in every doorway to be sure the senator wasn't around.

Ivy and Maggie stood by the makeup table, still chatting. "Sorry to cut this short, but do you have an empty office we can use?" Ben held up his phone. "There's a crisis back at the office."

Maggie nodded and led them to a room at the end of the hall. "Hope nobody got jilted," she said with a half-laugh as she closed the door.

Ivy immediately sat in the desk chair and picked up the phone, finger poised to dial. "Who called you? What's wrong? Is it Lily and Simon? Did his crazy mother finally drive that girl away? Last week, I told her the only way to cut the mother out of the planning process was to elope. I should've made a bet with Daphne on it."

"Slow down. There's no crisis. Well, there is, but not related to Aisle Bound in any way." Nervous energy kept him on his feet, pacing a loop between the desk, a file cabinet and a window with a view of Lake Michigan. "I just caught Senator Lawrence Newsome doing drugs in the bathroom."

"Oh my." She absorbed the news for a beat, then shook her head. "Doesn't surprise me. It's always the most vocal opponents who are unmasked as having problems, whether it's sex, drugs or alcohol."

"This is huge. We have to do something. We have to report it."

"Oh, Ben." Ivy looked at him with sad, dark eyes. "You can't. You've told me that, right or wrong, your credibility is shot. Without any proof, without another eyewitness, you can't take it to anyone."

The instinct and adrenaline that kicked in full force

the moment he recognized the senator drained away, as if someone flushed his emotional toilet. He leaned against the window frame and stared, unseeing, but unwilling to look at Ivy.

"I forget sometimes. For months, I spent every waking second thinking about my career tanking. Then I spent a few more months actively trying *not* to think about it. Just in the last couple of months, I'd finally gotten to the point where I didn't have to work at it. I could go days at a time without getting a crushing sense of failure every time I saw the news."

"You're not a failure. In fact, I think that's the single stupidest thing I've ever heard you say." He felt the comforting weight of Ivy's arms circle around his waist. She stood on tiptoe to tuck her chin up over his shoulder. "Forces beyond your control changed your life. Zigged when you wanted to zag."

"Dress it up in whatever pretty words you want. Story still ends the same way. My career ended a year and a half ago in Alaska, the minute I passed out and dropped my camera. I failed."

"Nope. You flourished. Against all odds, you persevered. Forged a new path for yourself. Succeeded so well you were promoted after a year. You're not a quitter, and you're certainly not a failure. That took courage, and strength, and drive and talent. I'm so proud of you, Ben."

The break in her voice undid him. He turned into her embrace, wrapped his arms around her and hugged like he'd never hugged before. How did she see things in him he didn't even know were there? Ben breathed deep of her sunny scent, burying his face in the silken brown strands cascading across his face like a soft river.

"You make me sound like an amazing man. A guy I'd like to sit down with and have a beer." He pulled back to drop a kiss in the center of her forehead. Better lighten the mood, before he broke down into a blubbering fool at Ivy's knees to thank her for propping him back up. "And then pick his brain for tips on women, because anyone that awesome must have an easy time scoring."

"I don't think you require any help in that department. Your bedpost is probably whittled down to the width of a toothpick from all the notches it's racked up."

"Ouch. From hero to man-slut in two sentences. You know how to keep a guy's ego in check."

"All part of the package." She pinched his cheek, then eased out of his arms to balance on the wide sill. "But I do have a serious question, if you don't mind."

Uh oh. Nothing good ever came out of a serious question. And perversely, women loved to ask them. Ben hitched himself onto the corner of the desk. Otherwise he'd start nervously pacing again. "Sounds ominous. I can't promise I'll answer—or give you an answer you want to hear—but give it a whirl."

"Do you truly hate your job?"

"Are you kidding? I get paid to stare at your beautiful face all day. Where's the downside in that?"

"Come on, I honestly want to know. After traveling the world filming crisis after international crisis, weddings must be, well, tame in comparison. Do you dread getting up in the morning, or have you accepted this unexpected twist in the road?"

Part of Ben wanted to make another joke and slither around an answer. Introspection wasn't his thing. On the other hand, after what Ivy had just done for him, she deserved a genuine answer.

"If you'd asked me this when we met, I'd have given you a different answer. I wasn't happy. It's why I applied for the producing job. And that was the right move. It was a shot in the dark, but I've discovered I really like it."

"Why?"

"News coverage is about recording the moment. With reality television, we still film the moment. But also the reaction to the moment. Then someone else's reaction. I get to weave all of these disparate pieces together. Make one, wonderful story out of them. It's challenging, and fun. Plus, I kind of enjoy not worrying about getting shot at, or having a deadly snake drop onto my head. So no, I don't hate my job." Surprisingly, just the opposite.

"Good to hear. Because that means you'll be able to handle this suggestion: give the tip away."

"Sorry?"

"Don't go through official channels with a network. Call one of your friends from the old days. Give them your tip about Senator Newsome. They won't be able to swoop in and do a sting in the next five minutes, but they will be able to start nosing around. Try to find his supplier, maybe. He's bound to slip up and use in public again. When he does, they'll be there to get him."

"You want me to just hand over what could potentially be the juiciest political scandal of the year?"

"In order to become the big scandal, the facts have to make it to the light of day. And it'll only happen if you're not involved. If you want this guy brought down, you've got to step away."

Damn it. Ivy was right. It galled him not to be able to dial up a network producer and instantly swarm a dozen cameras and reporters all over this guy. But he did have one or two old poker buddies who would at least listen to what he had to say. They'd start from scratch, and it might take weeks, or even months to verify Ben's story. But they would eventually, and that would have to be good enough.

"I can call Mitch. He's almost as low as you can get on the reporting totem pole in D.C., but he's friends with everyone. If he drops a pointed hint in the right place, it could work. He's a good guy—he'd keep my name out of it." It still stung Ben, the fact that his integrity, his word wasn't enough. Would, in fact, taint the entire thing. But he'd pass on the tip and put it out of his mind.

"Just proves what I said before. You're a brave man, Ben Westcott."

"Don't I know it. I'm going to your parents' anniversary party, aren't I? A man's either got to be dumb as dirt or have titanium *cojones* to do that."

"Nope. No bravery points there. It does, however, make you sweet, and much appreciated. And it won't be a hardship for you. Great food, free-flowing alcohol, and I'm pretty sure if you last the whole night, you'll get lucky at the end of it."

For a long time, Ben had been convinced his luck had run out. Now, though, it appeared the fickle Lady Luck had her eye on him once again. "Big talk, Ms. Rhodes. I'll believe it when I see you naked."

"Stay tuned," she teased with a sultry smile.

CHAPTER NINETEEN

I have great hopes that we shall love each other
all our lives as much as if we had never married
at all.

—Lord Byron

BEN RAN A finger around the inside of his collar. For
about the twentieth time. Next he'd fiddle with his green
tie, then smooth the ivory lapels of his linen suit coat.
Ivy knew this because she'd watched him repeat the
sequence incessantly over the past hour. Odd, since
normally he reminded her of a jaguar: eerily still, but
ever observant.

"You strike me as a party-loving man. So what's the
matter? You've been moody since you picked me up."

"I do like parties. But I think your definition is different than mine. This," he threw out his arms to encompass the black and white ballroom with windows on
three sides, twenty-three floors above the city, "shindig
for your parents—not a party."

Ivy ran her hands down a black velvet curtain, and
tweaked the red tassel that held it in a perfect vee. Her
mother had a whole princess-and-the-pea thing when
it came to events. One mis-draped curtain, a single
crooked napkin out of dozens of tables, and she'd bird-
dog right to it. Ivy had spent the last half hour circling

the room to ensure perfection. "People. Food. Conversation. You don't need to reference Merriam-Webster on this one."

"You, of all people, should know the devil is in the details. To me, a party's where I can talk smack with my colleagues, get a little too drunk, and then flirt with a smorgasbord of women."

"Wow. You just hit a new level of insensitivity."

"How is a discussion of semantics insensitive?" He drained his gin and tonic and gestured for the bartender to refill. When they'd arrived, he'd made a beeline for the bar and had kept at least one elbow propped on it ever since.

"Do you realize I'm standing right in front of you?" Ivy tried to tamp down the temper he'd stoked. "Here's a tip: avoid discussion of an all-you-can-eat female buffet when you had your hand down my dress in the cab twenty minutes ago."

"See? This is the difference between the sexes. Deep-seated insecurity about your ability to hold my interest got your dander up. I didn't say I wanted to stick my tongue down the throats of a dozen different ladies tonight—you just assumed it."

"First you insult me, then you psychoanalyze me? Are you trying to piss me off?" And then it hit her, and she wondered why she hadn't seen it sooner. "You're trying to piss me off. Let me guess, your big plan is to make me mad enough so that I kick you out of the party?"

"Depends." His lips quirked to one side in a half-grimace, half-smile. "Is it working?"

"Not on your life." She'd spent weeks planning this party. Her parents and grandparents would be able to

meet Ben under ideal circumstances—a crowded room
with lots of other people as distraction, so they didn't
give him a full court interrogation. "You'll have friends
to hang out with; Sam and Gib are coming. Daphne,
too. I won't abandon you in a sea full of strangers, I
promise."

"Ivy, I don't do parents. The last time I had to meet
a girl's parents was before my senior prom."

If she hadn't seen it with her own two eyes, she never
would've believed it. Bennett Westcott was nervous!
"Do you think my dad's going to charge in carrying
a shotgun and demand to know if your intentions are
honorable?"

"Yeah. That's more or less how it plays out in my
mind."

So adorable! "Look on the bright side," she said with
a reassuring pat on his arm.

"What—that at least I haven't gotten you pregnant?"

Her smile tightened until it felt like she'd left her
apricot cleansing mask on two hours too long. "Well,
I can't argue with you there. But I meant that at least
you won't have to panic much longer, because my parents just arrived."

Ben straightened off the bar so fast his drink sloshed
over the edge. He also took two steps back, as if scared
to be caught within arm's length of Ivy. The cloud of her
mother's perfume swept ahead like a rose-scented carpet unrolling for her. Samantha wore flame-red satin.
Ivy presumed her mother chose the color to show off
the anniversary gift her father would present after dinner. Forty years was the ruby anniversary, a fact Samantha had probably reminded David of every month
for the past year. He trailed slightly behind her, dapper

in a tuxedo. Like a shadow, he was for the most part quiet, but always right at her elbow.

Ivy kissed the air near her mother's cheek, then gave her father a warm embrace. "Congratulations on being the happiest couple I know. You put all my newlyweds to shame."

"Well, when you live with your favorite person in the world, what's not to be happy about?" Her father's attention turned, as ever, to Samantha. Ivy didn't know how they survived being separated during the workday. Their devotion, even after forty years together, was nothing less than inspiring to behold.

To his credit, Ben stepped forward, hand outstretched. "Congratulations on forty years with the most beautiful woman in the room. You're a lucky man, Mr. Rhodes." David pumped his hand heartily.

"He is indeed," twinkled Samantha. "But I didn't exactly get the short end of the stick."

Ivy laid a hand on Ben's arm, drawing him into the tight family circle. "Ben, as you've already guessed, these are my parents, Samantha and David Rhodes. Mom, Dad, this is the man who's been trailing after me for six weeks."

Because she knew no better way to relate to the male of the species, her mother simpered, then turned the full wattage of her flirtatious attention onto Ben. With her index finger, she tapped on the end of her nose. Eyes the color of emeralds widened.

"Your reputation precedes you, Mr. Westcott."

Ben met the challenge head on. "Which one?"

"Touché."

David cleared his throat. "Let's not beat around the bush. We respect the work you did a few years back, and we respect the care you're taking while working now with Ivy."

The brittle, professional grin Ben wore like a uniform warmed a bit. "Duly noted." The five-piece jazz combo announced the beginning of their set with a trumpet flourish, then settled into the smooth beat of a bossa nova.

"Would you care to dance, Mrs. Rhodes?" Ben held out one hand, palm up. "That is, if your husband doesn't mind my usurping you for a few minutes."

For all of his earlier twitchiness, Ben rose to the occasion like a champ. Or a well-practiced gigolo. Ivy's stomach fluttered back into place, and she checked one major worry off her list for the evening. Her parents and Ben had survived introductions without any major fallout. Every bit of her plan was falling into place.

A blissfully happy father, a party-loving, grateful mother, and a boyfriend who, if she didn't miss her guess, was on the cusp of declaring his love. Especially as an adult, nobody went through the bother of meeting the parents unless they had serious plans for the future. Right on cue, guests began to trickle through the doors. Waiters began to make the rounds with trays of caviar-topped potatoes and mushroom dip. Another signature Aisle Bound event was going off without a hitch.

"You used to travel constantly for your work?" David asked. Ivy hadn't known the safest place to stick Ben at dinner, so she'd put her easy-going father on one side, and Sam on the other, next to her. Here they were halfway through the lobster and filet, and conversation still flowed freely.

Ben shrugged. "Sometimes I'd be in three different

countries before dinner. Other times we'd hunker down in a city for weeks at a time. The only thing you could count on was the unpredictability. Of course, when I worked on *Wild Wedding Smackdown*, it'd be a different town every weekend. I figure I know the ins and outs of most airports better than the TSA agents do."

"How does it feel to have your wings clipped, staying here in Chicago all summer?"

"I like it." He leaned in closer, but Ivy could still hear him. "Maybe I'm getting old, but I've got to admit I enjoy having a hot shower every morning. Not taking malaria pills, or shaking out my shoes to check for scorpions or snakes. Even better, Gib's managed to get me running with him most mornings."

"Ah." David nodded knowingly. "You must jog along Lake Michigan. The path where all the girls in spandex and bikinis run."

Huh. She wouldn't have pegged her father as an ogler, but if it helped him stick to an exercise regimen, more power to him. Truth be told, Ivy particularly enjoyed doing her yoga at the North Avenue beach so she could watch the shirtless guys playing sand volleyball.

"Certainly keeps me motivated." Ben shoveled in food like he hadn't eaten in three days. Then he drained half a glass of an excellent pinot, and motioned for the waiter to fill his glass. Ivy had lost count of his drinks by this point, but knew it to be enough she couldn't believe he could still form coherent sentences. With a subtle jerk of her head, she shooed the waiter off in the opposite direction. She'd never seen Ben drink like this. If it took this much alcohol for him to cope with her parents, he'd need a liver transplant by Christmas.

"Harder in winter." David winked. "Come October, I switch from running outside to Zumba at the club."

Ivy almost choked on her asparagus. "You what?"

"Zumba. You know, it's like aerobics, but set to salsa music. All the ladies love the class. I still get to watch all the jiggling, then I go home and show off my sweet moves to my main squeeze. Everybody wins."

No. She refused to imagine her father shaking his booty to Shakira in sweat pants. There were some things a child just shouldn't learn about their parents.

"You should come with me, Ben. It'd be nice to get a little more testosterone in the class."

Ben paired a vague, unintelligible sound with a nod.

To her great relief, Sam dove into the breach. "How's fishing this season up at the cabin, Mr. Rhodes? Catch any big ones?"

"Work's piled up. We hadn't planned to go until July."

Samantha chimed in from the other side of the round table. "But now we'll need to go up at least a few days early to start the search."

Oh no. Ivy knew exactly where this conversation was going. Kind of like watching a semi that had lost its brakes careen down a mountain road. Unstoppable.

"We've got to start looking for a new cabin," David announced.

Sam shook his head. "Aw, did that last blizzard in February do in the roof?"

"No, she's in great shape. But family tradition says the cabin passes down from each generation at the wedding of the oldest child. A wedding present. Does your family pass down any traditions, Ben?"

"Just a curse."

The whole table laughed, thinking he'd told a joke. Ivy knew better, and noted the tic in his clenched jaw. Her dad pushed away his empty plate, patted his stomach, then continued.

"From the looks of things, this'll be our last summer before the cabin passes to Ivy."

Ivy could not risk looking at Ben. She assumed him to be either ghost white, slack jawed, or moving away from the table at the speed of light. "I'm not getting married. I'm not engaged. You didn't just jump to conclusions, Dad, you pole-vaulted."

"Now, now. Don't get your feathers ruffled. I'm being pragmatic, honey. We've already got four cabins at the compound. I'm not sure there's room to build another. If we want to find something in the immediate vicinity, we can't afford to drag our feet another three or four months until you've got a ring on your finger." David turned back to Ben. "Do you fish?"

"Not unless it's the only way to get dinner."

"Wisconsin is God's country. You'd love it up there. We fish and hike, and in the autumn we build enormous bonfires. And we all know that every man's got a little bit of a pyromaniac in him, right? Who doesn't like to poke at a huge, roaring fire?"

Daphne tapped on Ivy's shoulder. "You ready to give the toast?" she whispered in her ear, crouching down next to her chair.

"Not a great time," Ivy whispered back. Ben's lips were pursed, white around the edges. One hand toyed with the stem of his wine glass, tilting it this way and that, and his eyes were locked onto his plate. She needed to extricate Ben from her well-meaning but incredibly pushy parents ASAP.

Again, Daphne tapped on her shoulder, this time more insistently. "You asked me to coordinate tonight, and according to the timetable, you wanted to make the speech before dessert. They're already clearing some of the tables. We're not running late. Not on my watch." Gib stood behind her, ready to pass over the microphone in his hand.

"Bigger problems right now than sticking to the schedule, Daph." Ivy tuned back in to the conversation right as her mother dropped the conversational grenade in Ben's lap.

"How would you like to come to our cabin for Columbus Day weekend? We'll go to a fish boil. As authentically Wisconsin as beer and brats, but better for you."

"I can't."

Samantha doled out an indulgent smile. "Oh, I see the problem. Don't worry, we're all adults. We won't make you and Ivy sleep in separate rooms."

"Sorry, but I can't," he repeated.

Sam elbowed him in the ribs. "What's the matter, got a better offer?"

Ever so slowly, those storm-cloud eyes rose to meet Ivy's. "I'll be in Darfur in October."

Ivy felt like she was in one of those action movies, where the minute the bomb explodes, everything switches into slow motion. Her parents looked mildly surprised. Gib and Sam, who had a better grasp of what his words meant, looked stunned. Ivy reached down and grabbed Daphne's hand for support. Although petrified of the answer, she forced herself to ask the logical question in a calm voice. "Seems like an odd place to film *Planning for Love*. Why Darfur?"

"It's not for *PFL*. It's not for RealTV at all. After I called in that tip about Senator Newsome last week, people were grateful. Figured maybe I still had a nose for news and an eye for the right shots. I got the call this afternoon. I'm going to film a documentary about the ongoing conflict in Sudan." Ben paused for a second, as if giving a moment for the weight of his words to truly sink in. He took a swig of water, and when Ivy didn't respond, he cleared his throat.

"We start shooting in September, right after Labor Day, go for maybe five months. This kind of in-depth story, representing the humanitarian crisis and genocide on a daily basis, hasn't been done before. It'll bring awareness of their plight to the world in a whole new way."

Deep down, Ivy realized the enormity of this offer. It meant his colleagues had restored faith in his abilities. It meant validation. But, given that he'd been a coward and waited to spring the news in front of a crowd, she was pretty sure it also meant they were over. "You're leaving."

"Yes."

She tightened her grip on Daphne. "You're leaving me."

Ben dipped his head in acknowledgement. "I planned to tell you later tonight. I didn't want to spoil the party."

"Great plan," Daphne scoffed, sarcasm as deep as Lake Michigan. "How's it working out so far? Everyone still full of the romantic celebration vibe?"

"Stay out of it," Gib warned in a low voice. "Ivy and Ben have enough trouble right now without interference from onlookers."

Ivy reminded herself not to leap to conclusions, not

to fall into a full-blown panic. By its very nature, Ben's job was transient. But jetting off to San Diego for a week was one thing. It was another thing entirely to disappear for five months into a country so dangerous he might not survive.

In a tone that surprised her with its steadiness, she asked, "Am I supposed to wait for you?"

Ben's gaze slowly roamed the room in a full circuit. When it finally landed on her, his eyes had darkened to the indigo of a fresh bruise. Just like the one blossoming on her heart. "No."

"Why don't we go take a turn around the dance floor?" David suggested.

"No." Ivy cracked out the response like a whip. Damned if she'd let him hide her in a corner like an embarrassment, or worse yet, just walk out on her. "Ben, you're the one who decided this special occasion filled with my friends and family would be the appropriate place to break your big news. So you might as well finish it here. Saves me the trouble of re-telling the story to everyone later."

His eyes softened with regret. "Ivy, don't."

"Don't what? Don't make a scene? Don't care? Don't wonder what made you decide to turn your back on an amazing relationship?" Oh, she'd make a scene, all right. Certainly not in the place of her choosing, but the man of her dreams wouldn't walk out on her without providing some answers, and she'd do whatever it took to shake them loose.

"We could never have a real, lasting relationship. I'm Mr. Right Now, not Mr. Right. Look at all this." He flung out his arms, waved at Samantha and David, then at her grandparents seated at the next table. "I could never live up to your expectations for a relationship. I'm not built that way. This is why I left you back in April. This is why I said on that rooftop in Greektown, plain as day, we should enjoy ourselves for *six weeks*. Don't act surprised—I told you flat out that I'm not a long-term kind of guy. I don't want to hurt you, but I'm not capable of being the man you deserve."

Did he really think she was that stupid? Ivy stood and stalked over to stand in front of him. "That's a gussied-up version of *it's not you, it's me.* You are not laying that trite line on me. You don't get to disappear halfway around the world with nothing more than *it's not you, it's me.*"

He sighed. Did the whole finger-under-the-collar, lapel-smoothing thing again to give himself a minute to regroup. "Look, this job is a once in a lifetime opportunity. The second chance I never thought I'd get. A do-over that could completely change my life. You know how important my job is to me."

Did he even realize how his subconscious took over that last sentence? She doubted it. She doubted Ben realized anything except how easy running away would be, compared to staying put.

"Correction. I know how important your news job *was* to you. Not one week ago you told me how much you enjoy your current job. The one where you have artistic freedom, and yet don't have to stare death in the eye on a daily basis. I know you're passionate about politics and world events. The world needs more people in it who give a damn as much as you do. But come on, Ben. Five months in the Sudan? There probably isn't a more dangerous assignment on the planet. Is getting back into the news worth risking your life? Or is it that you'd rather shadow murderous tribesmen than stay with me?" She shook her head and crossed her arms over her chest. Ivy wouldn't let him leave until she damn well knew why. No way would she spend the next few weeks sobbing her eyes out without knowing the reason. "Have enough respect to at least be honest, with yourself and with me."

"Fine." Ben shoved back from the table and stood as well. "I've been upfront about this from the beginning. You represent everything I can't have—security, family, the perfect home behind a picket fence. Seeing what you have shows me what I'll fail at without even making an attempt."

"Or you could make the attempt, and surprise yourself. You work so hard, make such a point of not caring about anything. You're more scared to let yourself truly feel than anyone I've ever met." The harsh words flew out of her mouth. She'd harbored these thoughts since that weekend in April with him, but foolishly hoped he would change. And had feared pushing his self-reflection too far would end up pushing him away. No reason to shy away from confronting him with the truth now, though. "You're not just afraid of commitment—you're afraid of emotion."

"Sure, I'll cop to that." Ben shoved his hands deep in his pockets. "Safer that way. These statistics are outside your comfort zone, but do you know the divorce rate? Somewhere just short of astronomical. Hell, not even marriage. Do you know how many ugly, squabbling couples I see at weddings? Bitter, angry people who are so miserable together, they can't keep from fighting at their friend's big event? People who get more scarred and bitter with each failed relationship? I can't get hurt if I don't open myself up in the first place."

Yup. Bottom line—he was scared stiff. This man who'd traveled the world staring death in the face was nothing more than a yellow-bellied, emotional coward. "Please. Go back to filming floods, famine, a daily dose of death. You think that won't hurt? Won't eat away at your soul? You can't escape pain—but you can embrace joy to temper it. Where's your joy, Ben?" Ivy poked her finger into the center of his chest to drive home the question. Tried not to think about how it could be the very last time she touched that wonderful, muscled chest, even if in anger.

"The higher you fly, the farther and harder you fall. Joy's an aspiration I don't seek. My family's chased it for years, and never got within two miles of it. I got too damn close to it here in Chicago. Should've known the shit was about to hit the fan."

"Oh, right. Chicago's treated you so horribly. You've made a circle of friends, have a rewarding job, and you get to be with a woman who loves you. Nobody is pulling the plug on that life but you!"

"Ivy, you don't love me. You're in love with love itself."

All the burning pain and anger within her iced over. She lifted her chin. "Do not dismiss my feelings. You don't have to return them, but you certainly don't get to judge them."

"I don't buy this off-hand declaration of love. You're just spouting off in the heat of the moment. A last-ditch effort to make me stay. If you really were in love with me, you would've said so. Hell, you would've shouted it from the rooftops. You're physically incapable of keeping that emotion a secret."

He thought he knew her so well. She'd wipe that supercilious smirk right off his face. "I hadn't told you yet because I didn't want to scare you. The plan was always to wait until after you told me you loved me. After we made love, I'd tell you. The culmination of the perfect plan." Whoops. She hadn't meant to say that last part out loud. Even to her ears, it sounded a bit absurd. Her profession had taught her over and over again that there was no such thing as a perfect plan. Which is why she usually had contingency plans and back-ups for those. Except this time, when it mattered most, Ivy had no backup. No way to fix the yawning chasm between her and Ben, growing wider every second.

"A plan? You had a plan for our relationship?" Ben choked out a laugh, a harsh, scornful sound. Looked up at the ceiling, then drove his fingers through his hair. "Of course you did. Now I realize why you've been such a tease, why we haven't made it back to the bedroom after all these weeks."

His voice rose to a near shout. The musicians sputtered to a stop. Twelve tables of guests swiveled their heads to watch the action. "Well, what you call a plan? I call a trap. I'm not a puppet for you to manipulate. My life is my own, my choices my own. You can't plan for love, Ms. Rhodes. And you're sure as hell not going to get it from me."

Ivy stared, motionless, while the man she loved turned his back on her and stalked out of the ballroom. She watched his lithe, lionlike grace, his hair burnished the gold of ancient Roman coins by the crystal chandeliers. One last glimpse of his profile, those generous lips she adored locked down into a thin, grim line. Then he was gone. Forever.

Hand flailing, she reached out to grab the nearest wine glass and lifted it high in the air. "Since I'm quite sure I have everyone's attention, I'll take this opportunity to make my toast. Congratulations to my parents, Samantha and David Rhodes. They've stayed happy together for forty years. I think we've all just had a glimpse of what a rare, amazing accomplishment that is." Sheer willpower kept her tears at bay. Her parents deserved nothing but joy this night, and she'd already contributed too much sorrow to the evening. "They are a remarkable couple who make each other happy every single day. Thank you for being an inspiration to all of us, and wonderful parents to me. Here's to forty more blissful years."

As the entire room cheered and clinked glasses, Ivy kissed each of her parents on the cheek. Then the twisting, clawing knot in her stomach reached up through her throat. She tamped it back down by draining her glass. She wouldn't let Ben ruin her enjoyment of excellent champagne. No, she'd kick up her heels, dance with her father, and Sam, and Gib. Gib especially, since he was a whiz on the dance floor thanks to his fancy schools back in England. Yes, Ivy would stay to the end of this party, to have one last happy night before the empty string of tear-laden nights alone began. She'd just lost her best shot at happily ever after. Worst of all, it was her own fault. Her brilliant plan had backfired in a way she'd never anticipated.

CHAPTER TWENTY

The proper basis for a marriage is mutual misunderstanding.

—Oscar Wilde

BEN HATED MORNINGS. On the best of days, with the ferocity of a rabid tiger, the sun had a way of getting its claws into you and shaking until your head pounded and you wanted to beg for mercy. This morning proved to be a fresh level of hell.

After leaving the party, he'd hunkered down at a dark, squalid dive bar. Half a dozen shots and as many beers later, he concluded the answer to his problems didn't lie at the bottom of a glass. Staring sleeplessly at the ceiling for four hours hadn't exactly improved his filthy mood. Now his stomach turned over from the drinks, and his head throbbed from…well, everything else. Especially squinting at his laptop while firing off emails to get him the hell out of town.

Ollie could shoot without him for a few days until RealTV sent a replacement. He didn't care if they docked his pay, but he'd be damned if he'd show up at Aisle Bound with a camera on his shoulder. It took some serious web-surfing to snag any flight, thanks to a day's worth of backups from some East Coast hurricane. Now, with only one day left in Chicago, he could at least try to calm his stomach by laying down a layer of sugar and grease from Lyons Bakery's epic donuts.

He pushed through the door just shy of dawn, then paused at the threshold when he saw Sam loading the bakery case. Too late to cut and run, thanks to the damn tinkling bell on the door. Sam locked eyes with him, then jerked a chin toward a table at the back. Ben paused in front of the donuts.

"Does a condemned man still get one last meal? Because I don't think I can do this without a cruller or ten. And a vat of coffee."

Sam gave a nod, wiped his hands on his apron. "I'll set you up. We've got a special cherry fritter this morning that'll turn your world upside down. Take a seat."

Looked like Sam didn't plan on decking him anytime soon, and the prospect of a cherry fritter to top it off? There was a god after all. Ben rested the heels of his hands against his eyes. Whatever Sam dished out, he could take it. Couldn't be any worse than what Ivy served up last night.

"You look rough around the edges. Tough night?" Sam slid a plate onto the table, then deposited two giant mugs of coffee.

"One time in Afghanistan we spent the night with an Army battalion pinned down between two groups of rebels who didn't realize they were on the same side. No food or water. Our radio got shot, so we couldn't call for help. The lieutenant had a fractured leg, which meant running like hell wasn't an option." Ben took a long, life-giving gulp of coffee. "That night was a cakewalk compared to last night."

"Good to know you're keeping everything in perspective."

Here we go. "Let me lay it out for you. I only came here because Ivy told me you never work the early shift. I don't want to cause any trouble, and I don't want to rehash what should be a private matter between me and Ivy."

Sam did a spit take with his coffee, spraying it onto the floor. "Private? Buddy, stripping naked at center court at a Bulls game is more private than that show you and Ivy put on for all of us. So many people know about it there's probably a review in the *Tribune*. But I'm not going to bust your balls."

Another quick peek around the room confirmed Ben's suspicions. They were all alone. "Crap. No witnesses. You are going to beat me up, aren't you? Is Gib all lined up to swing by in half an hour to help you dump my body in the Chicago River?"

"We didn't have a formal schedule laid out, but..." Sam's voice trailed off, then after a second he burst out laughing and clapped Ben hard on the arm. "Don't be an idiot. Ivy didn't put a hit out on you. We're sure as hell not going to work you over. We're friends. Aren't we?"

He'd wondered all along if everyone accepted him because of Ivy, or if he'd made genuine friendships. Assumed, after last night's debacle, that the whole crowd would take Ivy's side without question. Throw a parade as soon as his plane took off from O'Hare tomorrow, waving *Good Riddance* placards. "Yeah, I guess we are. Does this mean I can eat my donuts in peace?"

"Nope. But on the bright side, I have no intention of talking about Ivy—"

"Great." Ben whooshed out a sigh of relief. The entire day loomed ahead of him, and he didn't have a damn thing to do, except avoid everyone connected to

Aisle Bound. If he wasn't going to get the third degree, he'd stay. Hanging out with Sam wouldn't be a bad way to pass the morning. Most importantly, it'd distract him from second guessing his decision about Darfur.

"—or what an incredible tool you were to her parents. Timing is not your strong suit."

"Hey, I didn't intend to ruin the party. Mr. and Mrs. Rhodes kept yammering at me about the future, trying to lock me down. You were there—you heard them. How else could I shut them up?"

"Not getting into it. But I do want to talk to you, as a friend, about your career."

Ben bit into a fritter, then bit back a moan. The cherry goodness exploded in his mouth, and lifted an ounce of the multi-ton lid of darkness currently suffocating his heart. "You want to tag along? I'm sure we could find room for a guy who knows his way around a camp stove."

"No way. The mean streets of Chicago are all the danger I can handle."

"Wuss." Ben licked his fingers and started in on the second fritter. If Sam wanted his fair share off the plate, he'd better be quick.

"Sure. But I know I'll live to see forty. Can you say the same thing?"

"I don't need a mother, Sam. Hell, I don't listen to the one I've got."

"Listen to me—as a friend—for five minutes."

After all the money he'd skimmed off him in poker, he owed Sam that much. "Okay."

"No secret I'm a news geek. It was a red-letter day when I discovered I could follow my favorite reporters on Twitter. I've been a fan of your work for years."

Weird. And strangely humbling. He'd never had a groupie before. After the incident, he'd shut down his Twitter account and Facebook. Enough people vilified him in newspapers and television. He missed Tweeting with other fans during ball games, but Ben sure as hell didn't need anyone snarking to him directly. "Want me to autograph your apron before I go?"

"You got a raw deal with the whole Cowering Cameraman label. But fair or not, the industry turned its back on you. Could've been the end. Instead, you turned it around, and made a whole new life. From what I can tell, you're good at it, and you like it." Sam leaned his elbows on the table. "Why walk away from a good thing?"

"Granted, *Planning for Love* is heads and tails a better show than *Wild Wedding Smackdown*. But it's still reality television. You going to sit there and tell me reality shows are as respected and important as the news?"

"You going to sit there and tell me you're going to risk your life in one of the most dangerous places on the planet because you're a television snob? Out of pride? What happens if this documentary goes nowhere? The news industry will still bar their doors to you, and you'll have shot yourself in the foot with RealTV. Then what? You'll be stuck coming here and helping me roll out pie crust for a living, because no one else will have you. If you even survive."

"I'm getting vaccinated, for Christ's sake. Chances are slim I'll die of malaria, or tuberculosis, or anything else."

"Right. Because rebel guerillas and pissed-off Sudanese National Guard always ask their victims to show a passport before shooting."

Ben dropped the rest of his fritter back onto the plate. Guess the sugar didn't agree with his roiling stomach after all. "I appreciate the concern. But I've been in more dangerous places and come out okay. Risk comes with the job. It's what I do."

"Is it? It used to be. Until circumstances forced you to try something new, something more artistic."

"*Wild Wedding Smackdown* was humiliating. Several steps below rock bottom. Maybe a hair above shoveling fries into a sack." But he'd had no choice. The networks castrated him, professionally speaking.

"Sure. But RealTV saw your talent, and gave you a chance to shine. A job that still challenges you, but in different ways. A job you admitted fulfilled you on a surprising level. You told us at poker last week how much you love producing. You're on the cusp of a whole new career. Why toss that chance away?"

"I've never heard you string so many sentences together at one time. Thought you were the one guy I could count on not to talk my ear off." No doubt about it, Ben couldn't get out of Chicago fast enough. He'd always been a lone wolf. All these people circling him, thinking they had the right to stick their noses in his business? It rankled him. Starting first and foremost with Ivy the puppet master. Well, he fucking refused to let anyone pull his strings. And he wouldn't sit here and suffer through a lecture, no matter how well meaning.

He pulled a couple of crumpled bills out of his shorts and tossed them on the table. "Thanks for breakfast. Since I doubt I'll be making my way back to the Windy City anytime soon, here's a tip to even the score: you've got a poker tell. I noticed it after just an hour of throwing cards with you. When you bluff, you start by taking three swigs of beer. See you around."

Ben slammed through the door with its damn tinkling bell and headed for the El stop. This morning officially sucked. Riding public transportation at dawn with a bunch of drunks coming off benders couldn't make it any worse.

"AHA." GIB POKED his head around the fitness center door. "Thought I'd find you here, old chap." The rich, plummy tones of his hearty greeting immediately raised Ben's antennae.

"Old chap?" he grunted as he continued to sweat through a never-ending set of pull-ups. "This is a weight room, not a nineteenth century club for members of the peerage. What unfurled the Union Jack up your ass?"

Gib crossed the window and leaned against the frame, crossing his ankles. "I see we're still in a mood. To be expected, I suppose."

"My workout, my mood. If you don't like it, go prop up somebody else's wall." Why wouldn't people leave him the hell alone? Shouldn't they all be shunning him, treating him like a pariah for breaking Ivy's heart? Ben grabbed his towel off the machine and swabbed his forehead. "What are you doing here, anyway? I thought you were off today."

"I am. These are my off-duty clothes." He smoothed a hand down the lapels of his blue sport coat. "See? No tie."

Ben moved to the weight bench machine and lay down. "Wow. You're really slumming it. Surprised the dress-code police didn't put out an APB on you."

"Your life may be little better than toxic sludge right now, but you've no call to take it out on me."

"My life's great." Bracing his feet on the floor, he began counting his bench press reps. Out loud. Maybe that'd shut Gib up.

"Bollocks." Gib snatched the barbell and placed it back on the rack.

Why couldn't he work out in peace and quiet? His sole goal for today was to avoid people. He'd texted Ollie instructions at midnight about flying solo for a few days. Emailed RealTV his plan to finish up the edits from New York for the next few weeks, and that they'd need to send another cameraman to Chicago to take his place. Then he'd turned off and packed his phone. In theory, that should've been enough to keep him off everyone's radar. In reality, it felt like he had a freaking homing device in his shoe.

Sighing, Ben rolled up into a stretch. "Seriously. Cut the Brit speak. You're freaking me out."

Gib sat on the fly machine across from him. "How are you?"

"Told you already. Life's great. My career's back on track, all's right with the world." Ben took a long pull from his water bottle.

"Don't be flip. Look, I came here today to check on you."

The troops were circling. Did they want him to have a security escort? Make sure he didn't do anything else to upset Ivy? Maybe they'd settle for house arrest—keep him here in the Cavendish. "Don't worry. I've got a flight out of town tomorrow morning. I'll give Ivy a wide berth until then. You don't have to protect her from me."

"Clearly the Queen's English isn't doing the trick." Gib rested his left foot on his knee, after straightening the pleat in his pants. "I'm not here about Ivy. I came to see how you were doing. Quite a bit of dirty laundry got aired last night. Wanted to be sure you're okay."

Ben assumed he'd been shifted to persona non grata status by Ivy's entire circle of friends and family the moment he left the ballroom last night. While he'd braced for a black eye from Sam, Gib wasn't the type to lead with his fists. Ben did expect he'd be black-balled from every Cavendish around the world. But first Sam surprised him, and now here was Gib acting suspiciously solicitous. "What's it to you?"

Something…off flickered in Gib's eyes. A moment later, his expression cleared. "We're friends. Friends look out for each other, offer a shoulder when one of them takes some lumps."

"You're Ivy's friend," Ben corrected.

"Quite right. In my capacity as Ivy's friend, I'll be popping by her place this evening with a cheery yet elegant bouquet. And a couple of bottles of chardonnay."

It took a lot to slam the door on the memory of Ivy's smiling face peeking over the rim of a wineglass. "Aren't you supposed to pick sides? Love her, hate the guy who walked out on her?"

"Not everything in the world is black and white. You're walking away from a rather nice life. Can't be easy. Are you sure this new job is worth losing everything you'll leave behind?"

Why did everyone insist on second-guessing him? "I'm returning to my old job, the one that put its foot on my ass and booted me out the door. If I don't grab this opportunity with both hands, I'll never get another one."

Gib stood. "Would that be so bad? You closed that door once, Ben. Just because it opens again doesn't mean you're obligated to walk through it. Think about what—and who—you have here. A second chance at life-long happiness doesn't come around very often. You sure you want to risk it?" He shook Ben's hand, grimaced, wiped his hand on a fresh towel and left the room.

Maybe some self-enforced house arrest would be the only way to get any peace and quiet, Ben thought as he whaled away on the heavy bag. He'd rather hole up in his room for the rest of the day than endure any more unwanted soul-searching from his friends. Hell, he'd rather go sit at O'Hare for the next twenty-four hours than sit through another conversation like that.

"BENNETT? ARE YOU decent?" Before Ben could answer, Julianna let herself into the hotel room. Cursing under his breath, he cinched the flimsy towel around his waist a little tighter. He held his ground at the threshold of the steam-filled bathroom.

"What the hell do you think you're doing? How did you get in here?"

"Gib gave me a key." She lifted the thin plastic card and waved it in the air. "Said he was quite sure you wouldn't let me in, and he believes you need to hear what I've got to say."

Great. Another person who thought they had the right to tell him how to live his life. Should've gone to the airport and parked on a barstool after all. "What is this, a fucking intervention? How many of you are going to come and butt your noses into my business?"

"I don't know." She closed the door and planted her sensible black flats right by his bare toes. "How long will it take you to rip the blinders off your eyes and face the truth?"

Christ. They were in Chicago—at this rate Dr. Phil would be the next one through his door to talk some sense into him. The redhead picked the wrong day to pick a fight. If she didn't get out in two minutes, he'd call security and have her removed. Ben braced his hands high up on the doorframe, leaning his bare, still-damp chest right into her face. Maybe the sheer power of his naked masculinity would scare her off.

"Here's a cold, hard truth. You've never liked me. I know it's because you think I hurt Ivy back in April, and you wanted to protect her. Believe it or not, I get it. I respect you for looking out for her. But I've had more than my fill of people who actually like me sharing their thoughts today. I'll be damned if I'll stand here and let someone berate me who treats me with disdain on the best of days."

"I'm sorry."

He'd expected an unending string of vitriol. Maybe a slap in the face, accompanied by a lot of cursing. Threats of dire retribution if he ever contacted Ivy again. But not an apology, of all things. Shocked, he dropped his arms and took a step back. "Come again?"

Julianna inclined her head with its smooth, short caplet of crimson hair. "I've been a stone cold bitch to you. Kind of became a habit. You didn't deserve the daily dose of animosity I dished out. So, I'm sorry."

Interesting twist. He didn't know what to make of it.

"Fair enough. You going to let me put on some clothes now?"

A flush almost as bright as her hair stained her cheeks. She backed into the hallway. "Sorry."

"Geez, that word just flows like water out of you all of a sudden. What gives?" Ben stalked past her and grabbed his orange cargo shorts off the bed. Took a beat to consider the fun of the shock value, deemed it the only bright spot in a miserable day, and dropped his towel without warning Julianna. Then stifled a chuckle when he heard her gasp. That'd teach her to barge into a man's room without asking.

"Well, first of all, I truly am sorry for the way I treated you."

"Duly noted."

"And second, I want to make sure you listen to what I'm about to say."

Ben zipped his pants, then pulled a yellow polo shirt over his head. After this, he was definitely checking out of the Cavendish. Immediately. "Fine. Spit it out."

Taking a few, tentative steps, she eased over to the desk and put her hand out for support. "I always thought you were selfish. But I never realized until today that you were self-sabotaging as well."

Unbelievable. An apology like that might as well come with a side of cruise missile and a body bag. "We're done." Hand on the small of her back, he ushered her to the door.

"Wait, I started wrong. I'm sorry." She threw herself back against the door, palms flat and fingers spread.

"Those magic two words only get you so far."

"I know. I'm nervous, because this is so important. Let me start over: I think you're perfect for Ivy."

Ben peered at her pupils. They seemed an appropriate size. But she sure acted like she was on something. "Are you high? 'Cause it's the only logical explanation for hating me, and yet saying I'd be the perfect match for your sainted mentor."

"I'm serious." Her words rushed out like rapids skipping over rocks in a river. "You rubbed me wrong at first. And you're right, I only wanted to protect Ivy. But you make her so very happy." Slowly, she eased off the door. When he made no move to stop her, she retraced her steps to sit in the leather desk chair.

"I made Ivy happy for a while. Past tense." Ben stayed in the doorway. He didn't want to give her any impression that she was welcome to stay.

"The thing is, though, she makes you happy, too. I've got a unique vantage point. I've been able to watch you, watching her. Day in and day out. And you know what?" She sighed deeply and put a hand over her heart. "You both light up like Christmas trees when you look at each other."

He didn't want to hear this. He hadn't wanted to hear Sam spout off about his career, or Gib talk about his happiness. But most of all, the one thing Ben wanted to accomplish all day, was to not hear about his relationship with Ivy. "Lust is sort of like fairy dust. It makes everything sparkle. For a while. Then it fades away."

She shook her head. "Might've started as lust. But it grew. You're right for Ivy. Walking away from her is a selfish, hurtful thing to do. The thing is, Ben," she steepled her fingers and rested her lips against them for a moment, "it hurts you just as much. I know your heart is broken into as many tiny pieces as Ivy's is right now."

"You don't know anything about me." The words

wrenched from his throat. If he wanted self-reflection, he'd go stand in front of a mirror. "I do. I know the longer I stay, the more I'll end up hurting her when I finally leave. Because I will, sooner or later. It's who I am. It's what I do." Belatedly, he realized he'd echoed the same words he tossed at Sam earlier, in reference to his job.

"It might be who you were. But every day is a chance to start fresh. You and Ivy love each other." Julianna popped out of the chair and stood with her hands on her hips. She looked pissed, and on the verge of yelling at him. Familiar territory. He knew she couldn't keep up the penitent act for very long.

"Ben, take your head out of your ass long enough to admit it, if only to yourself. Think about how you feel when she looks at you, when she laughs with you. Then ask yourself: Can chasing your old dreams down memory lane make you feel that good? Give you a happy ending?"

She'd tested his patience enough. "You want to know the only way to get a guaranteed happy ending? Tip an extra twenty percent at a massage parlor. In fact, thanks for the idea. Now I've got a plan for my afternoon." Ben opened the door and stood with a hand on the knob. "Unless you care to join me, your time's up." *That* sent her scurrying down the hall past the bathroom. His luck ran out when she stopped in front of the mirrored closet doors.

"When little kids are scared of the monster in the closet, you know what the parents do? They open the door. Prove there aren't any monsters. Well, you're scared of being happy. So what would happen if you opened the door on your fear?" With that parting shot, Julianna left.

Ben slammed the door behind her. Then he yanked open the closet door so hard it came off its rails. If it meant registering for standby on three different airlines, it didn't matter. He'd do whatever it took to get out of this town tonight. And, God willing, never come back.

CHAPTER TWENTY-ONE

The highest happiness on earth is marriage.
                    —William Lyon Phelps

IVY SCANNED HER appointment book. No more meetings today. Only a quick flinch as her eyes skipped over the words *dinner with Ben* she'd drawn a heart around earlier in the week. Refused to give in to the temptation to scratch it off the page with the dull tip of her letter opener. When she woke up for the second day in a row stuffy from a night of tears, realization dawned. Her whole, elaborate plan for love came about because she'd followed her passion. So how could she fault Ben for following his?

Being mature about his decision to leave didn't mitigate the pain, but it did allow her to face herself in the mirror this morning. That is, until she glimpsed the black circles and swollen redness caused from a night of wallowing. She'd flinched away from the sight faster than a vampire near holy water. Ivy checked her watch. Right on the cusp of four o'clock. Shut down the computer, picked up her purse, and threw open the door to her office.

"Time to celebrate," she yelled down the hall. That should get everyone's attention.

"Didn't expect to hear those words come out of your

mouth for a while," said Daphne. She stuck a handful of greens in her apron pocket and trailed after her to the reception area. "Aren't we still in the early days of Misery and Mourning Month?"

"Yes and no." Ivy plopped on the sofa, carefully arranging the myriad pleats in her favorite apple-green skirt. Standing in front of her closet this morning, she'd decided dressing up to be the best way to distract from the redness in her eyes and enormous bags underneath. "While I appreciate the effort you and Gib went to, coming up with an official name for my ongoing pathetic sadness—"

"At great personal expense," Daphne interrupted. "That fourth bottle of cabernet just about killed me. My headache didn't go away until an hour ago. But friends don't let friends drink alone."

"Hope you're ready to tie one on again, tonight. I promise this time it's for a happy reason." Which is why she'd insist they all celebrate. You'd think somebody died, the way everyone tiptoed around her in the two days since the abrupt and heartbreaking interruption to the party. While thoughtful and caring, their careful concern made her want to scream.

Thinking about Ben made everything hurt, from deep inside her heart to the tips of her freshly painted green nails. Ramdish, her yoga teacher, said the color green helped protect and heal the heart chakra. So today her panties, bra, nails, earrings, skirt, and even the bow in her hair were all the same color of a lush, late-spring leaf. While the ensemble had netted her a compliment from a drag queen sharing her morning commute on the El, so far Ivy's heart didn't feel even a little bit healed.

Daphne flopped down next to her. "We've got four

events this weekend. I, for one, need to get some sleep. Two nights on tear patrol's worn me out."

She never would've made it through the last two nights without Daphne, who let Ivy curl up and cry herself to sleep in her bed. "Have I mentioned you are the best friend ever?"

"Repeatedly. Especially every time I brought you another box of Kleenex."

"It bears repeating."

"Well, I love you." Daphne gave a quick, one-armed side hug. "We all do."

"Not all," Ivy corrected with a twist to her lips. "It's thanks to your support I can admit that, actually. I love Ben. I can't turn my love off just because he's gone. And he can't turn love on like a faucet, either." All this self-analysis made her heart ache. But Ivy figured it was like leg aches after going to the gym—a necessary evil. "Do I want my happily ever after to come right now? Yes. I'm sick of waiting. Except that, if he doesn't return my love, neither of us would be truly happy."

Daphne gaped at her. "Did you call a talk radio therapist in the middle of the night?"

"Even better. I looked through an old scrapbook. Pages of boys, and men, I fell for—some part way, some all the way. To figure out where I went wrong with Ben, I thought about why none of those relationships worked out. Starting with Derek Dillow back in the eighth grade."

"The ridiculous last name had to be a factor," guessed Milo.

"It didn't help." Nor did the fact she'd lapped him while swimming three days running. Some guys couldn't take a little healthy competition. "One of us was always more in love. And that never works. Both people have to be equally head over heels. No matter how hard I try, I can't force Ben to love me."

Daphne heaved a deep sigh. "I'm sorry. And I'm both proud of you, and sad for you."

"Me, too. And as of this moment, I'm going to leave all my moping out of the workplace. Now we celebrate. Except," Ivy did a double take of the office, "where's Julianna? Why isn't she here to share in my moment of triumph?"

Milo cleared his throat. "She never came back after lunch. Mumbled about how she lost a crown on one of her molars. But I guess her dentist squeezed her in, because she just texted me. Wants you to meet her for drinks in Wrigleyville. In half an hour."

Ivy beamed at him. "You guys are the sweetest. What did you do, sign up for shifts to take care of me? Well, this works out perfectly. We'll all go. Do our celebrating with Julianna, as it should be."

"You want to close the office early? Your news must be big. Milo, circle this one on the calendar," Daphne said with a lazy wave of her hand.

"Very funny. I'm too excited to work." She leaned forward to execute a mock drum roll on the coffee table. "Mira said yes. She accepted my offer to manage A Fine Romance."

Milo whistled through his teeth. "Good going, boss."

The phone call had been a balm to her bruised heart. It gave Ivy something to focus on aside from her endless wellspring of tears and heartache for Ben. She acknowledged her massive, strategic error. Learned her excruciatingly painful lesson—planning for love was impossible. But she could damn well plan for her business.

"We'll fly her out next week to get the lay of the land. Then she'll get started ordering merchandise while she ties up all her loose ends in Boston. Said she can be moved here completely by the end of August."

Daphne pulled down the side of her mouth in a grimace. "Isn't that cutting it close to the big opening?"

"A little." A lot, actually. "But Mira will be doing a lot on her end. And now that I have one fewer distraction in my life, I can spend all my spare time working at the store." Hopefully the long hours would give her something to think about other than how much she loved Ben. Or how worried she'd be every second he stayed in Darfur. Or how hopeless life looked now that he was gone.

Daphne leaned her head on Ivy's shoulder. "Honey, you can't bury yourself in work. It isn't healthy. You'll burn out."

"Don't worry about me. I'll be fine. I'll be fine faster if we all raise a glass to my new store!" She'd read somewhere that sharks have to keep constantly moving, even while sleeping, or they died. True or not, it perfectly embodied Ivy's approach to surviving this week. If she didn't keep moving, talking, *doing*, then she'd burst into tears and never stop. Ooze into a pathetic puddle of wretchedness.

According to Gib, Ben had left town this morning. But she'd felt wholly alone since the moment he'd walked out of the ballroom. Since he'd flung the love she offered right back in her face, without so much as acknowledging it. And, in fact, denying its very existence. Maybe he'd been right all along not to believe in happily-ever-after. Ivy certainly didn't believe it to be in her future anymore.

"WRIGLEYVILLE'S AN ODD choice," Daphne complained. "We never come here unless we're at a Cubs game."

Ivy elbowed her. If Julianna was going to go to all this trouble to cheer her up, then Ivy would make darn sure to at least project the illusion it worked. That meant everyone had to be cheery. Even Daphne, who'd griped the entire train trip about the turnstile prematurely eating her metro pass. "Keep an open mind. You know Julianna devours restaurant reviews like you do seed catalogs. I'm sure she's nosed out the newest, hottest spot in town."

"Her text did say she had something to show you," said Milo. "I'm thinking wine bar."

"Across from Wrigley Field?" Daphne wrinkled her nose. "Fat chance. My guess is a gourmet burger bistro. I hope they have duck fat fries."

Ivy couldn't think about food. She'd forced down a few slices of pizza last night, and a cup of yogurt this morning. But it was hard to eat with her stomach twisted in enough knots to tie up an ocean liner.

Shining like a beacon, Julianna's red hair bobbed ahead of them on the crowded sidewalk. She spotted them, waved, then frowned. "What are you doing here?" she called out as they approached.

Odd. "Meeting you for drinks. Or burgers. Daphne's convinced you've found us burgers."

"I only invited Ivy…" her voice trailed off. She shifted her weight from one foot to the other, then glanced sideways at the large tree next to her.

Hmm. Julianna could be very proprietary at times.

"Well, I asked the rest of the office to tag along. We're celebrating."

"Maybe."

"Cryptic much?" said Milo.

"Sorry." She laughed. "Guess that's my word of the week. As a matter of fact, I do know a great burger place around the corner. Ivy, meet us there when you're done. And good luck." She linked her arms through Daphne's and Milo's and rushed them across the street.

"Why do I need luck?" Ivy shouted after her.

"I think that was aimed at me." Ben stepped out from behind the tree. Dressed in a pale blue shirt and cargo shorts, he looked perfectly normal. Except there was nothing normal about him being here, on Clark Street, instead of on a plane bound for another continent.

His presence hit her on a physical level. All the air rushed out of her lungs, as swiftly as if he'd punched her. Gasping, she cradled an arm around her stomach. "What are you doing here?"

He twisted his lips into a wry grin. "Kind of a long story. Would you prefer I start with I'm a jackass, or go straight to I'm sorry?"

"The jackass part is self-evident. And I don't believe you're sorry about anything. You have to care to feel sorry. Goodbye, Ben." She didn't make it two steps before he snagged her arm.

"Hear me out. Please."

So hard to think with the welcome pressure of his fingers back on her skin. "I heard more than enough from you the other night. In the middle of my parent's anniversary party, in case it slipped your notice."

A nod. Then another. "Feel bad about that. It's why I took your mom flowers today."

Although she honestly had no idea what he wanted to say to her, that wouldn't have made it into her first hundred guesses. It definitely rooted her in place. "You visited my mother?"

"You bet. Took her an armful of lilies, to make her office smell nice. I apologized. Then I apologized again. I think she finally forgave me somewhere around the fifth apology. I'd fallen into a good rhythm by then."

Shock didn't begin to describe her reaction. What did it all mean? "I thought you didn't do parents."

He shuddered from head to toe, swishing his golden hair against his collar. "I don't. That is, I don't do just anyone's parents. Yours are special. Dropped in on your dad, too."

None of it made any sense. His words would make as much sense if he switched to speaking Swahili. Why break her heart, leave, but come back to make up with her parents? "You've been busy." His thumb slowly stroked the back of her arm. Ivy tensed against the soft caress.

"Well, I made the mess. Had to take the time to clean it up. David put me through the wringer. Took twice as long to come around as your mom did. His apology present stumped me for a while, but Julianna helped out there. Recommended a bottle of Laprohaig. Went over like gangbusters."

Maybe she was hallucinating. Lack of food and lack of sleep all caught up with her, and she was actually passed out on the floor of her office. It was the only rational explanation. Because in real life, Julianna would never help Ben do anything. "How does Julianna fit into this apology tour of yours?"

"Another long story. Let's just say she opened a door

for me, then helped me walk through it. Then helped me orchestrate my apology tour, and a few other odds and ends."

Ivy interlaced her fingers tightly. It was the only way to keep from reaching out, stroking the golden skin of his forearm. If she let herself touch him again, she'd probably burst into tears. For the four hundredth time. She still had enough pride intact to not want to fall apart in front of Ben. "Why? I don't understand. You're not even supposed to still be in Chicago."

"Well, I packed. I checked out of the Cavendish. Took a farewell walk along the lakeshore. Sat at the airport for about ten hours. Then I remembered one last, critical thing I had to do before leaving town."

"What might that be?"

"Grovel." Finger by finger, Ben unclasped her fingers, then threaded his own through. He led her over to a bus bench. "See, I remembered the first time I walked away from you. I swear, I did it to avoid hurting you. Didn't work. Backfired horribly, despite my good intentions. When I came back, we just sort of worked things out. I never apologized for hurting you. Truth be told, I've never stuck around before long enough to have to apologize."

He sounded different. He sounded aware his actions caused repercussions. It didn't sound like Ben at all. Ivy stared at the streaming traffic, rather than drown in the sea of his eyes. "It was very considerate of you to apologize to my parents."

"They were the warm-up act. I came back to apologize to you. To grovel, on my hands and knees, if that's what it takes. To convince you to take me back." He cupped his hands around hers, and held on tight. "Because I'm sorry. I'm sorry I've been a stubborn idiot. I'm sorry I said all those horrible things I didn't mean. I'm sorry when you offered me your love, I didn't grab onto it with both hands and hang on tight. Please forgive me, and give me another chance."

It sounded too good to be true. He was saying everything she wanted to hear. Which naturally made her suspicious. She'd been miserable the first time he left. The second time, she was barely holding herself together. Ivy knew she wouldn't survive a third rejection. "Why? What's changed so drastically in two days?"

"Me. Actually, I started changing weeks ago. As soon as I got to Chicago." He shifted on the bench. "Sam didn't beat me up yesterday."

"I'm not sure how I'm supposed to feel about that."

"He could've taken a shot, on your behalf. Would've been well within his rights as a friend. Instead, he talked through the long-term pros and cons of taking this job in Darfur. Pissed me off at the time. But it did make me realize two things. First off, revenge and pride drove me to take that job. Neither being an appropriate reason to change careers. But it wasn't until later the second piece hit me—Sam treated me like part of the family. Part of this big group of friends you've cobbled together into a family."

It hurt her heart, for him this time, that he hadn't realized that from the start. "Well, Sam likes you."

"Then Gib swung by to get his licks in. Not about how I'd ruined your life, but about the lack of happiness in my life. He pissed me off, too."

"No surprise there."

"I figured out the family thing applied to him, too. But the real kicker was when Julianna showed up."

Too fraught with emotion to filter her thoughts, Ivy blurted out, "She doesn't even like you."

Ben shrugged. "We had a rough start. She likes you, though. I guess great minds think alike. She hit me with the same accusation you did; that I was scared. When you hear the same thing enough times, it starts to sink in. A quote started running through my mind over and over again, like the news ticker at the bottom of a television screen: the only thing to fear is fear itself. Kennedy sure said a mouthful. And he was right."

Was this just an apology, to salve his conscience? Or could it truly be something more? "I'm sure his ghost has been pacing the grounds at Arlington Cemetery, waiting for your approval."

"Don't be a smart ass in the middle of my grovel. So I could either be a pussy my whole life, and be afraid of not living up to your expectations. Or I could confront that fear, and realize I was really afraid of not living up to my expectations. My irrational expectations that you'd only want me if I was perfect." Ben gently grasped her chin between his thumb and fingers, turning her to meet his gaze.

"I'm far from perfect, Ivy. But I love you. I've been falling in love with you since the day we met."

She couldn't listen to him for another moment. Not without sharing her own feelings. Not without making him realize how special she knew him to be. Her heart was so full it came bursting out of her mouth in a barrage of words. "I love you too, Ben. And I swear I mean it. I'm not in love with love, or hopped up on the idea of planning my own wedding. I love *you*. I love your resilience and strength and effortless charm and your obsession with pie and the way you hold my hand on the table while we eat and—"

"Whoa. This is my undying declaration of love. Wait your turn." Ben grinned, lifted her hands to brush a quick kiss over her knuckles. "I can't guarantee I'll be the man you deserve, but I can promise I'll die trying. I thought I'd spent my life running away from anything that could hurt me. In fact, I was running to something. To you, and to more happiness than I ever imagined possible. And in case you're skeptical about my change of heart, I've got proof." He picked her up, effortlessly, just like the day they met, and carried her to the edge of the sidewalk.

Ivy didn't see the growing crowd, and she didn't hear the buses lumbering by. Didn't even hear the ubiquitous symphony of taxi horns. All she saw, all she knew was Ben. His strong arm beneath her thighs, the safe, encompassing circle of his arm around her back. The brilliant, burning blue of his eyes just inches from hers. She wanted to stay in his arms forever.

"I figure I screwed up royally, accusing you of not loving me in front of more than a hundred people. The only way to make it right was to tell you how I feel. Very publicly." He set her on her feet facing Wrigley Field. The iconic red sign hung over the entry gates, and its digital readout read *Ben Westcott Loves Ivy Rhodes*.

He fell to one knee, and fished a robin's egg-blue box out of his pocket. When he popped it open, the sun glittered off the cushion cut diamond solitaire. Ivy's practiced eye pegged it at two carats. Between the serious sparkler for her ring finger and the public declaration of his love, Ivy didn't have to wonder anymore how he felt. Her nerve endings, inside and out, stood on end, knowing what he'd say next. Those magical words that would change her life forever.

"I love you, Ivy. The other night you said *where's your joy?* Well, it's not in Darfur—where, by the way, I'm not going. It's not spending every waking hour thinking about famine and genocide and hoping not to die of some unheard-of tropical disease. My joy is standing right in front of me. You are my joy. The question is, will you be my wife?"

The knots in her stomach budded into a panoply of cherry blossoms, then floated away on a warm breeze of happiness. "Yes. A million times over, yes. I love you, Ben." She couldn't decide whether to laugh or sob with joy. Luckily, Ben made the decision for her by crushing his mouth to hers, swinging her around in a circle while they kissed an epic, happily-ever-after kiss. Ivy dimly registered the sound of people around them cheering and clapping. The man of her dreams broke off the kiss to smile down at her.

"I never planned for love," Ben said. "But I'm so damn grateful you did."

* * * * *

REQUEST YOUR
FREE BOOKS!

2 FREE NOVELS
FROM THE ROMANCE COLLECTION
PLUS 2 FREE GIFTS!

YES! Please send me 2 FREE novels from the Romance Collection and my 2 FREE gifts (gifts are worth about $10). After receiving them, if I don't wish to receive any more books, I can return the shipping statement marked "cancel." If I don't cancel, I will receive 4 brand-new novels every month and be billed just $5.99 per book in the U.S. or $6.49 per book in Canada. That's a saving of at least 25% off the cover price. It's quite a bargain! Shipping and handling is just 50¢ per book in the U.S. and 75¢ per book in Canada.* I understand that accepting the 2 free books and gifts places me under no obligation to buy anything. I can always return a shipment and cancel at any time. Even if I never buy another book, the two free books and gifts are mine to keep forever.

194/394 MDN FELQ

Name	(PLEASE PRINT)

Address	Apt. #

City	State/Prov.	Zip/Postal Code

Signature (if under 18, a parent or guardian must sign)

Mail to the **Reader Service:**
IN U.S.A.: P.O. Box 1867, Buffalo, NY 14240-1867
IN CANADA: P.O. Box 609, Fort Erie, Ontario L2A 5X3

Not valid for current subscribers to the Romance Collection
or the Romance/Suspense Collection.

Want to try two free books from another line?
Call 1-800-873-8635 or visit www.ReaderService.com.

* Terms and prices subject to change without notice. Prices do not include applicable taxes. Sales tax applicable in N.Y. Canadian residents will be charged applicable taxes. Offer not valid in Quebec. This offer is limited to one order per household. All orders subject to credit approval. Credit or debit balances in a customer's account(s) may be offset by any other outstanding balance owed by or to the customer. Please allow 4 to 6 weeks for delivery. Offer available while quantities last.

Your Privacy—The Reader Service is committed to protecting your privacy. Our Privacy Policy is available online at www.ReaderService.com or upon request from the Reader Service.

We make a portion of our mailing list available to reputable third parties that offer products we believe may interest you. If you prefer that we not exchange your name with third parties, or if you wish to clarify or modify your communication preferences, please visit us at www.ReaderService.com/consumerschoice or write to us at Reader Service Preference Service, P.O. Box 9062, Buffalo, NY 14269. Include your complete name and address.

ROM11

FAMOUS FAMILIES

ReaderService.com

Manage your account online!

- Review your order history
- Manage your payments
- Update your address

We've designed the Reader Service website just for you.

Enjoy all the features!

- Reader excerpts from any series
- Respond to mailings and special monthly offers
- Discover new series available to you
- Browse the Bonus Bucks catalogue
- Share your feedback

Visit us at:

ReaderService.com

RS12